Megan Morrison

Tyme #2

Disenchanted

The Trials of Cinderella

Scholastic Inc.

Maps by Kristin Brown
The world of Tyme is co-created by Megan Morrison and Ruth Virkus.

Arthur A. Levine Books hardcover edition designed by Carol Ly, published by Arthur A. Levine Books, an imprint of Scholastic Inc., October 2016.

ISBN 978-0-545-64272-9

10 9 8 7 6 5 4 3 2 1 19 20 21 22 23
Printed in the U.S.A. 40
This edition first printing 2019

For Malcolm and Elinor, my fairy dust,
and for Devin, my solid ground

TYME

The Impenetrable Peaks
The Resplendent City
New Pink
North Silver
Silver River
Port Urbane
Reverie
Lilac Lakes
Violet Peaks
Dearth
Bright Bay
Commonwealth Green
Independence
Mimicry River
Venture
Vigor River
Blue Kingdom
Little Copper
Crimson Realm
Maple Valley
Republic of Brown
Copper Bay
Salting
Eel Grass
Quintessential
Little Copper
Ladle River
Silver Citadel
The Tranquil Sea
Yellow Country
Cornucopia
Grey
Golden River
Bay of Glad Tidings
Redlands
Fortress of Bole
Orange
Rapunzel's Tower
Vintage
Helio
Limestone River
N
E
W
S
The Olive Isles
The Impassable Swamps
Capital
City
Village
Other
0
25
50
100
Leagues

Quintessential

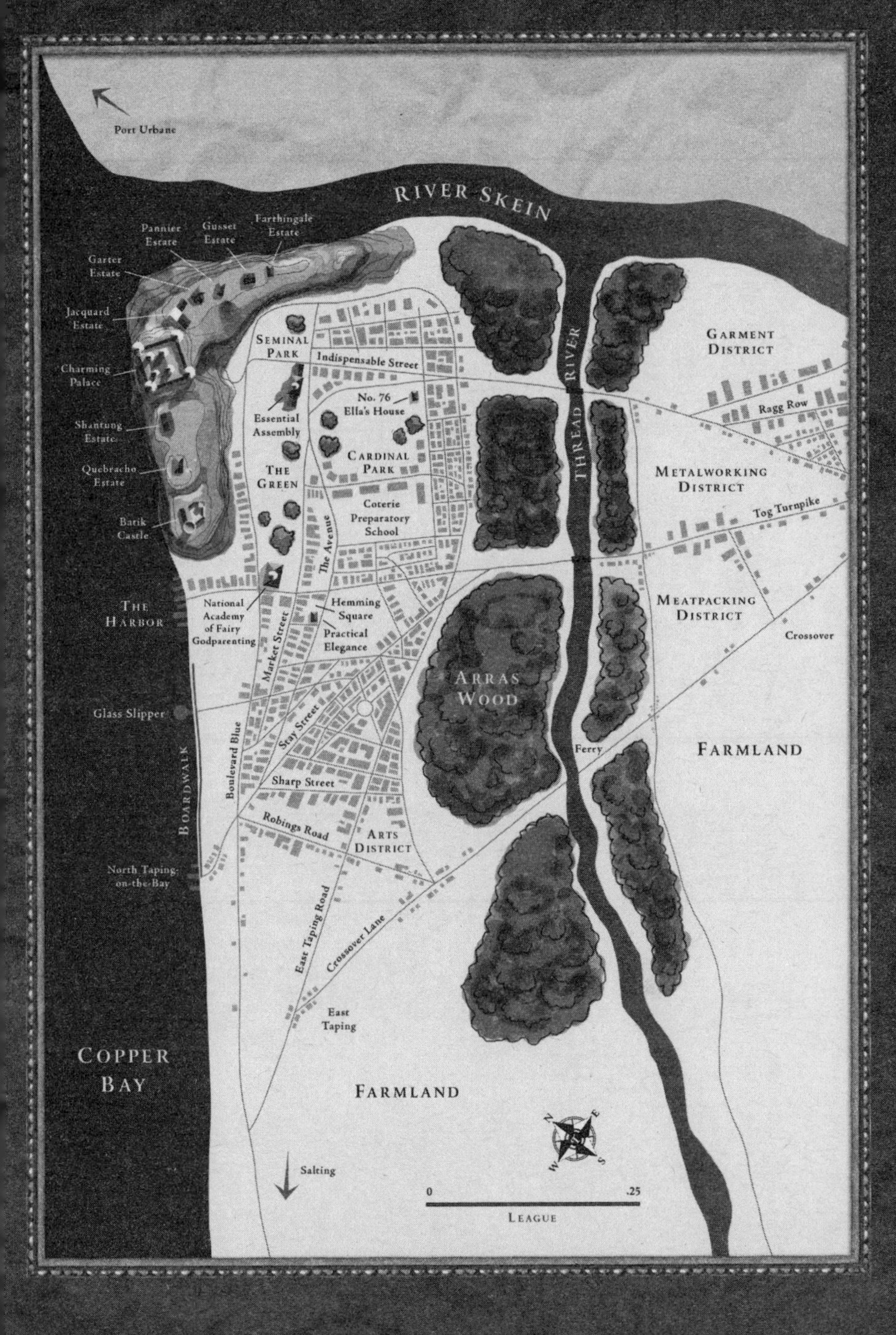

Port Urbane
River Skein
Pannier Estate
Gusset Estate
Farthingale Estate
Garter Estate
Jacquard Estate
Charming Palace
Shantung Estate
Quebracho Estate
Batik Castle
Seminal Park
Indispensable Street
Essential Assembly
No. 76 Ella's House
Cardinal Park
The Green
Coterie Preparatory School
The Avenue
Thread River
Garment District
Ragg Row
Metalworking District
Tog Turnpike
Meatpacking District
Crossover
The Harbor
National Academy of Fairy Godparenting
Hemming Square
Practical Elegance
Market Street
Arras Wood
Glass Slipper
Stay Street
Boulevard Blue
Boardwalk
Ferry
Farmland
Sharp Street
Robings Road
Arts District
North Taping-on-the-Bay
East Taping Road
Crossover Lane
East Taping
Copper Bay
Farmland
Salting
0
.25
League
N
E
S
W

Ella

WHILE her roommates dressed for Prince Dash's return to Coterie Prep, Ella Coach waited for her moment.

"Not like *that*." Dimity Gusset smacked her maid's hand away from her complicated upsweep of red hair. "That's last month's fashion. Skies, isn't it your job to know that?"

"If your girl isn't good, you should get a new one from Lady Trim's school," said Tiffany Farthingale, who applied a deep red stain to her lips while her own maid buttoned her clinging white dress up the back. "That's where Mother hired mine, and she's so current and clever."

"Father *says* I'm on the List for a fairy godparent from the Slipper," said Dimity with a sigh. "He's paid them an absolute fortune, so I *should* get my contract any day. Until then, I'll just have to put up with Miss Mediocrity here."

The maid plaited a tiny, perfect, gold-threaded braid and wound it into place around Dimity's tower of hair. The girl's plump fingers didn't stumble, but her blush told Ella all her feelings. Ella looked down at the woolen slipper she was knitting and started another row.

"I'm just so glad that Dash is back!" said Chemise Shantung, Ella's third roommate. "It's been so long, and there are so many rumors — do you really think he's bald?"

"I heard the witch cursed his hair off," said Tiffany. "Poor thing. He'll need comfort after all he's been through."

"You're dreaming if you think he wants your comfort," said Dimity. "You know he's Lavaliere's."

Tiffany rubbed a bit of red stain off one front tooth. "They're not betrothed."

Dimity rolled her eyes. "Hurry *up*," she said to her maid, who now knelt at her feet, buttoning up her high-heeled shoes. Dimity kicked at her, striking her fingers with a jewel-encrusted toe. The maid yelped in pain and cradled her hand against her chest.

Ella gripped her knitting needles with sudden force. "Button your own shoes," she snapped.

Dimity swiveled on her stool and pinned her narrow green eyes on Ella. "*You* look like a slum that someone set on fire," she said, raking her gaze over Ella's unfettered curls, her homemade clothing, and her battered black fishing boots. "You'll never get near the prince if you look homeless."

"Perhaps that's for the best," said Tiffany, wincing as her maid plucked an errant hair from between her brows. "Dash is used to a certain quality of company."

"The kind who can't put her own shoes on?" Ella retorted.

Dimity smirked. "Buttoning shoes and tatting socks, or whatever you're doing there, is servants' work," she said.

"Tatting is lace," said Ella. "This here is knitting. Your whole gown's covered in lace, and you don't know the difference?"

Dimity and Tiffany exchanged glances, and then both of them laughed — little tinkling laughs that made Ella want to shove her knitting needles right up their noses.

The assembly bell tolled. A general squeal of excitement arose both within the room and outside it, and Ella unclenched her fists. She didn't have to live with these people anymore. Chemise threw the door open. Ella's roommates squeezed themselves into the crowd outside, and Tiffany's maid slipped out through the servants' door at the back of the chamber. Ella was left alone with Dimity's maid, who still knelt by the vanity, clutching her kicked fingers, her face turned to the wall. Ella heard her sniffle.

"Is your hand all right?" Ella asked gently, kneeling beside her. "Can I help?"

The girl wouldn't look at Ella. "It's fine, Miss," she whispered.

"Call me Ella, hey? I'm no quint." Ella smiled, but the girl did not respond. "What's your name?"

The maid wiped her tearstained face and got up from the floor. "Excuse me, Miss," she mumbled. She curtsied and fled through the servants' door.

Ella looked down at her hands. Rough and worn. Funny how Dimity and her kind never missed that Ella was working class, but the servants couldn't see it. To them, Ella was just another rich quint they had to serve. They couldn't trust her, and she didn't blame them — but it left her nowhere, with no one to talk to.

She had to go home.

She grabbed her old knapsack from under her canopied bed, shoved her knitting into it, and slung it over her shoulder. She put her ear to the door and listened until she heard no more stragglers, and then she left the dormitory room and headed for the building's exit. She could catch the day's second coach to Salting if she hurried. All the school guards would be busy overseeing the prince's safety. Nobody would see her bolt.

She'd reached the top of the back stairwell when a loud rap behind her made her tense, and she turned. Mother Bertha, matron of the girls' dormitory, stood in the corridor, looking ominous, tiny and hunched though she was. "Make your way to the assembly," she croaked.

"Need the infirmary," Ella lied. "I'm going to retch."

"Don't give me any of your crass southern lip, Elegant Coach," said Mother Bertha. "Turn around and do your duty, or I will call a guard and have you dragged."

She would, too. She'd done it before.

Ella gave the stairs a longing glance, but for the moment she was beaten. With the tip of Bertha's cane against the small of her back, she proceeded to the welcome breakfast for Prince Dash.

Dash

CHARMING men broke hearts, and everybody knew it.

Nobody blamed them. It wasn't their fault. The Charming Curse had shackled them for seven generations, thanks to Great-Great-Great-Great-Great-Grandfather Phillip Charming. One hundred and fifty years ago, Phillip had broken the heart of the witch Envearia, and she had sentenced him and all of his descendants to be unhappy in love. Under Envearia's curse, every generation of Charmings bore one son, and every son broke the heart of anyone who fell in love with him. Some Charming kings neglected their spouses; others were cruel, insincere, or unfaithful. Each drove his partner into misery, and for a century and a half there was nothing they could do about it.

But Envearia was dead now. The Charming Curse was broken. Prince Dash Charming was glad that it was broken. He'd wanted to be free. More than that, he'd wanted his mother to be free. And in a few hours, Queen Maud *would* be free — of his father, of the palace, of this city.

As long as nobody caught her.

Dash ran a hand over his shaved head as he searched for what to say to her now. She sat beside him in the royal carriage, her jeweled fingers twisting in her lap, and she stared out the window as the horses brought them through the silver gates of Coterie Preparatory School. C-Prep gleamed at the heart of the city of Quintessential, a vast collection of impressive stone buildings, its torches and windows alight against the pale dawn sky. It was famous, this place, for educating the monarchs of Blue and all of their advisors — and today it would gain new fame. Today, Queen Maud would vanish from these buildings.

The carriage drew near the dormitory, and Dash's mother began to bite her nails — a distinctly unqueenly habit that she rarely indulged. She was afraid. She had a right to be. And Dash couldn't summon up a single word of comfort. He worked his jaw, but his throat was tight, and nothing would come.

"It's all right," his mother murmured, as though she could feel his distress. She stopped biting her fingernails and laid one cool hand on his. "It's a good plan."

Dash still wasn't sure. And since the plan was mostly his, if anything went wrong, he'd never forgive himself. "Maybe you *should* leave from the palace," he said for the hundredth time. These words came readily enough. Far easier to discuss strategy than emotion. "Our servants wouldn't stop you."

His mother shook her head. "They'd see me," she said. "They'd notice my direction, and your father would make them confess. Best that I slip away here, in the middle of the city, where I can be quickly lost from sight." She squared her shoulders. "It will work," she said. "Everyone is so mad to see *you* this morning that no one will pay attention to me. It's my best chance to go unnoticed. You were right about that."

Everyone *was* mad to see him. Dash swallowed hard. His classmates hadn't laid eyes on him since before Envearia had turned him to stone. Before the curse had been broken. He wasn't the same Prince Charming they all remembered, and he had no idea how they would respond to him now that he was just himself. Just Dash. No fancy speeches. No flattery.

"I'll keep their eyes on me," he managed, and he gripped his mother's hand. "You'll get away. I promise."

The carriage came to a halt in front of the boys' dormitory building. Footmen helped Queen Maud down to the pavement and Dash followed, his stomach in wretched, writhing knots. Every guard who worked at C-Prep stood in a great square around the dorm. His mother would need extraordinary luck to get past them. Extraordinary luck, an excellent disguise, and a little extra help.

He slipped his hand into the pocket of his satin breeches to make sure the Ubiquitous acorns were still there.

"Your Majesty. Your Royal Highness." Madam Wellington, C-Prep's headmistress, greeted them with a deep curtsy. In spite of a strong breeze, her two great, stiff wings of silver hair did not stir. "How glad I am to see you safe, sir," she said to Dash. "It gives me great joy to welcome you back to Coterie."

Dash bowed but did not reply. The curse had always forced him to flatter Madam Wellington, though he'd personally never liked her. He relished having the power to say nothing.

"Dash is delighted to be here," said his mother, giving him a sidelong look. "But he has been through a great ordeal."

"Of course — I understand. Will you honor us with your presence at the reception, Your Majesty?"

Queen Maud shook her head, and her circlet of sapphires twinkled in her golden curls. "This breakfast is for Dash and his friends. I am only here to settle my son into his rooms. If you will excuse us."

They proceeded into the dormitory through a private door. The queen's bodyguards flanked Dash and his mother as they climbed the steps to Coterie's royal apartments. The guards checked the rooms, then took up their positions outside the chamber.

Dash closed the door, shutting out the guards. He bolted the servants' entrance and untied all the chamber's curtains, which fell shut, obscuring the windows. His mother was already examining the parcel that sat on his school desk. A week ago, Dash had wrapped the parcel, marked it *Do Not Open*, and sealed it with wax that he'd stamped with his ring for good measure. Then he'd packed it in one of his school trunks, and his servants had brought it here.

With one fingertip, his mother traced the Charming crest, stamped into the bright blue wax.

"I'll miss him," she said quietly. "I know how weak that sounds. But he wasn't always like this. At first he was so wonderful —" She stopped short. Her eyes grew bright with sudden tears. "It will devastate him," she said. "Me leaving like this, without warning. No matter how he behaves, Dash, your father has a vulnerable heart. I don't know if I can do this to him in good conscience —"

"Leave," Dash blurted.

His mother stared at him. His new way of speaking still startled her.

It startled him too.

"Go," he corrected, but that was no better. He gritted his teeth to summon kinder words. "You need to get out." No. Wrong. He gave his head a sharp shake. "I mean — I think —"

He stumbled to a halt and looked at his shoes, perplexed. His heart was pumping too hard, making too much noise inside his head; he couldn't hear his own thoughts. Before the Charming Curse was broken, he would have spewed a sea of lovely, empty words, because the curse had made him a fount of insincere flattery. As charming as his name and as miserable as his ancestors.

His mother spoke gently. "You don't want me to be unhappy."

Dash exhaled and nodded. It had been nearly three months since the witch's death, and without the curse to speak his words for him, he found certain things difficult to express. But now when he spoke, the words were his own.

"You're so different." His mother chewed her thumbnail as she studied him. "So quiet and sincere. No pretty compliments, no platitudes. How can you have changed so much, and your father not at all? I can almost believe him when he says that he's still cursed —"

"The curse is broken," said Dash, emphatic.

"For you it is. But for him . . ."

"It's *broken*."

For twenty years, the Charming Curse had excused his father's famous unfaithfulness. King Clement had always sworn he *would* be true if he ever had the chance. But now the witch was dead. The chance had come. And still the king had gone off with Exalted Nexus Maven, just like he'd gone off with countless women before.

"We don't know everything about how witch magic works," said his mother. "I've consulted the Exalted Council and the House of Magic, and no one can tell me for certain if a witch's curse is always *entirely* broken when she dies —"

"He doesn't love you!"

Dash's mother recoiled as if he'd struck her. He clamped his teeth together. He hadn't meant to say it like that. Even if it was true.

His mother turned away from him. "I'll get ready," she murmured, and she took the parcel into the privy chamber and shut the door. When she emerged, Dash stepped back, alarmed. A dark wig and servants' clothes had transformed her entirely. For the first time in his life, Dash could envision his mother as the commoner she had once been: Maud Poplin, a serving girl in a southern tavern.

She packed her queenly attire into one of his trunks.

"I'll leave through the servants' door," she said. "After you head down to the reception."

"We should've done this at night. It would be easier for you in the dark."

"Ships leave by morning," his mother replied. "And we agreed that the Olive Isles is the best place for me to go. Your father will assume I've run to my sister, or farther south to Orange to stay with the Magnificents. He won't guess I'm on Balthasar. Not for a long while."

Dash pulled the Ubiquitous acorns from his pocket and pressed them into her palm. Her hand was moist; her nails all but gnawed off. "Take these," he said. "Ubiquitous Instant Fog. It'll hide you, if you need it."

His mother nodded and stuffed the acorns into her apron pocket.

"If I'm caught, it will only mean scandal. Your father would never punish me, not really."

But he'd watch her. Set guards on her. Make it impossible for her to try again. Either she got away now or King Clement would make sure that it was never.

She crossed the chamber and took Dash's hands in her own.

"I won't write for a while," she said. Tears glimmered in her eyes. "Trust that I'm safe."

Dash nodded, and his voice jammed in his throat. He wanted to tell her how much he would miss her, but it wouldn't come.

"Safe journey," he managed instead. "Maybe you'll even find Prince Syrah."

"I wish I would, for his mother's sake. To have a child missing — oh." She looked into his eyes. "I'm grateful every moment that Envearia is dead. That you're home safe." She kissed his cheek, let go his hands, and adjusted the shoulders of his jacket. She smoothed his royal sash and ran her fingers over the top of his shaved head. "Do grow out your hair while I'm gone," she said with a wet little laugh. "It looks so much nicer, darling." She hugged him with sudden fierceness, wrinkling his smoothed sash completely. "I love you," she said.

"Love you too," he mumbled.

She closeted herself in the privy.

Dash waited a moment until his eyes felt dry again and his emotions were under regulation. He pulled open the chamber door. The guards saluted him as he quickly shut the door behind him.

"Her — Majesty." Dash stopped. Swallowed. Tried to push past the lump in his throat. He had to keep speaking, had to say the rest of the lie and make sure that the guards did not go inside the room for any reason. "She — isn't. She doesn't —"

"Is Her Majesty unwell?" asked one of the guards sharply. "Does she require assistance?"

"No."

Lying had been so easy when the curse had done his speaking for him. Now anything but the plain truth required physical effort.

"She wants to be alone. Surprise. For me." He blushed as the words blurted out of him, disjointed and nonsensical. "Needs an hour of privacy."

Sweat beaded on his head and rolled down his temples. He pulled a handkerchief from his pocket and mopped his bald head.

"Her Majesty has asked for an hour of privacy?" said the guard. "Is that right, Your Highness?"

Dash nodded, grateful.

"Then yes, sir. Just as you say, sir."

The guards remained at their posts outside the chamber doors as Dash descended the steps, where another set of guards waited to escort him to the ballroom. Outside the dormitory building, clouds had rolled in to obscure the morning sun, and the air was cool and heavy. Rain was coming. He turned up his face for a moment, appreciative of the breeze; his dress jacket and royal sash felt stiflingly heavy and hot.

He crossed the Coterie campus, making his way through gardens that separated grand stone buildings all tastefully overgrown with flowering ivy. The place was eerily empty and calm; he could not remember it being so still. The entire school must be waiting for him in the ballroom. Every student, every servant, and nearly every guard would be congregated there to see what Prince Dash of the Blue Kingdom was *really* like, now that the witch was dead.

He came to the enormous building that held the assembly hall and ballrooms within it, and when he entered, the buzz of excited voices could be heard echoing through the antechamber. A thrill of terror shot through Dash. Outside the dining hall doors, he stopped and squared his shoulders, wishing he could stop himself from sweating. He set his jaw. All that mattered was that his mother made it to her ship without getting caught. For her sake, he would let all of Coterie focus on him.

Serge

"On behalf of the National Academy of Fairy Godparenting, certified by the Royal House of Magic, I wish you all my heartiest congratulations."

Serge smoothed down his fitted velvet coat with practiced, pale blue fingers. A glance at the mirrored wall on his right showed that his hair had withstood the hazy morning heat; a long sweep of white-blond fringe still waved perfectly over one eye.

"Many bright futures lie ahead of you," he said to the small crowd. He didn't read from a speech; he had spouted the same empty words to every graduating class of godparents for the last twenty years. "The futures of the children whose pain you will alleviate, whose hearts you will open, whose lives you will enrich — and even save."

As he spoke, he surveyed the new apprentices, all of whom were blue-skinned — except one. A young Crimson fairy, deathly pale, wore his hair in short ink-black spikes. His lips were as red as human blood, with wings to match. He gazed raptly upon Serge with large, shining crimson eyes, hands clasped under his chin.

"Mortal lives are swift," Serge continued. "We are called to illuminate their limited years with every kindness that magic can provide. This work is not easy — it will challenge your compassion and your inventiveness at every turn. But if you satisfy your clients, then you too will know the deepest satisfaction. And of course, as we like to say at the Slipper: Best wishes to you —"

"In making wishes come true!" cried the new godparents together. There were only a handful of them, but their applause was fierce enough that they might have been a hundred. The Crimson fairy was on his feet, applauding with his hands *and* his enormous wings, his tears turning to bright crimson roses as they splashed to the floor. Serge resisted the urge to roll his eyes. New apprentices were often passionate, but this one seemed particularly theatrical.

"And now, in accordance with Academy tradition, the fairy whom I take as my own apprentice will be decided by lottery."

Serge clenched his fist tight to summon his fairy dust. His wings grew hot with effort, but he maintained a cool expression so that the apprentices wouldn't see it. From within his palm, a sparse layer of blue dust emerged, fine and soft and slightly warm. Serge flicked a bit of it into the air, and a bright blue ring of names appeared just over his head, sparkling like a floating crown. He gave this ring a little tap, and it began to spin, faster and faster, until the names blurred together in a hoop of blue flame. He tapped it again, and the hoop came abruptly to a halt. One name floated up out of it and rose high overhead, where it expanded and began to rotate.

JASPER

The Crimson fairy clasped his hands over his mouth, his red wings and eyes both open wide. A faint, sustained squeal emanated from behind his hands.

Serge bit back a sigh and flicked the rest of the glittering names into oblivion with his fingertips. "Everyone else, please see Ascot in the back for your assignments. Thank you — and best of luck in your apprenticeships." He gestured for Jasper to follow him and fluttered out of the Academy with his apprentice on his heels.

"I'm Jasper," said Jasper, and he gave a nervous giggle. "But you knew that! I'm from Cliffhang, and I'm a hundred and twelve, and I love children — and *oh,* I can't *believe* I'm going to apprentice at the Glass Slipper. I can't believe I'm going to meet *Bejeweled*!"

"It's just Jules," said Serge. He gestured left, and Jasper flew with him past the stylish shops that lined the Avenue of Quintessential, toward the headquarters of the Glass Slipper.

"She's my absolute *heroine*, you've no idea. Have you any *idea?*" Jasper's crimson eyes gleamed. "The way she freed that camp of child soldiers in Pink, at the end of the war — has anyone ever done anything more wonderful? Were you there for that?"

"No, I was too young."

"All those sweet *babies*. No wonder the House of Magic put Bejeweled in charge of the Glass Slipper — she's a hero. Such an inspiration!"

Eighty years ago, Serge had sought out the Slipper for precisely the same reason. He had wanted to learn from Bejeweled, war hero, liberator of children, and defender of the weak.

Now he just wanted her to retire. Step down from the penthouse. Give him the Slipper so he could make it right.

"What's it like, being her Executive Godfather?" Jasper begged. "Does being in the same room with her just make you want to burst into *tears?*"

"There are days," Serge said, "when that occurs to me." He decided to change the topic of conversation. "So, you come from Crimson. How do you like Quintessential?"

"I love it," said Jasper at once. "It's so *fresh*. Have you ever been to Cliffhang?"

Serge had not.

"It's simply *crumbling*," said Jasper. "Everything's held together with magic, and it all looks like it might collapse on your head. And sometimes it does," he added, rubbing his temple.

This accorded with what Serge knew about the Crimson Realm; the duchies were eternally chaotic. The throne of Cliffhang was the only one that did not constantly change hands, and that was only because the fairy queen Opal, who had controlled that region for four centuries, was more dreaded than any fairy living. Serge turned right and flew down a hill, cutting in among ornate carriages and speeding toward the beach, wide and bright beneath the sun. His wings caught a sea breeze and he coasted to the bleached-wood boardwalk, where waterfront inns and restaurants stretched for leagues along the shore. Music and laughter spilled from balconies and patios, mingling with the sound of the pounding surf. Out past the shoreline, merfolk lounged on a jetty, their silhouettes slick and glinting. To the north, half a league away, Charming Palace sparkled like a giant sandcastle, its spires reaching for the golden clouds.

"Oh."

Serge glanced over, expecting to find Jasper's gaze fixed on the palace. Instead, his apprentice was looking in the other direction down the shoreline, his attention raptly focused upon a long, slim pier that appeared to be made of white sand. At the end of this pier, upon a circular platform, stood a building that looked like a great glass shoe, reflecting the sea and the sky.

"I'm going to the *Slipper,*" Jasper whispered, and Serge was surprised by the sudden sensation of a hand in his own. His apprentice didn't seem aware of what he was doing. "I've dreamed of this for so long."

Serge extricated his fingers and flew on.

It took them only a few minutes to reach the Slipper's famous headquarters. The building's spiked heel was the size of a castle tower. A crystal button in its wall, invisible to mortal eyes, gleamed first silver, then white, then blue under the press of Serge's thumb. A crystal door slid open, revealing a slender cylindrical room within.

"The Slingshot," said Serge as they stepped into it. "Blue fairy concept, gnomish design." He pointed to the handles that hung from the ceiling overhead. "Grab one."

The door slid shut. The little cylindrical room shot suddenly upward. Jasper shrieked and clutched a handle in each hand as they sped to the top of the heel. The Slingshot paused at the highest point, awaiting instructions.

"Reception," said Serge, and he adjusted his hand on the overhead strap. "Hold tight, Jasper." The Slingshot lurched forward, then dropped down again into the main structure, careening as though it would crash. Jasper screamed again. When the Slingshot came to a complete stop, Serge stepped into the lobby, and Jasper staggered after.

Ella

MOTHER Bertha marched her into the dining hall. Heads turned toward her as she walked, and people laughed in shock when they saw her. She glanced at herself in one of the high windows and took in the picture she made. Knitted skirt, homespun tunic, cheap canvas knapsack. Wild bronze curls. Warm brown skin with no makeup to enhance it.

She looked, she thought defensively, much more suited to eating eggs and toast than the rest of these glittering idiots.

"There he is!" cried someone on the other side of the hall, and that was all it took. Everyone was up, surging toward the windows, fighting for the best view of the prince.

"He really is bald!"

"Is his head tattooed?"

"I can't see, it's too dark —"

In the bustle, Ella found a seat at an empty table. She settled her knapsack in her lap, pulled out her knitting, and was tucking the tip of one needle under a pale blue stitch when she heard a faint noise of distaste from the table on her right. She turned her head slightly to see who it was, and she clenched her needles hard.

Lavaliere Jacquard sat a few feet away from her, looking like a crystal princess. The structured silk shoulders of her gown were exaggerated but artistic, slate blue and silver, framing her fall of glossy dark hair and her pale, slender face. She did not turn her large gray eyes upon Ella; instead, she raised her chin just enough to communicate that she, the only child of Lady Lariat Jacquard and the sole heiress of Jacquard Silks, did not consider trash like Ella Coach worth acknowledging.

Rage choked Ella. She looked down at the slipper she was knitting, and she forced her hands to keep stitching. She tried to breathe — tried to concentrate on the softness of the wool and the beauty of its sheen — tried to take comfort in the solid weight of her mum's old wooden needles in her hands. But her mum was dead. Her mum was dead and buried in the dirt, because working for Jacquard Silks had killed her. It had been two years, but coming to C-Prep had picked the scab clean off the wound. Breathing the same air as Lavaliere Jacquard was like breathing poison.

But Ella's stepmother wanted her at school here, and whatever her stepmother said, her dad went along with. This was the best school in all of Tyme, they insisted. It provided the best connections. The best education. The best opportunities for social advancement.

As if she wanted to advance among these people. Ella looked over her shoulder at the dining hall doors, ready to flee the second she had a chance.

The doors flew open. Madam Wellington hurried into the room and took her place, breathless, before the tables. "Be seated!" she commanded, and the throng at the window dissipated as students returned to their seats. "His Royal Highness has returned. As we welcome him back to us this morning, it is imperative that we are sensitive to his circumstances. Since the witch's death, he has fully recovered, at least in body —"

There were titters at this.

"In *body*," Madam Wellington repeated, frowning toward the giggling. "But in mind it is quite another matter. Do not question him about his ordeal, and do not betray any surprise you may feel at his changed manners."

The students hung on her words, more attentive to their headmistress than Ella had ever seen them.

"You will comport yourselves with the tact and dignity that His Royal Highness expects and demands of all Coterie students," said Madam Wellington.

The doors opened again, and everyone stood as the prince entered the room. From where she stood, Ella couldn't see anything but the back of his shiny bald scalp, but she could tell that he was tall. Really tall. A head above the others. She couldn't help a pang of curiosity — as long as she couldn't escape just yet, was there any harm in getting a glimpse of His Royal Highness? Once she ditched this place, she'd never get another chance.

With great pomp, Madam Wellington accompanied Prince Dash to the head table, where he turned and sat. His face was expressionless, but it didn't matter; the looks of him made Ella catch her breath. It didn't seem to matter that he was bald; his nose had a perfect little crook in its strong line, his eyes were startlingly green, and his mouth could have been chiseled out of marble. He was easily the most beautiful person she'd ever seen.

The C-Prep students formed a line around the outer edge of the dining hall and approached the prince, one by one, to curtsy or bow to him before they took their places for the meal. Ella found herself at the tail end of the line. She realized suddenly that her classmates had arranged themselves in order of importance — and they'd done it in swift, accurate silence. Every single one of these people knew exactly where they ranked. In terms of wealth, Ella calculated that she should have been about halfway up the line, but in terms of her actual social status, she was definitely in the right spot. Dead last.

First, of course, was Lavaliere Jacquard.

Lavaliere curtsied and glittered. She bowed her sleek dark head, extended a white hand to the prince, and settled herself at the head table on his right, still with her hand in his. A halo of light seemed to surround the two of them, radiating from their beauty and their jewels and the Jacquard silks that dressed them and their table. The line moved swiftly forward until Ella was only a few meters away from Prince Dash — close enough to feel her heart give an extra beat when she looked at him.

Then a loud *crack!* erupted in the dining hall, so near to Ella that she spun around to find the source of the noise. When she turned back again, the boy in front of her, Oxford Truss, was wiping his palm on his trousers. Ella noticed the smell of something burning. Something not breakfast. Something almost like hair. But there was no smoke, no flame. People began to titter as she turned full circle once more, confused.

Oxford scurried off to his seat. Ella now stood alone and last before Prince Dash and Lavaliere Jacquard and their friends. Dimity Gusset. Paisley Pannier. Loom Batik. Garb Garter. All of them looked at her clothes in open disbelief as she curtsied, or tried to. She could never seem to curtsy without wobbling like she might tip over. She felt warm — really warm, as though she had her back to a fireplace.

Suddenly, the prince shoved his chair back, looking almost wild. He grabbed a goblet from the table and hurled its contents at Ella. She gasped as the orange juice hit her full on, stinging her eyes and soaking her tunic. All around her, the students of C-Prep began to laugh. "Turn around," the prince shouted, and he grabbed another goblet. Ella flinched and turned away to keep from being soaked again, and this time the prince's liquid missile struck her square in the knapsack. She heard a sizzle.

"Your bag," said the prince, who was panting. "It was smoking —"

Ella's insides lurched. She dropped her knapsack to the floor and stepped back as the prince tossed the water from his glass toward the bag at her feet. He struck true. The flame went out. Ella crouched and rifled through her knapsack.

She drew out her knitting, singed and dripping and severed from the skein. It was ruined.

The last of the wool from Eel Grass. The last wool her mum had spun herself, on the great wheel back at the old cott. Ella had been making slippers out of it. Something small and warm to remember her mum by.

Stunned, she lifted her gaze to the head table, where she found Lavaliere Jacquard's laughing eyes upon her.

Ella dropped the ruined woolen slipper. She snatched up her knapsack, fled to the nearest door, and stumbled though it as waves of laughter swelled toward her from all around the room. She heard "Halt!" from one of the royal guards, and "Miss Coach! Stop!" from one of the teachers, but she bolted anyway. She didn't care anymore if they saw her run off. She didn't care who they sent after her. She was going home to Eel Grass and she was never, never coming back.

Dash

SHE ran. He tried to remember anybody ever running away from him before, and he drew a blank. People weren't supposed to run from him; they were supposed to be excused from his company. And they were definitely supposed to say thank you if he stopped them from being on fire. Whoever the strangely dressed girl was, she was profoundly out of place at Coterie. And she had left something soggy on the floor in front of the head table. It was grayish blue and looked like a dead rat.

Royal guards surged toward the door through which the strange girl had gone, and Dash realized that they meant to chase after her.

"Stop," he called out, holding up a hand. The guards halted, and Spaulder, their leader, turned to him.

"But, Your Royal Highness," he said. "She set fire —"

"To her own bag?" Dash shook his head. "Let her go."

The guards relented, but now Madam Wellington was before him, hands clasped to her heart. "Sir," she cried, "are you hurt? Are you burned?" Her voice quavered. "May I fetch a Hipocrath?"

Dash realized with a surge of deep discomfort that a hundred of his peers and the entire Coterie staff stood waiting, their gazes trained on him.

"No," he muttered.

The headmistress breathed a great, gusty sigh of relief. "What a dreadful event," she said. "When you have recovered, we will start the meal at your convenience. Would you like to address your classmates before we begin service?"

"No," he said again.

She looked at him, and so did his table companions. He knew they were all expecting more words. Glossier ones. But he didn't have to do that anymore.

He sat. So did everyone else in the hall. "You were heroic," Lavaliere murmured.

He wasn't sure. The strange girl had seemed terribly upset over the contents of her bag. Why had she looked so harrowed? She couldn't have cared about the soggy dead rat. A servant came to collect it from the floor, and Dash gestured for it, curious. The servant wrapped it in a napkin and passed it to him.

"She knits," said Dimity sourly. "You saw how she was dressed. Like a scullery maid."

"Worse," said Paisley, adjusting the ribbon in her hair.

Dash lifted the soggy thing in two fingers to inspect it. So it was made of wool. No wonder it smelled like wet, burned sheep. But though it was badly singed, he could more or less tell what it was supposed to be. A woolen slipper: the sort one wore to bed on very cold winter nights when one was up in Lilac for winter sports. "She knits?" he said, not sure what to make of it. "And she goes here?"

Lavaliere gave a sigh of revulsion and resignation neatly tied together.

"She's Earnest Coach's daughter," said Paisley. "You know. Practical Elegance?"

"The one who married that Gourd duchess from Yellow Country," said Dimity.

"Yellow *has* no royals," said Paisley with a rich snort. "Ella's stepmother is only a governor's cousin. She used to keep bees or something."

Dash frowned. "Ella?"

"The girl with the smoking bag," said Garb Garter, who was grinning. He had seemed to find the whole thing hilarious. "That Ubiquitous acorn must've sparked the fire. They're definitely getting less reliable."

Dash thought suddenly of his mother, who might be cracking Ubiquitous Instant Fog in order to escape. If all had gone well, she could be off the Coterie campus by now, and on her way to the docks. He wished he could know for sure.

Then he realized something. He peered down the table at Garb. "How do you know that a Ubiquitous acorn started that fire?"

Garb faltered slightly. "I — I heard the crack. Didn't you? And I saw Oxford Truss put it in her bag. He was standing right in front of her. You saw him, didn't you?" he demanded of Loom, who only gave a lazy shrug.

Perhaps it was true. But Dash wondered where Oxford had gotten the acorn and the idea in the first place. Ever since they'd been boys, Garb had thought that cruel practical jokes were funny, and the curse had made Dash laugh along jovially on more than one occasion.

Not anymore. He stared at Garb for another long minute and watched his face turn red, then very pale. His grin vanished. Dash turned away.

"I'm hungry," he said.

Breakfast service commenced.

Ella

NOBODY followed her. She raced from the hall out onto the campus grounds, heading for the nearest edge of campus. When she came to the dormitories, she found herself enveloped in a dense, dark fog that made her cough so hard she nearly lost air, but she pulled her wet tunic up over her nose and mouth just in time, and soon she came out on the other side of the dark cloud. She barreled down one of the long, narrow, honeysuckle-covered walkways that separated Coterie from the rest of Quintessential, and flung herself toward the busy city street, where, fortunately, a public carriage had already pulled over to one side.

She threw open the carriage door and leapt in, only to discover that the carriage was already taken — by an aproned maidservant with dark curls who screamed and clapped a hand over her mouth at Ella's abrupt entrance.

"Sorry!" gasped Ella, but she didn't back out of the carriage. Just because no one had come after her yet didn't mean that no one would. She had to get out of here. Now.

"Carriage is taken," shouted the driver over his shoulder, peering at them through the little window in the carriage front. "Unless you're headed south too."

"South," Ella agreed, her voice still raspy from coughing. She sat beside the dark-haired maid. "Please," she said. "Could we share?"

The woman's clear blue eyes traveled over Ella's soaked tunic, lingering on the Coterie brooch that was still pinned to her chest. She nodded and turned her face away.

"To the docks, hey?" said the driver.

"Yes, please." The maid kept her face to the window, though the curtain was drawn.

The horses clopped into motion, and the carriage drew away from C-Prep. Ella pulled her wet knapsack into her lap and opened the drawstring as wide as it would go to see just how much of her stuff was burned. She remembered the cracking noise that had come before the burning smell. It must have been a Ubiquitous acorn, which meant someone had done it on purpose.

Her eyes fell on her mum's old knitting needles, and her heart squeezed. They weren't destroyed, but they were badly charred. She withdrew them with a shaking hand and brushed flecks of ash from the long, scarred surfaces.

"Mum," she whispered. She had so little left that had been her mum's. Her mum had had so little to begin with. Ella hugged her belongings and started to cry. She tried to stop, but that only made it worse, and she ended up burying her face in the top of her open knapsack, which still smelled like burned wool and orange juice.

To her surprise, she felt a gentle hand on her back.

"What is it, hey?" In spite of her southern accent, the woman's voice was soft. Upper class. She must've been a lady's maid. "Is there anything I can do?"

"No," Ella managed. "They burned my mum's needles, and her wool, and I can't fix any of it now."

"Who did?"

"Those guildy quints at C-Prep," Ella spat. She sat up and wiped her eyes. "You know how they are," she said, turning to the maid, who drew back slightly. "You must work for one of those families. They don't care about anyone who isn't one of them."

The maid glanced again at Ella's brooch. "But you are one of them," she said.

"*No,*" cried Ella. "I grew up down south, and now everything's all changed and my dad has money, but I hate it and I just want to go *home*. . . ."

The maid heard all this with a look of some surprise, and Ella felt a swoop of sickening guilt.

"Skies, I sound as rotten as the rest of them," she said. "Complaining about having money. But living at C-Prep is miserable, and now my stepmum's moved into my dad's house, so I can't live there either."

"You don't get on with your stepmother?"

"My dad only pays attention to her, and she only pays attention to what people think. I don't *care* what people think."

The maid surveyed Ella's outfit. "Where will you live?"

"Eel Grass."

"Oh, Eel Grass." The woman smiled. "Lovely people there."

"Yeah." Ella dabbed her cheeks with her sleeve. "There are. Grats."

"But how will you earn your keep?"

"My friend Kit got me a job at the Corkscrew. You know, the big inn down in Salting? The one the queen's sister runs?"

The maid started. "I may have heard of it," she said, and she began to gnaw at a thumbnail.

"Yeah, well, I'm going to wait tables there and clean rooms."

"Won't your father want you to finish your education?"

"What education? How to kick your maid while she buttons your boots? How to dress up all plush for Prince Charming and then burn up people's bags? They set me on fire today, in front of the prince and everything. He had to chuck his juice on me."

The woman gaped at her. "Dash threw juice at you?"

"To put the fire out," said Ella. "That's why I'm soaked and I smell like breakfast."

The carriage lurched as it turned right.

"Two minutes to the docks," the driver shouted back, over the din of the streets.

The maid gathered her valise into her lap and clutched the handle. Ella couldn't help noticing that a sapphire nearly the size of a quail's egg glittered on one of the woman's fingers.

"Wow," she said, nodding at the ring. "That's plush."

The maid looked down at her hands. Her face went deathly pale. She worked the ring off at once and plumped it into Ella's hand. "It's not real," she said, laughing breathlessly. "And I don't care for it. Take it if you like it."

"Is it Ubiquitous?"

"Just paste jewelry." She refused Ella's attempt to hand it back. "Please keep it. You've had such a wretched day."

Ella shrugged and twirled the ring in her fingers as the carriage came to a stop.

"Docks," the driver shouted back. "Five nauts for the ride so far."

The maid fished the nauts out of a small purse, which was swollen with coin. Whoever she worked for, at least they paid her properly. She put her hand on the door, and then she turned back.

"I've been where you are," she said to Ella. "And I have no right to tell you not to run away — but it isn't going to work. Not forever. You'll have to come back." She gave a wistful little smile. "We both will," she said, and then she was gone, and the carriage door was shut.

"How far you going?" shouted the driver over his shoulder.

"Salting," Ella shouted back.

All she wanted was home. Eel Grass. Kit. The old cott. It had been four months since she'd seen it, and suddenly she longed for it, mice and all — longed to set foot in the leaking rooms, longed to sleep on the hard, musty bed. She wanted to light a fire in the belly of the old stove; she wanted to drink water from the village well. She wanted to shut her eyes and feel her mum still sitting there beside her. It was so hard to feel her mum's presence here in the city.

Feeling better for having had a cry, Ella tucked the ring and knitting needles into her knapsack. She leaned her temple against the cool carriage window as the driver steered them on toward Salting.

Serge

EVERYTHING in the Glass Slipper's lobby was glass, from the welcome desk to the waiting-room chairs, and all of it glowed with cool white-blue light. Serge loved the look of it. There were many things he'd change about the Slipper when it was his, but the lobby could stay precisely as it was.

"Serge," said the receptionist warmly from a deep, crystal-walled pool of salt water set into the center of the floor. Lebrine was a five-headed, many tentacled woman who turned only one of her heads toward him; the other four were engaged in consulting with other godparents. "Is this your new boy? A Crimson? Unusual . . ."

"Lebrine," he said, "this is Jasper. Jasper, Lebrine. Don't mind the fangs, she's delightful."

"Do you have a minute?" Lebrine asked, batting her eyelashes. "Because I have a problem. That mermaid, Nerissa, is demanding a Split. She's chained herself to the mer-window in protest, and Carvel's having quite a time getting her to see reason."

"If she wants to be human, she'll just have to wait until she's eighteen, and then she'll have to go through the usual processes. Nothing we can do about that. It's in the contract."

"But there must be exceptions!" said Jasper. "If she truly knows what she wants, then it's cruel to make her wait — how old is she?"

"Sixteen," said Lebrine. "Two years won't kill her." She patted Jasper's cheek with her tentacle. "You're a little softie, aren't you?

Toughen up, or you'll be as miserable as Gossamer over there." She jabbed her tentacle toward the other side of the reception pool, where a dark blue fairy with quivering wings wept as she pleaded with one of Lebrine's other heads.

"Serge!"

Gossamer had spotted him. She ran toward him, hands clasped, tears streaming, and he pulled a handkerchief from his velvet breast pocket. "Gossamer," he said as she snatched the handkerchief. "Meet my new apprentice. Jasper, meet one of our most committed godmothers."

"Jules won't even meet with me," Gossamer sobbed. "Duna's *ill*, Serge. She needs more than glass slippers and gowns, she needs *help*. Her contract's up tomorrow, but I need more time."

"We can't give anyone extra attention or we'd have to give everyone extra attention, and we'd never get to the rest of the List." Serge recited the words, but they were not his. They belonged to Jules.

"Pure nonsense!" cried Gossamer. "Plenty of clients get extra attention — they just have to *pay*. I Listed Duna with my own money, and it cost me every naut I had. I can't give Jules another fortune, but I *won't* leave my goddaughter. She'll suffer if you take me away from her!"

He knew it was true. But Jules had no interest in this kind of appeal, and one of his roles as Executive Godfather was to handle such denials himself.

Jasper's crimson eyes watched him.

"Jules listens to you," said Gossamer. "Please."

Serge hardened himself. One day, he would not have to say no. One day, he'd have the power to give all the contract extensions that anyone could want. One day, he'd be able to purge the List of privileged clients and fill it up again with the children who really needed godparents.

Just not yet.

"I'm sorry," he said. "The List is what it is."

Gossamer laughed wetly. "It is what it is?" she said. "A girl is going to die without my attention and 'It is what it is'? There you have it, Jasper. You came here thinking you were going to save lives, didn't you?" She shot Serge a swift, cold look. "Get ready to be disappointed."

She fled across the lobby.

"It's always emotional when contracts expire," Serge said to Jasper, watching Gossamer vanish into the Slingshot. "We get attached to the children in our care." He couldn't remember the last time he'd been really attached to a client, but that was beside the point.

"What about the mermaid?" said Jasper. "Nerissa. Her contract's not up, is it? Couldn't we help *her*? Why does she want to be human so badly?"

"Because she wants to marry Prince Dash, of course," Lebrine replied.

"Most of our goddaughters and several of our godsons have the prince on their wish lists," Serge explained. "But he's only one person."

"Did Serge tell you he knows the royal family?" Lebrine said to Jasper. "He's the one who located Prince Dash down in the Redlands after that witch turned him to stone. You're in the presence of the savior of our sovereign-to-be."

"Rapunzel told me where he was," said Serge, putting up a hand. "All I did was fetch him."

"Rapunzel!" said Jasper with an admiring look at Serge. "I read about her in the *Criers*! *You* gave her the brilliant boots that helped her on her journey."

"For a short interview, she talked an awful lot about those boots," Lebrine agreed.

"It was nothing," said Serge, who could not think back on Rapunzel without guilt. He'd abandoned her in Commonwealth

Green, with Envearia still alive, to go instantly after Prince Dash. He tried telling himself that it had been his duty to help the crown prince of Blue, but his conscience wasn't buying the excuse.

"He didn't tell any of us about how he'd helped her, not even Jules." Lebrine snaked a tentacle around Serge's shoulders and squeezed.

"Don't get the velvet wet," he warned.

"It reminded me of the old days." Lebrine sighed. "Remember, Serge? You used to take care of kids like Rapunzel all the time."

He shrugged off Lebrine's coil, slipped one hand into his pocket, and withdrew his watch. It was warm, so he flicked it open. Inside, there was no timepiece but a pool of glowing blue light. Written in this light, in silvery script, was *NEED YOU. COME TO THE OFFICE.*

"I think it's time we paid a visit to the woman at the top of the shoe," he said.

"You mean," Jasper breathed. "You mean . . ."

"I mean it's time to meet Jules," said Serge, and he put out a hand to catch Jasper, who fainted beside the reception pool.

Dash

It wasn't quite lunch when his father's guards dragged him into Charming Palace. The servants furtively watched his progress. They looked tense, Dash thought. Frightened, even.

"Your Royal Highness," murmured the chamberlain outside the throne room. His face was grave. "His Majesty awaits you in your quarters, sir."

Two guards bore Dash up the grand stairs and into his bedchamber, where they deposited him in a chair by the fire. King Clement lay on Dash's bed. In his hands he held a blue glass slipper that belonged to Queen Maud.

"Very good," he said. His voice was groggy. Slurred. "Did he tell you anything?"

"Nothing, Your Majesty," said Spaulder, the head guard. "The prince says he has no idea where she's gone."

"You searched his dormitory room?"

"Yes, sir. We found Her Majesty's clothes and jewels packed in one of the prince's trunks. There was also this." Spaulder set down a large piece of brown paper. "An empty parcel sealed with the prince's ring. The servants in the boys' dormitory also saw a strange woman with dark hair, dressed in servant's clothes, running from the dormitory. A gardener saw her vanish into a cloud of Ubiquitous Instant Fog. They reported her, but by then she was gone."

"I see." King Clement flipped the glass shoe by its heel and caught it again. He sat up, and Dash was shocked at the state of him. His tunic was unlaced at the throat and stained down the front with ale, and his eyes were rimmed bright red, making their piercing blue irises even more dazzling. "Go down to Salting. Arrest my sister-in-law and shut down the Corkscrew. Tallith Poplin will know where Maud is hiding."

The king's men left Dash's chamber, and he was almost sorry to see their backs. He'd never seen his father in this state and didn't know what to expect. Spaulder pulled the heavy door shut, and the chamber was silent except for the ticking of the tall clock and the sound of the sea beyond the palace walls.

King Clement hurled the glass slipper at the mantelpiece with sudden force, making Dash jump. The sapphire shoe smacked against the stones, but magic kept it intact; it fell safely onto a thick carpet, and the king flopped onto his back again. From his pocket he pulled a crumpled paper ball, which he tossed into the air and caught.

"Maud wouldn't really run to Tallith," said the king. "It's too obvious. So she's in Orange, I suppose?" He tossed the paper up again. "Or did she go east? I can't imagine she would, it's rather difficult to picture your mother roughing it in the Redlands, and she's not fond of Grey — the Silver Citadel depresses her." He gave an unpleasant laugh. "It must have been a marvelous adventure, smuggling her away from me. Where is she?"

Dash stood silent.

His father tossed the paper ball up again. "Your aunt will be stoic too, I imagine," he said. "She'll take her whipping like a hero. Good."

Dash's fists curled.

"Spare me the righteous look," said his father. "I have every right to punish any possible accomplices upon the *disappearance* of my *wife*."

"Aunt Tallith doesn't know —"

"I am king," bellowed King Clement. "No one helps my queen to leave me." He sat up suddenly and fixed Dash with his bloodshot blue eyes. "Not even you."

He leapt to his feet. He was a tall man, but Dash's most recent growth spurt had finally brought them level. They stood with gazes locked, and Dash willed his breath to slow down. His father had never struck him or his mother — never once. But he was not himself. Or maybe he was very much himself. Maybe, under the Charming Curse, his father had seemed a kinder person than he really was.

"Where is she?" His father took a step closer, bringing with him the stench of sweat and liquor. His golden locks hung in a damp fall over his tanned forehead. "Where. Is. She."

Dash held his ground, though he longed to take a step back.

The king's brilliant blue eyes burned furiously for another moment, and then his broad shoulders sagged under some invisible weight.

"She'll come back," said the king, but his voice was faint. "She loves me." He moved the hand that had the crumpled paper in it. "She said so in this letter. She left because she thinks I don't love *her*. But by the sea and the sky, I do." His eyes watered. "I've never loved another woman. There's only ever been your mother."

Dash laughed before he'd thought about it.

Rage distorted the king's expression. "I understood my father," he said. "We forgave each other — we were cursed, so there was no blame. But though you suffer what I suffer, you have no pity in your heart."

"No," said Dash. This lie he would not accept. "The curse is broken, and you know it. So does my mother. That's why she's gone."

"She's gone because *you* helped her. And until she returns, you will have no peace."

Dash gave his father what he hoped was an insolent shrug.

"You will not live in the dormitory. You will be here, with me, under full guard at all times. Every letter you write will be read before it is sent. Every class you attend, you will attend with escorts."

"You think I care?"

"Don't you?" said the king, holding up the crumpled letter. "Well, thanks to your loving mother, I can concoct a more fitting punishment." He smoothed the letter to make it readable once more. "She writes, 'Don't take this out on Dash. You know he has been hit hard by the witch's death, and though he is free, he is fragile. Be gentle with him, Clement. Don't push him into full society. Returning to school is enough of a challenge for now.'"

Dash heard his mother's private words with some bitterness. She was wrong: He was not fragile. But it was true that school was all he was prepared to handle. He had no wish for full society, with all it brought. The nobles, the *Criers*, the dancing, the gossip — no. Not *yet*.

"Let's have a ball," said the king.

Dash went cold all through.

"We haven't had a royal ball in ages. We'll invite the scribes and let them have a look at you — the *Criers* have been starved for months."

"No."

His father smiled. "But the country — nay, the world — is

desperate to hear about your encounter with the witch, and your wonderful good fortune in getting the old family curse broken — and your mother's departure, obviously. The scribes will want to know how you *feel* . . . And you'll want to dance with the girls in your class. I'm sure they've missed you."

"I —" Dash's mouth was dry. "I won't ask them."

"You won't have to," his father replied. "You'll be assigned a list of partners. Lady Jacquard will choose the girls and tell them beforehand that they're on your schedule. They'll all be so eager when they arrive, won't they? If you want to get out of the dances, you'll have to reject them one by one, in public."

Dash couldn't embarrass those girls like that. He'd already hurt most of them with his empty flirtations. He didn't want to humiliate them.

"Please," he managed.

"I'll make you a deal," said his father. "Tell me where your mother is hiding, and there won't be a ball." He waited several seconds in the silence. "Not going to give in so easily, eh? Very well. We'll see how your mother feels when she reads the *Criers* next week and sees that we're having a fine time together without her. I won't sit here heartbroken, if that's what she thinks."

King Clement plucked the glass slipper from the carpet and opened the door.

"Wait."

His father turned and fixed Dash with a questioning look.

"Leave Aunt Tallith alone."

The king snorted. "I'll do as I please."

"My mother doesn't hate you yet," said Dash. "But if you hurt her sister, she will."

For a long moment, his father was still. "Write an order," he finally said. "And sort out a messenger. I'll sign it."

He left Dash alone in his chamber.

Ella

THE Corkscrew Inn and Tavern was a big, delightfully ramshackle place that stood on a sea cliff overlooking the mouth of the busy Salting harbor. On the docks, sailors tied up their boats while travelers disembarked, hauling their baggage and gripping their children's hands.

Ella climbed out of the carriage. The tavern doors were wide open, and patrons milled in and out, some with drinks in their hands, others locked in embraces. Crouched beside the front door and fiddling with the doorstop was a skinny, aproned girl. Ella had never been gladder to see anyone.

"Kit," she cried, and Kit jumped up and whirled. Her whole face throbbed with the violently red pustules of a cankermoth infection. For one moment, Ella was sickened by the sight of them. Before leaving Eel Grass, she'd been used to the bumps; now, having had a few months' distance, they shocked her eyes. Nobody in Quintessential — at least not the plush western half of Quintessential — had to worry about cankermoth bites.

"Ella!" Kit seized her. "You're here! You really did it, you came back! Can't believe we haven't seen each other since your dad married that quint! What's her name again? Shirley?"

"Sharlyn," said Ella. "Not that it matters. I'm not going back there."

"'Course you're not. You're no quint. Come on, I'll get you something to eat and introduce you to Tallith." Kit pulled Ella into the Corkscrew. Lively pipe music greeted them as they navigated through the crowd of customers.

"Tallith's looking busy," said Kit, pointing to the bar, where a woman with frazzled blond curls and clear blue eyes was serving ale to what seemed to be ten people at once. Ella tilted her head, looking at the woman. She'd seen her before somewhere. Recently, even.

"That's Tallith Poplin?" she asked.

"Yeah, why?"

"She looks familiar."

"That's because there are always pictures of the queen in the *Criers*," said Kit. "They're sisters, you know. Right, well, I can only take a quick break for a chat." She steered Ella toward a small, empty table, where she sat on a wooden bench. "Then I've got to get back to serving. But we can talk all night, once I'm finished at midnight or so."

"You work that long?"

"Two to twelve is the best shift," said Kit, settling down next to her. "And Tallith's giving me six nights a week. I started with three, but she liked me — and she's a good one. Tallith doesn't hire kids just so she can pay them less. This is a proper lawful apprenticeship." Kit looked proud. "I get my meals and my days off for family, and I don't have to pay for my own aprons. I even room here nights."

"Since when do you work full-time, hey?" Ella asked. "I thought you still did half days at school."

"Dad got injured fishing, and I had to help. Apprentice wages are better than nothing. *You* know how it is," said Kit with a little sigh. "How's your dad's business?"

Ella didn't want to say that Practical Elegance was spooling millions. "Did my trunk get here?" she asked instead. "Did you get your present?"

Kit's eyes lit. "Yeah, and I love it," she said. "You knit the most beautiful things." She hesitated. "But I couldn't figure out the sleeves."

"They're not really sleeves, they're just long cuffs — where is it?"

"Your trunk's in my room upstairs."

"Do we have time to go up?"

"Just."

The two girls ran to the second floor of the Corkscrew, where Ella draped the knitted coat over Kit's shoulders and helped her wiggle her hands through the tight cuffs. The rest of the garment sat loosely over Kit's frame, just as Ella had pictured. Fat, horizontal cables wrapped about her shoulders and vertical ones draped almost to her heels in the back.

"It's not practical for work, I know," said Ella. "But it's pretty."

"Pretty?" said Kit. "It's *gorgeous*. I can't believe all the cables." She pulled the coat around herself and hugged it, and Ella tugged up the draped hood. "I feel like the Empress of Pink," Kit said. "All I need is a fur lining."

"Any Eel Grass gossip?" Ella asked as they made their way back downstairs.

"Not much," said Kit. "Except Mum's pregnant again. Oh, and she's got a job! But then, I'm sure *you* knew. She's in the workshop."

Ella stopped on the steps. "Which one?" she demanded. "Not the shop in Fulcrum —"

"Skies, no. That's why I got this job here. To keep Mum out of Jacquard if I could."

Ella exhaled. For one awful moment, she'd envisioned a pregnant Mrs. Wincey shivering through the winter in the dim, cramped Jacquard building, listening to people cough up blood and getting struck by the cane whenever she fell behind.

"There's roop up in Coldwater," said Kit.

"How many dead?"

"Near sixty people. The Jacquard and Garter shops both got hit."

Sixty people dead in Coldwater, and she hadn't even heard about it. News like that was serious in places like Eel Grass, but nobody cared in Quintessential. There hadn't been a single word about it in the *Criers*, just as there hadn't been a single word during the Fulcrum outbreak. Ella shook her head and started down the steps again.

"So where's your mum working if she's not with Jacquard or Garter?"

"She's at the workshop in Eel Grass, you mule. Obviously."

"In Eel Grass?" Ella repeated. "Who built a shop there? Batik? Quebracho?"

Kit's mouth hung slightly open, and now it was her turn to stop walking. "You don't know?"

"What?"

"Your dad . . . he didn't *tell* you?"

Ella's insides turned cold and jumpy. "Tell me *what*?"

Kit put a hand to her mouth. "Crop rot," she whispered. "I'd've told you forever ago, but I thought you *knew*."

Ella waited, frozen.

"Your dad built a workshop in Eel Grass," said Kit. "Oh, Ells, I'm sorry that you're finding out from me. . . ."

The wooden stairwell seemed to sway beneath Ella.

"Your old cott was knocked down months back," said Kit. "Now there's a workshop on the land. For making plush clothes, you know, and odds and ends."

"*What* workshop?"

Kit looked at her pityingly. "Your dad and Shirley's kind," she said. "It's a — what's it? Elegant Practices shop."

"Practical Elegance," Ella mumbled automatically. What Kit was saying couldn't be true. Her dad would never destroy their home to build a Practical Elegance workshop. He'd think of Ella's mum. He'd refuse. "Where can I borrow a horse?" she managed.

"Outside, stables. But it's ten nauts to get a horse for the day, it's too expensive; I'll just walk down with you tomorrow —"

"No," said Ella. "I'll be back." She ran from the Corkscrew.

Serge

REVIVING Jasper was difficult. He came halfway back to consciousness, babbling something about hopes and dreams, and Serge had to slap him to rouse him completely. He gave Jasper a moment to gather his wits before they vaulted up to the penthouse in the Slingshot.

The penthouse of the Glass Slipper afforded the most beautiful view in Quintessential. It was one big, clear crystal window gazing out in panorama upon the sunlit sea and the glittering city. The glass ceiling sloped steeply upward from the doorway to the apex of the slipper heel. At the high-ceilinged end of the room, at a massive crystal desk, in a stupendously tall white chair that was shaped like an egg, sat a short, curvy woman in a tight, glittering blue dress. Her hair was spiky and frost blue, to match her wings. Her eyes were closed, her eyebrows raised. In one hand, she held a glass of something liquid gold and smoking; with the other, she gesticulated in large, fluid circles as she dictated instructions to her tired-looking assistant, Thimble.

"Prince Dash won't be boarding at Coterie after all, and that's confirmed. Alert all godparents," said Jules in her husky voice. "And tell Gossamer," she continued, still waving her hand in circles, "to stop sneaking unauthorized names onto the List. Another charity case came up tonight — a girl from some village I've never even heard of. Eel Sauce?" She sighed. "Put Gossamer on my schedule. Ta, babe."

Thimble departed. Jules leaned back in her chair and took a long drink from her glass. Her gaze fell on Serge and Jasper.

"Serge." She had a way of giving just one word the weight of an entire speech. "Babe, it's *so* good to see you. It's been weeks, hasn't it? It feels like *weeks*."

It had been two days.

"You'll never believe this," she went on, "but I just got word that Queen Maud has disappeared from Quintessential. Apparently she ran away on *purpose*." Jules shook her head in disgust. "Some people don't know what's good for them."

Serge disagreed. It sounded like Maud knew exactly what was good for her.

"In any case, if the scribes try to get anything out of you, just tell them that we have no comment," said Jules. "There's no reason for us to be associated with the situation."

Except that we created it, thought Serge. Maud Poplin had been Jules's goddaughter, and Jules had sensed a big hit in the demure, impoverished beauty whose head was full of girlish dreams. She'd introduced Maud at a royal ball, where King Clement had been delighted by her beauty and simplicity. Within weeks, he declared he would marry her. The Essential Assembly opposed the match — he was a young king, and she was a villager who barely understood court life — but Clement always suited himself, and they were wed. It had been a huge success for the Slipper.

Now, of course, it was a disaster from which Jules would distance herself.

"Jules," he said, "this is Jasper, my new apprentice. He's quite a fan."

Jules flicked her frost-blue eyes to Jasper, and in one head-to-toe glance, she collected all the information she needed. It wasn't difficult, Serge knew. Jasper was leaning slightly forward, his hands were tense at his sides, and his crimson wings shimmered with emotion. And — Serge wished it weren't true — there were tears in Jasper's eyes.

"Jasper," said Jules, smiling a long, slow smile that spread across her blue face like a cat's. "Sweetheart, I just love you already, honestly I do. I want to hear *every*thing you have to say. Tell me what brings you to our little shoe."

Jasper drew a shaking breath. "Bejeweled," he whispered. "It's an honor — it's a privilege — it's —" He pressed one hand to his stomach.

Jules set down her glass. "You've come a long way," she said, her husky voice very soft. "It couldn't have been easy leaving home."

This hit the target. The tears that had stood shivering in Jasper's eyes spilled over, becoming miniature glittering butterflies that fluttered around his head. A tiny moan of embarrassment escaped him. "I promised myself I wouldn't do this," he said, swiping at his face as the butterflies dodged his fingers.

"I won't lie," said Jules. "I've never approved a Crimson godparent before. But I have a good feeling about you, yes I do. . . . What's your magic?"

"Hypnotics," he said, "but I don't use them. I swear you can trust me."

"Obviously. If anyone even suspected you'd used those eyes of yours, you'd be thrown out of this country in a heartbeat, wouldn't you?"

Jasper squirmed.

"But any Crimson can hypnotize," Jules went on. "I meant your *real* gift. Your own talent."

Serge looked curiously at Jasper. He hadn't thought to ask, but it was true: Crimson fairies were a bit like Kisscrafters in that way. Each one had a unique ability.

"Embellishment," said Jasper.

"Show me."

Serge's left sleeve began to glow. He nearly protested — this was his favorite jacket — but instead he watched as delicate, intricate webs of periwinkle light carved patterns into the blue velvet. When Jasper was finished, the webs of light flowed like tiny rivulets of pale water, illuminating the sleeve in a way Serge had never before seen. He extended his arm to admire the work. It was exquisite.

"I can undo it," said Jasper. "Or do your other sleeve to match."

"I prefer asymmetry," said Serge, and he met Jasper's anxious stare with a genuine smile.

"Truly Slipper-worthy," Jules said. "Clients will adore you."

Jasper clasped his white hands to his heart. "To hear *you* say that," he whispered. "You have no idea. Bejeweled, you are simply the *ideal*. The things you've done for children — the lives you've saved — you're everything. You gave me the courage to start a new life."

Jules's eyes glittered. "You remind me of Serge when he was new to the shoe. When I chose him as my apprentice, he fainted." She gave her husky laugh, and Serge's spine stiffened. "And now here he stands, my Executive Godfather. I mean, would you just *look* at him?"

Jasper's eyes went from him to Jules and back again, and as they did, his apprentice's eager expression faltered. He looked suddenly confused. He blinked his crimson eyes and gave his dark head a little shake.

"Be sure to listen to Serge, Jasper. He's the only one around here with a lick of common sense — which is why, eventually, the Slipper will be his." Jules gave Serge a wink. "I'm getting tired of this big chair, and there's no one better suited to take my place."

She had said it so many times that Serge had almost learned to curb his longing. Almost. His eyes roamed the penthouse as he imagined himself behind the glass desk, making the real decisions. Two new pairs of slippers stood on a long, slim table beside the window wall. He squinted at them.

"Whose are those?"

"Georgette's," Jules replied. "She said they were ready for my signature. Why?"

"Because *I've* never seen them."

"Oooh," sang Jules softly, laughing. "Look out, Jasper. Georgette was Serge's apprentice before you, and I'm sure he told her the rule."

"What rule?"

"I have the final say on all slippers," said Serge, picking up a glass ankle boot and inspecting it for flaws. "Nothing goes on any client's foot without my approval." He couldn't help a little hiss of revulsion. "These toes," he said. "The shape. I can't."

"So change them," said Jules. "You always do."

He always did. The Glass Slipper was so named because glass slippers were the symbols of mortals' most extraordinary dreams. Shoes so fragile and splendid that without magic, they were impossible. Glass slippers had to be breathtaking. Visionary. But *these* slippers were no such thing.

Serge thought of Georgette. She was a proud young fairy, and even though he detested her sense of style, he could empathize with her sense of pride. He shut his eyes to concentrate on that flicker of compassion and he closed his fist. He was just barely able to draw a fine layer of fairy dust to the surface of his palms, and he used a little bit of it to fix the offensive toes. When they were slimmer and longer, more exaggerated and artistic, he could almost relax — but the heels still looked clunky and empty. It only took a few final grains of dust to slenderize the glass stems and fill them with dark gray, swirling smoke. Jasper murmured appreciatively, and Serge smoothed his plume of hair, hoping that neither Jules nor Jasper could see how much effort that had cost him.

"There," he said, and he plunked the now-stylish boots down on Jules's desk so that she could affix the signature glass dots she loved so much. Serge hated the little dots — they marred his designs. But Jules was the one fairy at the Slipper whose taste he was not permitted to correct.

"Does *anyone* get to do their own slippers?" Jasper asked. "I could make a pair you'd like. I'm sure I could."

Serge raised an eyebrow. "Prove it. Fix these."

Jasper joined him at the table and picked up Georgette's second pair of slippers: red with black polka dots. "Ladybugs," he murmured. "But the insect trend is over. It's all about transparent details now."

"Good. So what would you do?"

Jasper steepled his crimson fingernails together. He giggled. As he gazed at the slippers, the black dots shifted and shrank until they looked like very small, inky fish. And then, to Serge's surprise and envy, the little fish began to swim within the red glass, schooling first on one side of the slipper and then on the other, swimming into the toe and then filling up the heel.

"Brilliant," cried Jules. "Serge, you wouldn't dare change that."

"No. They're flawless."

"Perhaps you've finally met your match," she said, grinning wickedly. "Oh *dear.* And for so long you've had no real competition. How exciting to see an apprentice giving my seasoned executive a run for his money."

Serge set his jaw. A faint blush stained Jasper's pale cheeks.

"Now, Jasper," said Jules, "are you ready to make somebody's wish come true?"

"Do you mean I can get a name? From the List?"

"Serge, show him." Jules relaxed back into her chair.

The List stood against the high glass window. It wasn't a scroll or a book, as Serge had expected upon his first visit; instead, it was a white stone obelisk, chest-height and slender, with a concave top. In this white basin, small orbs of blue light rotated slowly.

"What do I do?" Jasper whispered as they approached it.

"Put your hand in the basin. It will release the scroll with the most urgent client history."

"Urgent," Jasper repeated, glancing at him. "So the child who needs help most will come up first? That's what we learned at the Academy."

Serge nodded, though the truth was that the List was bought and paid for these days. There wasn't a child on it — besides the ones Gossamer sneaked through now and again — who was in truly dire need.

Jasper peered into the basin. He looked back at Jules.

And then he did something that Serge did not expect.

"Bejeweled?" Jasper's voice shot up nervously. "Earlier you said something about a *charity* case that came up tonight, and I was just wondering — will that name be *assigned* to anyone?"

Jules raised her pale eyebrows. "Never mind that," she said. "Choose a name."

"It's just," said Jasper, "that if there's someone who isn't getting served because they couldn't *pay* — well, I'm just an apprentice, so wouldn't I be a good fit?"

"I don't want to kill the illusion on your first day, babe," said Jules, smiling, "but the cruel reality is that we can't help everyone. If we aren't paid, then we can't do what we do."

It was, as Gossamer had said, pure nonsense. But Serge said nothing.

"Of course," said Jasper, nodding, "That's life — but could I see the contract anyway? The client contract, for that name? I'd love to read the history."

"I already sent it out."

"Isn't that it right there?" Jasper pointed to a dark green scroll that sat alone, half unrolled, near the corner of Jules's desk.

Jules was caught off guard. "I guess it is," she said with forced casualness. "Sure. Read it."

Jasper took up the scroll and unrolled it to peer down at the silvery script. "Elegant Herringbone Coach," he read. "Goes by Ella. That's pretty, isn't it? Listed by her mother, who died two years ago of roop. Mother's reason for listing the daughter . . ."

Jasper unrolled the scroll further. He scanned it for a minute without speaking, and then he looked up. "I want this one," he said.

Jules merely took another drink. "Stick to the List," she said.

"The only reason I would even *dare* to contradict you," Jasper said, "is that I look up to you *so* much. You'd never give up a client if your instincts told you not to. You'd break *all* the rules, I just *know* you would — and I want to be just like you. *Please* let me try."

He could not have played Jules more perfectly, and Serge began to wonder whether his apprentice's enthusiastic childishness was merely an act. A very good act.

Jules burst out laughing so hard that she nearly spilled her drink. "You are just too *much,*" she said. "Just too much. But we have our little systems for a reason. It looks like you're not quite ready for a name after all."

Jasper looked crestfallen, and even Serge was disappointed. For a minute there, he'd thought his apprentice might actually crack her.

"Don't be glum, babe," said Jules. "Stick with Serge for a while before you draw your own name. You'll catch on."

Jules held out her blue hand for Ella Coach's contract, and Jasper relinquished the scroll with a tiny sigh. Jules flicked the contract into a crystal tray at the corner of her desk, where it sat with several others among the rest of her correspondence.

"Now," she said, sitting back again with her drink in hand. "I need a little time to think. Serge, stop by tomorrow, would you? Alone. No offense, Jasper, but our most exclusive clients expect total discretion. This business is highly confidential." She swiveled around in her chair to face the moonlit sea. All they could see of her now were her little blue wings protruding through the oval hole in the back of her seat. The meeting was over.

Serge beckoned for Jasper to follow him. He strode to the Slingshot, opened the door, and turned back just in time to glimpse his apprentice tucking the edge of something up into the cuff of his sleeve. Something dark green and rolled up.

ELLA

SHE rode her borrowed horse hard along the main road that paralleled the shore, heading for Eel Grass. Kit could not be right. Ella's dad might've married a quint; he might've started dressing in the latest fashions and acting like a different person, but he would not destroy their old home without her knowing.

The salt wind cut across her face, but she didn't slow down until she came to the steep, rocky slope that led down from the outskirts of Salting into the northernmost corner of Eel Grass. The horse shied back, unwilling to hurry down the hillside, but Ella knew the way. She carefully maneuvered her ride to the bottom of the slope, where her home should have stood.

Should have. Didn't.

The old cott and the small field they'd generously called a farm were gone. The only thing left that Ella recognized was a grassy patch of ground marked with a stone slab chiseled in the shape of a keyhole. Her mum's grave marker. At the head of the plot where her mum was buried stood the tree her dad had planted there after he'd met Sharlyn, because it was some sort of Yellow Country custom to plant trees on the dead. That intrusion had been vicious enough.

This was worse. Looming over her mum's grave, there now stood an enormous, drab, rectangular building made of stone. A notice had been pasted to the front wall of it, and Ella urged her horse forward until she came close enough to read it.

PRACTICAL ELEGANCE

Garment and Accessory Workshop

Seeking skilled tailors and assorted fine crafters.

Send employment inquiries to Lady Sharlyn Gourd-Coach

76 Cardinal Park East, Quintessential

Ella shivered despite the late-afternoon sunshine and the heat that radiated from the sweating horse beneath her. She gazed up at the workshop, but all she could see was her mum kneeling on a mat at Jacquard, hunched and squinting, her raw fingers spinning strand after strand of Prism silk into spools. Ella could still feel what it had been like to sit there in that place in the winter, aching with cold, her hands stiff and chapped. Summer had been nearly as bad; they'd been near fainting in that dank oven, perspiration rolling down their necks and the backs of their knees.

Her mouth tasted bitter as memories coursed through her. Her mum's songs, hummed to make the working hours bearable. Her mum's tough hands demonstrating how to comb raw wool or thread the embroidery needle. Her dad's constant absence, and the way her mum had encouraged him to go. *"He's brilliant, Ell. One day people will see."* Running barefoot down to the seashore together. The bonfires they'd built. The swims they'd taken. The backbreaking work they'd done side by side, uncomplaining, because whatever else they didn't have, they always had each other. Every year on Shattering Day, her mum and Mrs. Wincey would put colored lanterns all the way down the road, over the dune and down to the beach, almost until the sea could lick them.

And then roop swept through the workshops in Fulcrum.

Ella remembered the first wet cough. The way her mum had tried to mask it with Ubiquitous lozenges. Pretended it was just a common cold, even while she spat blood.

"Mum, please, you've got to rest. I can go to the shop and work for you—"

"You get to school. I'll kick this, I promise you."

But she hadn't. No one recovered from roop unless they rested and got proper care. Her mum hadn't been able to afford either one.

Now her dad and Sharlyn could afford whatever they wanted.

Ella gazed up at the awful stone thing that stood in her mum's place, and then she slumped forward over her horse's neck and sobbed.

✦ ✦ ✦

"You all right?" Kit asked anxiously when Ella returned to the Corkscrew. "You were gone almost three hours."

"I'm fine, grats," said Ella, though she was not fine. Her home was gone. Her mum's grave was defiled. "Could I talk to Tallith now? Want to make sure I get this job." She was never going back to Quintessential. She couldn't stand to look her dad in his rotten, quinty face.

Kit led her into the kitchen, where Tallith stood at the wooden worktop, chopping fish and tossing it into a kettle. At Kit's introduction, she turned and wiped her hands on her apron, pushed back her yellow curls, and surveyed Ella.

"So you're Kit's friend from the city, hey?" she said. "She speaks highly enough of you. Swears you're a hard worker."

"I am," said Ella, who was struck once more by the familiarity of Tallith's face. She'd seen her before — and not just in the *Criers*.

"And you're looking for what?"

"Any job," said Ella. "With room and board if I can get it."

"I need another pair of hands on the evening shift. Six in the evening to four in the morning. You'd be preparing the boarding rooms upstairs, washing up the supper and drinks dishes, mopping up the tavern when it closes, clearing down the kitchen, and setting up for the breakfast shift. Probably some laundry too."

"I can do that."

"You'll start tomorrow night. Eat and sleep here, work the three-month trial period, and if I'm happy with you at the end of it, I'll employ you long term. Deal?" Tallith stuck out her hand.

Before Ella could shake it, the kitchen door flew open with a bang. Guards in royal armor marched into the kitchen. They flanked Tallith and grabbed her arms with unnecessary force. Terror flashed in Tallith's eyes, but her mouth closed in a hard line and she raised her chin.

Kit grabbed Ella by the back of her tunic and dragged her into a shadowy corner of the kitchen, where they stood together, still and silent.

"Tallith Poplin," said the largest of the guards in a deep voice. "By order of His Majesty King Clement, you are under arrest for your actions as an accomplice in the disappearance of Her Majesty Queen Maud."

Tallith's cool expression fled. "Maudie's gone?" she gasped. "What happened?"

"That's nearly a convincing performance," said the head guard. "But His Majesty believes you know the whereabouts of your sister. You can tell us what you know, or you can come with us to the dungeons."

"Is Maud hurt?" Tallith demanded. "What has he done to her?"

"You're speaking of your sovereign!" shouted the guard, and Tallith cried out as the back of his shining hand struck her across the jaw. Blood trickled from the corner of her mouth. "Your establishment here will be closed down till further notice," said the guard. "So it's not just you who'll suffer. All who are employed here will be out of a job until you confess what you know."

Kit gripped Ella's hand hard.

Tallith looked up at the guard in undisguised pain and confusion. "But I don't know where she is," she pleaded. "I swear it. I didn't even know she was gone, hey? When did she disappear — can you tell me that, at least?"

"Her Majesty vanished from Coterie Preparatory School at breakfast time this morning," said the guard. "She had a disguise, and a plan. She was running somewhere. Tell us where."

All at once, like a shock of cold water through her blood, Ella remembered where she had seen a face like Tallith's. It was the face of the maid in the carriage. The one who had been so kind to her and given her the big paste ring.

The genuine sapphire royal wedding ring.

Ella backed flat against the wall, as though by crushing her knapsack she could make the ring within it disappear. Her heart started beating like it wanted out of her chest; she was almost afraid the guards would hear it slamming against her ribs.

"Wait," said Tallith softly, turning her face to her shoulder to rub away the blood that had dripped to her chin. "You don't mean to say that Maud left him? Really left him? On purpose?"

"I think you know what I mean."

Tallith laughed — a sound of joy and vicious enjoyment both together. "She *did,*" she said. "Well then, take me to your dungeon. I don't know anything, but even if I did, I wouldn't tell you lot. There's nothing I would say to put her back in that wretched palace."

The head guard unlocked a length of chain from his belt. The two who held Tallith by the arms turned her roughly around and offered the head guard her wrists.

"Stop!" cried a breathless voice from the kitchen door. Every head in the kitchen turned to see a red-haired boy no older than Ella, dressed in royal livery and waving a scroll. He was sweaty and panting — he could barely gasp out his words. "By order of — His Majesty King Clement — stop the arrest!"

"What?" barked the head guard. He snatched the scroll from the boy's hand and read it. His frown turned to a snarl. He crumpled the missive in his enormous fist. "Let her go," he said, jaw clenched. "There's to be no arrest."

The guards instantly freed Tallith. The head guard surveyed the kitchen slowly, caressing the chain with his thumb as though he wished very much that he still had permission to use it. His eyes came to Kit and Ella. His gaze flicked to Ella's tunic, his heavy eyebrows arched, and she realized, too late, that she had never unpinned her silver C-Prep brooch — the same miniature silver gate that all C-Prep students had to wear on campus to identify them as belonging to the school.

"You," said the guard, advancing on her. "You're from Coterie. Were you at school this morning?"

Ella nodded, terrified.

"So you were there when Her Majesty vanished — and now you're here with Her Majesty's sister. That's no coincidence. What's your name?"

Ella tried to speak and found that her throat was dry. "Ella Coach," she whispered.

"Speak up," the guard commanded, and he reached out and seized her by the wrist to drag her into the light.

"Ella Coach!" she yelped, stumbling into the middle of the kitchen. Soon, surely, the guard would sift through her belongings and find the royal ring, and then — the dungeons? Execution? What happened to people who carried around royal jewels after queens vanished?

The door that separated the kitchen from the tavern beyond swung open, and a flood of music and conversation rolled in like a wave. In misery, Ella looked toward the happy noise — and gaped. In the doorway stood a woman — a tall, dark-skinned, impeccably dressed woman — whose eyes pinned Ella with a look so deadly furious that all of a sudden the king's guards were not the most frightening people in the room.

Her stepmother was.

"So you *are* here," said Sharlyn angrily, sweeping into the kitchen. "How *dare* you, Ella? And what have you done? Sir, what mischief has she done?"

"We have reason to believe," the guard replied, "that Ella Coach is involved in the disappearance of Her Majesty the Queen."

Sharlyn's eyes widened. A dry laugh escaped her painted lips. "Preposterous," she said. "She ran away from home is what she did. Let her go — she's coming back to Quintessential with me."

"By order of his Majesty the King —"

"Show me the order," said Sharlyn briskly, putting out a hand. "We will gladly comply with any mandate of His Majesty the King's."

The guard faltered. "She's under suspicion," he said.

"If you have no royal order," said Sharlyn, "then we're finished. When and if you *do* have permission to arrest my stepdaughter, please do so at number 76 Cardinal Park East in Quintessential, which is where she lives. My name is Lady Sharlyn Gourd-Coach. I am the cousin of Governor Calabaza of Yellow Country, and if you claim to speak on behalf of your monarch, you require official permission. Now let her go or I will report you."

The guard released Ella's wrist. Moments later, he was gone, and all the others behind him — except the red-haired messenger boy in livery, who was sitting on a barrel by the door, trying to catch his breath. Ella drew a deep breath herself and realized she hadn't taken one in a long time. She rubbed her wrist where the guard had kept hold of it.

"You arrived in the nick of time, hey?" Tallith said to the sweating messenger. She looked as relieved as Ella felt. "Name?"

"Tanner."

"Well, grats to you, Tanner. Stay the night, if you want — room and meal for free."

"That's kind," said the boy, waving a freckled hand. "But I'm wanted at the palace. Prince Dash will be anxious to know it all went off all right."

"Might've known I had my nephew to thank for the help," Tallith muttered. "Poor lad. Kit, you get Tanner as much stew and drink as he wants before he gets back on his horse."

"'Course," said Kit, and, with a brief, worried look at Sharlyn and Ella, she gestured for Tanner to follow her into the tavern. The door swung shut behind them. Silence fell in the kitchen, so thick and loud that Ella squirmed.

"I hope you feel as foolish as you are," said Sharlyn. "Look at the trouble you nearly got yourself into."

"I didn't —"

"Quiet." Sharlyn turned to Tallith. "My apologies," she said. "Ella is here under false pretenses. She doesn't need employment. She is more than adequately provided for."

"I'm *not* coming back to the city," said Ella. "I'm not living with you —"

"You are not of age to make that choice."

"Fourteen's the legal working age in Blue, so I'm old enough for an apprenticeship if I want one. Tallith's giving me a trial. We've already worked it out. I'm staying here — right, Tallith?"

"Sorry, Ella," Tallith said, almost gently. She shook her head. "I'm not interfering in family business. You go on home with your mum, hey?"

"She's not my mum." But Ella's shoulders sagged. Without a job, she couldn't stay. Kit's family would let her sleep in their cott, of course, but they had five children already to provide for, and she hadn't come down here to be their burden. "I have a trunk upstairs," she muttered.

"The driver will fetch it," said Sharlyn. "Get in the carriage. Now."

The private Gourd-Coach carriage was shining and white, with fashionable black trim, and drawn by two black horses and two white ones. Ella huddled to one side of the cushioned bench, putting as many inches between herself and her father's wife as possible. How her dad could've married this woman, Ella would never understand. And he'd done it just a year and a half after her mum's death.

Must've been nice to get over things so fast.

"Unbelievable," Sharlyn muttered as the horses started onward. She removed one yellow shoe and wiped mud from its heel with a handkerchief. "Unbe*liev*able. As if I have time for this."

"Then you shouldn't've come," said Ella. "It's not like I wanted you to. How did you even know I was here?"

"Your headmistress sent a messenger home saying that you had run out of the prince's breakfast reception — which is a whole separate conversation. I am absolutely *mortified*, Ella. Clover and Linden brought the message to my office, and I hurried straight up to your school to search for you. I met your friend Dimity Gusset—"

"She is *not* my friend —"

"— who told me she'd seen you throwing out a big packet of letters. I searched the bin in the privy, and I found them. Letters from your friend Kit, full of sympathy about your terrible school and your evil stepmother, inviting you down to work with her at the Corkscrew."

"Those letters are private!"

"You *ran away*. For a *tavern* job." Sharlyn snorted. "If you want to throw yourself away apprenticing for reduced wages, you should at least come to work for us on the Avenue, where you won't be robbed and murdered."

"There's nothing wrong with Salting! Just because it's not plush —"

"The Corkscrew is full of transients and criminals — and cankermoths, from the look of it. Do you want to end up bitten like that poor miserable girl in there, and spend the next seven years with a face full of hideous pustules?"

"You shut your clap! Kit's my *friend*! C-Prep is what's miserable!" Ella cried, furious.

"I weep for your misfortunes," said Sharlyn, wiping down her other shoe. She slipped it back on her foot and went about cleaning her bright red fingernails. "If you hated school so much, you should have asked to live at home," she said. "But of course you couldn't give me a chance, could you? My children and I have barely been in the city for a week. Ever since the wedding, we've looked forward to being near you and becoming closer as a family — and the moment we arrive, this is what you do? We packed up our entire lives in Cornucopia to move here —"

"Like it was some sacrifice!"

"It was an extraordinary sacrifice. It took four months and a lot of pain to sell the estate and settle the old family business into new hands, but I did it, and even though it was difficult for all of us, we left our home country to make a new life with you and your father —"

"Living in the city was *your* idea. You're the one who wants to be plush and fashionable. You're the one who made my dad's business the way it is now —"

"Successful?"

"Useless! He used to make real inventions, now he just makes quinty fashions —"

"Your father's inventions," said Sharlyn coldly, "are brilliant. That they also happen to be fashionable is why you are able to live like nobility. And while we're on the subject, though I can absolutely believe that you would insult *me* by running away, I can't believe you'd do it to your father. He adores you, Ella. Are you trying to break his heart?"

"He broke mine first."

"Skies, you're dramatic."

"Yeah," said Ella, laughing angrily. "That's me. You should both be ashamed of what you've done."

"And what *have* we done, precisely, to incur your righteous wrath?"

"You knocked down my old cott. You put up a workshop right next to my mum's grave."

"And you've been stewing over it for four months. Really, the way you hold grudges —"

"Four months? Try four hours. I saw it just now, today, when I rode down to Eel Grass."

Sharlyn blinked. "You didn't know about it before?"

"You never told me, so how would I know?"

Her stepmother was silent for a long moment. "I see," she said. "Ella, you should know that the area around your mother's plot is unfinished. Your father and I never intended for you to see it like that. We have plans to install some really quite beautiful fencing around the grave and the pomegranate tree, and a proper monument is being built —"

"That makes it all better, then," said Ella, and her voice wobbled in spite of her anger. She was close to tears. She clenched her teeth shut and balled up against the window as tight as she could, but her own reflection in the glass made her wince and she shut her eyes. It was no wonder that Tallith had mistaken Sharlyn for Ella's mum. Sharlyn's skin was darker brown, and her eyes were dark too, not clear brown like Ella's, but their features otherwise were similar enough that they could pass as natural family.

Beside her, Sharlyn sighed quietly but said nothing else. In silence they rode northward, until Ella jolted awake, thanks to the bumping of the carriage wheels in the rutted road just outside the city. She didn't remember falling asleep, but hours had passed and it was already twilight. The city streets were thick with noise: vendors shouting, the clattering of hooves on the stones, and the gonging of the great clock at the Essential Assembly. Here at the far outer edge of Quintessential, the buildings were ramshackle and low, with tiny, soot-blackened windows. A girl in rags played in a puddle with a boat made of driftwood and torn fabric. She looked happy enough with her makeshift toy.

The adults around her, however, looked gray. Their clothing, their faces — gray. Many outer-city dwellers were dragging themselves home now from long shifts in the workshops and warehouses that lay east in the labor districts: garment and slaughterhouse workers, blacksmiths and cobblers. The labor districts and the slums were hidden behind a long, dense thicket of forested land that ran south through Quintessential, dividing it. Within minutes of entering the city, the carriage pulled up alongside the forested divide, cutting the unsightly half of Quintessential off from view.

Eventually, the carriage turned onto Cardinal Park East, and the horses halted in front of number 76. Ella followed Sharlyn through the gate and up the steps to the enormous stone house that she and her dad had lived in for the past four months, ever since the awful wedding. Sharlyn opened the door, and the house gaped before them, all marble and tapestries and carpets. Ella couldn't have dreamed up this place, living back in Eel Grass. Sometimes she'd wished for a roof that didn't leak. Or walls without mice in them. That was as far as her imagination had taken her.

"Earnest!" Sharlyn called out in a strong, cheerful voice that suggested nothing at all was the matter. She strode into the house, and Ella trudged after her. "We're home!"

Dash

He paced his room, waiting. Many times he sat and tried to write some of his letters; many times he tried to read, but he couldn't concentrate on anything except what might be happening in Salting. He jogged down the long, private path that led from the palace to the sea, and he had a good, hard swim. When he emerged from the water, he realized that his father had been quite serious. Half a dozen guards — not his usual ones — stood on the beach, watching his every move.

He would have no privacy until his mother came back.

He toweled off and strode back to the palace, unfazed. He could handle a complete lack of privacy. *It will be worth it when I'm king,* he thought, stopping in his stride to gaze up at the breathtaking picture Charming Palace made, radiant atop the cliff ahead. However troubled his family line, he knew that he was fortunate to be a Charming, heir to the happiest and most prosperous kingdom in Tyme. His father was a poor example of a ruler, and the nobles could be shallow about their fashions, but Blue itself was as perfect as was possible. A land of beauty, comfort, and plenty, whose great army had crushed the mighty Pink Empire near a century ago, leading all of Tyme into an era of peace. He would be the first king in one hundred and fifty years to rule this nation without the shadow of the witch's curse upon him. Happiness might one day truly be his.

The scroll that awaited him on his desk, however, did not promise any happiness. It was gilt-edged and ribboned, and Dash unrolled it to find the swirling calligraphy of a formal royal invitation.

HIS MAJESTY KING CLEMENT
&
HIS ROYAL HIGHNESS PRINCE DASH
request the pleasure of the Company of

---

at a Royal Ball at Charming Palace, Quintessential
on 12th Greenwhile, 1088, at Nine o'clock

Evening dress and decorations
An answer is requested to the Equerry

Present this invitation upon entering

Dash took a deep, steadying breath, but it didn't help. The twelfth was tomorrow. How his father would manage to stage a royal ball by tomorrow night, he had no idea, but he didn't doubt that it would happen. Once his father had decided something, it always happened.

He collapsed into his chair and tossed the invitation onto the desk. Tomorrow would be a rush of frantic fittings and tailorings and scrubbings and tweezings and everything else that went along with public life. They'd anoint him with cologne and drape him in velvets and silks until he could scarcely breathe. He rubbed his scalp, where the short hairs were just beginning to poke through. At least his head was bare. *That* would be able to breathe, even if nothing else could.

Suddenly he realized that he could hear someone else breathing. Panting, in fact. He turned in his chair to see his messenger, Tanner, kneeling just outside his door, head bowed, waiting for acknowledgment. Sweat trickled from his freckled temples.

"Tanner," said Dash, jumping to his feet. "Did you stop the arrest?"

"Yes, sir."

"Did they hurt her?"

"Well, sir, I didn't see it, but her mouth was bloody."

Dash grimaced. They'd struck his aunt. But at least it had ended there.

"Then Spaulder started to arrest a girl from Coterie, sir," said Tanner. "He thought she'd helped Her Majesty to escape."

"Who?"

"Ella Coach, sir, her name was. She was there in the kitchen."

Ella. Same as the girl whose bag had been on fire that morning.

"Did she have curls?" said Dash. "And old boots on?"

"Yes, sir."

It had to be the same girl. So she had run away from Coterie and gone to Salting. Strange coincidence. He wondered what business she had there.

"The girl," he said. "Did they arrest her?"

"No, sir, not in the end. Her mother showed up, and they let her go."

Dash nodded. "Good," he said. "Thank you, Tanner, you're dismissed."

Tanner bowed and retreated.

Serge

SERGE arrived at number 76 Cardinal Park East, an impressive park-side home, and he hung back at the park's edge, hidden by foliage and the falling dusk. He pulled a folded evening *Crier* from his pocket to entertain himself while he waited. *HEARTBROKEN QUEEN MAUD ABANDONS CHARMING PALACE.* Serge skimmed the story, shaking his head. Maud had been a sweet girl with a good heart who'd deserved better. But then, no one had forced her to marry the king. She had adored him and thought that she could break the curse if she just loved him hard enough.

He folded the *Crier* and watched the street, where he expected Jasper to appear. They had eaten dinner together an hour ago, and his apprentice had seemed tense. Agitated. At the end of their meal, Jasper pretended to have an appointment at the Academy. But Serge had known exactly where he was really going.

Because Jasper had stolen Elegant Coach's contract.

Serge should have reported him for it at once. There was no question about that. He should have told Jules right at that moment when he'd seen Jasper stuffing the scroll into his sleeve, but something had stopped him — and whatever that something was, it scared him. He wasn't a rebel; he didn't want a mess. He wanted the Slipper, and that was all. He couldn't let Jasper have an illegal client. If Jules found out, they'd both be finished.

He was so very tired of Jules.

A moment later, Jasper flitted into view, his huge crimson wings as obvious as fire, even in the twilight. He looked shiftily around, then flew close to the gate that surrounded number 76. He gazed up at the house, and his mouth opened in dismay.

With effort, Serge dredged up a lick of fairy dust and flicked it into the air to make himself invisible. He stepped out of the bushes and sat on the bench directly across from number 76, rubbing his ears with the remainder of the fairy dust on his fingers so that he could hear Jasper even from across the street.

"She *can't* live here," muttered Jasper, still staring up in confusion at the splendid home.

Serge knew that she did. He had found the Coaches listed in the property register. Two years ago Ella might have been a charity case, but things had changed.

Jasper pulled from his coat pocket a small bright blue book that could only be the National Academy's *Official Guide to Fairy Godparenting*. He flipped to the center, where there were instructions on the best ways to approach a client for the first time. It was the trickiest part of the business, and it never happened on the first visit. The first visit was purely for getting a sense of the client's situation through a bit of careful spying — not in private chambers but in a parlor or garden. Serge wondered with some trepidation how Jasper would manage to spy. Unlike Blue fairies, Crimsons couldn't make themselves invisible.

A sleek black-and-white carriage turned the corner and approached number 76. Jasper pocketed his official guide and flew across the street to the park, where he alighted on the bench beside Serge, so near that if he flexed his wings, he'd knock into him.

Serge remained motionless.

He still didn't know what he was doing here. He told himself that he had come to talk Jasper out of this madness, but if that was the case, then why wasn't he saying anything? And why did he feel a strange thrill of excitement — the kind he hadn't felt in years?

A woman with a regal bearing descended from the carriage and went into the house. She was beautifully dressed, right down to her bold yellow shoes. Behind her followed a girl with a head of wild bronze curls. She wore a Coterie Preparatory School pin on her homespun tunic, old fishing boots that half swallowed her legs, and an expression of utter defeat.

"Ella," whispered Jasper beside him, and Serge felt, in his wings, a throb of empathy not his own as Jasper's heart leapt out of him. It was like that with first clients.

Jasper fluttered from the bench, crossed the road, and flew over the gate. He landed in the garden, where he folded his wings until they were two livid crimson stripes against the back of his jacket, making him appear almost human. He crouched low as he walked along the perimeter of the house, stopping beneath each window to listen.

Too nervous to watch any longer, Serge flew into the garden of number 76 and hovered behind him. He peered through the window his apprentice now crouched beneath. It looked into a tastefully arranged parlor graced with beautiful, understated furniture and one of the best-looking chandeliers Serge had seen in the last few decades. Three people stood in the room: the regal woman; a gaunt, awkwardly dressed man; and Ella.

Jasper straightened up just enough to peer over the windowsill.

"Where've you been?" asked the awkward man. The parlor windows were slightly open, and Serge was certain that Jasper could hear the man's voice even without fairy dust. "Your assistant told me you hurried off around lunchtime — what's going on?"

"Everything's fine, Earnest," said Sharlyn. "Ella and I were —"

"In Eel Grass," said Ella quietly.

The regal woman pursed her lips and crossed her arms. The man's face sagged. "Eel Grass," he repeated, and then he stood dumb for a full minute.

"I saw it, Dad," said Ella. "The workshop."

Ella's father nervously pushed back his rumpled dark curls. His hair was fashionably long in front, and when it fell down again, it obscured part of one of his eyes. "Why'd you take her there?" he asked the regal woman.

"I didn't," she replied. "I only went to fetch her when I found out where she'd gone."

Serge realized that he had heard of this family. The *Town Criers* had published a few pieces about Earnest Coach over the past couple of years. He had invented luminous blue shoe soles called Cinder Stoppers to protect work boots from getting holes burned through them in the forges — but it didn't matter what they were intended for. What mattered was that Queen Maud liked them so much that she put them on her slippers and wore them to a ball. Suddenly, everyone in Quintessential had wanted glowing blue soles on their dancing slippers, and Earnest Coach's rapid transformation from poor peddler to wealthy merchant had made for some very good gossip. He'd married his business partner, Lady Sharlyn Gourd of Yellow Country, who had brought her experience, her title, and her fortune into the marriage. As the owner of Sourwood Honey and Wax, that fortune was sizable.

Serge understood why Ella's father didn't look like he knew how to wear his own clothing. He probably had no idea what he was doing at this level of society — he or his daughter. And the poor girl was at C-Prep. They were likely eating her alive.

Ella's father still had not answered her when into the parlor loped a young woman who was perhaps a handful of years older than Ella, shockingly tall and angular, with close-cropped white curls on one side of her head and a blast of black frizz standing straight out on the other. She waggled her eyebrows at Ella.

"Linden, she's here!" the young woman shouted over her shoulder. "And she hasn't been skinned raw." She clucked her tongue. "Losing your touch, Ma? Taking pity on the poor little stepdaughter?"

"Clover," said Lady Gourd-Coach. "Please."

A young man entered the parlor. He was a head shorter than the young woman, and he sported spectacles and a floor-length leather coat with one sleeve sliced off to expose his right arm. This arm was dark purple from shoulder to fingertips with the Kiss of magic, and he raised his purple hand until his fingers were right in Ella's face. He snapped his fingers, and a shower of bright orange sparks burst from his fingertips and rained down over Ella's head like embers. She shrieked and recoiled.

"Hey," he said nastily. *"Grats* very much for making us feel so welcome. Or is running away from family an old village custom of yours?"

Ella looked to her father as though for support, but he said nothing. His eyes shifted away.

"Come on." Clover grabbed Linden's arm. "Let's rehearse."

"Gladly," said Linden, and he strode with Clover out of the parlor once more.

In the quiet parlor, the clock ticked. "Our cott's gone," Ella said when another minute had passed with no conversation. "How could you do it?"

"We needed a fourth workshop," her father replied. "The fastest course was to build on land that we already own."

"Our farm was there."

"It was bad ground, you know that. Just an empty field being wasted."

"Not empty to me or Mum. Just you, because you were never there."

"Ella," said Lady Gourd-Coach sharply.

"What?" Ella glanced at her. "It's true. He wasn't there. He was always traveling, always peddling, always somewhere else."

"For *you,*" her father said. "I traveled for you and your mum. To make a living."

Ella gave a low laugh but said nothing.

Her father shifted his weight. "I meant to tell you," he said. "The timing was always off. And I didn't think you'd care about the business plans."

"Didn't you."

"No, I didn't," he answered, his voice sharpening. "Why should you? Sharlyn's kids never cared about the honey business back in Cornucopia. They were busy with their music. I assume you've got interests of your own and don't need to know when we build another workshop."

"We don't *need* another workshop."

"How do you think businesses get larger, Ella? They grow."

"How come Practical Elegance has to grow? Three workshops aren't enough?"

"We're expanding our product line."

"Why? Who cares about shoe soles that never wear down, or shirts that can be worn inside out, or trousers that don't get wet in the rain?"

"My work," said Earnest Coach stiffly, "is extremely useful —"

"It would be to people who do hard labor, but that sort can't afford to shop at Practical Elegance, can they?"

"Ella, *stop,*" said Lady Gourd-Coach, but her husband shook his head.

"No, Sharlyn, let her go. If this is how she feels, let's hear it." He glared at his daughter. "You have a problem with profits? Where do you think this house comes from, and your school tuition, hey? You think it's magic? Fairies? Well, I can tell you it's not. It's hard work —"

"I don't want C-Prep or this house," Ella cried. "Especially not if people have to slave and die for you like Mum slaved and died for Jacquard —"

Her father moved forward with such quick, angry energy that Ella took a step back. "Your mother died of roop," he said. "Not of spinning silk. And until she died, as hard as it was on her, she was grateful she had that job —"

"Grateful!"

"Yes. Grateful. She *was* grateful, Ell. Just like the families who work for Practical Elegance are grateful to have a living."

"Quint," said Ella, and her father flinched. "That's what you are now. One of them."

He threw up his hands. "What do you want?" he shouted. "Do you want me to shut down the business? Move back to Eel Grass?"

"Yes!"

"You're being childish, Ell. You have no idea how the real world works." He paused and tried to straighten his cravat. "Now, I'm sorry I didn't tell you about the workshop before, but I care about you, and I didn't know how to tell you without hurting you."

"Right," said Ella. A tear slipped from her eye and raced down her cheek. "You care. You put a workshop on my mum's grave, that's how much you *care*."

"You're not the only person who has ever grieved, Ella," Lady Gourd-Coach interjected. "Other people have been through tough times —"

"And you'd know all about tough times, hey?" Ella turned on her stepmother. "With your chandeliers, and servants to cook your meals and dress you every morning —"

"I dress *myself*," said Lady Gourd-Coach, straightening her shoulders. "I'm a great deal more modern than the nobles around here. If you'd give me a chance —"

But Ella was laughing. "You dress your*self*," she mocked. "I haven't been proud of that since I was three years old."

"Ella!" cried her father.

"You *always* side with her," said Ella. "You do whatever she says — you've forgotten Mum ever existed —"

"Shut your trap! Get to your room!"

Ella ran from the parlor. At the windowsill, Jasper made a quiet noise of pain.

Serge, who had spied on many hundreds of family fights before, only drummed his invisible fingertips against his mouth. Perhaps fairy godparents would be useful to the girl; she presented herself dreadfully. A little styling would make an immense difference in her appearance, and he was rather a good coach when it came to elocution. They could be of real assistance here.

With some alarm, he realized what he was thinking. *They* weren't going to do anything. If Jasper wanted to pursue this lunacy, then he alone would bear the consequences.

"This could have been avoided," said Lady Gourd-Coach presently. "Why didn't you tell her earlier about the workshop?"

"Oh, not you *too*."

"Let's go up and speak in private. We need to decide on a punishment for Ella."

Earnest Coach sighed. "I know her attitude's not what it should be, but I don't feel right punishing her for it. It's one thing to send her to her room, but she's having a hard time. I don't want to make it worse for her."

"She ran away from school," said Lady Gourd-Coach. "She wasn't in Eel Grass for a visit, Earnest, she went down with the intention of staying there."

"She *what?*" Ella's father looked dumbfounded. "No, she didn't mean it. She's just upset —"

"She meant it. She sent a trunk of her belongings ahead of her, and by the time I got there, she'd nearly secured an apprenticeship at the Corkscrew in Salting."

"Skies," said Earnest Coach. He rubbed his eyes. "I've made her that miserable."

"She needs to move forward," said Lady Gourd-Coach. "This is her home now. She needs to accept that and start making friends here."

"I've pushed her to go to the parties. She won't."

"Then let's rectify that."

Still speaking quietly together, Ella's father and stepmother left the parlor.

Jasper unfurled his wings so suddenly that Serge jumped in alarm, and then, while he watched in horror, Jasper flew up to the second floor. People in the streets would be able to see him, with his ostentatious wings aflutter, zooming crazily around the Coach house. He hovered just beneath the upper windowsills, peering into each one, until he vanished around the side. Serge realized with a jolt what Jasper intended to do.

He was going to make contact with Ella.

Serge shot from the ground and flew after his apprentice, cursing himself for not having intervened sooner. Of course Jasper wouldn't wait and approach the client with subtlety; Jasper and subtlety were not on speaking terms. Serge hovered outside one window and then the next, looking for some sign of Jasper. He saw Ella's stepsiblings in one of the rooms, loudly playing on the drums and fiddle — and then he heard Jasper.

"I won't hurt you, I promise. I'm a *friend*." His voice seemed to be right in Serge's ear, and so did someone else's labored breathing — Ella's, he was sure. She must be terrified.

Serge flew rapidly along the outside of the house until he found the room where Ella sat upon her bed, pressed flat against the wall, staring wildly in front of her with her mouth open to scream. The window was wide open.

"Don't be scared," Jasper was saying now. "I want to *help*."

Serge flew into Ella's room and landed just in front of Jasper. With a quick shake of his fingertips, he made himself visible once more.

Now Ella did scream — and so did Jasper. But the drums and fiddle kept playing in the other room, and Serge was reasonably certain that no one had heard them. Even if they had, he needed to step in. The situation had to be controlled.

"Elegant Herringbone Coach," he said. "My name is Serge. I represent the Glass Slipper fairy godparenting boutique, making wishes come true for over three hundred years. You came up on our List, and we are here to offer you a contract. You have the right to retain our services for a period of one year. Be aware that we do not deal in love spells or romantic magic of any kind. No one, including you, can be forced to do anything. You agree to be bound by the laws and legal judgments of the Blue Kingdom . . ."

He realized what he was saying, and he stopped. He couldn't give his usual contract speech. He couldn't even be here.

"It's complicated," he said. "Perhaps you'd rather we left."

Ella remained flat against her wall, now looking more confused than afraid.

"Services?" she repeated. "Fairy —"

"Fairy godparenting," said Jasper. "Are you familiar with the idea?"

Ella nodded, barely. "But . . . doesn't it cost a fortune?"

Serge nodded. "Our services are usually expensive, Ella — or do you prefer Elegant?"

"Ella." She glanced warily from Serge to Jasper and back again as though waiting for one of them to attack her. "Sharlyn signed me up for this," she said. "Didn't she? My dad's *wife*." She said the word as if it tasted foul.

"Your stepmother did not contact us," said Serge.

Ella leaned forward, away from the wall. She looked puzzled — and suspicious. "Dad would never think of this," she said, almost to herself. "It had to be Sharlyn."

"I'm afraid not."

Jasper stepped up beside him. "Neither of them Listed you. Your mother did."

The room was very quiet.

"My mum's dead."

"It was two years ago," said Jasper. "Right before she died."

"Mum didn't have two nauts to rub together." Ella pushed herself up from her bed and stood before them, distraught. "And she'd never sign me up for this — she was no quint —"

"Read her letter," Jasper said.

Ella jerked. "Letter? From my mum?"

Jasper withdrew the stolen scroll from within his jacket, and Ella seized it. She unrolled it and stared at the handwriting. "I want to read it by myself," she whispered.

"Of course," said Jasper. "When should we come back?"

Ella did not answer.

"Tomorrow," said Serge, deciding. "When we arrive, you'll hear a chime. It means you have three minutes before we appear in this room. Do you understand?"

Ella nodded, never taking her eyes from the letter.

Serge glanced down at his palms and paused, surprised. He had somehow already generated plenty of fairy dust to transport himself and Jasper out of the house. Perhaps it was the look on Ella's face when she'd seen her mother's writing.

He grabbed Jasper's sleeve with one hand and snapped his fingers with the other, and the two of them vanished from Ella's bedroom. They materialized again beside the park bench across the street from number 76. Jasper put his hands out instantly to ward off Serge.

"Don't tell on me," he begged. "Please. I can explain."

"You stole Ella's contract. What were *you thinking*, Jasper?"

"The same thing you were thinking!"

"Oh? Enlighten me."

"You thought it was wrong to ignore a child just because she couldn't pay," said Jasper. "You proved it by letting me come here, didn't you?" His breath came fast. "We should do this together. We should help Ella."

"Presumptuous."

"What am I presuming that's not true?" said Jasper. "You haven't reported me to Jules. And you offered Ella *our* assistance, didn't you?"

"You invaded her privacy! If I hadn't intervened, it would have been disastrous."

"You could have just told her we had the wrong house! Instead, you told her we'd be back tomorrow."

"I know what I said," said Serge. "But we can't come back."

"We have to!" Jasper cried. "Can't you *feel* how unhappy she is? She's alone here. No one understands her —"

"Don't make the mistake of thinking that Ella is unique. Everything you've seen so far is classic client behavior. Running away from home, shouting at her parents — it's nothing new. And she's no charity case. She doesn't really need us."

"What about her mother?"

"Lower your voice," Serge hissed. Walkers on the park-side path were starting to stare. "It's very sad about her mother, but Ella is not the first girl whose mother died young and whose father remarried a woman she didn't like. Plenty of children would gladly trade places with her. We have our systems at the Slipper for a reason."

"Is that *you* talking," said Jasper, "or Jules?"

Serge drew a sharp breath.

"I thought so," said Jasper. "Are you coming back here with me tomorrow or not?"

Serge worked to recover his mental balance. "If I say no?"

"Then I'll come by myself."

"And if I turn you in?"

Jasper searched Serge's eyes with his crimson ones. "I don't live by other people's rules when I know they're the wrong ones," he said. "I did that for a century, just to stay in my grandmother's good graces, and it felt — oh. Horrible." He shuddered. "I had no idea who I was. I was whatever she wanted, that was all. I didn't come here to live that way. I came to be true to myself."

"Even if that means disobeying your inspiration?"

"What?"

"Jules," said Serge, folding his arms. "This morning you worshipped her. Was it an act?"

"Not at first," said Jasper. "Eighty years ago, I read a story in the *Criers* about an orphan boy in the north. Pierce was his name, I think."

Serge twitched. He hadn't thought of Pierce in decades.

"He'd been enslaved by an awful Kisscrafter — but Bejeweled rescued him," Jasper went on. "A wealthy couple from Lilac adopted him, and they were all so *happy*." He sighed, and little lights like stars floated from his lips. "Did you work for the Slipper back then? Do you remember?"

Serge nodded. Pierce had been his own first client. Jules had taken credit, but back then, he hadn't cared about that kind of thing; he'd been an apprentice himself, as full of passion as Jasper was now, and seeing Pierce adopted and free had been everything he'd ever dreamed of.

It had been a long time.

"I was young when I heard that story," said Jasper. "Afterward, I was *obsessed*. I read about how Bejeweled helped the mermaid who'd lost her sister, and about the girl who was imprisoned at the top of the glass hill. And then there was that orphanage full of children who were made to spin straw into gold — until Bejeweled freed them."

Serge listened with uncomfortable pleasure to this litany of good deeds, none of which Jules had actually performed alone. He had done the heavy lifting.

"So yes, I admire what she used to do," said Jasper. "But she clearly isn't doing it anymore. And I came to Quintessential to help people, so I will. What about you?"

"I am the Executive Godfather of the Glass Slipper."

"And you want to take over when Jules retires. So you can change things."

"Well — yes," said Serge, somewhat rattled that Jasper had read the situation so well. "Why shouldn't I? I've worked long and hard for the privilege, and I don't intend to lose it. I can't allow you to take Ella as a client."

"I'll be careful," Jasper began, but Serge put up a hand and silenced him.

"You've already broken nearly every rule in the book — you're a menace, Jasper! You could have been seen by anyone walking along the park tonight. For all you know, Jules has heard about this already."

For the first time, Jasper looked alarmed. "Do you think?" he whispered, looking both ways along the park. "Does she have spies?"

"All over the city," said Serge. "She knows the gossip before the scribes do — even *I* don't know how she does it. If we go behind her back to help Ella, we have to be more than careful. We have to be untraceable."

Jasper rose up on his tiptoes. "We?"

"That's not what I meant," said Serge, his insides roiling. He had to sneak Ella's scroll back into Lebrine's files before it could be missed. "We'll come back tomorrow — but only to get the contract," he said. "We'll explain to Ella that we've made a mistake."

"It's no mistake, Serge. This is where we're meant to be. I *feel* it." Jasper eyed him briefly. "And so do you."

Serge couldn't deny it. He *did* feel something here — his dust had come to him so easily. But that didn't mean he would risk the Slipper.

"Report to work tomorrow morning," he said to Jasper. "In the meantime, don't go anywhere near Ella Coach, or I *will* report you, and you will go back to Crimson."

He snapped his fingers and left his apprentice alone.

Ella

4th Blackwhile, 1086
Fulcrum Hospice

To the fairies at the Glass Slipper:
My name is Ellie Herringbone and I'm dying from the roop. We just wasted our last few nauts so a Hipocrath could tell us there's no hope for me. But a kind Blue fairy told me that there might still be hope for my daughter, Ella, if I put her on your List. The fairy said that every once in a while a charity case gets some attention so it's worth at least trying and she said she'll do her best.

Ella is a good girl. No mum could want a better. She should have had such a pretty childhood. Instead, she's had nothing but hardship, just like me, and she's never complained. And that's my fear.

I'm scared she'll think that this is all life can be, and it's all she's fit for. I'm scared the second I'm dead she'll take my place in that Jacquard shop with the mold and the roaches and she'll stay there. I'm scared she'll meet someone she loves more than she loves her own self, and pay for it with her life.

Ella can't waste herself here. She's got brains and strength. She should be somewhere that matters, where she can make something of them.

I've told her all her life that Quintessential's for the quints. But White skies, if I could make her one of those city children I'd do it. If she could have nauts like them, if she could have their education and their chances, I'd give anything for it. I'd die for it. As long as I'm dying anyway I wish I could die for that. Instead, I'm leaving her nothing and she's going to end up bent under someone's foot and I can't stand it. Oh, I can't stand it, I wanted to give her more than just survival but there's no changing places in this world, there's no going up the ladder. They keep you right where they want you, the Jacquards and the rest of them. Give you just enough to keep slogging through the muck, and never enough to get out of it.

So now I'm begging you fairies — who'll probably never listen, hey? You'll never see this letter. But if you do, my daughter, Ella, needs you. Save her from this life. Give her the same privileges as those children in the city, and I swear, she'll use them right. She knows what things are worth. She'll change the world if she gets her chance, I know it.

Since I can't anymore, please help her find her way.

~Ellie Herringbone

THE worst thing about death, Ella thought as she wiped her tears once more on her pillow, was that there were no more answers. Anything she hadn't asked her mum before she died, she could never ask her now. It would always be like that. She'd keep getting older, and she'd keep having new questions, but her mother would always be dead.

She closed her eyes, clutching the letter and wishing her mum could be with her for just a minute. Just to hug her. Maybe *that* was the worst part — not being able to hug her. But not being able to ask questions was a very close second.

Had her mum really wanted her to be a quint?

She opened her eyes and stared at the strange, silvery contract.

She'd stayed locked in her room all night, crying all the tears she'd kept bottled up since the funeral, reading and rereading her mum's letter. It made no sense. Her mum had always mocked city dwellers; she'd said that in Eel Grass the people were real and they knew what real life was about. But according to this letter, she'd wanted a plush life — or at least she'd wanted it for Ella.

Then again, her mum had been dying when she wrote that. Maybe she'd been delirious.

A brisk knock at the door made her sit up straight. Someone was rattling the handle.

"Ella, unlock this, please."

She hid the fairies' scroll deep in her wardrobe, down inside one of her fishing boots, and then unlocked her bedroom door but didn't open it. She went back to bed and rolled to face the wall. The door opened.

"Chef Alma made poached eggs," said Sharlyn. "Your father says you like them."

Ella didn't turn.

"Earnest and I have discussed your behavior," Sharlyn said, "and we've decided that what you need is encouragement to develop your new social life, starting today."

She already didn't like the sound of whatever this was.

"Get dressed and come downstairs to eat. You have an appointment in an hour."

"What appointment?" said Ella, but Sharlyn had already closed the door.

Not quite an hour later, she went downstairs. She grabbed a piece of toast in the dining room, where her dad and Sharlyn sat with the remains of their breakfast.

"Collect your school things," said Sharlyn. Her dark eyes raked over Ella's knitted skirt and long, hooded pullover. "Chemise Shantung is here to pick you up for a gathering."

"What gathering?"

"In fact," said Sharlyn, "there's rather wonderful news, Ella. You don't deserve it, given your little adventure to Salting, but every noble family in the city has been invited to attend a royal ball. Tonight."

Ella gaped. "A *ball?*"

"I know!" Sharlyn looked delighted. "It's short notice, but don't worry, I'll make sure you have what you need. In the meantime, your classmates are getting together this morning for a little work party, to help with some of the arrangements for the ball. Lady Jacquard will be your host."

The crumbs of toast in Ella's mouth suddenly tasted burned. "You want me to go to the Jacquards'?"

"You're going," said Sharlyn. "Right now."

Ella couldn't quite breathe. She met her dad's eyes. "Don't make me," she said. "Not the Jacquards'. I'll go to Chemise's if you want — or even Tiffany's, but —"

"Jacquard Silks is our supplier, Ell," said her dad. "They contract with Practical Elegance. You can't just snub them."

"Besides," said Sharlyn, "this is a wonderful opportunity for you to see your classmates outside of school. Once you make friends, you'll find your place here."

Ella's pleas went unanswered. Several minutes later, she was in the Shantungs' carriage, hugging her satchel. It was the cruelest punishment her stepmother could have devised, making her go to Lavaliere Jacquard's house.

"Isn't it exciting?" Chemise was saying. "A royal ball, tonight! There's never been one on such short notice — the messenger came round only this morning!" She twisted a dark, glossy lock of hair around one finger. "What am I going to wear? I haven't had a new gown in — well, you know, the fashions change so fast. . . ." She collapsed against the carriage cushions, biting her red bottom lip.

Ella took out her embroidery hoop, which she'd hidden in her school bag since Sharlyn said she couldn't bring her workbasket to a social gathering. She stretched a piece of dark blue linen over the inner ring, then flexed open the outer ring to fit it over the fabric before tightening the screw. The bumping of the carriage made it tricky, but Ella was well practiced, and soon she had made her way twice around the loop, tugging the linen and tightening the screw until the fabric was taut as a drum. If she concentrated on work, she could almost forget where the carriage was going.

"What are you making?" asked Chemise, watching Ella thread her embroidery needle.

"A first Shattering Day dress," Ella replied. "My friend's mum is expecting a baby."

"How lovely," said Chemise. "I've never learned to embroider, but I've crocheted things. I once made a potholder for our cook."

She sounded proud — as though potholders weren't the easiest things in the world, Ella thought. But still. That a Shantung heiress had ever crocheted anything was shocking.

"I've forgotten how since. I don't suppose you'd teach me again sometime?"

She asked so kindly that Ella was unable to refuse. "Yeah, if you want."

Chemise smiled, and Ella found herself smiling back just a bit.

"Did you make your skirt too?" Chemise's eyes flickered over Ella's outfit, which Sharlyn hadn't been able to get her to change. "It's intricate, isn't it? How long did it take?"

"Weeks," said Ella, gratified by Chemise's look of admiration. She'd always liked this skirt. It was full, and the cable patterns were interesting, and the hem was purposely uneven, coming up shorter in front to show her boots.

"What will you wear to the ball?"

"I'm not going," said Ella.

Chemise looked extremely embarrassed. "I'm so sorry," she said. "I shouldn't have assumed. I thought all the Coterie families were going — but perhaps it's just old friends of the Charmings."

"I'm invited," said Ella. "I'm just not going."

Chemise frowned in confusion and fell silent as the carriage brought them farther west. Here, upon the seaside cliffs that flanked Charming Palace, stood some of the most spectacular homes in Quintessential, belonging to old and influential families like the Garters and the Panniers, the Farthingales and the Gussets.

And the Jacquards.

When the carriage reached the top of the cliff where the Jacquards' vast estate sat, Ella's mouth sagged open.

"Isn't it perfect?" said Chemise wistfully as the carriage brought them through endless manicured gardens and up to the manor's principal entrance.

Ella followed Chemise out of the carriage, staring up at the intimidating height and breadth of the Jacquard manor. It was a palace, many centuries old, and it evoked a sense of grand history. But everything about it was newly refinished and fashionably precise. Against the backdrop of the Tranquil Sea, the buildings gave the impression of being light and airy: blue as a robin's egg, all trimmed in shining white, with endless windows and balconies.

Ella shivered looking at it. She stood rooted at the bottom of the imposing steps, clutching her satchel to her. Every stone of this place, every line of mortar, had been paid for in blood. Including her mum's.

The front doors opened, and Ella and Chemise went up the steps. A gloved butler ushered them in, and she had the suffocating sense that she was being swallowed. The ceiling vaulted overhead, and slim double staircases curved upward before her, leading to a balcony that overlooked the marble entrance hall. In the center of this hall stood an aquarium some fifteen feet high, designed to look like an ocean wave of glass rising up from the floor. Inside it, glistids glittered and azurefish flashed their bright blue fins.

Ella gazed at the opulent sight, numb. The Jacquards lived in impossible splendor. She'd always known it, but to see it was sickening.

"Why, Chemise Shantung! How lovely to see you."

A woman with a sleek dark bob cut in a sharp diagonal line across her forehead stood at the balcony above them, her smile as white as Sharlyn's — only hers was on a pale face. Her cheeks had a natural glow that Ella was certain came from a jar, her dark eyebrows were expertly plucked and penciled, and her clothing was loose and layered in shades of shell and flax, intentionally rumpled in style, meant to appear as though she had only just climbed out of bed and accidentally happened to look perfect. One of her sleeves had been spun so gossamer-fine that it was rendered transparent, and the jewels that twined up her arm showed through it.

"Lady Jacquard," said Chemise, curtsying. "Thank you so much for hosting."

Lady Jacquard descended the curving stairs. Her hand, resting lightly on the balustrade, glittered with white and blue fire. Ella tried and failed to fathom the cost of the diamonds and sapphires she wore. "How is your mother?" Lady Jacquard asked Chemise as she came to stand beside the crystal wave. "And Challis?"

"We're all very well, thank you."

"Perfect," said Lady Jacquard. "I hear business has been rocky — my sympathies, of course. Do tell your mother I'm thinking of her and that I send my very best wishes."

She turned her gray eyes upon Ella. They traveled the length of her, from her boots and knitted skirt to the fabric band on her head. Ella dug her fingertips into her satchel, which she still held in front of her like a shield.

"Elegant Herringbone *Coach*," said Lady Jacquard, apparently enjoying the taste of Ella's name. "Lavaliere didn't exaggerate your fondness for knitting. But family traditions are so important. And there's always room for talent at Jacquard. . . ."

Lady Jacquard laughed, and Ella broke out in gooseflesh.

"I'm joking, of course," she said. "Well, girls, I'd just adore a chat, but I've got such a lot to do — His Majesty asked me to arrange the details of the ball for him, you understand. Enjoy yourselves."

A servant led Ella and Chemise up the curving stairs and into a wide, mirrored hall lined with portraits of Jacquards that went back centuries. This hall led to Lavaliere's chamber — because it was certainly a chamber and not a room — which was already full of people when Chemise and Ella entered. Dimity lounged on a settee, brushing her hair; Loom relaxed, half asleep, in a brocade chair, his booted feet resting on a cushioned stool; Paisley and Garb stood out on the balcony, laughing. A maid worked unobtrusively in one corner, half hidden behind a screen, mixing powders and creams at a vanity table, and another maid sat before a tall, slim jewelry armoire, comparing fabric swatches against precious stones. Two more young women in serving uniforms stood on either side of a thronelike chair.

In this throne, elevated above the others, sat Lavaliere Jacquard. Her sleek dark hair was tied off with a flounce of Prism silk that fluttered without needing any breeze, dancing as only Prism silk did, picking up the sunlight and subtly shifting from gold to pink to faint, silvery blue.

Nauseating weight settled in Ella's chest at the sight of it. One hair-tie length of Prism silk cost fifteen hundred nauts. Before going to C-Prep, she'd only ever seen the stuff on looms in the Jacquard workshop. As a little girl, she'd longed to touch it, but she'd never been allowed. No one who spun Prism silk could afford a scrap of it.

Lavaliere's elbows rested on the cushioned arms of her chair. The maids on either side of her were hard at work on her fingernails, no doubt for the royal ball.

"Hi," she said to Chemise. She did not acknowledge Ella. "Didn't you bring your maid?" With her chin, Lavaliere gestured toward a corner of the chamber. Ella looked over to see a small group of servants all making silk flowers.

Chemise blushed. "I didn't know we were supposed to," she said. "I'll send for Flaxine."

"No need," said Lavaliere, flashing her beautiful smile. "You can take her place at the maids' table and make the flowers yourself."

Chemise's face flushed redder still. For a second, Ella almost thought she might cry.

"I'm joking," said Lavaliere with a laugh that sounded just like her mother's. Chemise sucked in a breath of relief.

"Why don't *you* sit with the servants, Cinderella?" said Dimity with a smirk. "Give them a hand with their knitting."

Ella tensed at the nickname. The scribes had called her that because of her dad's Cinder Stoppers, and when Dimity realized she didn't like it, she had made sure it stuck. But working with the maids wasn't a bad idea. It would make the time go faster than just sitting around and being useless. She went to the corner table and sat herself down.

Behind her, Dimity giggled nastily. "She's really *doing* it," she whispered, quite loudly enough to be heard.

The servants stiffened when Ella sat among them. She tried to smile at Dimity's maid, whom she recognized from C-Prep, but the girl would give her only a polite nod.

"Where's Tiffany?" asked Chemise. "I hope she isn't ill."

"I hope she *is*," said Dimity. "She honestly thinks she might catch Dash for herself. It's so pathetic. She'll see tonight, won't she, Lavaliere?"

"She's on his dance card," Lavaliere replied. "He has the fourth with her."

"But your mother's arranging his partners! Can't she fix it?"

"Let her dance with him," said Loom dispassionately. "Nothing could put him off more."

Lavaliere laughed.

"Dash is strange now, though," mused Dimity. "He was positively dull at breakfast yesterday. He used to be such fun."

"Will he be quiet all the time now, do you think?" asked Chemise.

"He'll come around," Lavaliere replied.

Ella watched the hands of the servant sitting across from her. He picked up five small circles of cut white silk, stacked them, and used a small pair of scissors to make small slits all the way around the outside. When he was finished, he pinched one of the circles with tweezers and held it over a candle flame until the "petals" began to curl up. When all five circles were done, he artfully restacked them, gave them a twist at the bottom, and put a few stitches through the twist to keep it strong. Then he fluffed out the curled petals and inserted a sparkling pin into their middle.

"Lovely," said Ella admiringly, and she took a stack of blue silk circles from the table.

"Please don't trouble yourself, Miss," said the young maid who sat beside her. The Jacquard *J* was embroidered into her apron. She smiled too brightly at Ella. "We'll do the work."

"I don't mind helping."

The maid's smile became strained. "Miss, please. If the flowers aren't perfect —"

"It's your hide," said Ella. "I get it. I promise I'll make them right."

The maid watched anxiously as Ella copied what she'd seen — little slits, curling petals, a twist and a few stitches, and finally a pretty pin.

"There," she said, holding up the finished flower. "Does it pass?"

The maid smiled — a real smile. "It's good, hey?" she said, nudging Dimity's maid on the other side of her.

Dimity's maid glanced at Ella's handiwork and then at Ella herself. "It's good," she said, and she smiled a bit too.

Gratified by their acceptance, Ella buckled down to work, making one flower after another until she had the rhythm of it.

"You're quick, Miss," said the servant across from her. "You've done this before?"

Ella shrugged. "I've done work like it."

"I don't see why *I* can't be on his dance card," said Loom with a great sigh. "It's so unfair."

"Dash doesn't court men," said Paisley, who had just come in from the balcony with Garb.

"He doesn't court *you* either," said Loom. "But you get to dance with him."

"And you get to dance with Mercer Garrick," said Dimity. "Who is besotted with you, by the way, if you haven't noticed."

"I know." Loom's voice was sour. "He wrote me a poem."

"You could do much worse than the son of the Exalted Nexus," said Paisley.

"Are the Garricks actually going to show their faces tonight?" Garb demanded. "I didn't think they'd be invited after — *you* know."

"The king's affair with Mercer's mother?" said Paisley.

"He's had a million affairs," said Dimity. "What makes this one any different?"

"This one made the queen disappear," said Garb. "Where do you think she went?"

"My father says Lilac," said Paisley.

"My mother's for Orange," said Loom.

They were both wrong, Ella thought. The queen was on a ship. There was no other reason for her to have gone to the docks yesterday morning.

She fluffed the petals with her fingertips, thinking of how compassionate the queen had been to her. It was sad, really, that the king had made someone so kind feel so miserable. She wondered what she ought to do about the royal wedding ring. She certainly couldn't keep it.

"Let's have a wager," said Garb, pulling out his coin purse and throwing an obscene amount of money onto the table. "Where will Queen Maud be found? Who's in?"

All but Lavaliere and Chemise added to the pot. "I say she's still in the Blue Kingdom somewhere. Probably Port Urbane," said Garb. "Loom's for Orange, Pay's for Lilac — Dimmy, what's your bet?"

Dimity brushed her hair for the thousandth time and pursed her lips. "Grey," she finally said. "Hiding at the Silver Citadel."

Loom gave another gusty sigh. "How long is this little party supposed to last?" he complained. "I need to get ready for the ball."

"There won't be a ball if Mother doesn't find a band to play the first hour," said Lavaliere. She hissed and recoiled from the jewelry maid, who was now holding an enormous emerald earring next to one of Lavaliere's ears. "Don't *touch* my face," she said coldly. The maid skittered away, and Lavaliere sank back into her throne.

"There might not be a ball?" asked Chemise in dismay.

"Pulse said they'd play — but only for the dancing," said Lavaliere. "They're so famous it's an insult to ask them to play the first hour. Someone else has to play during arrivals."

"But your mother will think of something, won't she?"

Lavaliere shrugged. "It's short notice."

This was followed by a period of silence. The quiet was punctuated only by a shrill giggle and Chemise saying, "Oh, don't . . ." Ella paid no attention to whatever they were doing. She held out her tweezers to poise a silk petal over the candle flame.

Something cold and slimy oozed down the back of her neck. She yelped and dropped the petal into the fire, where it smoked, and she reached back to slap the slimy thing off, but it only slipped down into her tunic. She jumped up from the table and shook out her clothing, and the offending thing dropped to the carpet. A snail. She picked it up and looked around at her classmates, who had clearly enjoyed the entertainment. Only Chemise looked unhappy.

"A real one this time," gasped Garb, who was laughing so hard he'd nearly given himself fits. "Better than Ubiquitous."

"So it was you who put that acorn in my bag yesterday, then?" Ella demanded. "*You* burned my knitting?"

"That pile of wool?" said Garb, grinning. "Who cares, Cinderella? You want more wool, I'll get you some."

Ella set her jaw. She walked out onto the balcony and deposited the snail in a plant, and then she went back to the maid's table, but she did not sit. She didn't want to stay here for one more minute.

"I need the privy," she whispered to the maid in the Jacquard apron. "Where is it?"

The maid led her down the corridor to the privy chamber, and Ella dawdled within it, taking as much time as possible before she put her hand to the door — and stopped.

"How *dare* you mention that while there are guests in this house?"

The furious whisper was Lady Jacquard's.

"Forgive me, my lady, but she asked me to tell you. The pain —"

Ella heard the sound of a hard slap and the sharp cry of the maid.

"Shut up," said Lady Jacquard while the maid sniffled. "You know what happens when you forget your place in this house. You lose it."

"My lady —"

"You'll spend the next month on Ragg Row," said Lady Jacquard. "On a spinning mat. And while you are there, you'll reflect on how fortunate you are to have a position in my home."

"Please —"

"One more word and you will lose your position permanently."

The maid's footsteps pounded away down the corridor. Ella grabbed up her satchel and flung open the privy door, shocking Lady Jacquard, whose face lit with rage. In an instant, however, she appeared relaxed again; she laughed ruefully and pushed back her sharp, dark fringe of hair.

"Why, Ella." Her voice was so sugary she could have iced a cake with it. "Haven't you ever heard that you shouldn't startle people?"

"Sure," said Ella quietly, staring at her. "I hear lots of things."

Lady Jacquard kept smiling, but her eyes turned as cold as her house.

"It's my fault she was out here," Ella said. "I asked her where the privy was — she was only showing me. Don't send her to your workshop."

Lady Jacquard's pale cheeks flushed ever so slightly, and Ella realized that she'd just insinuated that the Jacquard workshop was a bad place to be. But it *was* a bad place. And Lady Jacquard knew it, or she wouldn't send her maid there as a punishment. The maid couldn't stand up for herself — she'd lose her living if she did — but Ella had no job to lose. She was not vulnerable like that maid was, or like her mum had been. As this realization struck her, so did the certainty that she had to do something about it, then. She had to act.

"She'll catch roop if she goes there," she said. "Please. Don't send her."

"My dear." Lady Jacquard's smile was awful. "Jacquard is perfectly safe."

Ella could not accept this. "There was roop in Fulcrum two years back," she said. "There's roop up in Coldwater now."

"You take such an interest in the welfare of my employees." Lady Jacquard slipped an arm around Ella's shoulders and gave her a hard little squeeze. "How kind."

She steered Ella back to Lavaliere's room, and Ella reentered the chamber, nauseated. The servants glanced at her, questioning, and she felt like a traitor to them — she should have been able to do something to save that maid's position. But what? She was wealthy now, and she lived in the city, but that didn't give her authority here. Lady Lariat Jacquard was Director of the Garment Guild and held the highest seat in the House of Mortals, in the Essential Assembly. She was nearly level with the king. To really stop her, it would take money. Power. It would take the Charmings themselves, or the Exalted Council.

Or the fairies.

Ella went back to making silk flowers, but her mind was elsewhere. When the work party was done, she returned to the carriage with Chemise, and by the time the Shantungs' driver stopped the horses in front of Ella's house, she was deep in thought.

Fairies had magic. *That* was power. If anyone could put a stop to Lady Jacquard and her workshops, they could.

Dash

THE ball was in eight hours.

Dash willed the hands of the clock to stop progressing, but seconds ticked by, and minutes, and soon the few hours that buffered him from humiliation would be gone, and he'd be standing at the foot of the grand staircase beside his father, facing the horde of glittering Quintessentialites who wanted to look at him and dance with him.

He was sitting in the reading corner of the king's office, which was as far as he could get from his father's desk without throwing himself out the window. Lady Jacquard stood at the desk beside his father's chair, reviewing the arrangements for the ball.

"I'm sure it will surpass all expectations," the king said when she was done. "Are things in Coldwater improving?"

Lady Jacquard made an irritated noise. "Those laborers are so irresponsible," she said. "Refusing to stay home when they're ill. They spread disease to everyone, and now scores of them are dead and the whole shop is infected. You'd think they'd look out for their own, but no — they come to work and poison each other."

"Your managers ought to turn the sick ones around. Send them home."

"Believe me, I've told them to — but it's difficult to know who's ill. People hide the sickness with Ubiquitous lozenges. The magic stops the coughing. It's madness."

Dash only half listened. He flipped through his *Crier*, looking for any news about his mother. There were several columns speculating about her disappearance and her whereabouts, but none of them came close to the truth. She was still safe.

"That's Dash's dance card there, is it?" Lady Jacquard turned her smile upon him. "I hope you're pleased with the arrangements," she said, extending the card as she approached. Dash could see that it was crammed with names. He took it from her fingers without touching her and laid it on the reading table before fixing his eyes once more on his *Crier*.

"Are you feeling well?" Lady Jacquard asked him.

Dash glanced at his father, but the king shrugged as if to tell him that he was on his own. Lady Jacquard was already speaking again.

"You've been missed," she said. "Lavaliere has been sleepless with worry. Your encounter with the witch nearly frightened her to death."

He doubted it.

"And you know what gossip is," Lady Jacquard went on. "Everyone has a theory about what it must be like for you now that the curse is broken." She gave his shoulder a motherly pat that made him stiffen. "Is there anything you would like me to make known to the public before your appearance this evening? Of course, if I'm being too forward —"

"You are."

A frost settled over the king's office. Lady Jacquard was silent, and the flush that rose in her pale cheeks was somehow frightening.

"I mean," said Dash, realizing at the look on his father's face that he might have gone just a step too far. "I just —" He stammered to a halt. He'd meant what he said, and he had no idea how to cover it.

"My apologies, Your Highness," said Lady Jacquard. She went to his father. "Your Majesty," she said, and curtsied, but the king took her by the elbow and whispered to her.

"I see," said Lady Jacquard. She gave Dash a look that was one part false pity, two parts real calculation, and then the king kissed her hand and she departed.

King Clement didn't speak until Lariat's footsteps receded.

"That was unwise," he said, his countenance more serious and kingly than Dash was used to seeing it. "I thought you were old enough to understand that our position relies upon keeping our friends. You've never insulted her before — the curse wouldn't let you, I'm sure — but now that you're free to say what you like, I order you to *hold your tongue* with Lady Jacquard."

Dash said nothing. His father advanced on him and stood before his chair.

"Answer. Now."

"Yes, sir," Dash muttered.

The king gave him a long, hard look, and then his serious manner vanished. He plucked Dash's dance card from the table and swung it back and forth by its ribbon, like bait.

"Curious, son? Want to see who's first?" He flipped the dance card over. "Chemise Shantung! Well, that ought to get the night going for you. Delightful women in that family."

Dash tried not to listen, but his father's voice and choice of topic were difficult to ignore.

"Paisley Pannier, Dimity Gusset . . . Ah, now for some fun. Your fourth partner is the fragile Miss Farthingale — still in love with you, I imagine. And number five is lovely Lavaliere." He smiled. "Very clever, Lady Jacquard, very clever. Two dull dance partners followed by an uncomfortable one, and then she schedules in her daughter, knowing that Lavaliere will dazzle you by comparison."

Dash recognized his father's insight as accurate.

"Numbers six through nine don't have Lavaliere's looks," the king continued, pacing away to his desk. He thumped the dance card. "The Shantung girl is first because she's the only one who's equally attractive, and the first dance is always a bit stiff. This schedule is deliberately arranged to make Lavaliere the brightest star of your night." The king looked both amused and unsettled. "That child does whatever her mother tells her. And her mother certainly wants her on the throne."

Dash snorted.

"You don't like her?" said his father, watching him now with narrowed eyes. "The Assembly expects the match, you know. So do your friends."

Dash tried to picture Lavaliere in a wedding gown and found it was easy. Picturing himself beside her, however, was more difficult.

"In any case," said King Clement, "the two of you are already together."

Dash couldn't deny that Lavaliere was essentially his girlfriend. Or at least it seemed like she was, because she'd positioned herself beside him at every social occasion since the curse had first seized him, and Dash had flattered her lavishly because he could not help himself. But for all their proximity, there had always been distance between them. They had barely even kissed, except when it was publicly appropriate.

Still, as irritating as it was to have the world assume he was destined to marry Lavaliere, he preferred her cool aloofness to Tiffany Farthingale's clinging. He hoped Tiffany wouldn't cry tonight.

"The tenth dance is Prince's Preference," the king said, returning his attention to the dance card. "Choose Lavaliere for that one. It will erase your little misstep with her mother just now." He tossed the dance card onto his desk. "I think I'll have a walk," he said. "I'm looking forward to this evening. If your mother can have her fun, then so can I." He raised an eyebrow at Dash. "Unless you want to tell me where she is — or just give a strong hint if you want to be virtuous. There's still time to cancel the ball."

Dash pretended to return his attention to the *Criers*.

"She's in Orange, isn't she?" the king pressed. "Orlaith the Magnificent never cared for me — she'd give Maud sanctuary, and she could hide her well at that labyrinth of a university. Or perhaps your mother sailed for Olive. She and Claret were always friendly."

Dash remained relaxed. He couldn't show, by word or flicker of motion, that his father had gotten it right.

"I admire your loyalty," said his father. "Very touching stuff. But you're punishing yourself for no reason. Your mother will be back, and you know it."

Dash hoped it wasn't true, even though he missed her. One word from her would have stopped all of this. Little as his father had respected the queen in other ways, he had always deferred to her judgment where Dash was concerned.

"Have it your way," said his father. "We'll be two Charming bachelors tonight, enjoying a ball together. Just like it was with my father and me." He strolled out, whistling.

Serge

Afternoon sunlight flooded the penthouse of the Slipper. Serge leaned against the glass wall, watching Jules pace in circles around her desk, her short frame elongated by shoes so high-heeled that no one without wings could possibly have balanced upon them. In his pocket, his watch burned. When he flicked it open, names and addresses swam into view.

LOOM BATIK. BATIK CASTLE.

LAVALIERE JACQUARD. JACQUARD ESTATE.

FLINT QUEBRACHO. 21 SEMINAL PARK SOUTH.

TIARA ZORI. 6 HEMMING SQUARE.

Serge snapped his watch shut.

"The nerve of Clement," Jules seethed. "Giving a ball without any prior warning. Every single godparent is out in the city, but they'll never get to everyone in time, and we'll never be forgiven if they don't — but we're responding as fast as we can! What do these people think we're *made* of?"

"Magic," Serge replied. "Don't panic, Jules. I've drawn up a schedule and delegated tasks. I'm confident that every client will be seen in time."

"What about *your* clients?" Jules demanded. "They're our most deserving, and they'll be furious if you don't give them what they want — you should be with them by now."

"I stayed here to ensure that everyone else was managed efficiently," said Serge. "I'm capable of seeing to my clients' needs in the time that remains."

"Then go," Jules snapped. "The clock is ticking. Stop making me nervous."

"What about Lavaliere Jacquard?" he asked her, making sure not to sound accusatory.

"What about her? You take care of her."

"Won't Lariat expect you personally?" Serge could hardly bear visiting the Jacquards. If only Jules would take that one visit off his hands, he knew he could handle the rest of it.

"I've got a *beastly* headache," said Jules. She collapsed into her oversize chair. "I know you can do it, babe," she said, closing her eyes. "Ta."

Serge left the penthouse and went to find Jasper, who was sitting in a glass chair beside the reception pool, whispering with Lebrine.

Before he could reach his apprentice, someone jostled him with such energy that it nearly sent him to the floor. Gossamer the perpetually tearful had knocked into him. Tears glistened as usual on her dark blue cheeks, but this time she carried a box of her belongings, out of which stuck a purple seaweed scroll. Serge regarded it with some surprise. Purple scrolls meant termination.

"I'm fired," said Gossamer. "I'm not the right *fit* for the Slipper. I've had one too many lapses in judgment — that's what Jules calls it when I do my real job, which is to help children in *actual* need, instead of the entitled brats we call clients. Right after she fired me, the royal ball was announced, and do you know what she did? She actually tried to get me to stay and work through the end of the day." Gossamer laughed angrily. "You know what I told her?"

Serge did not, but he was very, very curious.

"I told her I don't exist for her convenience, and I wished I'd never taken this job in the first place. I knew the Slipper wasn't what it used to be, but I thought I could make a difference. I thought I'd have the resources to change lives." Gossamer shook her head and hefted the box in her arms. "This place is poison. I don't need a contract system or a List. I have *magic*. I'm *bursting* with it, because I still have compassion, unlike the heartless witch who runs this place."

Serge stared. "You said all that? To Jules?"

"And more," said Gossamer with a satisfied flick of her little wings.

"She'll have the House of Magic revoke your license."

Gossamer snorted. "License," she said. "What am I, human? Who's going to stop me if I want to use my magic?"

"Jules can try."

"Jules can barely make a glass dot anymore, and you know it. That's why she needs so much money — she's magically bankrupt." Gossamer lowered her voice and moved closer to him. "I know about you. You're running out of fairy dust, aren't you."

Serge stepped back, caught off guard. "Excuse me?"

"If you don't get out of here soon, you'll dry up just like Jules. Is that what you want? To spend your life in a penthouse, pretending you have a headache, when the truth is you're not *magic* anymore?"

An ugly shock coursed through him. "Get out," he said. "You've been terminated."

Gossamer fluttered away as commanded but turned back when she reached the Slingshot. "Good-bye, Serge," she said. "Best wishes to you in making wishes come true."

Only after the door slid shut behind her did Serge remember that Jasper was there, waiting by the reception pool and listening to every word. He took a moment to collect himself before joining his apprentice.

"You've been reinstated for duty," he said, forcing a smile and trying to organize his insides, which were all in pieces. "The ball begins at nine, which gives us very little time before clients are climbing into their carriages. I didn't want to overwhelm you on our first rounds, but it looks like we'll have to take on Gossamer's clients as well as our own."

"If we split up, we can cover more clients in less time," said Jasper.

"Apprentices may not work alone until the trial period is complete."

"But what about Ella?"

"Not *here*," Serge hissed, and he headed for the Slingshot. In moments, he and Jasper were flying briskly toward the first client's address.

Batik Castle sat atop the cliffs that rose up along the seaside just north of the harbor. The vines that crawled over its shining battlements were laden with large blue flowers.

"Gorgeous," said Jasper as they approached.

"Isn't it?" said Serge, grabbing with relief at this bit of normal conversation. "Some segments of this fortress date back almost as far as the Shattering."

Jasper sighed. "We have castles that old in Crimson," he said. "But they don't look like this."

From the breast pocket of his gray coat, Serge pulled a tiny bell. It looked like a fresh bluebell flower, and the music of its chime was enchantingly delicate. As they waited their contractual three minutes before entering the client's room, Serge tried to calm his disordered nerves by smoothing the fall of hair he wore over his eye. Ocean mist made his hair unruly; he'd have to use magic to hold it in place today, though he didn't have much to spare.

Because he was running out of dust. And, apparently, everyone knew it.

"You should try Preen Creme." Jasper indicated his own black spikes of hair, impervious to the sea breeze. "I brought just *roomfuls* of it with me from Cliffhang. Here, let me fix you."

Serge would have declined the intervention, but Jasper's fingertips were already on his blond wave, applying a substance that smelled refreshingly of lime.

"Don't you love the scent?"

"It's nice," Serge admitted, glancing at himself in his watch's mirrored case. Jasper had given his plume a nice sense of lift and bounce. "Three minutes are up." He grabbed Jasper's sleeve and snapped his fingers.

They vanished and reappeared in Loom Batik's bedroom. Loom sat with his feet propped on his vanity table, looking bored, as usual. His glass slippers changed hue in the sunlight, turning from deep amber to sunset gold. They were precisely what he had requested upon signing his contract, and Serge still enjoyed seeing them; they had tremendous depth of color. They were marred only by Jules's glass dots affixed to the heels.

Gossamer was wrong, Serge thought. He wasn't like Jules. He still had empathy — he felt things; he cared for people. Jules just didn't give him enough chances to show it anymore. That was why his dust was harder to summon.

Loom kicked down his feet and pulled off the slippers. "About time," he said. "I've been wearing those things all morning, calling you."

"They're sublime," said Jasper, picking up one of the amber shoes. He ran a fingertip over the glass dot and frowned.

"Who's *this?*" Loom demanded. "Where's the girl you used to bring?"

"Georgette is now an official godmother," said Serge. "She has her own clients to manage."

"This one's not even a Blue fairy," said Loom. "What is he, Red?"

"Crimson."

Loom drew back. "*Crim*son? Don't they hypnotize people and send them off cliffs?"

Jasper did not defend himself, but his look of quiet hurt prodded Serge into speech.

"Jasper is my apprentice," he said. "If that troubles you, I will reassign you to a more suitable godparent."

Loom glowered and fingered the spike in his ear. "He can stay."

"Good. Now, what can we do for you?"

"I want shoes," said Loom, flexing his bare feet. "I can't wear the glass ones again. They were impressive at first, but everyone's seen them now — too bad, since sheer is the fashion. And I'm sick of these spikes," he said, touching a blue-black hairstyle that was almost exactly like Jasper's. "I want something *fresh,* if you have any creativity."

Jasper stepped up to the challenge. Under his pale fingers, Loom's coarse black hair grew long, straight, and shiny. It hung in artistic, jagged lines around his face and past his shoulders, with one thick lock in front that was not white but actually clear as glass. The boy's mask of boredom was momentarily pierced by this sudden, dramatic change in his appearance; he exclaimed over how much he liked it.

"Now do shoes," Loom said to Jasper, whose Crimsonness he had apparently forgiven. "Can you make ones as good as my hair?"

Jasper could. When they left Batik Castle, Loom was satisfied, which Serge could not remember happening before. "Impressive work," he said to Jasper. "Loom is famously particular."

"Thanks for backing me." Jasper's voice was soft. "People usually won't."

They visited Gossamer's clients in rapid succession. There were pimples to disguise, hairstyles to arrange, and accessories to fashion according to the latest trends. There were carriages to embellish and shoes to conjure. Jasper's whole performance continued to impress Serge. He had the knack of dramatically transforming faces with his hair arrangements, and his taste was faultless — everything he touched was improved. Even more remarkable: Jasper knew just how to speak to each child, and in reply the children listened to him and seemed instinctively to trust him. Serge had never worked with an apprentice so gifted. He found himself wondering whether, once he had taken over the Slipper himself, Jasper might not be his own Executive Godfather.

They left Gossamer's last client's home. Serge alighted on the grass in a small park, and Jasper came to rest beside him.

"What is it?"

Serge forced his wings to relax. "Nothing," he lied. He took out his watch, which was hot with the call he could put off no longer. He flicked the watch open.

LAVALIERE JACQUARD. JACQUARD ESTATE.

LAVALIERE JACQUARD. JACQUARD ESTATE.

LAVALIERE JACQUARD. JACQUARD ESTATE.

His stomach hurt.

Serge clicked the watch shut and pocketed it. "I'll be engaged for the rest of the afternoon," he said. "I'm afraid you can't come. This client prefers anonymity."

"But what about Ella?"

"What about her?"

"You told her we'd come back. She must be getting ready for the ball too — aren't we going to help her?"

"No."

Jasper pressed his red mouth shut.

"Look," said Serge. "After all you heard Gossamer say, I know you must be having doubts about Jules. And the Slipper doesn't live up to its old reputation these days, I know it. But see it from my perspective, Jasper. If I just wait a little longer, I'll be the one in charge. Think of the good I'll be able to do. If I have to fulfill a few spoiled children's petty whims between now and then, it's worth it."

"Is it?"

Serge stiffened. "I just said that it was."

"How old is Jules?"

"Three hundred and four."

"So she could live another century and just keep stringing you along, couldn't she?"

It was something he tried not to think about.

"I like you, Jasper," Serge said after a moment. "You're talented. But you are not to interact with Ella Coach without my say-so — and don't ever bring up her name again while we're at the Slipper. Do you understand?"

Jasper's giant wings drooped. Tears spilled from his eyes and, where they splashed, dead orchids bloomed from the lawn and crumbled into ash.

"I'll take that as a yes," said Serge. "See you tonight."

Ella

ELLA stood at her window, looking outside for the fairies. When they came, would they fly in? They had said they would chime her, but she didn't hear a thing. Maybe they had come to visit while she'd been away at Lavaliere's house, and she'd missed their visit for the day. She hoped not.

"So?"

Ella turned to find Sharlyn just inside her bedroom door, holding a parcel in her arms.

"How was Lavaliere's?"

"Great," said Ella sarcastically. "We're all best friends now."

"You didn't give them half a chance, did you?"

"Garb Garter put a snail down my back."

"I've heard the Garter boy likes his pranks," said Sharlyn. "But what about Chemise? She seems lovely."

"She's the nicest of the lot," Ella admitted. "By about a thousand leagues."

"That sounds promising. Perhaps you can pursue that friendship tonight at the ball."

"I don't want to go."

"You don't turn down a royal invitation, Ella. It simply is not done."

"What if I'm sick?" Ella faked a cough. "I'm feeling really sick."

"Absolutely not." Sharlyn brought the parcel in and put it on Ella's bed. It was stamped with a big blue G. Gusset Gowns. Dimity's family. Nearly every garment they sold was made from Jacquard silk. Sharlyn opened the parcel and drew out the gown — rose-colored silk with massive shoulders all built out of silk rosettes, and a thin ribbon of Prism silk fluttering around the high waistline. It must have cost enough to pay the Winceys' rent for a year.

Sharlyn laid the gown across the bed. "You can borrow jewels from me, and I'll send in my hairdresser after supper."

"But —"

"No buts. Tonight, I hope you'll finally appreciate what opportunities you have here in this city. This is how business is really done, Ella. Not in offices, but on ballroom floors."

"Oooh," said Clover, appearing suddenly at the door beside her brother. She was so tall that her blast of black curls nearly brushed the doorframe as she gave the rose-colored gown an approving nod. "Nice choice, Ma. Looking forward to the ball, Ella? Even *you* have to ditch the attitude and get excited about a royal invitation, don't you?"

"The best part is always the music," said Linden, who held his drumsticks in his hands. "It would be great to meet the main musical act. Start to get our name out there. You don't know who's playing, do you, Ma? I will *die* if it's Pulse."

Ella suddenly remembered what she'd heard in Lavaliere's room.

"It's Pulse," she said. "But they won't play the first hour, and it's such short notice that Lady Jacquard can't find anyone else to do it."

"She needs musicians?" said Clover, grabbing Linden's arm. "For tonight?"

"This is just what I mean!" said Sharlyn. "Here's a tremendous opportunity for Clover and Linden, and you know about it because you were in the right place with the right people. It isn't as if chances like this are advertised. You simply have to be connected."

"Ma," said Clover, now pacing frantically across Ella's room, her half-pouf of hair vibrating with every step, "talk to Lady Jacquard — you're better at that bit than we are."

"Done," said Sharlyn. "Come with me, Ella. We'll visit the Jacquards, then shop for shoes."

But Ella would not go back there.

"I don't want to go to the ball," she said again. "I told you about the music thing, and I went to Lavaliere's like you asked. Please let me stay home."

Sharlyn actually hesitated.

"Go on," said Clover.

"Yeah, she's shy," said Linden, pushing up his spectacles with a purple finger.

But Sharlyn shook her head. "You're going. End of discussion."

"Sorry, Ella," said Clover. "We tried."

"Thanks for the tip about tonight," said Linden. "We owe you one. Come on, Clo — let's tell the others." He raced from the room with Clover on his heels, leaving Ella alone with Sharlyn.

They regarded each other in the quiet.

"I can't wear that gown," Ella said. "That's Jacquard silk."

"Ella, I understand that your mother —"

"No." Ella cut her off. "You don't. And I have my own dress."

"An *appropriate* dress? For a royal ball?"

"If I can't dress myself, I'm not going."

Sharlyn looked pained, and Ella thought for one second that her stepmother might give in.

"Then I ask you to make an effort," Sharlyn finally said. "A real effort. This is your first appearance at the palace — do you fully comprehend the magnitude of this? If you wear a knitted smock, you'll humiliate our family and injure Practical Elegance — and you'll hurt your own prospects too."

"I get it," Ella said. And she did. But Charming Palace wasn't her world. She could dress in the queen's own gown and she would still be out of place there, so she might as well wear something that didn't make her skin crawl.

When Sharlyn was finally gone, Ella reached under her bed and pulled out the box that held her mum's Shattering Day dress. She'd packed it away after the burial, and she hadn't looked at it since. Now, with gentle hands, she unfolded the old garment and held it up. She'd almost forgotten how beautiful it was — a white linen sheath, simple in shape, made special by the embroidery that blossomed in intricate patterns across it. The embroidery thread had once been bright royal blue, but with years of wear and washing it had grown dull. Still, the designs were extraordinary. Her mum had been as much of an artist as her dad.

Ella grabbed the seam ripper from her workbasket. It was strange to know that her mum would have told her to go to the ball. She'd acted so proud, but underneath it all, she'd wanted Ella invited to royal events. She'd wanted her in the city. She'd even wanted her in the care of fairy godparents.

She sat on her bed and pulled her mum's dress into her lap. She hadn't spent four months at C-Prep without absorbing something about the latest styles. A decade ago, this dress had been perfect, but now the sleeves were too long, the waist too low, and the neck too high. The skirt needed letting out too. Stupid big shoulders she would not do — nor sheer panels either. But she could make it modern without those things. She could make herself a gown fit for a palace. A gown that even Sharlyn couldn't fault.

Determined, Ella pulled out the stitches.

Serge

HE left Jasper in the park and flitted sluggishly toward the Jacquard Estate, grateful that Jasper had taken on the bulk of today's godparenting effort and left him some dust to spare. Lavaliere would require every speck of it.

Three minutes after chiming, he appeared in Lavaliere's chamber. Lavaliere, in a Prism-silk dressing gown, paced from her silver-framed oval mirror to her great four-poster bed, her glass slippers sinking into the sheepskin carpet. The heels of her hands were pressed to her temples. On her face was an expression of agony.

"Where have you been?" she whimpered, kicking her slippers aside when she saw Serge. The prismatic shoes fell sideways in the carpet, sparkling. They were exquisite — cut all over into tiny facets so that they seemed to be constructed entirely of diamonds — and they were the only ones Serge had made in the past fifteen years that Jules hadn't insisted on disrupting with her signature dots. For the Jacquards, Jules always made exceptions.

"I've been calling all day. I've called hundreds of times. Hurry, please, it hurts so much —"

Serge ushered Lavaliere into the blue chair. "Don't move," he said. "Relax if you can."

She shut her eyes. Her neck muscles stood out like cords.

Serge closed his fists. He genuinely longed to see her out of pain, so his dust emerged at once. He moved his hands close to her face until he could touch the illusion that lay flush against her skin. Carefully, he pinched this invisible mask in his fingertips and pulled it from her face and neck, as if tugging a sheet from a statue. Lavaliere cried out, and so did Serge. He was not prepared for the sight of her.

Every bit of skin on her face was packed with purple cankermoth pustules.

"How bad is it?" she whispered. "How bad?"

Two years ago, on her way back from a holiday in Lilac, Lavaliere had been bitten. Under Jules's command, Serge had hidden the first outbreak on Lavaliere's face, but the sores had steadily grown worse. Once a month, Serge removed the illusion so that Lavaliere could treat the pain, but the pustules had never looked as bad as this. Some had turned black. Some were open and weeping.

"It's serious," Serge said, trying to keep the alarm out of his voice. "You must have an infection. You need real treatment, Lavaliere. Numbing the pain isn't enough. I can send you up north to a Hipocrath specialist. You have to leave the illusion off and let him do his work —"

"Twill!" Lavaliere interrupted. "Where are you?"

A waiting maid scurried from her corner with a white glove and a jar of cream. She smeared the cream over Lavaliere's pustules with her gloved hand, and though Lavaliere never opened her eyes, her face contorted in pain as Twill's fingers traveled over the weeping bumps.

"Almost out," said Twill, digging around the bottom of the jar with her gloved fingertips.

"I still need it on my neck," said Lavaliere. "*Hurry.*"

Twill did her best to spread the last bit of cream thin enough to cover all the pustules. It was just enough to do the job. "It's all gone, my lady."

"Serge will get more." As numbness set in, Lavaliere's muscles relaxed.

"Pain doesn't lie," said Serge. "You put the last dose of cream on three weeks ago. It's supposed to numb the pain for a month at least. You're getting worse."

"Put the illusion back on."

"Lavaliere. You need to go up north and get treatment."

"And what, live in Port Urbane for the next five years with my face uncovered?" She laughed harshly. "Not a chance."

"Five years is nothing compared with the rest of your life."

"Dash Charming is the rest of my life," she said. "Put the illusion back on me. Now."

"I need your mother's permission."

"As if she won't give it."

"She might not this time," said Serge. "She needs to see how bad it's gotten."

Lavaliere sank back into her chair. "Fine."

Serge pulled the bell cord and held the door nearly shut so that the maid who responded could not see into the room. She returned minutes later, panting.

"Her ladyship is busy," the maid gasped. "You have her permission for anything. She asks that you hurry, because she'd like to look Lavaliere over before you go."

"Tell Lady Jacquard it's a contractual issue. I need her consent in person."

The maid looked terrified, but she went.

Lariat Jacquard appeared in the corridor several minutes later, her smile tight. "Serge," she said when she reached the door. "What's the problem?"

Serge let her into Lavaliere's chamber. As soon as Lariat was inside, she gave a shout of disgust and turned her back on her daughter. Serge quickly shut the chamber door.

"I *told* Jules," Lariat hissed. "Keep it out of my sight. It's humiliating enough to know it's there without having to look at it."

"The sores are infected," Serge said. "Lavaliere needs treatment, and soon. If I put the illusion back on her now, it might hurt her."

"What will *hurt* her," said her mother, still facing the door, "is being seen like that. A cankermoth bite never killed anyone. Just cover her face. And do something about her mouth while you're at it — make her lips fuller, would you? Then Chemise Shantung won't have anything on her."

She left the chamber, and Serge heard Lavaliere's muffled sobs. Both her hands were pressed to her mouth. She still had not opened her eyes.

"Cover it *up,*" she managed through her tears. "*Now.*"

But he couldn't bring his dust to the surface. He strained internally, but everything in him rebelled. Masking her face was wrong, and his heart couldn't be fooled by any argument to the contrary. To trick himself, he had to think of something else. Someone else. He tried thinking back on Rapunzel — the memory of her had helped him to drum up his dust a time or two — but to his surprise his mind fastened on Ella Coach. He saw her clearly, standing with her mother's letter clutched in her hand, her face hungry and lonely.

He had to meditate on this vision for several minutes before he could begin the process of constructing Lavaliere's illusion. He pictured her face as she wished it to be — the texture, the colors, the contours. He imagined a smooth throat. Dark eyebrows, long lashes. The new shape of her mouth. When his mental image was exact, he flung fairy dust into her face.

In a moment, it was finished. The infection was concealed. Her mouth was not so changed that anyone would suspect she had been altered, but it would satisfy Lariat. He sank down in the nearest chair, exhausted at heart, as Lavaliere opened her eyes. She ran to the mirror and examined her face, first on one side and then the other.

"Mother was right," she said, touching her lips. "I'm perfect now."

"Shall I bring out the gowns, my lady?" asked Twill, peeking out from her corner.

Lavaliere nodded. "Mother bought a few of the latest things, but only for inspiration," she told Serge, as though nothing had passed between them. "Do something like these, but not *quite* — it has to be unique. When I arrive, everyone should look at me. Make that happen."

When she was satisfied, Serge left her chamber. He trudged to the edge of the Jacquard Estate, sat heavily on the rocky cliff top, and gazed out at the Tranquil Sea. A spectacular sunset lit the waves and sky, but he was numb to beauty. He didn't even think he could fly. He tried to flutter his wings, but they were leaden.

There had to be a way. A way he could give Jules and her clients what they wanted without losing his magic. A way to hang on long enough that he could get the Slipper for his own. He just needed something true — something to keep his dust flowing.

He thought he knew what that something might be.

Ella

SHE had been cutting and sewing for nearly five hours when it happened.

She'd taken in the waist of her mum's old gown and removed the sleeves. The hem had been let down, but it was still too short to be a proper gown; the skirt hung just past her calves, and the bottom edge looked raw. She shimmied into it to test the fit, being careful not to pull out the loose stitches that held everything temporarily together, and turned to the mirror to see how bad it was.

She gaped.

Somehow, her mum's embroidery had turned bright blue. It even glinted like royal blue metal — Ella had seen gold thread that shone like this, but never blue. She twisted this way and that, watching the frock shimmer in the lamplight until she was certain that she wasn't hallucinating.

The thread was not the only change. The old linen was somehow clean, pure white again, with a heavy, flaxen sheen. Against it, the blue metal thread stood out a league; the contrast was sharp and perfect. Even the length of the skirt had changed since she put it on; it brushed the floor around her feet.

For a minute, she could only stare at the dress and wonder if she had gone mad.

Then it struck her. The fairies. Maybe they were here.

"Hello?" Ella whispered, looking around. There was no answer. Quickly, she fished the seaweed scroll out of her boot and unrolled it, looking for the fairies' names, which she'd forgotten. They weren't written there. "Blue fairy?" she whispered. "Red fairy?" But no, that hadn't been a Red fairy; she'd read that they were tiny and had red skin. The one who'd appeared in her room yesterday had been tall and pale as death, with the most outrageous and terrifying set of eyes she'd ever seen. "Crimson fairy?" she whispered. "Is that you?"

Something changed in her reflection. Ella looked quickly into the mirror and saw the charm that hung from the simple necklace at her throat, the golden *E* that had been her mum's, turn to blown glass full of what appeared to be liquid diamonds.

"No," she said impulsively, putting her fingertips to the *E*. "Please — it was my mum's." The charm returned to normal, and Ella looked around, both delighted and disturbed. "Um," she said to the empty air, feeling a little foolish. "Where are you?"

No answer.

"The dress is perfect," she said. "It's so good of *you* — but I have to take it off so I can stitch it up properly. So if you could, you know, not look at me . . ."

Even as she spoke, she realized that removing the gown would be unnecessary. Along the lines she had basted together, an invisible force was at work. The waist cinched closer; the bodice hugged her ribs; the hem straightened until the gown hung perfectly around her, showing not a single excess thread.

"Grats," Ella whispered. She gazed at herself in the mirror for a moment and then whipped her head toward the window, where she thought she heard someone giggle.

A knock at the door made her gasp.

"Ella?" called Sharlyn.

She grabbed her old robe and threw it on over the dress, then opened her bedroom door.

"Lady Jacquard agreed to let Clover and Linden play the first hour," said her stepmother, beaming. "They've already left for the palace. You've given my children a huge gift tonight. Thank you."

Ella nodded.

"I came to see your gown so that I can choose the right jewels," Sharlyn went on. "I do wish you'd at least consider wearing the gown I bought for you. . . ."

Ella untied her robe and removed it.

Sharlyn drew a breath. "Where in all of Tyme did you get that dress?"

"It was my mum's. I remade it."

"*You* made this?"

Ella glanced toward her window and nodded. For a second, she thought she caught sight of something fluttering again — something dark red.

"It's strange," said Sharlyn, raising her pince-nez to study the embroidery. "It's not the fashion, but somehow . . ." She shook herself slightly and lowered the glasses. "Shoes?" she asked.

Ella hadn't thought about shoes. She went to the wardrobe and pulled out the clogs she usually wore on Shattering Day, knowing full well they wouldn't pass inspection. As she picked them up, however, they changed in her hands. The leather became soft and supple, studded with beadwork. The toes tapered and lengthened. When she slipped her feet into them, they glittered pale gold, like the *E* on her necklace.

"Lovely," said Sharlyn. "I have the perfect earrings."

"My mum's necklace is all the jewelry I want."

Sharlyn sighed. "Well, I'm sending in my hairdresser," she said. "That's nonnegotiable."

When she left, Ella ran to the window and threw it open. She stuck her head out and looked around but saw nothing fluttering except the leaves in the trees.

"Grats," she whispered again anyway. "I appreciate it."

She sat before her mirror when the hairdresser came, and she wondered whether she would have to dance with anyone. She hoped not. She was pretty sure she remembered all the court manners — they'd made her take an etiquette course first thing upon her enrollment at C-Prep — but there was a stupid huge number of court dances, and they were all complicated. She was sure she'd forget some of the steps.

When the clock struck eight, she left her bedroom, hesitated, and went back. She fished in the pocket of her mum's old cloak, where she'd hidden Queen Maud's ring, and she tucked it into her bodice. Maybe she could leave it at the palace somewhere. That was where it belonged, after all.

"Ella," she heard Sharlyn call. "The carriage is waiting."

She hurried downstairs. When her dad caught sight of her, he made a noise of joyful pride.

"I recognize that dress," he said, his voice creaking a little. "Don't I?"

"Yeah." Ella turned in a circle to let her dad see the whole thing.

"And wearing Ellie's necklace too," he said, really choking up now. "I wish she could see you, Ell. She'd be so proud."

There, for a brief moment, was the dad she knew.

She sat between him and Sharlyn in the carriage, barely listening as they talked about the evening ahead. Charming Palace came into view, aglow with countless torches in the near-darkness. Ella pressed her hands to her stomach, reassured by the feeling of her mum's embroidery against her palms.

"I imagine he's doing it to prove that there's nothing to worry about," her dad was saying. "That even though Queen Maud's gone missing, everything's under control."

"And to give the scribes something else to talk about," said Sharlyn.

"True, true . . ."

They came to the grand front staircase. On the wide steps were dozens of people wearing shoes and gowns and headdresses so fine that she probably looked like she was going to a picnic by comparison.

But these people didn't matter, she reminded herself. Their money didn't make them better than the people back home. She thought of Lady Jacquard's maid, sentenced to a month on Ragg Row. She thought of the sixty dead laborers up in Coldwater that the *Criers* hadn't mentioned once. She thought of the letter her mum had written to those fairies.

She would not be afraid to go to a ball with these people. They only ran the world — they didn't know anything about it.

Ella lifted her chin.

"That's it," Sharlyn said quietly. "Shoulders back."

The carriage door opened, and Ella followed her stepmother onto the steps of the palace.

Dash

GREETING guests at a ball was uncomfortable work. Standing under the weight of his formal suit and royal sash, amid the heat of candles and lamps, Dash sweated profusely. His hose itched and his feet hurt, but families kept marching through the doors and down the long blue carpet that led to the grand staircase, where they presented themselves to him and his father. Music thumped through the ballroom as the first-hour musicians played. They were called the Current, and Dash had never heard of them, but the beat was stirring and the fiddle was intense. He thought he would have liked it if he hadn't been so miserable.

"EXALTED MAVEN GARRICK, NEXUS OF THE BLUE KINGDOM," the herald cried. "TAM PERIWIG GARRICK. MERCER PERIWIG GARRICK."

The Garricks moved toward them, and no one's face showed a shadow of the distress Dash knew they all must feel. The king's affair with Nexus Maven had ended, but that made things no less uncomfortable.

"Exalted Nexus," said his father, smiling. "Welcome. How are all the Garricks this evening?"

"Delighted to be here, sir," said the Nexus. Her amulet gleamed against the bodice of her gown.

Her husband's face was placid as he bowed to his sovereign. He bowed in exactly the same way to Dash, who blushed with guilt that wasn't his. Their son, Mercer, had long been among Dash's circle of friends; now Mercer gazed at him without expression, like they'd never met.

Dash worked for something neutral to say to his classmate. "So awkward," was what blurted out of him. And though it was true, this was not a moment for truth; it was a moment for superficial pleasantries, for making pretend that nothing was the matter.

The Nexus's expression froze. The king went still. Dash flushed with horrible heat.

Both Mercer and his father, however, appeared to thaw slightly. They glanced at Dash, who thought he saw a smile touch the corner of Mercer's mouth as his family retreated.

"Oh, excellent," the king muttered. "Is this what's left of you, now that the curse is broken? A social illiterate?"

"You wanted me at this ball," Dash managed. "You've got me."

"LADY CAMEO SHANTUNG. CHALLIS SHANTUNG. CHEMISE SHANTUNG."

"The Shantung fortune is all but gone, you know — Jacquard Silks has put them nearly out of business," said his father. "Perhaps you'd like to throw that in their faces when they greet us."

The king fell silent as Lady Shantung and her daughters drew close enough to hear him. If they were on the edge of ruin, it didn't show; they were dressed in sharp gowns with sheer panels peeking from the skirts, and high, jeweled shoes. They curtsied, and Chemise regarded Dash with interest. His voice caught in his throat as he remembered the things he'd said to her under the curse. Satin skin, graceful hands, eyes that hypnotized his heart. Lips as succulent as berries. He'd actually said that while kissing her. *Succulent.* His face boiled.

At least during the formal greetings he wasn't expected to speak much. If anyone asked him his name right now, he didn't believe he could choke out the syllable.

"SIR GORE FARTHINGALE. CHANTILLY FARTHINGALE. TIFFANY FARTHINGALE."

His father chuckled. "Here comes your lovesick pup."

"Shut up," Dash said hoarsely. He had not recovered from facing Chemise; he could not deal with Tiffany. But on she came, with her father and sister, and she positioned herself right in front of him. Her limp blond hair was tortured into a system of curls that looked like a fancy hat. Big glass baubles the size of lemons hung from her earlobes. Dash knew it was all meant to impress him, but it only infected him with the impolite urge to laugh — an urge that was quelled by the desperate gaze Tiffany fixed on him, her big blue eyes full of unchecked hope.

"How marvelous to see you, Sir Gore," said the king cheerfully. "Your daughters are the picture of loveliness. Aren't they, son?"

Dash willed himself to say something polite, but no helpful lie occurred to him. Tiffany ducked her head demurely, and her glass earrings wobbled. "Your earrings," Dash said. "Very — big. Very clear."

His father was right. He was socially inept. A complete buffoon.

"Thank you, sir," Tiffany whispered, glancing up at him again. "I hoped you'd like them."

Dash was relieved when the Farthingales moved on. His father laughed heartily.

"You know," said the king. "There's nothing wrong with a simple 'Good evening.' You should try it."

They greeted the Batiks and the Panniers, the Brogues and the Zoris, the Quebrachos, Trapuntos, and Whipcords. Dash said nothing but "Good evening," to any of them.

"LADY SHARLYN GOURD-SOURWOOD-COACH," cried the Herald. "EARNEST GOURD-COACH. ELEGANT HERRINGBONE COACH."

Dash looked at the ballroom doors and was arrested.

Ella. The girl with the smoking bag. The one who had run away from him.

She stood between her parents, looking like one of those statues in the War Museum, with her shoulders flung proudly back and her chin thrust out like she was issuing a challenge to the whole room. Her bronze curls, simply arranged, shone around her face. Against the brown of her skin, her white gown shocked the eye, and as she drew closer, Dash saw that she was unembellished except for the embroidery on her dress — no feathers, no heels, and no jewels — just a simple golden chain at her throat.

"New blood," the king murmured. "Always interesting."

The whole ballroom watched the Gourd-Coaches approach. Scribes scribbled furiously in their corners. Students from Coterie pointed at Ella and whispered to one another. Some of them glared at her, Dash noticed; others laughed behind their hands.

"Your Majesty." Lady Gourd-Coach curtsied, and Earnest Coach inclined his head. Ella bobbed awkwardly. "Your Royal Highness."

"I don't believe we've been introduced," said King Clement.

"Our family has not had that pleasure, sir." Lady Gourd-Coach met the king's gaze with ease. "My cousin, Royal Governor Calabaza of Yellow Country, sends his regards."

"Calabaza! My best wishes for his health. I understand that our talented musicians tonight are your children?" Upon the dais at the side of the ballroom, the drummer shot showers of colored sparks from his fingertips, making people's faces glow purple, then gold, then green.

"My daughter and son, sir. Their band is the Current."

"An auspicious debut. And is this your youngest?"

"Ella's my daughter, Your Majesty," said Earnest Coach, speaking for the first time. He had a slight southern accent; it reminded Dash of his mother's voice. "She and I have lived in Quintessential for just about four months, since moving our headquarters to the Avenue — Practical Elegance, if you've heard of it."

"The famous Cinder Stoppers, of course," said the king. "Little Cinderella, isn't that what the scribes call you?"

"Yes, Your Majesty." Ella looked ever so slightly pained.

"Dash left Quintessential about six months ago, so these two won't have met at school. Say hello, son," his father prompted.

Ella flicked her eyes to Dash's, and he stood dumb, burning inwardly. The triumphant way she carried herself made him nervous.

"Good evening," he managed.

"Good evening, Your Highness," she replied.

Her family joined the crowd. The king followed them with his eyes. "Reminds me of Maud," he said. "With her country necklace and her terrible curtsy. Watch out, son."

They greeted another handful of Coterie families, and then the line of entrants came to an end with a final flourish.

"LADY LARIAT JACQUARD, DIRECTOR OF THE GARMENT GUILD, FIRST CHAIR OF THE HOUSE OF MORTALS. LAVALIERE JACQUARD."

"*No* insults." Dash's father glanced at him. "I mean it. Speak well or be silent."

The first ladies of Quintessential glittered at the opposite end of the velvet carpet. With faultless poise, they approached the staircase, and the crowd watched their progress like one many-headed monster, alive with curiosity and envy.

"Your future bride," the king said in a low voice. "And looking like it."

Every bit of Lavaliere Jacquard was beautiful, graceful, and restrained, from the crystal circlet that bound her dark hair to the shimmering silver gown, delicate as a spiderweb, that clung to her elegant figure, its train floating in sheer wisps behind her.

"Lariat, you've outdone yourself," said the king, gesturing overhead at the lights and flowers that cascaded with elegant effortlessness around them. "I hope you'll save me the fifth dance. Let's all of us make it the highlight of the evening, shall we?"

"I would be honored, sir," said Lariat.

Lavaliere extended her hand to Dash. Out of habit, he kissed it, which was far more attention than he'd paid to any other girl. It sent up murmurs all around the room. Lavaliere lowered her long lashes. Lady Jacquard and King Clement exchanged smiles. The scribes at the walls nearly broke the nibs of their pens writing down every detail.

The musicians finished the last song of the hour with a flourish of bright white sparks that elicited a noise of approval from the crowd. As the Jacquards swept away from the grand staircase, the Current left the stage and Pulse replaced them, oozing into position with their instruments poised, long blue hair hanging in sheets past their elbows.

"Time to dance," said the king.

Dash approached Chemise without meeting her eyes and led her to the center of the blue-and-white marble dance floor. He'd danced in public a hundred times, but the eyes of Quintessential had never crushed him like this. He felt faint. He held up his sweating hands, palms out. Chemise placed her fingers against his and stepped close, smelling of lilacs.

"It's good to see you, Dash," she ventured. "I couldn't picture you without hair, but it looks nice, actually." She paused and lowered her voice. "Are you feeling all right?"

He knew she meant the curse.

"I don't want to talk," he choked.

Chemise's eyes registered hurt, but she quickly turned the subject. "I love Pulse, don't you?" she asked. "All the old dances feel so fresh to their music. . . ." She chattered amiably on to fill the uncomfortable silence, and Dash shut his mouth before anything else unpleasant fell out of it.

At a nod from the king, Pulse struck up the first song. The rhythm rolled and undulated, stirring the dancers into motion. Dash raised his arms along with Chemise and mirrored her in the series of angular, jerking motions that had been in fashion for the last few years. Under the curse, he had always been a fine dancer, confident in his movements. Now his arms didn't seem to belong to him. He couldn't remember the next move — he panicked and went the wrong way, nearly slamming into Mercer and Loom, who sidestepped him with twin looks of reproach. He lunged back toward Chemise and smacked her arm, hard. She sucked in a breath.

"Sorry," he gasped.

She gave him a weak smile, but in her eyes he saw the light of judgment flicker. She thought him strange. He *was* strange. When the dance ended, she evaporated from his side.

Paisley Pannier stepped up for her turn, wearing a gown so elaborate that Dash had no idea how to get near enough to hold her by the waist. He had to try a couple of angles before he figured it out, and Paisley watched him struggle, one eyebrow raised. Fortunately, she was happiest when she was listening to herself talk, so Dash was not required to speak for the duration of the second dance.

Dimity Gusset was not so easily borne. Her gleaming red hair was piled on her head and topped with a crystalline ornament that looked like a bird's nest full of transparent eggs. When Dash gaped at it, she laughed at him. "You used to say such *nice* things about my hair," she teased, and throughout the course of their dance together, she acted almost like a scribe, asking personal questions and pushing for details, though he did not answer. She needled him until the end of the dance, then made her way over to Lavaliere to gossip about him, no doubt.

The dancers changed partners, and he turned. To his horror, Tiffany Farthingale was before him. Dash stared at her in shock. He'd forgotten it was the fourth dance. Tiffany was already on the verge of tears; her chin wobbled as violently as her earrings.

"I missed you," she whispered. "I'm so glad you're home."

They had been math partners in school last year. Every day, for that hour, the curse had given Tiffany Farthingale its full attention. The other girls in his set had always seemed to understand that his flattery couldn't be helped and shouldn't be believed, and apart from a few kisses, they'd left him to Lavaliere. Only Tiffany had treated his attentions as though they were real.

She held out her hands to him. Dash took them because it was part of the dance. She clasped them and leaned in close. "I don't care about the curse being broken," she whispered. "I've always known the *real* you."

But she hadn't. No one had. She laid her head against his shoulder, though that was *not* part of the dance, and he cringed as every scribe in the room began to scribble madly.

"Don't." He shrugged his shoulder to get her off it.

Tears appeared instantly in her eyes. "Before you left, you said I was the only girl who —"

"That was the curse! You *knew* it wasn't real."

He didn't mean to shout it. Around them, dancers stilled. Scribes nearly combusted in delight.

Tiffany fainted.

Guards bore her away. Everyone was talking — laughing — their voices were an oppressive buzz. Dash saw Lariat Jacquard going from guest to guest — he saw his father speaking with Cameo Shantung, who gazed at Dash with pity. There was only one thing he could do.

He ran.

Ella

SHE hid in the royal privy for the second and third dances.

Somehow, like magic, Sharlyn had managed to arrange a dance partner for her within five minutes of their being in the palace, and Ella had been forced to endure Oxford Truss, whose cologne smelled like medicine and who spent the entire dance instructing her to be lighter on her feet. At the end of the song, when she saw Sharlyn beckon, she ducked into the crowd and made her way to the far end of the grand ballroom, where she asked an attendant for the privy chamber. She was shown down a corridor, and she gratefully escaped.

But she couldn't stay in here all night.

The sound of heavy footsteps in the hall decided things. Somebody needed the privy, and she would have to hide somewhere else. Ella pushed the door open, stepped into the corridor, and collided with a very tall person who was running like someone had set dogs after him. He tripped and brought himself to a brief halt, panting.

"Sorry!" she said. "Sir," she added, as she realized whom she'd slammed into. Prince Dash stared at her in wide-eyed panic. His

WHEN she returned to the party, Sharlyn found her at once.

"Where have you been?" she hissed as she and Ella's dad flanked her on either side, swift as dragons. "I arranged dances for you — it's been embarrassing. You can't just disappear like that. You'll hurt the company."

"How does my not dancing hurt Practical Elegance?" Ella asked, glancing over her shoulder to see if Prince Dash was after her and hoping very much that she wasn't about to get into royal trouble. The prince hadn't been too happy to see her with his mum's ring.

"You're making us look socially incapable," Sharlyn hissed. "That matters to these people just as much as their profits do. Stay right here, do you hear me? I've arranged for the Garters' son to dance the fifth with you."

"What?" said Ella, snapping out of her thoughts. "No, not him."

"Garter Woolmakers is a major supplier —"

"He doesn't like me, I promise you. He'll be glad to get out of it."

"Lower your voice," said Sharlyn. "You've already insulted the Batiks and the Trapuntos — don't you care at all that your behavior might cost us our business relationships?"

"Ell," her father said quietly. He met her eyes. "Please. For me."

Ella hesitated. She had already done many difficult things for her dad's sake. She wondered if he'd ever realize it.

"Fine," she said. "But this is it, hey? I don't want any other dances."

Sharlyn gave a sharp *"Shh"* and smiled at something just over Ella's shoulder. "Good evening, Buckram. Are you enjoying the ball?"

"Please call me Garb, Lady Gourd-Coach," said Garb smoothly, smiling back at her with all his teeth. "All my friends do."

He offered Ella his hand. Reluctantly, she took it. He had shaved his head like the prince, but it didn't suit him one-tenth as well. The Garter crest, heavy with rubies, glittered at her from his breast. They took their places on the dance floor, and Ella prayed to the Beyond that it would be the shortest song ever written, or that Pulse's instruments would fail, or that the lights and flowers that hovered magically overhead would crash like Ubiquitous acorns and force the party to a halt.

Instead, the song was a slow one, and the dance that accompanied it was intimate. Ella did her best to stand close to Garb without touching him, but it was impossible. As they turned in slow circles, she kept her eyes on his shoulder, hoping that no conversation between them would be necessary.

"Homemade?" Garb asked. "Or bought?"

"Excuse me?"

"Your dress. We've got a wager on it," said Garb, pulling her closer. "Did you make it, Cinderella? Or buy it in a shop?"

Disgusted, Ella turned her head and did not answer. She caught sight of her dad dancing with Sharlyn.

"Most people are betting you bought it," said Garb. He was holding her waist too tightly. "But I think you made it yourself." He lowered his voice conspiratorially. "My father told me how it is with your family. You've got your money now, but you used to live in a hut, and your mother spun silk in a Jacquard shop for years. So the way I see it, you can probably do the same menial labor she did."

Cold circled Ella's heart like a snake and squeezed it.

"Menial labor?"

"You know, sewing and the like," said Garb. "So, do I win the bet?"

Ella wrested herself from his grip. He tried to catch her again, but she deflected him.

"Come on," he said, glancing around them. "Can't you take a joke?"

"A joke?" People around them were starting to take notice, but the angry hum in Ella's head drowned out any embarrassment she might have felt. "Everything you're wearing, everything you have, you have because of someone else's *menial* labor. Don't you get that?"

Garb flushed. "Of course you'd say that," he said. "You're loyal to your class."

Ella walked off the ballroom floor.

Dash

DANCING with Lavaliere was easy. She took her place and went through the movements and didn't speak a word.

It was a relief.

It was also a strategy, of course. If he insulted his partners whenever he opened his mouth, then Lavaliere would give him no reason to open it.

They twined arms and turned in a slow circle. Dash caught sight of his father dancing with Lariat Jacquard. Beyond them, Ella Coach was dancing with Garb Garter, but they weren't doing the steps. Ella jerked away from him, Garb flailed for her. . . . She pivoted and left him there alone. Red-faced, Garb stalked off the dance floor.

Dash missed a step. Lavaliere pulled him instantly back into formation and glanced back to see what he was looking at.

"She's bizarre," she said quietly.

She replaced her head upon his shoulder and said nothing more. When the dance ended, she gave him a brief, meaningful smile, then swept regally toward her next partner as though a crown already balanced on her head.

He got through the next four dances without incident, mainly because he was focused elsewhere. He kept track of wherever Ella went in the ballroom; her bronze curls picked up the light. When it finally came time for the tenth dance, he made his way to her. His father wanted him to choose Lavaliere for Prince's Preference, but he had to talk to Ella.

When he reached her, she was standing with her family and the Shantungs.

"Your slippers are beautiful," Chemise was saying. "What a lovely shape — I haven't seen anything quite like them."

"Yours are pretty too," Ella replied. "I like that shade of green . . ." She caught sight of Dash and her voice trailed off.

Dash bowed and put out his hand. "May I have this dance?" he asked.

Her father looked shocked; her mother, gratified. Ella only looked afraid. She drew back and didn't answer — for a moment, he thought she might actually turn and run away from him *again* — and then Ella's mother spoke for her.

"Ella would be honored, Your Highness."

Ella put her hand gingerly into his, as though she might retract it at any moment, and she allowed him to lead her to the dance floor. Her hand was small and cool, a little rough. People around them whispered as they went together to the center of the ballroom floor, but Dash wasn't in the mood to care what anyone thought. Protecting his mother was paramount.

They took their places, and Pulse began to play. The dance was simple, just a few steps and a few turns, but Ella fumbled almost at once and went in the wrong direction.

"Sorry," she muttered.

"How did you come by the ring?" Dash asked, pulling her close and keeping his voice very low. "Tell me everything, exactly as it happened."

Ella glanced up at him. "I was trying to before," she said. "I ran off from C-Prep at the same time the queen did, and we wound up in the same carriage. I didn't realize who she was at the time; it only struck me later when I was down in Salting at the Corkscrew, and I saw your aunt, and it hit me that the maid in the carriage looked awfully like her, so it must've been Queen Maud."

"But why did she give you her ring?"

"I don't know," said Ella. "I noticed it and said it was plush, and she turned white as death and took it off. She told me it wasn't real, and if I liked it, I could have it. She wouldn't take it back."

They crossed wrists and took each other's hands, and Dash considered her story. It made more sense than he had anticipated. It would have been easy for his mother to forget to remove her wedding ring, and if she was caught with it, she would have been identified.

"All right," he finally said. "But why did you go to visit my aunt?"

"Oh, that." Ella looked embarrassed. "I was trying to get a job at the Corkscrew."

"What? Why?"

"So I wouldn't have to live here anymore."

Dash regarded her in complete confusion. "You would rather work in a tavern," he said, "than live in Quintessential?"

"By about a thousand leagues," she muttered, and then she seemed to realize to whom she was speaking. "I don't mean to insult the capital, sir," she said. "I just miss home."

"Where is home?"

"Eel Grass. Down south."

They turned their backs on each other, took two steps, and pivoted again. They joined right hands and raised them, and as they stepped close, Dash dared to whisper: "Are you going to tell anyone what you know?"

Ella looked bewildered.

"About my mother," Dash added.

"Why would I?"

"Money," he said. "Attention."

Now she looked insulted. "I've got more than I want of both," she said. "And anyway, she was really kind, your mum. I was in a bad state, and she took care of me."

Dash's heart thumped. "Did she?"

"Yeah. She was gentle."

Gentle. Yes, that was the word for his mother.

He twirled Ella under his arm, and it occurred to him that he was perfectly comfortable now, for the first time all evening. For the past few minutes, his dance steps had been fluid, and he hadn't struggled once for what to say. Funny how easy it was to talk about things that were real.

"Thank you," he said.

"What for?"

"Keeping quiet. And giving back the ring. Most people wouldn't have."

Ella smiled a bit. "Then most people aren't worth much," she said. "Are they?"

ELLA

THE prince smiled back at her, such a beautiful smile that Ella completely forgot the next steps of the dance. Dash had to pull her in the right direction to get her back on track.

He was a serious melter. The flickering candlelight illuminated his golden face; his cravat was partly undone, and he gleamed with a faint sheen of sweat that only made him lovelier. No wonder Tiffany had fainted. No wonder he was always in the *Criers*. Her pulse got heavy just looking at him.

She was glad that he seemed to believe her now, about the ring. He seemed nice enough, really, for royalty.

A shout of pain and the thud of someone falling to the floor startled her out of admiration. Ella turned to see Chemise Shantung collapsed on the blue-and-white marble next to them. Her feet were bare and smoking like fire.

Ella dropped to her knees beside her and waved the smoke away. Chemise's feet were raw, glistening red, like they'd been skinned. "What happened?" she gasped.

Chemise grabbed Ella's arm and dragged her close.

"My shoes crashed," she said in an agonized whisper. "Help me. I don't want anyone to know they weren't real. . . ."

It was too late for that. Their classmates closed in around them, gaping, while the whispered condemnation flew from one gossiping mouth to the next:

"Ubiquitous."

Chemise closed her eyes. "You need a Hipocrath," said Dash, crouching. He picked up Chemise and carried her off the dance floor.

As soon as the prince was out of hearing range, their classmates began to laugh.

"I told you," said Dimity to Lavaliere. "She's been faking it for months."

"I knew Shantung was losing business, but this is just *sad,*" Paisley said gleefully. "Do you think she can afford to finish school with us?"

"She'd better not show her face," Garb replied. "She nearly set me on fire. I can't believe she had the nerve to dance with me in those things. If she singed my stockings, I'll send her a bill."

Even the adults joined in the discussion. Ella heard Oxford Truss's father saying, "I keep *saying* those acorns will hurt someone."

"And look, she's already making friends at her new level." Garb's eyes traveled over Ella's gown. "They can sit around and *knit* together."

Paisley snorted. "Chemise and Cinderella," she said. "How sweet."

"Go to Geguul," Ella spat. A few people around her gasped. Dimity and Loom both looked at her with revulsion. "My language bothers you, hey?" she demanded. "But it's fine to laugh at someone who's hurt?" Her voice cut through the gossiping crowd. "She's bleeding, and all you care about is her money. You're savage!"

"Look what's calling *us* savage," murmured Paisley.

"When she's frothing at the mouth," said Dimity. "Like a dog."

"Like her mother," added Garb under his breath.

Lavaliere Jacquard laughed, and Ella snapped.

"Shut your traps, you murderers!" she cried, taking a step toward Lavaliere, who gasped. "That's what you are! You don't care when people get sick or hurt — you don't care when they *die*!"

The whole ballroom was watching her now. Even the king. Ella saw his crowned head swivel toward her, along with Lariat Jacquard's, and a cold hush fell across the crowd. The only sound came from the great clock at the Essential Assembly as it tolled midnight.

"Filthy quints," she shouted. "Hearts as White as witches —"

"Ella, *stop*!" cried Sharlyn, gripping one of her arms.

"No more." Her father gripped the other.

"They killed my mum!" she cried. "They're the problem, not me —"

Her father and Sharlyn dragged her from Charming Palace.

Serge

By the time he mustered the energy to fly again, the Jacquard Estate was dark. He flitted down the coast until he reached the Academy, and he made his way to the apprentices' boarding house.

When he arrived at Jasper's apartment, he heard muffled voices behind the door. He knocked, and the voices were silenced.

"Who is it?" Jasper sounded higher-pitched than usual.

"Serge."

There were sounds of frantic shuffling. Jasper threw the door open, and Serge peered over his shoulder.

"Who's here?"

"Me," said Jasper, and he caught Serge's eyes with sudden focus. Uneasy, Serge glanced away. "Come in." Jasper grabbed his hand. "Skies, you're freezing."

In a minute, Serge was bundled in a big chair by the window, thawing under a blanket, holding a cup of ruby-colored hibiscus tea. He looked around Jasper's tiny, cozy boarding space. Framed along the walls were several old news clippings — a history of Jules's great successes at the Slipper — from little orphaned Pierce all the way to Queen Maud. Serge's eyes roamed listlessly from one story to the next.

Jasper fluttered over and sat at his feet. "Tell me what's wrong."

"It's confidential."

"Should it be?"

"No." Serge stared into his tea. He wished he could tell Jasper about Lavaliere. He hated being all alone in it. "But there are contracts in place, and there's so much on the line, and . . . I'm not a rule breaker, Jasper."

Jasper reached out and laid a hand on the pointed black toe of Serge's boot. "Then why are you here?"

Because I need something real, he thought. *Because if I don't do something good, and soon, I'm going to run out of fairy dust.*

Aloud, he said: "I'm here to help you with Ella." He expected a high-pitched squeal of excitement, but Jasper only waited. "Secretly, of course," Serge added. "I meant what I said before. We have to be untraceable. I'll make us both invisible when we go to see her."

"I already went to see her."

"What?" Serge hastily set down his teacup. "I told you —"

"Just listen," Jasper pleaded. "I didn't make contact, and nobody saw me. But I had to help her prepare for the ball! I stayed outside her window in the branches while she made her gown —"

"Made her gown? She didn't buy one?"

"No," said Jasper. "She's got a good sense of line, and she's skilled, but the fabric was old. I gave her a tiny bit of assistance from afar. That's *all*."

Serge considered him. "How did she look?" he asked.

"Perfect," said Jasper happily. "Very simple, very lovely — very *her*, I think."

"Don't do it again."

"I won't." Jasper clasped his hands. "When can we go to her?"

"Now, if you like," said Serge. "She'll probably be at the ball, of course, but —"

Jasper was on his feet instantly. It required uncomfortable effort, but Serge dredged up a bit of dust, enough to make them both unseen, and they arrived at 76 Cardinal Park East.

The house was nearly dark, but behind Ella's bedroom curtains, light shone. A carriage approached along the dark park-side avenue. It pulled up to number 76, and a footman began to unload what appeared to be musical instruments from the carriage roof. Two figures stepped out of the carriage, and Serge recognized them as the same young people he had seen in the house yesterday, playing the drums and fiddle.

"Clover and Linden Sourwood Gourd," whispered Jasper. "Ella's stepsiblings. They have a band — the Current." He grabbed Serge's arm. "They're talking. Let's go closer —"

"No need." His fingertips still bore a touch of fairy dust; he rubbed a bit into Jasper's ear and the rest into his own. Clover and Linden's conversation now sounded as though it were happening right beside them.

"— like a lunatic, screaming at everybody."

"You thought she was wrong?" A womanly voice. Clover, the stepsister.

"You thought she was right?" Linden snapped out his words.

"I'm not sure." Clover climbed the stairs to the front door. "The people in this city . . . no offense intended . . ."

"They're snobs," said Linden. "Offense intended. But insulting every noble in town? I can't see the benefit. It definitely doesn't help *us* any. And Ma will kill her."

"Slowly, I imagine."

"Anyway, the new trend had better change soon, or I'm going to start wearing both sleeves again." Linden sounded deeply affronted. "Did you see how many people tonight had one missing, or sheer? That's been my thing for *years*."

The door closed, and their voices became indistinct.

"Chime Ella to let her know we're coming," said Serge.

For the next three minutes, he concentrated, trying to bring enough dust to his palms to transport them both into Ella's room. Finally, he produced a thin layer. He found Jasper's sleeve and snapped the fingers of his other hand, bringing them right to the middle of Ella's bedroom. She was sitting on the carpet, still in her ball gown, leaning against her bed with her bare feet sticking out. Her face was tear-streaked.

Serge made himself and Jasper visible once more. When they materialized, Ella jerked but didn't otherwise move.

Jasper crouched next to her. "What happened?"

"Are you hurt?" asked Serge.

"Yeah," said Ella. "No — I don't know. I really . . ." She pulled her knees up and hugged herself. "I tangled it," she whispered. "I said things. Bad things. To everyone — even the king. And now Sharlyn thinks I've got one foot in prison, and my dad thinks I'm out to destroy Practical Elegance, and I'm *not*. I just don't understand how he can be nice to the Jacquards and the rest of them. Guess I'm supposed to get over Mum and forget how she died, but I *can't* — and everyone here is so awful —"

She doubled over and cried into her skirt.

Jasper looked at Serge, who shook his head, perplexed. He had heard many outbursts from many children, but this was something new. "When you say that you said bad things," he said, leaning against Ella's wardrobe and folding his arms, "what precisely do you mean?"

She was quiet for a long moment. "This girl, Chemise Shantung, wore Ubiquitous shoes tonight. Her family is nearly out of money, I guess. Her shoes crashed in the middle of a dance and burned her feet, and it was awful — she was crying — and they just laughed."

Serge knew the Shantung family. He had been Challis Shantung's godfather a decade ago, and he knew that Shantung Silkworks was in decline, but he hadn't realized that the situation had deteriorated as far as this.

"The prince was the only one who tried to help — the rest of them don't care. They don't have a stitch of feeling. Their employees drop dead of roop, but they just keep going to parties, and living in castles, and slapping their servants, and laughing. And nobody stops them, ever." She looked at Serge. "My mum worked twelve years for Jacquard, spinning silk."

He started.

"She died two years ago, during the roop outbreak in Fulcrum. Did you know there's been another one, in the workshops up in Coldwater? Near sixty people are dead."

Serge glanced at Jasper. Both of them shook their heads.

"Nobody around here knows," said Ella. "It's not in the *Criers*, because nobody cares if peasants die — peasants are just dirt to step on." She looked from Jasper to Serge. "You're fairies," she said. "Can't *you* make things right? Can't you stop Lady Jacquard and the rest of them?"

"Stop Lady Jacquard," Serge echoed.

"You're powerful," Ella insisted. "My mum said Blue fairies could do so much to make this country better if they'd bother, but instead —" She halted.

"Go on," said Serge, pushing himself away from the wardrobe.

"No," said Ella, her eyes still on Jasper. "You'll turn me into a swan or something."

Jasper regarded her thoughtfully. "You've heard that story?"

"What, about the six brothers who got turned to swans by that fairy queen in Crimson?" said Ella. "'Course I have. Mum told me when I was little, to scare me out of messing with magic folk. It's probably not even true."

"It's absolutely true," said Jasper. "The fairy who did it is my grandmother."

Ella gaped, and even Serge could not help staring. The grandson of the dreaded Queen Opal of Cliffhang — that made Jasper one of the Crimson royals. He hadn't just left a country behind, he'd left influence. Position. A throne.

"We'd never hurt you," said Jasper. "We'll help you, Ella."

"With what, hair and shoes?" Ella replied. "Because I don't want that."

"What *do* you want?" asked Serge.

She sat up straight. "I want the Garment Guild shut down," she said. "I want Jacquard ruined. Jacquard and Garter and everyone else."

Serge blinked. "If the wrong people hear you, you really could end up in prison," he said. "You didn't say that at the ball, did you?"

"No." She chewed her bottom lip a moment. "But I called them all murderers."

Serge and Jasper drew a simultaneous breath.

"And I have to go back to school with them next week," she whispered. "They hated me already. Now it's going to be ten times worse."

"All right," said Serge. "From the beginning. Tell us every word."

Ella told them her story, beginning with her childhood at her mother's knee in a miserable Jacquard spinning room. She told them about her mother's slow death and her father's quick remarriage, and how he and her stepmother had demolished Ella's old home to make way for Practical Elegance. She told them about her burned schoolbag, Queen Maud's ring, her old friend Kit, and the job in Salting that she'd had to leave behind. She spoke for half an hour, her hands in fists, pacing from her bed to the window and back again. Finally, she told them every detail of what had happened at the ball, where she had exploded just like Chemise's shoes, shouting at the nobles of Quintessential that they were White-hearted witches.

At the end of her story, Serge sank into a chair by the window. When Jules had reformed the List to serve only the Jacquards of the world, he had done nothing to stop the change. Not one thing. He'd feared angering her. He wasn't willing to risk his reputation, his inheritance, his position at the top of the pile.

Ella was.

He uncrossed his arms and flexed his hands — then blinked at them in surprise. Fairy dust. A healthy layer of it. He hadn't even tried.

"You can't shut down the Garment Guild without throwing every one of their employees out into the gutter," he heard himself say. "Tens of thousands of people depend on that work. It's the largest industry in Blue. The workshops may be terrible, but half the labor class would starve if you got your wish."

Ella sagged and sat down on her bed. "You're right."

A moment of quiet passed. She scrubbed a tear from her cheek.

"So nothing can change," she said. "People either work themselves to death or starve. Those are the choices."

"It's not that simple," Serge replied. "But you can't deny that most people will take a bad job over no job at all."

"Yeah." She looked down at her hands and rubbed her fingertips together. "What should I do?"

"What do you mean?"

"How do I fix it?" She looked over at him. "*Can* it be fixed?"

"I truly don't know," said Serge. "But if you want to try, then I want to help you."

"Do you mean it?"

Serge nodded. He did mean it. More than he had meant anything in quite some time. But this was not a problem he could solve with fairy dust. For the first time in decades, a worthy dilemma was before him, and he had not the first clue how to approach it.

"You know, my grandmother likes to say that people will do anything they *want* to do," Jasper mused. "The trick is getting them to want what *you* want. Of course, her methods aren't exactly *legal*. . . . But she has a point."

Serge and Ella both looked at him in perplexity.

"What we need," said Jasper, "is to convince the members of the Garment Guild that they *want* better lives for the working class. If they want to change things, then they will."

"But why would they want to?" asked Ella. "There's nothing in it for them."

"I don't know," Jasper admitted. "We'll have to think about it. Work on it."

Ella looked crestfallen.

"But even if we can't change Quintessential overnight," said Jasper, "we can still do *some*thing. You mentioned your friend Kit. Couldn't we help her family?"

"You'd do that?"

"Of course."

Ella dug under her bed and came up with a dilapidated fishing boot. Out of it, she pulled her Glass Slipper contract.

"Didn't know what to do with this," she said. "Do I sign it?"

Serge came to himself at the sight of the scroll. "Don't sign anything," he said. "You're, er — a special project."

"You're illegal," Jasper whispered. "We're not supposed to be helping you, because your mother couldn't pay, so this has to be *completely* secret."

"Jasper!"

"What? We have to tell her so she can keep it secret too."

"You're sneaking around to help me?" said Ella, looking somewhat cheered. "Really?"

Serge smiled in spite of himself. "Take my hand," he said. "Let's make this official."

"But you just said it couldn't be official."

"It's not contractual," said Serge. "It's still official."

"Can we make glass slippers for her?" asked Jasper, getting up from the carpet.

"No slippers," said Serge. "If anyone sees them, we'll be found out. We'll charm something else." He studied Ella. "Something you wear all the time, if possible, so that you can call us from anywhere. A ring, perhaps?"

Ella's fingers found the golden *E* charm on her necklace. "It was my mum's, though," she said protectively.

"We won't change it," said Serge. "I promise."

Ella unclasped the necklace and handed it to him. He took it in fingertips that were thick with fairy dust. The last time he'd made this much effortless dust, he'd been standing in a Ubiquitous shop with Rapunzel.

"Hold out your hand," he said, and when Ella did, he wrapped the golden chain around her outstretched palm, coating the chain and her skin with soft blue glitter. He cupped one of his own hands beneath Ella's so that he too was touching the chain, and Jasper laid his pale hand on top of hers, connecting the three of them.

"This magic is old," said Serge. "It's what Blue fairies used to do, long before slippers or contracts — I've only done it a few times myself, under special circumstances. Ready?"

Ella nodded, her eyes fixed on their three hands.

"Ella Coach," said Serge. He closed his eyes and felt the energy of compassion move through him, into his hand, into the chain that wrapped Ella's hand. The gold grew hot but did not burn. "I take you as my godchild. I take you as my godchild. I take you as my godchild."

Throughout this invocation, Jasper shivered madly. Tears sprang into his eyes. As they spilled over, they turned to tiny, silent fireworks. "Ella Coach," he said solemnly. "I take you as my godchild. I take you as my godchild. I take you as my godchild."

A zinging sensation moved through Serge's fingers as the Crimson magic pulsed into them, and now it was his turn to shiver.

Ella made a high-pitched noise. "My hand," she whispered. "It feels like it's humming."

"Now you," said Serge, nodding to her. "Serge and Jasper, I take you as my godfathers."

"Serge and Jasper," whispered Ella, "I take you as my godfathers. I take you as my godfathers. I take you as my godfathers."

The gold chain glowed brightly, lighting their faces. When it faded, he and Jasper withdrew their hands from hers, and Serge unwrapped the chain. Ella took it and replaced it around her throat.

"So warm," she said, touching it with a fingertip. "It's really magic now?"

"It has the power to summon us," said Serge. "Call our names three times. Wherever we are, we'll feel your call, and we'll come to you as quickly as we can."

Ella looked a bit dazed. "All right," she said. "But when should I call?"

"Anytime," said Jasper. "For anything. If you want to talk with us, or plan with us — or if you're in trouble and you need our help. Don't ever hesitate."

Serge took the contract from Ella's desk. "We won't be needing this," he said.

"All right . . . but could I keep my mum's letter?"

He detached it for her. Fairy dust smudged the corners and the writing on the letter glowed with faint silver light. His eyes followed the illuminated script across the page.

She'll change the world if she gets her chance, I know it.
Since I can't anymore, please help her find her way.

Serge hoped that he could.

Dash

EACH morning, courtesy of the Exalted Council, *Town Criers* boxes in locales across Tyme filled up with stacks of magically reproduced parchment covered in whatever news the Council deemed relevant to each particular city or nation. People often said they were glad to live in the time of *Town Criers* rather than a century ago, when news had been harder and slower to come by.

Dash disagreed. Having been the object of the *Criers* since his birth — and Quintessential boasted the most boxes of any city in Tyme — he could not marvel at them. A few mornings after the royal ball, when it was time to return to C-Prep, he sat in the royal carriage and stared straight ahead at the upholstered wall in front of him. His father's guards flanked the royal carriage on horseback as it passed through the palace gates. As the gates swung shut, the scribes closed in.

"Do you have nightmares about Envearia?" called one voice.

"How long before you propose to Lavaliere Jacquard?" cried another.

"Who's Queen Maud having an affair with?"

Dash ignored them. As the royal carriage rolled northward along Highborn Avenue, the scribes began to give up. One by one they peeled off, until only the most persistent still rode alongside him.

"Were you offended by Elegant Coach's insults at the ball?" cried a man's voice.

Dash made the mistake of glancing left. Through the window, he met the eyes of the scribe, a skinny man with a leering smile.

"Is that a yes?" the scribe asked eagerly. "Some people are calling it disloyal, the way Miss Coach was talking. They say she's dangerous. Do you agree?"

Dash hadn't heard her outburst, but he knew every word. After making sure Chemise was safely in the care of her mother and the royal Hipocrath, he'd come back to the ballroom to be accosted by Paisley and Dimity, who recited Ella's litany of insults. He'd listened in disbelief. Never had such a thing happened at Charming Palace. Ella had seemed like a decent person when they'd been dancing; he could not imagine what had possessed her.

He ignored the scribe the rest of the way and finally arrived at school. The first morning back at Coterie was an endless and exhausting string of social interactions. Mathematics was his first class, followed by Natural World, and by the time he dismounted from his horse at the end of sports hour, he was drained. He asked that his meal be brought to him in the carriage, where he ate alone.

After lunch, he made his way to Fundamentals of Business with the guards at his heels.

"Your Royal Highness." A stout middle-aged woman bowed to him outside the classroom door. "I'm Professor Linsey-Woolsey," she said. "The ball was absolutely splendid — very kind of His Majesty to include the professors in his invitation. A delightful treat. Don't forget to take a smock. . . . Good afternoon, Miss Kalamkari. Did you catch up on the reading?"

Dash entered the classroom, leaving the guards outside. The chamber was lofty and bright, with high, arching windows along two walls. Within it were rows of slate-topped tables just big enough for two, most of which were already full. Garb and Paisley sat together at one, Loom and Mercer at another. Sari Kalamkari chose the seat beside Tiffany, who reddened and angled her chair away from Dash as he passed her.

Lavaliere sat alone at the head of the class, at the table next to Paisley's. She cast a glance over her shoulder, smiled when she saw Dash, and ran her fingertips over the back of the empty chair beside her, telling him it was his. Then she turned back to Paisley and continued her quiet conversation.

Dash grabbed a smock, made his way to the front, and sat beside Lavaliere.

"Are you all right?" she asked, turning to him. She actually looked anxious.

"I'm fine."

She shook her dark head. "The way that awful girl behaved at your home. She completely spoiled the ball. I felt terrible about it — I *told* my mother we shouldn't have invited that family."

"New money never knows how to behave itself," said Paisley, patting her intricate braids.

"My father says they won't last half a year in this town," said Garb, leaning past Paisley to get in on the conversation. "After that display, Practical Elegance will lose all sorts of business. My father's even considering canceling their wool contract."

But he won't, thought Dash. Lord Garter would never turn down a profit, no matter how badly someone's daughter behaved.

"She should be grateful to be invited to a royal ball at all," said Garb with a toss of his head. "Given her history, it's a massive honor that you'd let her anywhere near Charming Palace. You did her a real favor, dancing with her. Not that she'd know a favor if it slapped her in the face." He sneered. "You saw the way she treated *me*, I'm sure."

Dash frowned. He wondered what Garb meant by Ella's history. The way he said it, it sounded like she was some kind of criminal.

"We did wonder," said Paisley, eyeing Dash. "Why you danced with her, I mean. Not that anyone would question your choice, of course. It's just . . . interesting."

Lavaliere turned her big gray eyes upon him, and he realized too late that he should have concocted an answer to this question in advance. Of course his friends would want to know why he'd sought out Ella at the ball.

His mouth dried up as he attempted a reasonable lie.

"Her bag," he managed. He licked his lips. "The fire last week — just checking to —" He took a deep breath and forced out the rest of the words. "Make sure she wasn't injured."

Poorly delivered as the falsehood was, it seemed to satisfy them all.

"That was gallant," said Lavaliere. Under the table, she briefly touched his hand. "She didn't deserve it."

"What do *you* think of the fit she threw?" Dimity asked from behind him, leaning forward over her desk. "Are you simply furious?"

This question was far easier to answer. "She should have more respect for the kingdom," Dash said, and Lavaliere nodded her agreement.

"She's in this class," said Dimity. "Ella Coach. Just to warn you."

"She wasn't at archery today, though," said Paisley. "Maybe she's been expelled."

"We can dream." Dimity wrinkled her nose. "Either way, at least she doesn't board here anymore. Honestly, I can't believe I had to room with that beast for four months."

Dash glanced around the room, but Ella was not there. Neither, he realized, was Chemise.

"Do you know if Chemise is all right?" he asked Lavaliere.

Her expression tightened. "I'm sure she'll be fine. Such a shame about her family."

Dash thought it was rather more of a shame about her feet — although it *was* sad to see a family as old and as integral as the Shantungs sink out of favor. It showed, he supposed, that a reversal of fortune could happen to anyone.

"Look, she's here," whispered Paisley. "She came to school after all — the *nerve*."

Every head turned. Sure enough, outside the classroom door, a mess of bronze curls glinted just on the other side of Professor Linsey-Woolsey.

Ella Coach had arrived.

Ella

COMING back to Coterie was the very last thing that Ella wanted to do. She had begged her dad to let her go to another school instead — any other school. But her dad, of course, had let Sharlyn make the decision, and no amount of pleading had softened Sharlyn. "You're fortunate that Madam Wellington is willing to meet with me," Sharlyn had said. "I'm sure she thinks your behavior was nothing short of seditious. You deserve to be expelled."

Ella wished for expulsion, but no such luck. Sharlyn's meeting with the headmistress lasted all morning, and by the end of lunch hour, Ella was forced to don her C-Prep uniform once more.

She slouched her way to Fundamentals of Business, terrified.

What would her classmates do to her when they saw her? What would they say? She tried to remind herself that she didn't care what they thought, but that didn't mean she wanted to endure a chorus of nasty insults and laughs and looks. "You brought this on yourself," Sharlyn had said before departing from the campus. "I told you, didn't I, that you would damage your own prospects, and not just the business?"

Practical Elegance would lose money today, Ella knew. The *Town Criers* had made a full and gleeful report of her outburst at Charming Palace, and, as the scribe put it, "The loyal citizens of Blue will surely withhold their coin from Practical Elegance to show their displeasure."

"Good afternoon, Miss Coach," said Professor Linsey-Woolsey as Ella came to the door. Ella tried to sidle past her, but the professor put out a hand and held her back. "A moment," she said.

Ella glanced over the professor's shoulder into the classroom and flinched. Every head had turned. Her classmates stared at her, cold-eyed. The prince included.

"Step this way," said the professor quietly, and she pulled Ella aside, where they could not be seen. "I was at the ball," she said.

Ella looked at the ground.

"Between your running away from Coterie last week and your outburst at the palace the other night, it's clear that you have reached a boiling point."

Ella scuffed one boot against the stones. "If you don't want me in your class, I'll go."

"Not at all," said the professor. "You see, I have a theory. Would you like to hear it?"

Ella wasn't sure. She gave a half nod, half shrug.

"My theory is that you have not found your education here at Coterie to be . . . relevant to your experiences, shall we say." The professor eyed her with interest. "Perhaps we can change that."

Ella had no idea what she was talking about.

"Now, come in," said Professor Linsey-Woolsey. "Don't forget to take a smock."

The classroom was silent, and Ella was sure that everyone in it had been trying very hard to hear her conversation with the professor. Without looking up from the floor, she went to the hooks at the back wall and took down a smock. She donned it to protect her uniform from chalk dust, and she sat down at the back of the room, in the only available seat, beside Oxford Truss.

"Wonderful," Oxford muttered, scooting his chair away from her.

Needing some distraction to keep her face from burning up completely, Ella dug into her knapsack and pulled out the little Shattering Day dress she was embroidering for Mrs. Wincey's baby. She propped the hoop against her desk and began to stitch.

"Your next project in this class," said Professor Linsey-Woolsey in a clear voice, striding to the front of the classroom, "is meant to prepare you for the responsibilities that await you in the world. Many of you will be Garment Guild leaders and Assembly members, and your decisions will influence the health of the kingdom. It is imperative that you understand the repercussions of those decisions. Starting today, therefore, you will work in partners to create an original business and solve the kinds of problems that arise in real-world situations. You will create business plans and budgets, develop advertisements, and prepare a detailed presentation to be delivered to the class in a few weeks' time." She folded her arms. "Miss Coach. Kindly give me your full attention."

The room erupted in vicious laughter. Ella shoved her embroidery back into her bag.

"I will assign your partners," said the professor. "When I call your names, please reshuffle yourselves accordingly."

"Can't we pick our *own* partners?" Garb complained. "This is like primary school."

Professor Linsey-Woolsey ignored him. "Chelsea and Loom," she said. "Garb and Oxford."

Garb gave an audible groan of despair as Oxford jumped up and hustled to the front of the classroom, getting away from Ella as fast as he could.

"Lavaliere and Tiffany."

Paisley and Dimity both sucked in their breath. Ella could practically feel a chill in the air as Tiffany pushed back her chair and made her way to the front.

"Kente and Paisley. Dimity and Mercer. Prince Dash and Ella."

Dash

THERE were actual shrieks of dismay. Dash looked up at the professor, astounded. She had been at the ball. She *knew* what she was asking of him.

Lavaliere clutched his hand under the table. "Tell her no," she hissed. "Refuse to do it. She can't make you."

But Dash's mother had made him promise long ago that he would not use his title and position to command such trivial favors. He was to be always a gentleman, never a spoiled tyrant. He was to respect his teachers and lead his peers by example.

He shook his head slowly and rose from his chair.

Ella Coach it was.

Ella

ELLA'S head went cold and light. Her blood pounded in her ears. The prince would never put up with being assigned to her — surely he hated her guts.

To her shock, a few moments later, Dash Charming sank into the chair beside hers. She kept her eyes on her lap so that her classmates' looks of fury and disgust would not smother her. It was enough that she could hear their every noise of outrage.

"Weft and Sari, since we have an odd number, you will work as partners for now, but when Chemise returns to school, you will be a trio," said the professor. "All right, class. Your attention, please. Attention!"

But the room was so socially disarranged that nobody could concentrate. Ella heard whisper after awful whisper.

"That foul, canker-bitten peasant."

"Poor Dash — I hope the smell isn't too much for him."

"At least he's bald and can't catch lice!"

This comment, uttered by Garb, was greeted by a classroom-wide cascade of sniggering laughter that never seemed to end. Ella gritted her teeth. *Do not cry,* she commanded herself. *Not here, not in front of them.*

"The first step," said Professor Linsey-Woolsey loudly, to recapture the attention of the class, "is to decide what your business venture will be. To do this, make three lists. One, what are your skills? Two, what are your interests? Three, what are your resources? Use your answers to help you determine a line of business that plays to the strengths of your partnership."

Slowly and reluctantly, the students turned their attention to the task before them. A few began to list things in chalk on their slate desks, while others glanced back at Dash and Ella again, their faces full of judgment.

Dash picked up the chalk and wrote three headings on their slate desk. *SKILLS — INTERESTS — RESOURCES.* His writing was swift and perfect. He poised the chalk under *SKILLS* and cast a glance at Ella, and she wondered what to say. Should she apologize to him for losing her temper in his home? There was probably etiquette for apologizing to royalty, but she didn't know what it was.

It was safest to concentrate on their schoolwork. "I can sew," she said.

Dash wrote *Sewing* under *SKILLS*, and then he continued to write. *Riding, Jousting, Swimming, Sailing, Skiing. Tennis.*

Ella picked up her chalk and drew stars next to *Riding* and *Swimming.* When the prince looked questioningly at her, she explained "I can do those too, so we have them in common."

Dash laid down his chalk and sat back, and Ella leaned forward to add her skills to the list. Beside his, her writing looked childish; for the first time, she felt somewhat embarrassed by her village education.

Knitting, she wrote. *Embroidery. Spinning silk. Unrolling raw silk. Shearing sheep. Carding wool. Spinning wool. Cleaning. Cooking. Sickbed care. Gardening. Driving a wagon.*

Prince Dash starred the very last one, and that was all. A flush had risen in his pale cheeks.

"We could do a messenger service, maybe," Ella ventured. "Since we both know something about riding horses and driving wagons."

The prince's eyes traveled over to the table beside theirs, where Weft and Sari were working. *Mathematics,* their list began. *Public speaking. Social skills. Dancing. Dress sense.*

Ella followed his eyes. "Should we add any of that?" she asked.

In reply, Dash took up his chalk once more and wrote *Mathematics.*

"Not social skills?" Ella asked, surprised, drawing a star beside *Mathematics.* "Or public speaking?"

The prince gave a dry laugh. "No."

Ella hesitated. "You *can* dance, though," she finally said, and she scribbled the word *Dancing.* "But I can't star it, because I'm terrible." She laid down her chalk, not sure what to do next. "There we go, then," she said lamely. "Let's make a business."

DASH

HE surveyed their list, unhappy with his contributions. Nearly everything on his list was a leisure activity, while nearly everything on Ella's was an actual working skill. His embarrassment surprised him; he wasn't sure what to make of it. It wasn't as though he would ever need to card wool. It wasn't even as though he wanted to.

She drew a squiggly line under *INTERESTS*. "What do you like?" she asked.

Dash wrote out his interests, uncomfortably aware that he had nothing new to say. His interests very closely matched his skills. Swimming, riding, skiing . . . these were the things he liked, so these were the things he could do.

Ella's list was different. *Knitting, Embroidery,* and *Swimming* were there, but so were many new items. *Eel Grass. Salting. Shattering Day. My friends back home. History. Travel.*

"You enjoy traveling?" Dash asked, glad to see something he could relate to. He starred it.

Ella looked a bit shy. "I think I'd like it," she said. "One day it's something I'd like to do."

"Then you've never traveled at all?"

She shook her head. "From home to here," she said. "That's the longest trip I've taken."

He could barely comprehend it. He had been to Orange to study, to Lilac for winter sports, to the Olive Isles for sailing competitions. He had been all over Tyme. How strange it would be never to go anywhere.

"One day, I'd like to go to find one of the Siddae, on the Golden River," she said absently.

Dash ran a hand over his bald head, which the Siddae, with their hairless, tattooed scalps, had partly inspired. "So would I," he admitted.

"Really?" Ella looked at him with interest. "You'd want to go and meditate by the river?"

"I'd like to try."

She nodded. "My mum always wanted to," she said. "But it didn't work out."

"She could still go, one day," said Dash. "Perhaps when she retires."

Ella looked at him strangely. "Oh, I see," she said, after a moment. "No — the woman at the ball wasn't my mum. Sharlyn's my step-mum. My real mum died two years back."

"I'm so sorry," Dash said. "I didn't realize."

Ella's face was suddenly expressionless. She worked her lower jaw back and forth, and he realized that she was trying not to cry. He looked away from her to give her a moment of privacy in which to collect herself, and he wondered what he would do if his own mother died. If her ship sank and she drowned on her way to the Olive Isles.

The idea was unbearable. To drive it out, Dash considered Ella's list of interests and busied himself drawing stars beside *Shattering Day, History,* and *Salting.*

"You know Salting?" Ella's voice was disbelieving.

"My aunt lives there."

"Oh, right . . . So you've been?"

"A few times."

"And you *like* it?"

"Is that surprising?"

"It's just so common compared with Charming Palace."

Dash supposed that was true. "I like the music," he said.

"Oh, music! Obviously," said Ella. She wrote it under *INTERESTS,* and Dash starred it. Then, on impulse, he reached over to write under the *SKILLS* column again.

Keeping secrets, he wrote, and he glanced at Ella. "And giving things back," he added quietly. "Thank you again for that."

Her face softened. And then she snickered and wrote *Putting out fires.* Under that, she added *Excellent aim when throwing juice.*

Dash laughed aloud and instantly regretted it — Loom was at the desk in front of them, and he glanced over his shoulder to see what was going on.

Ella, however, was grinning. She shot Dash a quick look, then reached over in front of him. Under *INTERESTS* she scribbled *Fair treatment of the labor class.*

~ Ella ~

SHE wasn't sure what possessed her to write it. She blamed it on his laugh. The sound disarmed her, like his smile, and for a moment, she was bold.

But only for a moment. Then she realized how stupid she was.

The prince stared down at her words. His face had drained of color.

"What do you mean?" he asked in a voice that suggested he knew what she meant, and he did not like it.

She was relieved when Professor Linsey-Woolsey swooped in front of their desk to survey their lists. The prince casually used the wet rag at the corner of the desk to wipe away *Fair treatment of the labor class.* He wiped out the silly things they had written at the bottom of the *SKILLS* list too.

"Have you decided on a venture?" asked the professor.

"Not yet," said Dash, and Professor Linsey-Woolsey moved on to the next table. When the prince remained silent, looking at her, Ella knew she had to answer.

"I didn't mean anything by it," she said.

"Don't lie," the prince said quietly. "Just explain."

"It's — look, it's just that people working in the shops aren't treated fairly," Ella managed, keeping her voice a whisper.

"What shops?"

"You know — the silk shops. The wool shops."

"Are you accusing the Garment Guild of injustice?"

Ella swallowed. The Garment Guild *was* unjust. It was also the oldest and most powerful institution in Blue, and its members had built this kingdom — even little children knew that. Many times, in her village school, they had sung the wretched old anthem: "The Guild That Made This Country Great."

If only there were some way out of this conversation. If only she could fly.

Ella wished suddenly for the fairies. Maybe if Serge and Jasper were with her, they could do some sort of magic to make the prince forget what she had written. But then, that wasn't what her mum had wanted, was it? Her mum had died believing that if Ella had her chance, she could change the world.

Well, here she was, talking to the prince himself. If this wasn't a chance, nothing was.

"How much do you know about workshops?" she asked under her breath. Most of their classmates were the children of Guild members. The last thing she needed was for everyone else in the room to hear what she was saying.

"I know enough." The prince's voice was formal now. Distant.

"Do you know about the roop outbreak in Coldwater?"

The prince frowned. "You mean the sick people who went to work," he said. "The ones who were supposed to stay home. Yes, I heard."

"You *did?*" said Ella, surprised. "Scores of people died at —" She lowered her voice still further. "At Jacquard and Garter."

His frown deepened. "Isn't that their fault?"

"*Whose* fault?"

"The sick people."

Ella's blood pumped faster. "How?"

"They used Ubiquitous, didn't they?"

"What, to hide the roop?" said Ella, who was near trembling now with the effort to keep her voice a whisper. "Yeah. They use lozenges to hide their coughing, and they keep working until they drop dead. If they don't, they get sent home without a single naut to buy bread with, and their babies starve. But I guess they don't deserve to have babies if they can't feed them, hey? After all, it's their fault they were born poor. They should be punished for being so stupid. If they were clever like you, they'd've been born with crowns on their heads."

The prince gaped at her, and Ella's heart slammed. She was sure no one but him had heard her. But she'd gone too far. She was being — what was the word Sharlyn had used? *Seditious.*

Professor Linsey-Woolsey was back. "Something wrong?" she asked, her brow creasing. "Is there a disagreement?"

"Yes," said Prince Dash, still staring at Ella.

"May I help?"

"No."

The professor looked alarmed but left them to themselves, and the prince's frozen expression of angry shock began to frighten Ella. What had she been thinking? Why had she been so honest? Had his beauty melted her brain?

"Let's just do a messenger service for our project," she whispered. "All right? I'll make the budget. Just *please* forget what I said."

Dash

HE would not forget what she said.

He was stung beyond words. He was born to his crown, but he wasn't stupid. He could see logic. He'd been in his father's office when Lady Jacquard had spoken about Coldwater, and Lady Jacquard knew everything there was to know about business. By refusing to stay home, the laborers had made one another ill.

Suddenly, he saw Ella as his peers must have, vulgar and swearing in the middle of the ballroom. No one but his father had ever insulted him so openly — and his father was king. Who did she think *she* was?

Ella wrote the words *MESSENGER SERVICE: BUDGET* on their desk. Underneath this she frantically listed a column of words. *Saddles — Stirrups — Reins — Bridles — Feed — Shoes — Pay — Sick Leave —*

Dash took his chalk and underlined *Sick Leave*. "What's this?"

She scrubbed the words out with the side of her hand. "Nothing," she whispered.

"What *is* it?" he demanded.

She pressed her lips together. She looked frightened. "Well, it's pay," she whispered. "For people who can't work because they're sick or hurt."

"You'd pay people," said Dash, "for not working?"

"No, I'd pay them so that they don't starve to death while they get better."

"They're not earning it."

"I know, but —" Now Ella looked confused. "They're still skilled," she finally said. "They're still valuable — they're just sick. Everyone gets sick, don't they?"

"It's money. For nothing."

"Orange doesn't think so." She was barely audible now. She gripped her hands in her lap. "Commonwealth Green doesn't think so. Yellow Country has a system. Even the Redlands takes care of its people."

Dash was stung anew. How dare she suggest that the Blue Kingdom was less than those other nations? "How do you know that?" he demanded.

She fidgeted. "I heard it," she said. "My mum used to tell me —"

"You have no proof?"

"Well, no, but —"

"Enough."

Lavaliere had been right in advising him to refuse this partnership — he wished now that he'd listened to her, even if his mother would have disapproved. Ella Coach was mad.

Ella

SHE was sick with fear. The prince would tell the king what she'd said, she was sure of it.

When Professor Linsey-Woolsey checked on them again, Ella jumped. "What did you decide on?" the professor asked.

"Messenger service," Ella said, and the professor walked away, looking disappointed.

Ella and Dash neither looked at each other nor spoke as the professor took her place before the class and gave them their homework: to speak with an adult about their work so far, and to get advice on how to proceed. Ella wiped their slate tabletop clean with the wet rag, and the chalk marks vanished easily. She wished it were so easy to wipe out the things she'd said.

Dash

THE professor brought class to a close. Ella pushed back her chair at once, and Dash watched as she hung up her smock on one of the hooks behind them. The C-Prep uniform, neatly tailored and silver-buttoned, looked all wrong on her. His eyes traveled over it, down to her big, battered boots and her socks that were thick as blankets, slouching around her knees.

She touched the cheap gold *E* that hung from her necklace.

"You're lucky, hey?" she said to him. "Nothing wrong with being lucky. I just wish everyone could be. That's all I meant, I swear."

She grabbed up her satchel and hurried from the room.

"That must have been dreadful."

He turned to find Lavaliere standing before his desk, looking down on him in concern.

"I'll tell my mother," she said as he stood and hung his smock on a hook. "I'm sure she can fix it. You can't be forced into acquaintance with that — *thing*." She tucked her arm into his and gave him a protective, possessive squeeze. "I'm not going to stay partnered with Tiffany either," she went on. "We have to stand up for ourselves, you and I."

Dash walked with her toward their next class, quietly simmering. The things Ella had said nagged at him; the more he thought about them, the angrier he felt. If she thought that keeping silent about his mother gave her special privileges with him, then she was wrong. She was wrong about all of it. She knew nothing about the Garment Guild. Nothing about the Blue Kingdom. She was new to Quintessential — new money, new blood — and she didn't know the first thing about anything.

Serge

WHEN he left his office at sunset, everything was in meticulous order. "Anything before I go?" he asked, rapping on the glass desk that rimmed the reception pool. All of Lebrine's heads remained engaged in other conversations, so he gave her a parting wave, glad there were no emergencies for him to handle. It meant he could make his way to Ella's house all the sooner. "Tomorrow, then," he said.

A sudden surge of heat in his pocket stopped him on his way to the Slingshot. He took out his silver watch and flicked it open.

MY OFFICE. NOW.

When he arrived in the penthouse, Jules crossed her legs and kicked her pointy-shoed foot in a slow, deliberate rhythm.

"So, babe," she said, leaning back in her chair and fixing him with frosty eyes. "Why the interest in Elegant Coach?"

Serge was caught so much by surprise that he barely managed "I'm sorry?" in a tone that, he was pretty certain, could only be described as guilty.

"You had her contract," said Jules. "I requested it an hour ago, and it turns out that *you* just filed it last night." She paused. "Care to explain?"

Serge's mind grasped for a good lie. He used to be quite nimble at thinking up excuses for all manner of things — back when he had been a godfather with actual challenges to face.

"I wanted to see her," he said. Best to stick close to the truth.

"Why?"

"Because the scribes have been sniffing around for dirt on Maud. I was looking for a way to distract them."

"So you visited Elegant Coach." Jules picked up her drink. Swirled it. "Make sense, babe."

"I thought we could use a good, old-fashioned rescue story," said Serge. "You know. Impoverished beauty turned to fashion darling. That sort of thing."

Jules tilted her head. "Not a terrible idea," she said. "Except that Elegant Coach isn't impoverished."

"I know that now," said Serge. "I didn't at the time."

"Regardless, you had no business taking that contract," said Jules. "I was perfectly clear with your apprentice." She leaned forward, studying Serge. "I hope he hasn't fooled you with those eyes of his — you're not hypnotized, are you?"

Serge laughed. "Jasper's harmless. He'll make an excellent godfather — he's just idealistic."

Jules scanned his face. "Elegant Coach's mother's letter was gone," she said. "Why?"

Serge shrugged. "Jasper's the sentimental type. Don't worry — I won't let him become another Gossamer."

Jules laughed, and the suspicion vanished from her expression. "At least someone around here lives in reality," she said in her husky voice.

Serge smiled thinly, glad she hadn't seen through him. "Why did you go looking for the Coach contract, anyway?" he asked, sitting down across from her. "Sudden change of heart?"

"Research," said Jules. "Apparently, the girl's a troublemaker. She threw a fit at the royal ball — insulted the nobility, ruined the party — but before she did that, when it was time for Prince's Preference, Prince Dash made quite a show of choosing the Coach girl for his partner. Apparently, they had themselves a very intense conversation on the dance floor — nobody knows what they spoke about, but according to Lariat Jacquard, it was the most the prince spoke all night, to anyone. And *now* the girl is partnered with Dash for a project at school. Lariat is *not* happy."

"Why? What does she care if they're partners at school?"

Jules leaned forward. "Think back, Serge," she said. "Lariat Jacquard almost had Clement twenty years ago, and then in swept Maud Poplin from Salting — a nobody who showed up at a royal ball one night and stole the crown right out from under her."

"Thanks to you."

"And you," said Jules. "And now here's Ella Coach, another southern nobody — and of all the girls at the ball, Dash asks *her* to dance?" Jules shook her head. "Lariat Jacquard will not see her daughter supplanted by another Maud Poplin. If she has to, she'll strike."

"How?" he asked, taking care to keep the fear out of his voice.

"She'll crush the Charmings," said Jules. "Remove them from power."

Serge sat up, startled. "Does she have that kind of sway?"

"Oh yes." Jules chuckled. "Clement's been in a precarious situation for years, but he hasn't paid attention. While he's been gallivanting, Lariat has been demonstrating to the Essential Assembly that they don't need a king in order to make decisions. They just need *her*."

"But they can't just oust the king."

"They can call a vote," said Jules, "to eliminate the royal seat from the Assembly. If the House of Mortals votes to annul Clement's leadership, and the House of Magic allows it, then what can Clement do?"

"He has an army."

"True, he could start a civil war." Jules snorted. "But he won't. He has no iron in his spine."

"You honestly believe that the House would vote against the monarchy?"

"I know they would. And if they do," said Jules, "Lariat Jacquard will take direct control of the Blue Kingdom."

Serge digested this awful idea. Clement was not a great king — indeed, the Charmings had not been great kings since Envearia had interfered with them. But Lariat Jacquard was monstrous. The woman had no compassion, even for her own daughter.

"Will she call the vote soon, then?" he asked.

"Not necessarily. She doesn't *want* the monarchy dissolved. She believes Lavaliere will be queen, so she'd prefer to keep the throne a seat of power, for now. No — if the Coach girl proves to be a true threat, then Lariat will find a way to get rid of her."

Terror shot through Serge, but he masked it. "What's her plan?"

Jules shrugged. "How should I know?" she said as the music of a rather shrill fairy chime filled the glass office. "There's Thimble," she said with a sigh. "She's got a *sense* for interrupting me, I swear. I'll call you when I need you, babe, all right? Ta."

Serge left the Slipper. He made his way north along the seashore, flying quickly past Batik Castle, Charming Palace, and the Jacquard Estate, then cut east across the city to Cardinal Park.

When he arrived at Ella's home, the sky was dark.

"Finally!" Jasper cried, leaping from the park into the lane. "Where have you *been?*"

Serge flicked fairy dust at him. They both vanished from view, and Serge seized Jasper by his invisible shoulders. "Ella's in trouble," he said, and he divulged all that he had just learned.

But Jasper did not grow still or sober. Instead, Serge could feel him bouncing up and down. "Prince Dash is partnered with *Ella?*" he squealed. "Really?"

"Is that all you heard me say?"

"No, there were other parts too; I'm sure they were important —"

"This isn't a game. Lariat Jacquard has the power to ruin Ella's life." He rang the chime. "Let's go see her."

Three minutes later, they were in Ella's room, where they found her curled up on her bed, embroidering a small circle of dark blue linen with bright white thread. The stitching wasn't quite finished, but already it was beautiful — a keyhole, embellished all around with delicate vines that blossomed into tiny symbols of the different fairy tribes and their nations. Serge had seen many Shattering Day garments, but Ella's was a particularly eloquent design. He admired it for a moment before remembering his purpose.

"Ella, what happened at school today?"

"Did the prince sit with you?" added Jasper. "Tell us all about it."

Ella gave a dull laugh. "It's not like he sat with me on purpose," she said. "The teacher made him. By tomorrow, I'm sure he'll figure out how to get a new partner."

"Why would he?" cried Jasper.

Ella recounted every step in her disagreement with Prince Dash over the labor class, the Garment Guild, and sick leave. "I insulted him and the whole kingdom," she said. "Again. Could one of you put a spell on me so I won't keep saying stupid things?"

"My grandmother once took someone's mouth away," Jasper said. "It was one of the scariest things I ever saw." He shook himself and perched lightly on the foot of Ella's bed. "It was brave of you to say the things you did."

Ella shrugged. "Doesn't matter," she said. "He didn't get it."

"Then show him."

"How? Drag him to a workshop?" Ella snorted. "Hey, Your Royal Gorgeousness, how about a trip to Ragg Row? You'll love the stink of mold and mouse droppings — it's really *fresh*."

"Don't suggest any such thing to him," said Serge. "You're in a vulnerable position already. It would be best if you avoided Prince Dash from now on."

Jasper looked up in dismay. "Why is that best?"

"How am I vulnerable?" asked Ella at the same time.

"Some people," said Serge, "don't want you near the prince."

"Because of what I said at the ball?" said Ella. "Are people watching me?" She went to her window as though she might find a horde of Assembly members there. "How can I avoid being near him? I'm assigned to work with him."

"As your godfather, I urge you to choose another partner if you can."

"And as your *other* godfather," said Jasper, "I say don't. You want to make change? Influence the prince."

"Do you want her in danger?" Serge demanded.

"Do you want her to give up her cause?" Jasper shot back.

Serge did not. But he didn't want to see her crushed by Lariat Jacquard either. He opened his mouth to make another point, but Ella sighed quietly, stopping him.

"I can't influence him," she mumbled, stabbing her embroidery needle into her work. "My mum used to say a fish knows nothing but water. He's the fish."

"We're *all* fish," said Jasper. "You included. Have you considered his perspective?"

Ella made a noise of disgust. "No," she said. "'Cause he's wrong."

"Try to understand him anyway."

"Why should I?"

"Because if you don't, you'll lose this chance," said Jasper. "Imagine yourself in his position. Imagine what's going through his head. Then approach him with facts, not emotions — though I can hardly believe *I'm* saying so."

Ella pulled herself up against the headboard of her bed and chewed on a thumbnail for several minutes while Serge and Jasper waited.

"I know some facts," she said finally. "What if I told it to him like this?"

Dash

THAT evening, Dash kept to his chamber, stewing in thoughts unlike any he'd ever entertained.

She couldn't really believe that the Redlands and Yellow Country had better systems than Blue. This kingdom was the greatest country in Tyme. The most powerful, the most affluent, the most forward-thinking.

Wasn't it?

He longed for a talk with his mother. He had questions that she would be able to answer better than anyone else. She was from the south, after all. She'd worked in a tavern for years. She'd been a poor laborer, she knew the world outside Quintessential just as well as Ella Coach did, and *she* had never mentioned any great injustice. Surely if there were a genuine problem in the kingdom, the queen would have brought it up.

He lay in bed, unable to sleep. With his mother gone, whom could he turn to? He couldn't trust his father's opinion, and none of his friends had the faintest idea of what the world of labor was like. He could ask Aunt Tallith — she would know plenty — but if he wrote to her, his father would read the letter, and if he tried to visit her in Salting, his father's guards would tail him.

He could think of only one person who might help him. It was already after eleven, but the matter felt urgent. He sat up in bed and rang the bell, and when the page came, he asked for Tanner.

The red-haired messenger was there in minutes, bowing and stifling a yawn both at once.

"Did I wake you?" Dash asked him.

"No, sir, of course not, sir. How may I be of service?"

"I have questions."

"Of course, sir."

"How long have you served here in the palace?"

"Two years, sir."

"Have you ever fallen ill in that time?"

"Yes, sir, once."

"Tell me what happened. How long were you ill? Were you able to work?"

Tanner looked a bit surprised. "About two weeks, sir," he said. "And I was wretched, flat on the floor. No, I couldn't work a stitch."

"And you didn't lose your position here during that time?"

Tanner's neck reddened. "I was lucky to keep my job, sir, and I know it. I'm grateful beyond reckoning. I hope I haven't forgotten to say so. If I have, sir, then I beg your forgiveness."

"No, no — you're in no trouble," said Dash hastily. He was quiet for a moment, uncertain of how to proceed. "I'm just trying to work something out," he said. "Never mind. You may go."

Tanner seemed to want to say something, but he closed his mouth and bowed as though to leave.

"Yes?" Dash prompted. "What is it?"

Tanner straightened up. "If it's not too bold to say so, sir, I've worked other positions before this one, and I've seen other servants thrown out in the dead of winter when they're sick like I was. Is that what you're after finding out?"

Dash sat forward. "It is," he said. "Tell me, where do servants go when they're thrown out in that way?"

"Well, sir." Tanner looked uncomfortable. "If a body's lucky enough to have family that can take them in, then they go to that family. Lots of times, though, a body's supporting a family themselves. So it's not just them out in the street, it's their children too."

"But who would throw out a servant with a family of dependents?"

Tanner gave a shocked laugh, then checked himself. "Ah, sir." He was very quiet. "If I tell you honestly, it'll seem like cheek."

"Tell me."

Tanner swallowed visibly. "Everyone would, sir," he finally said. "Everyone throws us out. Servants are only useful if they're serving — same as any worker anywhere. My cousin Grommet and I worked in the same house a few years back. He was a groom there, but he lost that job when a horse crushed his foot, and then he had to take the next job he found — shearing sheep up north in Coldwater. He could barely hobble, but he did the work anyway, till he died of roop. A lot of them up there died."

"Why did he keep that job if people were dying?"

"He had two babies to support. If he left that position, he might not get another, and then his family would starve. He was dead either way."

Silence fell in the chamber as Dash worked these ugly ideas through his brain. He supposed he had known these things to be true. Servants were servants; they had no money or protection. That itself was no surprise. But he had never fully examined what that must mean.

"Whose house were you in when Grommet was thrown out?" he asked, almost afraid to hear the answer.

"Lady Jacquard's, sir."

Dash thought of what Lady Jacquard had said to his father the other day. *Those laborers are so irresponsible.* But was it irresponsible to want to provide for one's own children? Was it irresponsible to continue to work, even when one was sick enough to die?

"I'm sorry about your cousin," he said when he remembered himself. "Truly I am."

"Thank you, sir."

"I'm sorry to have disturbed you — you may go."

Wider awake now than ever, Dash sat up against his pillows, thinking.

Ella Coach thought that people should be paid when they were sick, and she thought that other countries were providing such pay. Insulting as her comments had been, had there been some truth in them? *Did* other countries have sick leave? How were such things even done?

Dash could sit still no longer. He got out of bed, pulled on his dressing gown, and made his way down to the palace library, hoping that the Royal Librarian would be awake. She was not, but her assistant was there, busy atop a stepladder. Dash asked for his help finding information on current labor regulations across Tyme.

"A fascinating request, sir," said the librarian, who looked both intrigued and apprehensive. He brought out a few scrolls and a small pamphlet for Dash's perusal. "These aren't precisely what you're searching for, I'm afraid," he said. "But I'm certain that the University of Orange would keep such records. Shall I request a loan, sir?"

"Please do." Dash drummed his fingers on the pamphlet. "We keep copies of old *Criers*, don't we?"

"Of course."

"How hard would it be to find articles on a specific topic?"

"Quite easy, sir." The librarian looked proud. "We keep a thorough index of every possible subject. What may I find for you?"

"Everything that's been written about Practical Elegance — or the Coach family."

True to his word, the librarian quickly retrieved a substantial stack of *Town Criers*, and Dash sat paging through them in the reading room until the sky grew light.

When he dressed for school that morning, he was exhausted and his head ached, but his research had been worthwhile. He couldn't fully trust the *Criers*, but there was one article, by a scribe called Nettie Belting, that was particularly powerful in sketching a picture of the Coach family's history. If Nettie's facts were accurate, then many things were clear.

Ella Coach might have understood things better than he'd given her credit for.

Ella

THE next day in Fundamentals of Business, she slipped into the chair in the back corner, where she began to embroider. One stitch.

Two. She concentrated on the evenness of her stitching, and she tried to block out the hissed insults of her classmates as they passed.

"Peasant."

"She's probably got cankermoth eggs nesting in that bramble on her head."

"Don't touch her — you'll catch roop just like her mother." Garb's words struck Ella like a hit to the gut. She dropped her needle, and it swung from its thread as she fumbled to grip it again.

"That's cruel," said Lavaliere, but she was laughing.

Ella heard the scrape of the chair beside hers being pulled out. Felt the thud of a person dropping down next to her. A radiantly warm person, who smelled like soap and cedar.

"Hello," he said quietly.

She glanced sideways at him. "Hello." She knew exactly how to explain herself to him — it was so simple she should have thought of it yesterday — but he was probably still furious.

He didn't seem furious, though. He regarded her with sober concern.

"Don't worry." Lavaliere came to his side and laid her hand upon his shoulder. She flicked her big, contemptuous gray eyes over Ella. "It's all taken care of."

She had no sooner finished saying this than Professor Linsey-Woolsey approached their desk. Lavaliere swept away, dark hair swinging, and settled herself at the front desk beside Paisley. Tiffany was no longer her partner but had been displaced to the back, where she now sat partnered with Kente.

Ella had a feeling that she herself was also about to be displaced.

"Your Royal Highness," said the professor, looking troubled. "May I have a word?"

Dash stood and went out with the teacher, and Ella tucked her embroidery away in preparation. In a moment, she knew, the world would be restored to order. The prince would be partnered with one of his friends, and she would be reassigned to whoever was left over. Maybe, if she got lucky, it would be Chemise. She looked hopefully around the room, but Chemise still wasn't back. Ella hoped that her feet were healing up all right.

She was surprised when, a minute later, Dash dropped down beside her again. He did not relocate to another table but sat still with a flush in his cheeks and his eyes pinned on Professor Linsey-Woolsey, who was making her way back to the front of the room.

Lavaliere had turned in her chair and was frowning. *What's wrong?* she mouthed, but the prince only shook his head. Lavaliere gave Ella a deadly look and spun away again to the front, whipping her tail of hair behind her like a horse smacking a fly.

"By the end of next week," said the professor, "each partnership must turn in a thorough draft of a business plan. Begin to flesh out these plans in class today, and I will be around to check your homework. Raise your hands if you have questions."

Throughout the classroom, chatter struck up. As soon as no one was looking at them, Prince Dash picked up his chalk with one hand and reached for the washrag with the other. Ella looked on in surprise as he wrote on the table in very small, neat strokes.

I heard what Garb said to you. I'm sorry.

He scrubbed out the words with the washrag, and she stared at the wet patch of slate where they had just been.

I researched you last night, Dash wrote in tiny letters. *I know about your mother.*

He wiped these words away just as Professor Linsey-Woolsey appeared before their desk.

"Miss Coach, did you speak with an adult about the project?"

In fact, Ella had forgotten the homework completely — but she had done it all the same. "Yeah," she said, thinking of her conversation with Serge and Jasper. "I talked to my — uncles." She gave Dash a quick look. "They said I should prepare my facts and not be so emotional. So I've got my facts ready."

The prince met her eyes.

"And you, sir?" said the professor. "To whom did you speak?"

"One of the palace librarians," Dash answered, holding Ella's gaze. "I asked him to find information on current labor laws across Tyme."

"Excellent. Continue in your efforts." The professor left them to themselves.

Dash

IT was a cool day, but Dash felt warm. Ella's clear brown eyes had lit at the mention of labor laws; she looked at him now as though he had done something heroic.

"You — er. You said you — had some facts?" he managed, confused.

Ella gazed at him for another moment. "Look, I'm sorry I got upset with you yesterday," she said. "I was out of line."

"It's all right."

"No, it's not," she insisted. "Sir," she added. "I'm sorry about that too; I know I'm supposed to be calling you sir, I'm just not used to any of this, so it's —"

"Don't call me sir," Dash interjected. "None of my friends do."

Ella's eyes lit again, brighter.

"Just, er." Dash swallowed hard. "Tell me your facts. I'm — I'm listening."

She picked up her chalk. "Right," she said. "You mentioned yesterday that laborers make each other sick — and it's true. They do. But they don't *want* to. No one wants to work when they're dying. They want to stay home and get good medicine — they just can't."

He thought of Tanner's cousin Grommet, and he kept listening.

"We both like math, so I'll explain it in math, hey?" She put the chalk to the slate. "If you have a family of three people," she said, "two parents and one child, then your expenses might look something like this."

He paid close attention as Ella wrote out the cost of renting a small house in an average village. It wasn't very much — he was surprised. Then she wrote out the cost of food, candles and lamp oil, fabric, shoes, and tools. She tallied the cost of keeping one horse and giving one gift on Shattering Day, and she calculated taxes — she left out nothing. He marveled at the details she knew and understood.

"And this is how much a person gets paid for spinning ten hours a day at Jacquard," Ella said. She wrote out the number and multiplied the daily rate by days, weeks, and months, until she had a total yearly income.

"So let's multiply it by two, assuming there are two living parents who both work," she said, and she did so. "And this is why it isn't fair," she finished as she wrote the total yearly income beside the total cost of supporting a family.

The sum of both parents working ten-hour days was barely equal to their daily expenses. And their daily expenses were meager.

"Now imagine," said Ella, "that one of the parents gets sick and can't work."

Dash watched as Ella drew a line through the sum of the two salaries and reduced it to half again.

"And when someone is sick," she said, "you have to add on new expenses for medicine and travel and specialists."

She wrote them out. She knew them well. The details were intimate.

"So this is what you're left with."

She scribbled a new number on the slate.

"And that," she said, "is why people go to work when they're sick."

Ella

HE was listening. He looked heart-struck too, as if he understood.

She grabbed the damp rag from the corner of the desk and started to wipe the slate tabletop, scrubbing out the math she'd scrawled all over it, but the prince's hand stopped hers.

"Reading," he said.

Ella drew back and let him study the numbers. When he was done, he leaned back in his chair and blew out a long, slow breath.

Professor Linsey-Woolsey paused beside Ella's chair.

"That looks interesting," she said. "What were you calculating?"

"Nothing," said Ella.

"An idea," said Dash at the same time.

They looked at each other.

"A business," he continued. "One that . . ." he paused. "Pays fair wages. And gives sick leave. Is that right?" he said, searching Ella's face.

"Yeah," she said, heat sweeping through her. "That's right."

"I see," said the professor, glancing from one to the other of them. "And what will the business do?"

"We're working that out," said Dash. "Should we create a garment company?" he asked in a low voice when the professor had walked away again. "Use Practical Elegance as a model?"

"We *could*, but I'd want to change everything," said Ella. "I'd want to implement sick leave and shorten working hours and make sure the workshops are decent." As she spoke, her enthusiasm for the idea mounted. If she could create a better plan for Practical Elegance, then maybe she could share it with her dad. Maybe he'd even pay attention. "We'd have to change the whole budget," she said. "Raise prices, raise wages — and I'd want to change most of our suppliers. I only want to contract with people who treat their laborers properly."

"Then let's do it."

"Seriously? You'd want to work on a plan like that?"

Dash nodded.

A moment later, the professor brought class to an end. Ella regarded the prince with new admiration as he packed up his books. To think, an hour ago, she had expected him to reject her for another partner. She had underestimated him.

"I'll ask my dad about Practical Elegance tonight, hey?" she said. "Get some information to start us off."

A gleam of Prism silk danced suddenly at the corner of her vision. Lavaliere paused beside their desk. She did not acknowledge Ella; she only smiled a little at Dash. "Walk me to history class?" she asked softly, and rested her polished fingertips on the slate tabletop before him.

The prince rose. He doffed his smock. He cast a look at Ella that she could not read, and then he followed Lavaliere out of the classroom. Dimity lingered after them, just long enough to laugh in Ella's face, and then she was gone too.

Slowly, Ella gathered up her things. It was strange that the prince could be such a decent person when his friends were the biggest quints in Quintessential. Even if he didn't completely act like it, he was still one of them. She had to be careful.

Dash

HE was by the fire, reading, when his father walked in.

"Son," said King Clement with a breezy air that was incongruous with the sleepless trenches under his eyes. "How is Ella?"

Dash let go of the scroll in his hands, and it rolled up in his lap. "What?"

"Ella," his father repeated, slowly and clearly. "Elegant Herringbone Coach."

Dash didn't know what his father was getting at. "I imagine she's well," he said. "Why?"

"I understand you chose her as your partner at school," said King Clement.

Dash shook his head. "The professor assigned us."

"And then today, you had an opportunity to reassign yourself. Isn't that so?"

"Who told you that?"

"Lariat Jacquard." His father watched him carefully. "You refused to change partners, and you stayed with the Coach girl. True or false?"

"True, but —"

"You made quite a point of asking that girl to dance at the ball."

"I didn't —"

"Everyone noticed, son. Ella Coach commanded your full attention, and the two of you had a very intimate conversation. What *were* you talking about?"

Dash shook his head again. He wasn't about to tell his father that Ella had spoken with his mother. The king would haul Ella in for questioning — and she, unlike Dash, would have no choice but to give him answers.

"I think you have a little infatuation."

"No!" Dash blurted the word. He felt his face go hot. "Ridiculous."

"Is it?" said his father. "A country girl can be irresistibly appealing, and I should know; I married one. Of course, mine was tame. Yours has teeth. That was quite a scene at the ball — she must fancy herself a revolutionary. Is that what you find so bewitching?"

Dash reopened his scroll and tried to focus on it. Defending himself was pointless. His father had made up his mind about something that wasn't true; protesting would only make it worse.

"Lavaliere is unhappy," said his father. The words hung in the room until Dash looked up, irritated.

"Why should I care?"

"Because she's your girlfriend."

"Barely." He didn't want to be together with her. He didn't even want to talk to her anymore. The way she had laughed when Garb made that crack about Ella's mother — he couldn't tolerate it. He expected such viciousness from Garb. From Lavaliere, it was something new.

Or maybe it wasn't. Maybe she'd always been nasty, and he'd simply been too consumed in his own cursed misery to notice.

"When Lavaliere is unhappy, son, so is her mother." The king moved closer until he stood before Dash's chair. "So I told Lariat a story to explain your behavior. I told her that you very much wanted to partner with Lavaliere today, but I *made* you stay with Elegant Coach, because I have suspicions about the girl after her outburst at the ball."

Dash looked up, outraged. "You told Lady Jacquard I'm *spying* on Ella?"

"You're 'keeping an eye on her activities,'" said King Clement. "To see if she's a threat."

"A *threat?*"

"It's only a story," said his father, waving a hand. "It will keep Lariat from pouncing. Partner with the Coach girl for this project, then give her up as soon as you have a chance, and we'll say it's because

I've determined she's harmless. In the meantime, give Lavaliere your attention whenever you can. Persuade her that you care."

"I'm *sick* of Lavaliere," said Dash. "Acting like I'm —" He couldn't find the word for it.

"Claimed?" his father supplied.

That was it.

"Her mother was the same," said the king. "It rankles, doesn't it? It's enough to drive a man straight into the arms of a nobody from Salting."

"My mother is *not* a nobody."

"No." King Clement's voice was quiet. He searched Dash's eyes. "Where is she?" he asked in a tone so plaintive that Dash's heart ached, in spite of what it knew. "Please. I can't sleep."

Dash looked away from him.

"I'll let you finish school at home, with tutors."

He wished he could give in.

"I'll stop hounding you about the Jacquards," said his father desperately. "Have the Coach girl if you want — let the monarchy go to Geguul. Just tell me where to find Maud."

"The monarchy?" said Dash, nonplussed. "What do you mean?"

"We're close to losing it," said King Clement, holding up his thumb and forefinger a hair apart. "*This* close. Do you think I push you toward Lavaliere because she's such a lovely child? I told you, our position relies upon keeping our friends. If Lariat thinks the throne is out of Jacquard reach, she'll make it worth nothing. The House of Mortals will call a vote to get rid of me."

Dash was completely thrown. "You're king."

"Oh, I'd still be king," said his father with a harsh laugh. "King Clement the Powerless."

"But the Assembly," said Dash. "They'd back you."

"Lariat owns them," said his father. "She's worked all of them onto her side."

"How?"

"Blackmail, probably. Who can say? What matters is that if I cross her, she'll take control. We're cornered, son. If you won't play the game, you won't be king. Not in any way that matters."

Dash considered what his father was saying. Lady Jacquard in power. Lady Jacquard, who threw injured fathers onto the street and called her dying workers irresponsible.

"You know what you're up against now," said his father. "Behave yourself accordingly. Understand?"

Dash nodded slowly. He did understand. But he did not like it.

Ella

SPORTS hour at Coterie was torture. She didn't mind archery, though she was no good at it, but she hated being near Lavaliere and her friends. She'd tried to trade for another class, but water and horseback sports were both full.

"Lavaliere," called Miss Halfdrop, the games mistress. "Your turn."

Lavaliere stepped up to the shooting line and placed one foot on either side of it. She rotated her chin over her shoulder and nocked her arrow on the bowstring.

"Perfect stance," said Miss Halfdrop. "Ella, look how Lavaliere rotates her hips. That's what you need to do."

Lavaliere glanced back at Ella. She smirked. And then she faced her target, drew the bowstring back past the side of her face, and released her arrow. It flew, sharp and sure, and struck dead center. Miss Halfdrop whooped approval. Lavaliere pivoted and returned to stand with Dimity and Loom, cradling her cheek in her hand. Ella thought she saw tears in her eyes, but Lavaliere turned her back before she could be certain.

"What's wrong?" she heard Dimity whisper. "Are you hurt?"

"It's just the string," Lavaliere murmured. "I pulled it too close to my face. I'm going to sit out for a while." She left the shooting range to sit in the shade of the trees with her eyes shut, grimacing as though she had a bad headache.

"Ella, your turn," said Miss Halfdrop, beckoning. Ella stepped up to the shooting line.

"Traitor," Dimity said, so quietly that Ella almost didn't hear it. Ella nocked her arrow and raised her bow. She had been called so many names this week that she was starting to feel immune.

"Hips!" called Miss Halfdrop, and Ella tried to rotate hers. She raised her bow. "Fingers!" shouted Miss Halfdrop, and Ella adjusted her grip. She drew back the bowstring.

"So Dash is actually spying on her?" she heard Loom say.

"Because of what she said at the ball?" said Mercer.

"The king thinks she might be a threat," Dimity whispered.

Ella accidentally released her arrow early, and it flew wide of the target.

"She heard you." Loom sounded amused. "So much for spying."

"Try again," called Miss Halfdrop, but Ella did not. She turned on Dimity.

"What's this about, hey?" she demanded. "How am I a threat?"

Dimity looked at her in disgust. "Do you think Dash *wants* to stay your partner?" she said. "Do you think he'd go anywhere near trash like you if —"

"Shut *up*." Lavaliere was back, clutching her bow and looking as if she wanted to shoot Dimity right through the heart. "I *told* you."

Dimity flushed, then turned very white. She hung her head and followed Lavaliere away from the range and out of earshot, while Ella stood still, stricken.

Prince Dash was spying on her for the king?

She left the shooting range and hurried through the woods to the equipment room, where she hung up her bow and put her uniform back on. She'd get into trouble later for walking out of class, but just now she couldn't care. She ran up the hill to the main campus, skipped lunch, and went instead to the empty business classroom, where she was an hour early. She tucked herself into the corner and concentrated on finishing the dress for Mrs. Wincey's baby, but even stitching couldn't soothe her. The knot in her stomach only hardened.

When the classroom door finally opened, and chattering students spilled into the chamber, Ella turned her back on them and tucked her embroidery away. She felt Dash drop down next to her. Heard his melancholy "Hello." She replied with a curt nod, unsure of what to do. If he was really spying on her, then she didn't want to give him anything.

Professor Linsey-Woolsey addressed the class, looking quite serious. "Chemise Shantung has withdrawn from C-Prep," she said. "Her injuries are too grave for her to return."

There was a general murmur of surprise — and amusement.

"Injuries?" said Garb with a laugh. "To her purse, maybe."

"One peasant down," said Paisley, cutting a look back at Ella. "One to go."

Beside Ella, Dash stiffened.

"That's awful," Ella said quietly. "Chemise was the nicest one here."

"Yes."

They were quiet together for a minute.

"Did you get information from your father?" Dash finally said.

"No." It wasn't true — she had information to work with, although her dad had said that Sharlyn was the one she should really talk to — but if Dash was watching her and reporting back to the king, then she didn't want to tell him any of it. "Sorry," she said. "Maybe we should pick a different project, hey?"

Dash looked at her in surprise.

"We can do a messenger service," said Ella, looking down at her desk. "Like I mentioned the other day. We both know some about wagons and horses, so that would work."

"You don't want to do a garment company that pays fair wages?" Dash paused. "I thought that was important to you."

Ella twisted her fingers. "Let's just keep it simple and get a good score."

The prince was silent. He tapped his chalk against the desk. Then he bent close to the slate and wrote in very small letters, *Did someone say something?*

"About what?"

About me spying on you. Which I am not.

Ella sat back, thrown.

Was it Lavaliere? He wiped out all of his writing and looked at her. Waiting.

"I overheard people," Ella whispered. "Dimity and Loom —"

"They're lying."

"But . . . you'd say that, wouldn't you, if you were spying."

Dash clapped the chalk onto the desk and ran a hand over his bald head. "I wouldn't say *anything*," he said. "I wouldn't mention it. That's how spying works."

"I'm not a traitor," said Ella as quietly as she could.

"I know!"

"Good. Then let's just do a messenger service."

Dash made a noise of sheer frustration. *You don't trust me?* he wrote.

I want to, she wrote back. *But if I'm wrong, what happens to me?*

NOTHING. Dash wrote the word with sharp, emphatic strokes. He was pink-faced, and his scalp was sweating.

"But I said those things at the ball," Ella whispered, uncertain. "I insulted you the other day. If the king thinks I'm plotting treason or something —"

NO. Dash wrote. *Believe me. Please. I want to do our real project. Do you?*

Ella looked into his eyes. They were very green.

"Why do you even care?" she heard herself say.

"Because I care about my country —"

He took a sudden, sharp breath and stopped speaking, then grabbed the wet rag and scrubbed out every word on the slate. A moment later, Lavaliere was standing beside him. She looked paler than usual.

"I don't feel well," she said. "Walk me to the infirmary?"

Dash stood without a word, and Lavaliere leaned against him. He escorted her out of the chamber with an arm around her waist, leaving Ella to wonder what the truth was.

Serge

THEY were finishing up with one of Gossamer's old clients when Ella's voice rang out in his head, as clearly as if she were standing beside him.

Serge, Serge, Serge!

He put a hand to his heart. It had been many years since he had joined with a godchild by the old magic, and he'd forgotten how personal it was to be called in this way. The pang of Ella's emotions came through clearly — anxious, confused, fearful — but her condition was not dire. She was in trouble, not peril.

That old magic pulled him straight to 76 Cardinal Park East, with Jasper right behind him. When they reached Ella's room, they found her cross-legged on her bed with schoolwork spread out all around her, chewing on a fingernail that was already gnawed to the quick.

"What's wrong?" said Jasper, leaning over the foot of her bed to read what she was doing. Serge took a seat at her desk.

"There's this rumor going around that the prince is spying on me," said Ella, and Serge listened to the rest of her tale with narrowed eyes. So this was how Lariat Jacquard planned to undermine her. Gossip. Lies. "I don't know if I can trust him," Ella finished. "I *want* to. I could've sworn he meant it when he talked about fair wages and sick leave. He seemed like he was listening to me — really listening."

"I'm sure he was," said Jasper.

"The prince isn't spying on you," Serge said. "His interest in your cause is genuine, I have no doubt."

"Then why are people saying it?"

Jasper gave him a desperate look, but Serge shook his head. Lariat's threat to the monarchy was dangerous knowledge, and Ella should not have it. She couldn't control her temper. She might damage herself. "It's a rumor," he said instead. "A deliberate rumor, meant to keep you and the prince from getting too friendly."

Her face registered understanding.

"Lavaliere," she said. "She wants to make me look bad. Is that it?"

"This rumor is serious," Serge said, sidestepping the question. "It doesn't matter that it's false. Find another partner in class, and let it all blow over."

"But what about our project?" Ella laid a hand on her school notes. "What if he remembers it when he's king? Isn't it worth trying to show him how things could be run better than they are?" She looked around at the scattered parchment. "Except I don't know exactly how Practical Elegance is run. Sharlyn's the one who really knows, and I can't ask her."

"Why not?" said Serge and Jasper at the same time.

Ella looked uncomfortable. "She's barely spoken to me since the ball," she said. "She'll never get over it. She said I humiliated this family beyond repair."

"Soften her up," said Jasper. "Give her something she wants."

"A present?"

"Not exactly. What does your stepmother want from *you?*"

Ella's expression hardened. "She wants me to dress like the other girls."

"Ah," said Jasper. "That makes sense. This is business, and business is just theatre with numbers. If you want to be convincing, then you have to look the part. What do you have to wear?" He opened her wardrobe and gazed in dismay upon its barrenness. The only garments in it were C-Prep uniforms, a pile of knitted stockings, and a few old tunics and skirts.

"I won't buy clothes from the shops on the Avenue," Ella declared, folding her arms. "Most of those merchants get their supplies from Jacquard and Garter and —"

"I'll make your clothes," said Serge. "Problem solved."

Ella hesitated. "I'd still be a hypocrite," she said. "Dressing up like a quint — it's the same as giving in."

"How?" Serge sat forward. "You're not abandoning your values. You're simply showing your stepmother that you can see her point."

"It shouldn't matter what I wear. It won't change anything about me."

"Exactly," said Serge. "It won't change anything about you, except that you'll appear professional, and your stepmother will take you more seriously. What's wrong with that?"

Ella pursed her lips but could apparently find no other argument to give.

Jasper took Ella's hand and pulled her to stand. "At least let us show you what we mean," he said, walking around her to inspect her hair from all angles. With a few deft motions, he parted it and swept it back. A crimson shimmer made a nimbus around her face as magic took hold of her voluminous curls and settled them into a professional twist. Jasper tucked one last curl into place, and the crimson shimmer faded. He turned Ella toward the mirror.

Her eyebrows shot up at the sight of her reflection. Jasper had drawn attention to all the right features. Her forehead was high, her eyes bright. Her cheekbones stood out a league.

"I didn't know my hair could change my face so much," she said softly.

Jasper beamed. "Serge will get you dressed," he said.

Serge closed his eyes. He pictured Ella in dark gray riding breeches and a long, fitted coat in deep red over a simple, severe undertunic. He saw her clearly, chin up and fists clenched, her whole heart in her expression. His own heart thrummed in reply. His dust came easily, warming his palms and filling them like soft chalk, and he squeezed his fists to feel it there. His chest was tight.

He opened his eyes and flung the dust at Ella. It exploded in a cloud of glittering blue, and as it faded, Ella looked down at herself and drew a breath of awe. She touched the lapels of her dark red coat, then put out one foot and gazed at the simple, perfect gray boot.

"Wow," she whispered. She looked in the mirror, and the usual hard edges went out of her face. She touched her hair. "Sharlyn's going to die of shock," she said, and then she looked away from herself with a little shake of her head. "I'm sorry," she said. "Forgive me, all right?"

"For what?" said Serge, startled.

"For calling you here and complaining like I have real problems, when I know —" She paused and seemed to struggle with herself. "I know I'm lucky. I'm grateful my mum wrote you. I'm grateful you're here, I mean it."

It had been so long since any godchild had thanked him that Serge stood without replying, unsure whether he could speak. Ella meanwhile retrieved a tiny garment from her scorched schoolbag and pushed it into his hands.

"For Mrs. Wincey," she said. "If you visit Kit any time soon."

He held up the little gown, struck again by the complexity and evenness of Ella's embroidery. "Lovely work." He ran a fingertip along one of the small, swirling vines. "Jasper was right, you're quite skilled."

"Grats," she said with a proud grin. "I like doing it."

"It shows," said Serge. He glanced at Ella's paltry clothing collection. "*I* like dressing people too," he said. "Especially people who appreciate it. So if you don't mind, I'm going to make you a few more pieces. Just in case you decide to upgrade your wardrobe permanently."

Ella looked at her reflection once more. "D'you think if I dressed better at school, Dash would take me more seriously? My ideas, I mean?"

"*I* think he's taking you seriously already," said Jasper. "But we'll leave you a few new things anyway. You can decide what's best to do."

Ella nodded, and the fairies went to work. It was not long before her wardrobe was full of shoes and accessories for Coterie, as well as clothing for social visits. Ella stared at it all, mouth open. "I've never had this many clothes at once," she said. "How do I know what to pick?"

"Call us for help if you want to," said Jasper fondly, taking Serge by the elbow. "Good night, Ella."

"Good luck," said Serge. With a flick of his dusty fingertips, he and Jasper were invisible, and with a snap, they vanished from her room. He brought them to the front garden of number 76, just outside the large sitting room windows. Within the well-lit parlor, Lady Sharlyn Gourd-Coach sat at a large mahogany desk, wearing her pince-nez and writing steadily.

A moment later, Ella entered the room, tasteful and tailored, hair and boots gleaming. Her lips moved, saying something the fairies couldn't hear.

Sharlyn paused in her writing and laid down her pen. She looked up, and her eyebrows arched. "Why, Ella!" Her rich voice could be heard through the windows. She rose from her chair, looking mystified and delighted together. "What's this?"

Ella's lips moved again, and her stepmother went to her. They spoke too quietly to be heard without fairy dust, but Serge didn't need to listen. They were talking — that was what mattered.

He had done something good here.

"Let's go," he said.

"No, let's listen! Do that thing with my ear —"

"Let's *go,*" said Serge, catching Jasper by his invisible hand.

He flew off, almost giddy. He couldn't remember the last time he'd felt like this. To have so much dust all of a sudden, after feeling dry for so long — he had to do something with it. To hold it back would be a crime. A waste.

Jasper allowed himself to be pulled across to the park, where they alighted, still invisible. "Where are we going?"

"I thought I might cut through the fairywoods down to Salting," said Serge. "I'd like to see what I can learn about the Winceys. Find out what they need. Will you come with me?"

Jasper was quiet for such a long moment that if Serge hadn't felt his apprentice's sleeve against his own, he would not have been certain that he was still there.

"I'd love it," said Jasper finally. Serge thought he heard a sniffle.

Together, they flew into Cardinal Park, toward the fairywood at its center.

SHARLYN was so thrilled with Ella's "show of maturity" that she told her almost everything she wanted to know about the inner workings of Practical Elegance. Ella walked away from the conversation with a head full of ideas and a pile of disorganized notes. She brought these with her to business class the next day, where she plunked them down on the slate in front of Dash. She heard her classmates' scattered whispers about treason, saw them look pointedly at her fine new satchel and fashionable boots from Serge. She ignored them as best she could and took her seat.

Dash gazed at her papers in obvious surprise. "What's this?"

"Stuff my stepmum told me. About Practical Elegance."

"You mean you want to do the garment business after all?" He glanced at the table in front of them, where Loom was putting down his bag, and he lowered his voice. "You believe I'm not spying on you?"

Ella shrugged a little. "I guess."

"You *guess?*"

"Well, I can't *know,* can I."

The prince did not look satisfied, but Professor Linsey-Woolsey spoke from the front of the room, cutting their conversation short. "Today and tomorrow, we will spend our time in the library," said the professor. "Use the time to do research that will enhance your business plans. For example, you might strengthen your advertising strategies by looking in the *Criers* for strong campaigns. Take your things with you, please, and let's make our way."

Coterie's library was a tall brick building covered all over in ivy except for the shining panes of its windows. Of all the places at C-Prep, Ella liked it best. It was cool inside, and quiet, and it never closed — she couldn't count the number of times she had escaped her old dorm room and come here for some peace.

Most of their classmates headed toward the periodicals to flip through old *Criers*, but Ella made right for the stairs.

"Where are we going?" asked Dash, climbing behind her.

"Philosophy," Ella replied. "Maybe we can find something on business ethics." She stopped on the third floor and chose a table near the windows, looking out over the gleaming athletic fields, where the younger students were out playing games. "This all right?" she asked.

The prince nodded and set down his things as two royal guards took up positions just ten feet behind him, where they stood motionless. Watching. One of them was the same man who had bullied Tallith Poplin in the kitchen of the Corkscrew, and who had accused Ella of helping the queen. The guard narrowed his eyes at her now, something like a smirk playing at a corner of his lips. Her skin prickled, and she looked away.

The prince took his seat without seeming to notice the guards' presence. But then, he was probably used to being followed and stared at.

"Shouldn't we look for books?" Ella asked.

"May I read your notes first?"

She sat across from him and handed over her notes from the meeting with Sharlyn. "There's a list of products there," she said. "And a schedule showing how many of each item gets produced, and when they're released."

Dash sank into reading. He paged through her writing, making notations from time to time in his beautiful, princely script. At one point, he frowned. "What does this say?" he said, tapping his pen beside a cluster of words that Ella had written very quickly, and very poorly.

She blushed. "See separate list for metalworking supplies," she muttered. "Sorry. My old teacher down in Eel Grass didn't have us practice our handwriting much."

The prince glanced up from his reading. "Is Eel Grass anywhere near Barnacle Cove?"

"*You* know Barnacle Cove?"

"My mother was born and raised there."

"Oh, right! Yeah, BC's just south of home. Fun place. Twice as big as my village, and lots more young people. I used to go to dances in the village hall with my friend Kit."

Dash looked interested. "What were those like?"

"Imagine the opposite of the royal ball, and you've got it."

"Is it really so different?"

"It's another world," said Ella honestly. "Decorations are ribbons and lanterns. There're no gowns or fancy dancing either. People just put their arms round each other for the slow ones."

"That sounds nice."

"It is."

He considered her. "And you'd really rather live there than here? Down south, I mean?"

"Well . . . it's home. This is your home, so it makes sense you'd rather live here than anywhere else, hey?"

The prince didn't reply right away. He looked out of the window, down at the young students who were now mounting their horses.

"Six months ago, I wouldn't have said that," he replied eventually. "I was so tired of . . ." He stopped. "I was just tired," he amended, but Ella got the feeling there was much more to it. "I needed time away," he continued. "I went down to Orange to attend the University for a while."

"You've studied at the University of Orange!" Ella leaned forward. "That's where I want to go — tell me what it's like."

"I don't know if I can really describe it," he said, but it was obvious he was glad to be asked; he spoke with some eagerness. "Orange is a nation of learning. Enlightenment. The royal family lives at the main University, in the center of it all. I stayed with them, and it was — just very different. From home."

His expression turned pensive. He looked out across the campus, toward the city beyond.

"I thought you went to the Redlands," Ella ventured. "Because of . . . well. The witch."

He shook his head. "I traveled to the Redlands from Orange about three months ago," he said, "after I attended a special lecture on witches by Nexus Keene. His ideas gave *me* ideas, and I —" He stopped, shook himself slightly, and turned his green eyes on her. The full force of them was disorienting; Ella forgot, for just a moment, where she was.

"I haven't shared that with anyone," said Dash. "I'd appreciate it if you didn't mention what I said."

"I wouldn't do that."

"I don't mean to offend you," Dash added, and the color in his cheeks intensified. "It's just that usually —" He stopped. "It's self-protection," he said.

It was sad, really, Ella thought. The way he assumed that his confidence would be broken. He was so beautiful, and he had so much, but he couldn't open his perfect mouth without fearing that what came out of it would end up in the *Criers*.

"I'm not offended," she said, and she kicked him a little under the table. "Anyway, it's not like you said anything really juicy, is it? 'Prince Dash Enjoyed University of Orange' doesn't make much of a story."

"You'd be surprised what they can turn into a story."

"No, I wouldn't. The scribes wrote steaming piles about my dad and me when we first moved here. I don't know how you put up with it. I could barely cope with it for two months, and you've had it all your life — you have a lot more strength than I do."

He gave her a smile so warm that everything inside of Ella went soft all at once.

"Thanks," he said quietly.

The head guard who stood posted behind Dash took a step closer to them, eyeing Ella all the time. She had almost forgotten about the guards; now she had the sudden sense that they could see right into her brain, and she blushed hard. "Do they just stand there staring like that?" she muttered. "All the time?"

Dash glanced back and scowled. "Yes," he said. "Excuse me." He got up with sudden energy and strode over to the guards, fists clenched.

Dash

He stopped in front of Spaulder, whose expression was thoroughly insolent. Beside him, the other guard, Bevor, looked more appropriately nervous.

"Give me space," Dash demanded, his voice low. "Take a few steps that way." He pointed to the other end of the floor, where the guards might stand out of earshot.

"I have my orders, Your Highness," said Spaulder. "My apologies." But he didn't look apologetic. The man was actually smirking; under his bushy eyebrows, his eyes were full of amusement.

Dash looked back at his and Ella's table to see if she was listening, but she wasn't there any longer. He saw her hair gleam from the other side of the stacks, a few rows of books away.

"Please," he whispered, turning back to Spaulder. "I know you're supposed to listen in on me in case I slip up and say where my mother is. But I'm never going to accidentally blurt that out, am I? Can't you just let me have a conversation with a friend? That's all I want."

Spaulder snorted. "*All* you want, sir?" he said, and his lewd tone made his meaning clear. "His Majesty wants me to listen in on plenty of things. Including your private moments with your *friend*."

Dash flushed, furious. "Just because you're my father's man doesn't mean you can't be replaced," he said coldly. "Do not overstep yourself with me."

Spaulder's smug expression flickered. Fear flashed in his eyes, and Dash felt a measure of satisfaction to see it there.

"Sir." The guard bowed his head. "I beg your pardon. Truly, I have no choice in my duty. His Majesty's wish is my command." The man's face was red. He was embarrassed, Dash knew, to be cowed like this in front of a fellow guard. He was frightened too of losing his position.

Perhaps he had a family to support.

The thought came to Dash quite suddenly. He had never thought of Spaulder as anything other than a thug for the king, but Spaulder was a man, and a grown one.

"Do you have children?" Dash asked.

Spaulder cringed. "Your Highness, if I've caused offense to you, I beg you to visit the consequences on me alone —"

"No, that's — that's not what I meant," said Dash. His anger at Spaulder drained from him, replaced by the uncomfortable heat of shame. He held this man's whole happiness in his power — and he had been ready to abuse that power, to give himself a moment of personal pleasure. Spaulder was a bully, but that did not excuse tormenting him. "It was only a question," Dash managed. "To know you better. How many children do you have?"

"Three, sir."

"How old are they?"

Spaulder dared a glance up at him. "A son near your age, sir, and two daughters, one the eldest, and the other one still quite small."

A boy his own age. Dash considered this. Considered, for the first time in his life, how little he knew not only about Spaulder but about any servant in his house.

"Stay where my father told you," he said. "Don't jeopardize your family. I shouldn't have asked you not to do your duty."

Spaulder bowed his head once more, but not before Dash saw the surprise that registered in the man's eyes. "Yes, sir."

Dash turned back to his table, and he swallowed when he saw that Ella was back in her seat, looking at him. How much of that had she heard?

He sat across from her, nervous. She opened her mouth. Closed it.

"Say it," he said recklessly. She probably thought him a miserable brute, the way he'd threatened Spaulder's livelihood.

"You're a good person," she blurted. "And see?" She jerked her chin toward his shoulder, and Dash glanced back at his guards. They had moved a good twenty paces away. They still watched him, but they wouldn't hear his conversation.

Not that Dash had any idea what to say anymore. The way Ella was gazing at him, he didn't even know where to look. He hadn't noticed before, but she'd changed her hair. It was up in a twist, though a few of her curls had escaped confinement. With her bright eyes on him and her soft curls glinting around her face, he wasn't sure he could muster up two words.

His father wanted Spaulder to report on his interactions with Ella.

His father thought that he was infatuated with her.

"We should —" Dash managed, but the words were strangled. All his earlier ease was gone. "What's — next? With — er." He pulled at the neck of his shirt. It felt too tight. "The . . . the garment project?"

Oh, well done.

Ella looked at him curiously. "Class is probably almost over," she said. "And I need to check out these books. Should we go downstairs?"

Dash nodded and gathered up his things without a word. He followed Ella down to the library's front desk, where the rest of their class already stood listening to the professor.

"We'll meet here again tomorrow in order to spend the full hour researching," she said as Lavaliere turned her head and flicked her big gray eyes from Dash to Ella, then back to Dash. He could not read her expression, but he knew that whatever she was thinking, it was not good. It surely didn't help that his face was burning.

"What did you find there, Miss Coach?" asked the professor. Ella, who had been approaching the librarian, turned and offered her book. The professor took it and held it up. "Business ethics — an excellent idea," she said. "The rest of you, be sure to branch out in your thinking tomorrow."

"Oh, we *will*," said Lavaliere. She shot Dash a smile — the kind that indicated a private joke, only he wasn't sure what was funny.

"Class dismissed," said the professor, and a moment later, Lavaliere was at Dash's side, propelling him out of the library toward his next class. He wished he could look back at Ella, but it wasn't prudent. It hadn't been prudent to sequester himself upstairs with her either. Tomorrow would have to be different — but Ella would still be his partner. He'd still see her, talk to her. That was something.

He realized what he was thinking at the same time he realized that Lavaliere was speaking.

"Don't you agree?" she said.

He nodded, though he had no idea what she was talking about. His mind swung straight back to Ella. Her boot nudging his under the table. Her kindness. How she'd called him strong and good.

". . . is my opinion," Lavaliere said. "But Paisley always thinks she knows everything."

Dash made a noncommittal noise.

"You and Ella were a long while upstairs," Lavaliere said casually.

He came out of his reverie, alert.

"It's a shame you have to endure her," Lavaliere went on. "Even for a noble cause."

Dash hesitated, uncertain. "A noble cause?"

Lavaliere gave him an arch look. "For His Majesty," she said. "For the Blue Kingdom."

Because he was supposed to be spying on Ella.

"It *is* for the Blue Kingdom," he answered, and he had no trouble saying it. It was not a lie.

"Well, I'll make sure you're not stranded with her tomorrow," Lavaliere said, untucking her arm from his as they came to the door of her history class. "You won't have to be noble all on your own." She kissed his cheek and slipped into the classroom, leaving him alone with his guards and his sinking heart. Tomorrow, it wouldn't matter how far away Spaulder stood from him; he wouldn't get a moment with Ella. Not a real one.

Not with Lavaliere watching.

Ella

THE last day of the school week found Ella in a state of high distraction. She barely noticed poetry class or history; even archery didn't bother her. She only wanted to get to the library again so she could work on the project.

And be with Dash.

She mentally swatted the thought away. It was the project that mattered, not the prince. She couldn't like him — not *like* him. It was stupid of her if she did. He was dating Lavaliere, or seemed to be. That was what everyone said.

But it was hard not to like him. Very hard. If he'd just been pretty, she could've gotten over it, but his looks weren't all of him.

Not by a league. He was up so high that he didn't have to care about anybody else — but he did care. When he'd carried Chemise off the ballroom floor without laughing at her, she'd thought it was good of him, but still — Chemise Shantung was one of his own. It meant more to Ella, far more, that he thought about his servants. That he considered their families — that he noticed they were real people, with real lives.

When she reached the library that afternoon, she didn't see Dash right away. She headed upstairs at a jog, too excited to walk. On the third floor, she spotted him reading at their table, and when he looked up at her, she grinned before she could help herself.

He glanced down at his book without returning her smile.

Her grin faded and she approached him, feeling silly. Maybe she'd misjudged things yesterday — maybe he'd just been acting polite. When she passed the bookshelves and came closer to the window, she halted. Lavaliere and Paisley were seated at the table directly behind Dash, Lavaliere facing him. She lifted a dark eyebrow at Ella. Paisley turned in her seat and dragged her dark-eyed gaze over Ella's fairy-made shoes and satchel and her carefully upswept hair.

"My, my," she said. "Someone is obviously trying a little harder. I can't imagine *why*."

Ella's skin went hot; she turned her back on them and sat across from Dash, who flicked his eyes to her again. Embarrassed, she looked down.

"We need financials by next week," he said tonelessly.

"What?" Ella managed.

"The assignment," Dash replied. "The next step in the project. Create a budget."

"Oh."

They were silent. Ella took out her notes and her borrowed book on business ethics.

"Do you have a sample budget from your stepmother?" Dash asked.

"No, Sharlyn says the money stuff's private."

"What about a list of vendors?"

Ella could feel Lavaliere and Paisley watching her. Listening to her. She couldn't answer the question honestly with those girls right there — but she had to answer. She wished they were back in Professor Linsey-Woolsey's classroom with their slate and chalk.

She pulled a bit of parchment out of her bag and wrote, *I know the vendors my dad uses, but if we're going to do this right, we can't buy silk from Jacquard or wool from Garter. If we want companies who really treat their people properly, we might have to look outside of Blue.*

She pushed this across the table to Dash, whose jaw tensed when he read it. She'd insulted him again. Insulted the country. Before she could try to fix it, Lavaliere was beside them — Dash crumpled the note in his fist not a moment too soon. Lavaliere looked narrowly at his closed hand.

"I need help finding the ethics section," she said. "Show me?"

"Ella knows where it is," the prince replied. "I don't."

Lavaliere tossed her tail of hair and waited.

Dash rose and followed her in among the bookshelves, and the two of them vanished from sight. Behind Ella, Paisley laughed softly. "You can change your shoes," she murmured. "But you can't change your birth."

"As if I'd change my birth," Ella snapped, and she bent over her notes. With angry energy, she filled a sheet of blank parchment with columns and rows, and she began to list as many cost categories as she could think of, deliberately driving everything out of her head except for the business budget. There were loads of costs to consider — soon she needed another sheet of parchment, and then another. The task almost kept her mind from wandering back to

Dash and Lavaliere, off behind the bookshelves, doing whatever they were doing.

The prince returned at the end of the hour, his face expressionless, his hand clasping Lavaliere's. He slung his schoolbag over his shoulder.

"I'll do a budget this weekend," he said. "Will you do a vendor list?"

"I already started the budget," Ella replied.

"Then I'll do the vendors," said Dash, never meeting her eyes. He turned as though to leave, but before he could take a step, Lavaliere leaned in and kissed him. Dash seemed to freeze for half a second, and then, unmistakably, he kissed back.

Ella looked out the window at the athletic fields, her heart beating hard. She tried to tell herself that she didn't care who he kissed, but that was a lie and she knew it. So she told herself instead to get over Dash Charming — fast — before her feelings got any stronger.

She just wished she knew how.

Dash

LAVALIERE would not come unglued from his side. She was worse than having guards.

"We can share a carriage to school next week, since I'm not boarding here anymore," she said before they parted ways to their own carriages that afternoon. "What do you think?"

"If you'd like."

"I obviously would," she teased. "So just say yes."

"Yes."

She glanced at him with laughing eyes. "So you'll pick me up?" she prodded.

"Yes."

"And you'll drop me off again after school?"

"Yes."

"Good; let's try a harder one. What should we do this weekend?"

"I don't care."

He said it too loudly; she squeezed his hand hard. They had an audience — a few dozen students were lolling about on the yard in front of the Admissions building, waiting for carriages.

"I mean —" He focused hard to force out the lie. "Whatever — makes you happy."

Lavaliere relaxed. "My mother got us tickets for a matinee tomorrow. Will you take me to the Curtains?"

"Yes."

She kissed the corner of his mouth — for the benefit of the onlookers, he was sure. He fixed his mind on Ella's note, and the idea that they would have to look outside the Blue Kingdom for vendors who treated their employees with respect. It couldn't be true that not one single member of the Garment Guild was ethical. Some of them must have been doing the right things. He'd ask the Royal Librarian for records.

He walked Lavaliere to her carriage and helped her in. "See you tomorrow," she said, looking pleased as she sat back.

At home, the library didn't have what he wanted, although the librarian did give him copies of international labor laws and various other labor records that had been Relayed by the University of Orange. Dash would have to ask his father for the Blue Kingdom's records himself. He stayed in his bedchamber for an hour after dinner, rehearsing what he wanted to say so that he wouldn't draw suspicion, then found the king in his office, writing.

"I need help with school."

His father did not look up. He looked wild with sleeplessness. His hair was unkempt, and his eyes were unusually dark. "Ask the librarian," he said. "I'm busy."

"The library doesn't have what I need."

"Then how am I supposed to help?"

Here it was. He had to be smooth now. "I need information on the Garment Guild," he managed in one breath.

Now his father stopped writing and looked up sharply. "Is this about the Coach girl?"

"No, it's for class," said Dash, who had anticipated this.

"You need Garment Guild records for class? Why?"

"Just to find vendors. For our business," said Dash, forcing out the words. "So we can — get a decent score." He was sweating. He hoped his father wouldn't ask more questions.

The king bent his head and kept writing, apparently satisfied. "Fine. I'll call for some papers. When do you need them?"

"It's due next week," Dash said.

The king snatched a fresh sheet of vellum from a golden tray. "Not that you have a lick of sympathy," he said, "but I'm sending a copy of this letter to every person I can think of who might be harboring Maud. Wherever she is, she'll hear what I have to say."

Dash stepped forward to look at the pile of letters. The one on top of the pile was addressed *Care of Queen Claret of the Olive Isles*, and there was nothing Dash could do to stop it being sent without giving his mother's whereabouts away. He only hoped that when the letter arrived, she would ignore it and stay where she was.

"How is Lavaliere?" his father asked. "Happy with you, I hope. Her mother hasn't set the House of Mortals upon me, so I assume you're behaving yourself."

"I'm taking her to the theatre tomorrow."

"Good boy."

The next night, Dash was sitting up in bed, reading carefully through the labor records from Commonwealth Green, when messengers delivered a stack of large crates filled with various kinds of information on the Garment Guild. He got out of bed at once and went to his study, where he opened one crate and then another until he found what he wanted. Each company licensed by the Garment Guild reported not only their financial details every year, but also the total number of citizens they employed. Employee numbers were arranged by workshop locations, areas of skill, pay rates — and ages. There were plenty of fourteen-year-old apprentices listed among the employees at Aglet Laceworks. There were thirteen-year-olds too — even a few twelve-year-olds. Dash frowned at this, but he supposed it was to be expected that some children would start working younger than was strictly legal.

The report from Batik Dyes, however, was worse. Of the five hundred Batik employees in Quintessential alone, almost a hundred of them were children, some as young as nine.

He paged through the other files to see if anyone else hired young children and was dismayed to discover that some were worse than Batik: Garter employed children as young as eight, and when Dash found the record for Jacquard Silks, he had to stand up and walk away from his desk. What could Lariat Jacquard possibly want with six-year-olds? What could a child of six *do* in a workshop?

When he was king, he would forbid it. He couldn't believe that no Charming before him had ever done anything to stop this.

He went to his father's chamber and found him drinking by the fire, staring out the window at the sea. Queen Maud's glass slipper sat on the table beside the crystal decanter, glimmering in the firelight.

"I thought fourteen was the legal working age."

His father turned his head sluggishly. "Hmm?"

"Fourteen. I thought you had to be fourteen to start an apprenticeship in this country."

"Ah." The king drank deeply. "You've been reading labor reports."

"Isn't it illegal to hire small children?"

His father gave a lazy shrug. "Illegalities only matter if they are enforced," he said. "To maintain the peace, we turn a blind eye to our friends' failings."

"You let the Garment Guild do whatever they want, you mean."

"Why shouldn't children find apprenticeships as early as they can?" The king drank again. "Their families might need the income."

"Six-year-olds, Father. That's not apprenticing, that's — that's —" Dash shook his head. He had no word for what it was.

His father laughed somewhat sadly. "My boy," he said. "You are the first Charming in one hundred and fifty years who will rule this kingdom without the curse over your head. You have a chance at happiness. Don't spoil it by becoming an idealist."

"Other governments enforce their apprenticeship laws," Dash pressed. "Commonwealth Green — Yellow Country — I requested their records. *They* don't allow this."

His father focused on him, and for a moment he appeared completely lucid. "This *is* the Coach girl's influence," he said softly, smiling. "It is, it is . . ."

And it was. Dash said nothing, afraid of what might slip from him if he spoke.

King Clement picked up the queen's glass slipper and caressed the heel with his thumb. "Never mind," he murmured, turning his gaze once more to the sea. "You can't help what you feel. I know."

Dash left him there. He went back to his chambers, where he paged through every recent Guild record, taking notes as he went. He didn't realize how long he'd been working until he had to call for more candles.

Hours later, dawn broke, just as Dash replaced the Zori file in the final crate. He sat back in his chair, overwhelmed. There were so many wrongs. So many problems to be solved. He caught a sudden glimpse of his future — saw himself as king as he had never seen himself before. Not the mighty occupant of a throne, but a person hard at work, grappling with the Garment Guild. Ideals might be impossible to achieve, but he *would* try. What did it matter if he was the first Charming who could have a happy marriage? Why should that be his priority when so many in his country were suffering? When his kingdom was not all that it should be?

He looked down at his pile of notes. A measly beginning, but maybe Ella could make something of it.

At least she would see that he was on her side. Even if he had to stand at Lavaliere's.

Ella

WHEN the new week began, she walked into business class to find Lavaliere and Dash standing in the aisle between the desks, Lavaliere smoothing down the front of Dash's uniform jacket with slow, deliberate fingers. Ella hung back by the smocks, unwilling to go closer until Lavaliere made her way to the front of the classroom.

Dash sat heavily in his chair. Ella slid behind him and into her seat.

"I made up some numbers over the weekend," she said. "Costs and profits and all. They're not real, but they'll do. Did you decide anything about vendors?"

Dash pulled a sheaf of vellum out of his schoolbag. There must have been twenty pages of closely written notes, all in his handwriting.

"What's this?" Ella asked as he placed the stack on the desk in front of her.

"Numbers," he said. "Vendors."

Ella picked up his notes and began to read as he watched her. She read and read, turning page after page of detailed research. Profits, skill groups, ages, payment — everything she could have wanted to know about every member of the Garment Guild except for the physical conditions in their workshops, which could be seen only by visiting them in person. She sat engrossed, reading the columns on Shantung Silkworks, and she didn't realize that her mouth had opened or that her fingers were jittering until the prince asked:

"Is it — useful?"

"Useful?" she cried. From the front of the room, Paisley turned to glare at her. Ella was too excited to trust her voice; she picked up the chalk.

It's brilliant, she wrote. *Where did you get all this so fast?*

"I can get things," he said, blushing.

"We should have put that on your list of skills, hey?" she whispered. "I can do a real business proposal now — not just for school. I can make this into a serious plan for my dad's business and actually try to get him to follow it."

He grinned, dazzling her. And then he picked up her chalk and wrote swiftly on the table:

Happy?

Ella gestured for the chalk. Their fingertips brushed. They looked at each other, and she flushed hot and cold together.

"Yeah," she said. "I am."

Dash

THE way Ella looked at him — it made him feel like he was really someone. Which he was. People had admired him all his life.

But not like this.

She pulled her hand away from his. On sudden impulse, he grabbed it.

Ella

DASH seized her fingers, and she jumped. Stared at him. He pulled her hand under the desk and held on to it. His palm was hot — or maybe it wasn't; she couldn't be sure. Her insides had gone up in flames.

What was he *doing*? Was he serious? They were in class — and he had a girlfriend. She had to pull her hand away.

She couldn't make herself do it.

Dash

WHAT was the *matter* with him? Ella Coach was out of the question. He couldn't do this — he had the Jacquards to please. His future throne to save. They were in the back corner of the room where nobody could see them, but still, he was chasing trouble. So much trouble.

Ella gave his hand a tiny squeeze. Dash squeezed back.

"And how are we coming along?" asked Professor Linsey-Woolsey, pulling up unexpectedly in front of their desk. Dash yanked his hand into his lap and choked. He couldn't issue a sound.

"Nearly done with the draft." Ella spoke much too rapidly. She handed over their outline. "Still have to put the numbers in, but here's our notes."

Professor Linsey-Woolsey glanced through Dash's research.

"Very thorough," she said, and she left them again.

"I'm . . . surprised about Shantung," said Ella, after a moment. Her eyes were still fixed on his notes, which she clutched much harder than was necessary. "They don't hire anyone under age fourteen. Now I want to shop there and see what their silk's like. I bet Sharlyn will take me, if I ask."

Dash thought of the six-year-olds at Jacquard. The idea still sickened him.

"What do the smaller children do?" he asked, his voice a rasp.

"What, in the workshops?" Ella's mouth twisted in a joyless smile. "They unroll cocoons," she said. "They have little fingers. Kids as young as four do it."

"Four!" he exclaimed, shocked out of his embarrassment. "How?"

"You catch on fast when someone hits you," said Ella, rubbing her fingertips together. "And you're tied to the chair so you can't mess anything up."

"You've seen them? Tied to chairs?"

Ella looked askance at him, and Dash realized his voice had risen. At the table in front of them, Loom and Chelsea sat working quietly. Too quietly. He shut his mouth.

Children are cheap, Ella wrote. *Apprentices get half wages.*

But four-year-olds can't apprentice, Dash wrote back.

"They can if nobody stops it," Ella muttered. *Shantung pays better than Jacquard too,* she continued on the slate. *It's why they're out of money. Who's going to buy Shantung when they can get Jacquard for less? Even my dad buys Jacquard.*

"But — your mother."

Ella glanced at him. "Yeah."

Together, for the rest of the hour, they filled in their business plan. They worked mostly without talking, pointing to various charts and notes to get their ideas across. When class was done, Lavaliere rose and packed her schoolbag. They were nearly out of time.

Dash glanced at Ella. He wanted to speak to her — wanted to see her. Alone. Without Lavaliere, without guards. He was mad to consider it; there was no point in pursuing this.

But he would. Somehow he would.

"Tomorrow," he blurted. "I'll see you." It was all he could think of to say, and then Lavaliere was upon them.

Ella

How was she supposed to stop feeling things when he only got better every day? He listened, and he cared, and he'd given her massive piles of restricted financial information, and she was going to make something real out of it. She was going to make a business proposal for her dad and Sharlyn, and they were going to listen to her, because she'd have every single number worked out. Maybe Jasper was right and she couldn't change the whole Garment Guild overnight. But she could start small. With Practical Elegance.

She made a fist in her lap with the hand Dash had held. Why had he grabbed her hand when he was with Lavaliere? How could he *kiss* Lavaliere? He knew it was wrong to hurt people and starve them and put little children to work in shops — it didn't make sense that he'd tangle himself up with a Jacquard, not even if she was beautiful and plush. He was better than caring about all that. He *was.*

Ella watched Dash leave the classroom. He was stiff-backed. Wooden. His face had no spark in it. He held Lavaliere's hand, but only just politely, like holding hands with a dance partner he'd been assigned.

He didn't like her at all.

Ella felt suddenly sure of it. Dash didn't care two stitches about Lavaliere Jacquard. So why was he always stuck to her?

"Stare at him a little longer, why don't you," said Dimity, pausing next to Ella's desk. "You're pathetic."

"Shut your trap," Ella muttered. Dimity sauntered out of the room.

"Everything all right, Miss Coach?" asked Professor Linsey-Woolsey, who was the only one now left in the classroom with her. She peered at Ella from her desk.

"Yeah. It's fine."

"Good. I must say, I'm impressed with your project. I'm glad to see you working to your potential, in spite of your critics. They fear you, you know."

Ella snorted.

"They do," said the professor. "What you have to say is worth saying, so many people will try to silence you. Don't let them."

Ella stood. She swung her bag onto her back and lifted her chin. "I won't," she said.

Serge

ELLA hadn't called them for a week. Every other client had, many of them more than once, but Ella had stayed quiet. He tried not to feel disappointed.

He and Jasper did go down to help the Winceys. Kit had been startled — even frightened — at the idea of a fairy godfather, but at the mention of Ella and the sight of the embroidered baby dress, she relaxed. The Winceys' drafty stone cottage was heartily disorganized; every corner and surface was cluttered with debris. Mr. Wincey was laid out on a stained, threadbare sofa, one leg propped up on yellowed cushions. A baby sat on an unraveling blanket in the corner, proudly banging a chipped spoon against a dented pot; two tangle-haired children of about five and seven fought boisterously, and a skinny boy of ten or so sat in a wobbling chair, squinting at his book. It had been a long time — much too long a time — since Serge had done work in a house like this. It was a home full of love but with few resources to manage all the jobs that must be done. He looked around the place, his fingers tingling readily, and got to work.

Before they left, Serge took Kit aside. He had made her an account at the nearest apothecary, with enough money in it to cover the cost of her pain treatments until her affliction ended. Kit looked embarrassed at the mention of her pustules, but she expressed only gratitude. "It's our biggest expense by far, that pain cream," she said. "It's a huge weight off. I can't believe you mean it — I don't know how to thank you."

"Just like that," Serge said.

He and Jasper left the humble cottage and headed for the nearest fairywood. Outside, along the weedy, sandy village road, stood another handful of wood-and-stone huts, some even dingier than the Winceys'.

"We could be here for a week," said Jasper. "A month, even."

"There is no end of families in need in Tyme," said Serge. "We could visit a different cottage every day for the rest of our lives and we'd never get to them all."

"Let's do it anyway."

"What — you mean start our own service?"

"Why not? You're leaving the Slipper," Jasper said matter-of-factly. He covered his mouth with his hands. "I absolutely did not mean to say that," he murmured.

"Leaving the Slipper?" Serge was too surprised to be angry. "You're ridiculous."

They came to the edge of Eel Grass, where the Practical Elegance workshop stood at the bottom of a steep, rocky hill. Serge paused to survey the place, thinking of all Ella had told them. It felt good to help Ella. It felt good to help her friends. These deeds had mended him; his dust was coming freely again. He wasn't leaving the Slipper. He didn't have to now. As long as he had projects of his own on the side, he could do what Jules wanted and keep his magic flowing. He didn't know why he hadn't thought of it years ago.

"I've been doing research, you know," Jasper said, alighting on a large boulder. "On certain historical events. A girl on a glass hill. Children who spun straw into gold. And Pierce, the little orphan from the apothecary's shop. Do you know what I found out about them all?"

Serge flushed.

"They were yours," said Jasper, tilting up his pale face to study Serge with his crimson eyes. "It was your work I admired all my life."

"Not *just* mine," said Serge quickly. "It was always Jules who had the society relationships. Pierce wouldn't have been adopted by that wealthy family if it hadn't been for —"

"You're the one I was waiting to meet," said Jasper. "You're my inspiration, the reason I left home. Your deeds gave me that courage."

Serge suddenly felt fifty again, and very hot in his wings.

"You don't need a penthouse to do what you do. You don't need the Slipper. You're the most gifted godfather in the history of Tyme."

Serge was caught too much off guard to answer right away. He waited until he could be sure of the evenness of his voice. "I did a little research too," he said. "Prince Jasper, Earl of Cliffhang, second in line to the throne. I ought to be calling you Highness."

"Don't. I came to the end of my path there, like you have at the Slipper. I simply wasn't that person, and as soon as I let myself admit it, I had to move on."

"I'm not at the end of my path."

"Fine." Jasper fluttered to his feet. "Let's go visit Ella."

"She hasn't called us."

"No, but she wants us."

"You seem very certain of what other people want."

Before Jasper could reply, Serge's pocket watch grew hot.

JACQUARD ESTATE. NOW. JOB TONIGHT.

He clicked the watch shut. "Jules has a job for me," he said, trying not to let his dread show in his face. He didn't want to see Lavaliere Jacquard. Not because he didn't want to help her, but because he knew she wouldn't let him.

Jasper traveled with him back through the fairywoods and to the shoreline of Quintessential. They stopped on the beach, and Serge flew out over the sand, toward the darker shoreline. He looked back at the city. A full, bright moon hung over the silhouette of the Assembly clock tower. Serge gazed at the picture, longing for a moment to be a Grey fairy, responsible for the night sky and only the night sky. To know what his role was, and his purpose, without ever having to question it and without moral dilemmas to complicate things — that would be freedom.

"You wouldn't like it in Grey," said Jasper quietly, sidling up to him. "You're too much an individual."

Serge supposed it was true.

And then he realized what had just happened.

He turned on his apprentice, stunned. "How?" he demanded. Jasper's eyes gleamed by moonlight, and Serge rubbed his own eyes furiously, fear spiking in him. "Did you hypnotize me? Did you — *how* did you —"

"I can't do hypnotics at all," said Jasper simply. "Very rarely — not even once a century —you get a Crimson who can do something else."

"Read minds?"

"Not exactly minds. More like emotions."

Serge rubbed his chest over his heart. "But that was a very specific emotion," he said angrily. "Like a thought."

"Yes, well." Jasper spread his hands. "The more intense the individual, the more specific the reading. You're an open book, Serge."

"Don't you dare. Don't you *dare* read me again."

Jasper folded his wings into two stripes on his back, and he sat down in the sand. "I didn't ask to be able to tell what people are feeling." He sifted sand in his fingers. "It's as much a curse as a gift. My grandmother knew exactly how to use it for her benefit, and for much too long I let her steer me."

"Why even *tell* me this?"

"Because I can't wait any longer," said Jasper. "Your feelings aren't my business, so I was trying to stay out of it. But now you're my friend." He looked up at him. "And whatever it is that Jules wants you to do tonight — you can't do it."

Serge pulled his jacket more tightly closed, as though by doing so he could ward off further probing into his heart. "What do you know?" he asked.

"Lavaliere Jacquard," said Jasper. "She's suffering, and you're helping, and you're so sick about it that it's making *me* sick just to be near you. So you can't do it. I won't let you."

"Let me?"

"You heard me," said Jasper hotly. "You're admirable and good and you're my hero and I won't *let* you be warped like this. You're not going to Lavaliere tonight. You're free. Throw that pocket watch away and don't look back."

Serge did not answer.

"I know it's brutal, but you have to do it soon. Jules is far worse than you realize."

"You've only met her once."

"Once was enough," said Jasper. "She and my grandmother have a lot in common. Jules will stay in that penthouse till the day she fades, just like my grandmother on her throne. By the time the Slipper's yours, you'll be ruined."

"I'll be barely two hundred," said Serge. "I'll still have centuries ahead of me."

"But who will you *be*?"

"I will not discuss this with you."

"Serge —"

"You lied to me, Jasper. You invaded my privacy — my heart."

"I couldn't tell you until I knew that I could trust you."

"How fortunate I feel to be so trusted," said Serge. "Go back to the Academy. I have work to do, and you can't come with me."

"I said I wouldn't let you go."

"If you really have the gift you claim, then you know how important the Slipper is to me — and you know better than to get in my way." He made himself invisible. "Don't follow me," he said. "Stay away from me, Jasper."

He flew away north to the Jacquard Estate, where Lavaliere was waiting.

Dash

HE sat hunched over his desk in his chamber, concentrating. He dipped his pen in ink and started the note for the third time.

Ella ~

I need to talk to you. Meet me halfway through sports hour, in the yard behind the equipment shed.

He crossed it out, crumpled up the parchment, and flung it into the fire. What was he going to do behind the shed? Kiss her? And then what? Lavaliere would still be waiting for him half an hour later. Was Ella supposed to put up with that? No, he was not his father; he would not court two girls at once. And Ella might not even want him.

That was ludicrous. He was Prince Charming. Everybody wanted him.

But Ella was not everybody.

He pushed back his chair, paced to the window, and looked out at the sea. He longed for his mother. He could have confided all this to her — his feelings for Ella, his fears about the Jacquards, his ambitions for the country — and she would have known how to listen. How to help him. She was the only one in his life who had never been charmed by the Curse. Who had always seen him for what he really was — a real person.

Like Ella did.

He went back to his desk, grabbed a fresh sheet of parchment, and started again.

Ella ~

I wish we could see each other in private. Just to talk. It would be a relief to me to talk openly with you; I feel I can trust you with anything. I can, can't I?

For us to speak privately would require sneaking around, and I don't want to get you into more trouble than you've already been in lately, so I'll understand if you would rather not try it. But if you are willing, then I'll find a way to avoid my guards, and we can meet.

I promise not to be offended if the answer is no.

Yours in friendship,

Dash

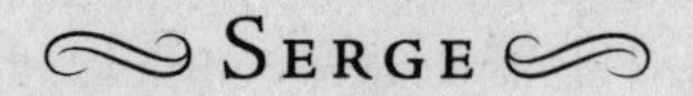

Serge

"Monthly visits are too far apart."

Serge stood with Lariat Jacquard in her office, his mouth shut tight.

"Her pain is too intense. She needs to see you weekly, Serge. Jules told me it would be no problem at all, and of course I've made a sizable donation to the Slipper, to make sure that everything is fair."

Lariat smiled at him. "You're so good to help us," she said. "I'm sure you'll understand that I do *not* want to be called to her room when you are working. It's a sight too terrible for any mother to bear — truly it breaks my heart to see her suffering. I therefore give you absolute authority to replace the illusion on her face, no matter what."

Serge left the office. Slowly, he climbed the stairs.

Lavaliere awaited him, sitting in the center of her chamber with her chair angled away from all mirrors and glass so that she could not catch sight of herself. He peeled the magic from her face, and it was everything he could do not to gag. Open sores had grown together across her face and neck; she glistened with them. The smell was rank. She was weak, too, and feverish — the infection must be spreading. To ignore her condition and disguise it with magic now was nothing short of abuse.

"It doesn't matter if your mother doesn't want to see this. She needs to know —"

"She doesn't care," Lavaliere said.

Serge fell silent. The girl was right.

"Just cover it up. My head hurts." Lavaliere kept her eyes pressed shut as Twill worked the pain cream over her mangled face. "I'm so tired. I don't think I can go to school tomorrow . . ."

He could quit. Right now. He could refuse, walk out, and be finished.

And never inherit the Slipper.

Serge squeezed his hands shut and dug into himself, forcing the dust to come to him, wrenching it from the deepest reserves of his power. But when it broke through the skin of his palms, it burned like he'd grabbed hot pokers in his fists. He looked down, alarmed, to find that his dust was wet and clumped.

"You couldn't visit Dash, could you?" Lavaliere murmured. "Make him normal again? He's so awkward."

"No," he said, hardly paying attention. He stared at the strange, wet dust. Was he bleeding? Sweating? What was this?

"I wish that witch were still alive," she said. "He used to be lovely. Now he's dull. And bald. Couldn't you at least make his hair grow back?" She paused. "Why aren't you doing my face?"

He flung the strange dust at her, and it exploded, concealing her illness. Afterward, he tried to leave but found that he couldn't snap his way out of her room. He didn't have the strength. He couldn't fly from her balcony either; his wings would not support him.

With his last few grains of strange, damp dust, he made himself invisible and walked out of Jacquard manor, just as a heavy rain began to fall.

Dash

THE next morning, Lavaliere was too ill to come to school. Dash went to Fundamentals of Business feeling almost like a free man, except that his father's guards still tailed him from door to door.

He got to class before Ella, and when she sat down beside him, he made a lightning-quick reach under the table for her hand. He touched her fingers and pushed the folded letter into her palm.

She unfolded it at once. Dash burned with anticipation as he watched her read it. Her eyes flicked quickly over the lines. He didn't miss that her fingers were trembling.

"Yes," she whispered when she was done. "I'd risk it. Where —?"

"I'll find somewhere."

Ella nodded. She buried the note at the bottom of her bag and picked up her chalk. It took her a moment to start writing.

I asked my stepmum if we could visit Shantung last night, and we did. Since their workshop practices are so different, I wanted to see if the silk was different too.

One bronze curl had come loose from Ella's twist. It bobbed beside her cheek as she kept writing.

It was amazing. Their people are artists, and their silk is heaps nicer. I don't understand why nobody talks about that.

Dash made himself concentrate on what she had written. "Isn't it all just silk?" he asked.

Ella pulled two stockings out of her satchel and handed them to him. "Shantung and Jacquard," she whispered.

"Which is which?"

"Feel them."

He did so and was surprised to find that it was easy to sense the difference in quality. One stocking was slightly rough to the touch. The other was as smooth as . . . well, silk, he supposed. "Shantung?" he guessed, lifting the smoother stocking slightly.

She nodded. *So here's what I don't get. People in this city love to flaunt their nauts and buy top quality, right? They don't care how much things cost. Why do they buy Jacquard when it's inferior?*

To this, Dash had an answer.

It's not about quality, he wrote. *It's about fashion. Look around. Have you seen how many heads are shaved lately? People just copy each other.*

"They copy *you*, you mean," she said.

Dash sat back and considered. It was true that people had followed him all his life, doing whatever he did.

They'll buy what you buy, Ella wrote. *Look at your mum. She wore Cinder Stoppers to a ball, and now Practical Elegance makes millions. Couldn't you do the same thing for Shantung?*

Perhaps he could. But if he started telling everyone how much better he liked Shantung silk, he doubted Lady Jacquard would take it very well. And so he was back in the same old trap.

But was his whole life really going to be dictated to him by Lariat Jacquard? Was he going to keep on courting Lavaliere and pretending things were settled between them, while Lariat tied little children to chairs in her workshops? He couldn't. He *couldn't.* But he also couldn't see his way out.

When class was done, he stayed in his seat, rifling through their half-finished draft. Ella kept her seat as well, busying herself with something in her satchel. The other students drifted out of the chamber, but Dash waited. With Lavaliere away, he could steal a minute with Ella right now. Just one.

Dimity was the final lingerer. She stopped beside him, arms folded.

"We'll be late," she said.

"Go on," Dash muttered, bending over the outline and writing in a few figures. Eventually, Dimity had no choice but to leave them, and the heavy chamber door fell shut. They were alone.

They looked at each other.

He opened his mouth, but nothing came. He reached out instead and brushed her loose curl back toward her ear, dragging a fingertip across her cheek.

She flinched. "Why are you with her?"

He froze.

"Is it just because she's approved?" said Ella, whose hands were clenched tightly in her lap. "Because she's such a — I mean, you don't even seem to —" She faltered to a stop.

He withdrew his hand.

"You're offended." She bit her lip. "I shouldn't've said anything. But yesterday, I thought — I mean, it *felt* like you might —" She stopped, looking as strangled as he felt. "Our project," she finally said. "It matters. I hope we're still friends, because I can't see this through without you."

"Can't you?" he managed.

"'Course I can't," she said. "You've been amazing, don't you know that?"

Dash felt certain that he had been no such thing. "All I did was get the numbers."

"No, that's *not* all." She leaned toward him. "You've thought about the problem. You've admitted it exists, you've tried to imagine how to solve it. Now you just need to see the workshops." Ella's eyes darkened. "Are you ever allowed to go places on your own, or do those guards follow you everywhere?"

"Everywhere."

"Well, if you ever get a chance, go to the garment district. East of the woods, over by the slums. Ragg Row. That's where Jacquard is, and all the rest."

Ragg Row. He'd heard it mentioned. It wasn't a place where decent people went. But thousands of citizens went there every day to work, of course. Children went there.

"I'll try," he said.

"Will you really?"

He nodded.

To his intense surprise, Ella grabbed one of his hands in both of hers. "You're so good," she said fervently. "You'll be such a good king."

Dash flushed with pleasure. "It's your influence," he said, and when she shook her head, he tugged her hands to bring her closer. "Yes it is," he whispered. "Ella —"

The classroom door banged open, and they gasped. Ella snatched her hands away and Dash sat back, breathing hard as Spaulder and two other guards stomped into the chamber. "Your Royal Highness." Spaulder folded his arms, resolute. "You're running late, sir."

Dash let the guards steer him out. At least this time, with no Lavaliere to watch him, he had the luxury of looking back. Ella's eyes were still on him.

That night, his father visited his bedchamber.

"You were alone with the Coach girl," he said. "Getting quite cozy too, I'm told. Care to explain, son?"

Dash turned from his desk, where he had been studying a map of Quintessential. East of Arras Wood, across the Thread River, lay an entire half of his home city that he knew nothing about. "Ella —" His voice cracked on her name. "She couldn't — stay after school. And — we were behind."

"So you stayed after class instead? A flimsy excuse. When you tell Lavaliere, do try to sound less like a liar."

Dash gave his father a cutting look and turned back to the map. A moment later, the king was behind him, one hand on his shoulder. He bent until Dash could feel breath at his ear. "Do not risk the throne for that girl. I've never met a woman who didn't have ulterior motives."

Except my mother. But Dash had no wish to prolong the conversation, so he said nothing, and his father left the room.

Ella

LAVALIERE was back at Coterie the next morning. Everywhere Ella went, she saw Lavaliere's head on Dash's shoulder, her hand in his hand, her arm in his arm. Whenever he caught sight of Ella, she saw in his fixed and motionless expression that he was miserable. Trapped. She wanted to help him, but she didn't know how.

When she sat with him in class, she tried to focus on the business proposal. But when Dash leaned over to write figures in front of her, he was so close that she could feel the warmth of him and the dampness of his jacket from the rain. His knee brushed hers under the table — he quickly jerked it away. Then he leaned in again, deliberately.

He was torture.

Class was over. Lavaliere was coming. Dash wiped out his writing and turned his back on Ella, who gazed at the wet slate. Her knee burned. Her stomach ached.

Even without that curse on him, he was going to break her heart.

Serge

He sat on the beach in the rain all night, and the next morning he could barely move.

He went to the Slipper because he had never missed a single day of duty, but he didn't even have the strength to change his clothes first. When Lebrine saw the state of him, all her mouths dropped open. By the time he reached his office, his head ached so viciously that he had to ask Carvel to handle his clients. Carvel didn't protest, but he did want to know where Jasper was. So did Lebrine. And Thimble. Even Georgette asked after him. Nearly all Serge's colleagues were concerned by Jasper's absence. Serge didn't remember when they'd had time to get to know him.

The next day was worse. He tried to dredge up his dust, but none came. Not even enough to make himself invisible. If Ella called for him, he wouldn't be able to respond. He tried to focus on her, hoping that thoughts of a worthy godchild would restore some of his better feelings, but instead he felt ashamed, and his palms felt strangely numb, as though some of Lavaliere's pain cream had wormed its way into them.

He hid in his office, slumped over at his desk with his head on his arms, barely able to flick his wings. When Thimble stopped by with scrolls for his signature, he heard himself say the words that had been said to him so many, many times.

"I have a headache."

Looking grave, Thimble left him.

Maybe Jules really did have headaches. Maybe, when fairy dust ran out for good, that was the result. A permanent pounding grief in the middle of the brain, reminding him of every wrong he'd ever done in the name of the Glass Slipper.

His pocket watch grew hot.

COME BACK UP. REMEMBERED SOMETHING.

How satisfying it would be — how freeing — to take the watch and throw it out the window, right into the sea. Jasper would tell him to do it. Jasper had *told* him to do it.

Serge willed himself to his feet and made his way to the penthouse.

Dash

THE week at Coterie ended with buckets of cold rain and Lavaliere's head affixed to his shoulder.

"My mother wants to throw a party," she said at the end of the day when they walked together to the carriage. She tucked herself very close to him under his umbrella. "Dinner just for us first, and then a gathering afterward for all our friends. Your father already agreed," she said before Dash could have an opinion. "Do you like Pulse for the dancing?"

"I like the Current."

Lavaliere gave him a sidelong look. "I doubt Mother will invite that family."

Dash pretended he didn't know what she meant.

When they reached the Jacquard Estate, scribes enveloped them at once. Lavaliere put out a hand to let them know she would not speak. She did, however, turn to Dash, close her eyes, and put up her face.

Dash kissed her, thinking of Ella. Her accent. Her curls. The slight roughness of her cool hand in his. He kissed her harder.

"Dash," she murmured in surprise.

"Ell —"

His stomach turned to ice. Panicked, he opened his eyes. There was no fatal scribbling around them. The scribes hadn't heard him — he'd only just breathed it.

But Lavaliere's expression was brittle. She pivoted and stalked into her home, leaving Dash alone among the scribes.

"Something wrong, Your Royal Highness?"

He shut himself up in the carriage and pulled the curtains.

He was done for.

Ella

SHE was in her bedroom, putting final touches on the speech she and Dash had outlined together for their presentation when there came a tremendous *slam* from downstairs. Ella stuck her head out into the hall. Down at the other end, Clover and Linden stuck their heads out too.

"What did you do now?" asked Linden, pushing up his glasses.

"Nothing," said Ella. For once, it was true.

"Ma's had a bad day, then," said Clover. "Let's go down and give her some good news."

They went downstairs, and Ella followed at a distance, curious.

"Hey, Ma," said Linden, as they entered the office. "That hour at the palace set us up. The bookings keep coming in."

"We're busy every weekend for the next three months," said his sister. "Up in Port Urbane and Tarnish on the Sea, and out in Fetchington — and two private parties right here in town."

"We'll be able to move out soon, at this rate."

"Excellent," Sharlyn muttered, though she didn't seem to hear a word of it. She wore her pince-nez and bent over papers at a desk in the corner, scratching so violently with her pen that it was a wonder the nib didn't break.

Ella looked at her dad, who sat at his own desk, looking wan and grim.

"What is it?" Ella asked, coming to stand by him.

"Lady Jacquard has stopped the supply of silk to Practical Elegance," he said slowly.

"We've just had a letter from her — not even a meeting." Sharlyn turned her chair fully toward Ella. "What happened? Did you insult Lavaliere up at school?"

"Ell?" said her dad.

"I haven't done anything," said Ella. "Not since the ball. Nothing, I swear." She fidgeted. "I guess there was a rumor. . . ."

Her dad and Sharlyn waited.

"Just, you know, after the ball. People at school started saying I was a traitor."

"What?" cried Sharlyn. "Ella, that's extremely serious. Why didn't you say something? Earnest, I was afraid of exactly this. People think she's disloyal —"

"No they don't!" said Ella.

"Then why did the Jacquards break from us, Ell?" asked her dad. "Can you explain it?"

"No," said Ella, folding her arms. "Unless Lavaliere's all twisted up because Dash — Prince Dash, I mean — he's my partner in business class."

Her stepsiblings' mouths both opened. Her dad's face turned sharply toward her. "Prince Dash?" he said. "The two of you —"

"We're friends."

Clover and Linden looked archly at each other while Sharlyn tapped her pen against the desk. "So this is how Lady Jacquard plays the game," she said. "I knew I didn't like that woman. I should have trusted my first instinct. Well, if she thinks we're that easy to shut down, she's going to be disappointed. Practical Elegance can stay on schedule without Jacquard Silks."

"How?" asked Ella's dad.

"Shantung," said Sharlyn and Ella at the same time.

Sharlyn looked startled.

"They're more expensive," said Ella. "But if we budget elsewhere, then we can take the hit."

Now everyone was staring at her like she'd turned into a mermaid, but she kept going anyway. It was too good an opportunity to miss.

"Shantung's worth the extra money," said Ella. "They don't hire young children, for one thing. And more of their profits go to providing their employees with proper pay — which is why their stuff's higher quality. But it's also why they're going bankrupt," she said. "If people don't start buying Shantung soon, they'll shut down, and there'll only be Jacquard left. And now you see how important it is that there's an alternative, hey? If it's just Jacquard, then they get to decide who's in business and who's not."

She was stealing from her own proposal, but the timing was right, and she was glad to be prepared.

"We have lots of ideas for Practical Elegance," she said. "We're almost done with our business plan for class, and then I want to share it with you both."

"We?" said her dad. "You and Prince Dash?"

"It's a good thing, Earnest," said Sharlyn. "If he likes her, we'll be fine. We just need to move quickly. In fact, I should finish this letter to Cameo Shantung and get it off tonight. If I could have some peace and quiet?"

Ella went upstairs with Clover and Linden right behind her. They followed her all the way to her room.

Clover smirked. "Caught yourself a royal ally, did you?"

"It's a business project."

"You're awfully passionate about it. Sounds like you've been putting in extra hours."

"Oh, *Dash,*" said Linden in a high-pitched voice. He turned away and hugged himself, moving his own hands up and down his back. "You're so *business*like."

Ella's cheeks burned. "We never —"

"Deny nothing, temptress," said Clover.

"Hold me," piped Linden. "Whisper sweet words of labor reform . . ."

Ella locked herself in her room, and Clover and Linden burst out laughing.

Dash

He waited for the hammer to fall.

At supper with his father, he expected to be upbraided for his stupidity, but nothing happened. The king spoke only once. "I sent your mother's letters by Relay," he said, pushing back his chair. "I wanted her to hear me immediately. I don't care that this makes the Exalted Council privy to my business. I don't care if the *Criers* publish every word." He laid down his knife and fork and left the dining room.

The next morning, Dash scanned the *Town Crier,* looking for a story with his name in it. Something about how the Jacquards were offended and the monarchy was in peril. But there was no story. The Jacquards didn't even send a private letter to the palace.

When the school week began and the royal carriage reached the Jacquard Estate, he braced himself for retribution. But Lariat only smiled and waved, and Lavaliere melted against him, overflowing with affection. She kissed his cheek and twined her hands with his before letting him help her into the carriage. Even once the door was closed and they were alone, she was unusually friendly. She spoke of nothing but the party her mother was going to throw, and how lovely it would be to have a bit of relaxed fun with all their friends. By the time they reached C-Prep, Dash was almost convinced that she hadn't heard his mistake.

At lunch, Lavaliere did not come to the dining room. Since he was untethered, Dash went to the business classroom early and found Ella already in it, alone.

"Are you by yourself?" she asked in surprise.

He nodded and sat beside her. They might only have half a minute, but at least it was theirs.

"Jacquard Silks pulled out of Practical Elegance," said Ella in a rush, keeping her voice low and her eyes on the open classroom door. The guards were watching them. "All of a sudden they won't supply us. I don't know what I did."

So Lavaliere had heard his mistake after all.

"I — said your name." His whole body throbbed with embarrassment. "While I was —" He could not say this part of it. How could he say this part of it?

Ella frowned at him, waiting.

"Kissing her."

Ella looked confused — and then she didn't.

The classroom door swung open. Lavaliere walked in looking triumphant, with Dimity and Paisley and several other girls behind her. Every one of them but Lavaliere glanced at Ella, and most of them smirked. They dispersed to their tables, and Lavaliere floated to the front of the room.

Dash's stomach sank. Five minutes after class began, the hammer dropped at last.

"Elegant Coach," announced an office messenger who appeared at the door. "Madam Wellington wants you at once. Bring your things."

The classroom fell silent. Every head turned. Lavaliere gave Ella a brief, triumphant smile.

Ella's expression hardened. She threw off her smock, snatched up her belongings, and left the classroom.

Lavaliere let out a brief sigh. "I feel so much safer now," she said, and this was enough to set the rest of the room talking. Professor Linsey-Woolsey could not quell the raucous chatter, and Dash heard snippets of heated conversation all around him:

"— deserves what she gets."

"— actually *bleeding*."

Garb Garter snorted richly. "What did anyone expect?" he said. "She's a danger to decent people." A chorus of agreement greeted this statement.

Dash looked over at Kente. "What's going on?"

Kente looked reluctant to speak.

"Ella attacked Lavaliere in the changing room during archery," said Chelsea, turning around at the table in front of him. "Ella came out last, except Lavaliere never came out at all, and then Dimity went back and found Lavaliere bleeding, lying on the floor. Ella ripped up her arm and knocked her down, and Lavaliere hit her head and blacked out." Chelsea shuddered. "I hope they expel her."

Dash looked in disbelief at the front of the room, where Lavaliere sat twirling her hair tie of Prism silk around one finger. Her arm was viciously scratched, from wrist to inner elbow; Dash could see the bloody red stripes from where he sat. That she'd scratched it herself, he was certain.

He got up and went to Lavaliere's table. "Your poor arm," he announced, loudly enough to be heard by his classmates. "I'm furious."

Lavaliere gave him a look of simmering dislike, but he had done his job. He left the classroom and ran to the front of the school with the guards close behind him. The door to Admissions burst open when he reached it, and Ella stormed out in tears, clutching a letter written in red ink.

"Suspended," she said before he could speak. "Lavaliere said I attacked her." She laughed roughly. "Madam Wellington wouldn't even listen to my side. I'm dismissed from campus, and I can't come back for a month." She hiccupped and swiped under her eyes.

It was his fault. If he hadn't made a mistake . . . "I did this," he said. "I'm sorry —"

"*She* did this," said Ella. "And I don't care. I never wanted to be here anyway." She hiccupped again. "Until you showed up," she mumbled. Then she whirled and ran to her carriage.

Dash pursued her.

"Will you still meet me?" he whispered when he caught her at the carriage door. His father's guards were closing in — he had only two seconds.

"How?"

"I don't know — I'll send a message."

She nodded and he stepped back, to return to class and Lavaliere.

Ella

It was almost six o'clock before Dash's messenger came to the house. Ella had been watching for him, and she raced to the front door and flung it open to prevent Sharlyn's butler from answering. The messenger was a boy her age, wearing no livery, but she recognized him from the kitchen of the Corkscrew.

"Tanner, hey?" she whispered.

"My lady," he replied, and bowed slightly as he held out a note. "The gentleman who sent me asks you to read this and give me your answer at once."

I think I can get out tonight, but I don't know where to go. I'd say meet me in Salting, but the guards might expect that, and I don't want trouble for my aunt.

Do you know a place? Tell me where and when, and I'll be there.

She bit her lip hard.

"Could you wait, please?" she whispered to the messenger. "Just for a few minutes, while I write back?" He bowed and went across the road to the park, and Ella ran upstairs, despairing. What could she write? Where could she see him? He couldn't come to her house; that was too obvious. She ran to her room and twisted the *E* charm in her fingers. "Serge, Serge, Serge," she whispered, but she felt no warmth from her charm in reply, and a quarter of an hour later, Serge was not there. If he and Jasper were busy, then waiting for them might take too long. From across the hall, she heard a low, sweet singing voice coming from behind Clover's bedroom door.

She approached. One knock, and the singing cut out.

"Make it good," Clover called.

"It's Ella."

The door opened, and Clover stood in it, teasing her half-blast of hair with her fingertips. "Hello, hello," she said, smiling. "To what do we owe the pleasure?"

Ella peeked past Clover into the room. The Current's singer, Bonnie Brae, lounged on Clover's bed, reading over some lyrics. "It's secret," said Ella under her breath.

Clover stepped into the hall and pulled the door shut behind her. "All right, tell me."

Ella dragged Clover to her room and shut the door. "You can't say anything to my dad. Or your mum. Or anyone. I'm serious."

"No problem."

"Can I trust you?"

Clover shrugged. "Yeah," she said. "But either you know that or you don't."

Ella shoved her hands into her hair, setting all her curls awry. "All right," she said. "I lied about Dash. We're friends, but . . ."

"There's a little more to it?"

"I want to see him, and he wants to see me, but there's nowhere we can go."

"So you need a place to meet."

"Yeah. His messenger's outside waiting for me to give him an answer."

"I've got a place." Clover bent over Ella's desk and scribbled on a scrap of parchment. "Here," she said, handing it over. "Tell the messenger that you'll be at this address by eight." She scribbled something else. "We'll put this on my mum's desk in the office."

Ma —

Ella wants to meet the band and relax with some new people. We'll have her out late, but no worries, we'll take care of her.

Big kiss,

Clover

"Your mum won't believe I said that."

"'Course she will," said Clover. "Do you know how much she wants the three of us to get along and be best friends?" She threw down the pen. "Come on," she said. "We'll go downtown to meet the crown — there's a song begging to be written. Watch out, or I'll write a whole set about you." Grinning, she pulled Ella from the room.

Dash

It was seven when Tanner returned with an address. Dash seized the slip of paper and checked the street name against his city map. He followed a route with his eyes and retraced it a few more times to make sure he could tell a driver how to get there. If he left now, he could just make it by eight.

Now all that remained was to get past the guards. They didn't follow him around inside the palace, but that was only because they had him completely penned in; his father had posted a sentinel at every door that led outside, including all the entrances to the servants' stairways.

So he'd use a window.

He dressed in black and shoved a fishing hat into his schoolbag. He grabbed his coin purse and tore through his desk drawers, looking for the pouch of Ubiquitous acorns that Garb Garter had given him last year when he'd been handing them out to everyone in fistfuls. There were twenty or so — enough to create a little chaos, he hoped. He sifted through them, checking their stamps in the hope of something that could aid him in getting down the wall. He found an acorn with a rope stamp and kept it separate from the others. The rest of the pouch he stuffed into his pocket.

Downstairs, he made sure the librarian saw him perusing the history section and choosing a few volumes, which he carried upstairs to the reading room. The sun had set and the garden outside was growing dark; Dash snuffed out the reading-room sconces to conceal his movements at the window from the guard who stood below. He donned the fishing hat and pulled it low to obscure his face, unlatched the window that was nearest the corner, and pushed it ever so slightly open. He peered down, and a thrill of fear shot through him. The jump down to the parapet was farther than he'd thought — perhaps fifteen feet.

Slowly, Dash inched the library window open until he'd created a wide enough passage to fit through. He grabbed a fistful of acorns out of the drawstring pouch, and he flung them as hard as he could out the window, toward the other end of the garden. They exploded against the far wall in a cacophony of clattering drums, smashing glass, and the braying of a Ubiquitous donkey.

"Intruder!" shouted the guard at his father's office door, and he sprinted toward the sudden cacophony, pulling his sword as he ran.

Dash clambered through the library window, and dropped down to hang from it. Breathing hard, he edged along the stone sill until he was directly above the garden wall. He let go of the sill and fell.

One ankle twisted under him when he landed, and he had to bite his lips shut to keep from shouting — but he was out of the palace and atop the wall. He stayed low, sparing just a brief glance toward the other end of the dark garden, where the guard was slashing his way through the Ubiquitous items, making them crash one by one as he shouted for reinforcements.

Lying on his stomach, Dash dragged himself to the edge of the parapet and looked down the outside of the palace wall. Another fifteen feet, at least. Guards stood positioned at intervals along the perimeter, and torches were mounted along the outer wall. He crawled along the parapet until he found a section of the wall that was in shadow, and he cracked his rope. It funneled from his fist, and a grappling hook appeared at the end of it. He secured this on the stones, then quickly dug out his last handful of acorns and threw them as far from the palace as he could, out toward the tree line. The two guards nearest him both pulled their swords and took off running toward the resulting racket. Dash tossed the rope. He gripped it, hauled himself over the wall, and dropped with speed onto the lawn.

Pain lanced his ankle when his feet struck ground, but he had no time to limp. He forced himself into a hobbling run and kept running until he reached the busy main road. He put out his hand to flag down a carriage, and he hoisted himself into the back, pulling his hat down as low as he could to shield his face from the driver.

"Sharp Street," he said. "Take Boulevard Blue south to Robings Road, then go left."

The driver set his horses in motion just as two royal guards barreled onto the street. Dash slumped down in the seat of the chaise. When the driver turned right onto Boulevard Blue, he dared a glance back. No one had followed. In spite of his throbbing ankle, he couldn't resist a grin.

He was out.

Serge

WHEN the moon rose that night, Serge was still curled in his own bed, where he'd been since the night before. For the first time in eighty years, he had not reported to work. He hadn't even responded to Ella's call. He felt as feverish as Lavaliere, all hot and cold shivers and clammy blue skin. He had never been ill in this human way — he'd never even heard of a Blue fairy with a fever. It frightened him.

Almost stranger than his sickness was the fact that Jules hadn't called for him once all day. It was lucky she hadn't. He wasn't sure he could fly all the way to the Slipper.

He had no sooner thought this than his watch lit up with such heat that it startled him. He tugged it out and silver messages flashed into the blue light in rapid succession.

LARIAT JUST LEFT.

BIG NEWS. HUGE.

GET HERE NOW.

He pushed himself to his feet and barely managed to get himself dressed. His wings were sore and heavy and he knew he couldn't fly; even walking was out of the question. Once on the street, he flagged a carriage, like a human would. He climbed up and slumped in his seat.

"Where to, sir?" asked the nervous-looking driver, eyeing Serge's wings.

Serge thought about telling the driver to take him to the Academy. He could go to Jasper's. Say he was sorry. Tell him it was over.

"The Glass Slipper," he said instead.

He found Jules in her office, standing with one blue hand braced against the window wall that looked out on Quintessential, lighted up in the darkness. Serge sank into a chair, exhausted.

Jules didn't seem to notice the difference in him. "Apparently, that Coach girl really did have her claws in the prince," she said. "But after today, I doubt we'll hear much more about her. Her family might as well leave Quintessential. When the Jacquards are against you, you're out."

Serge's wings stirred. For the first time in days, energy pulsed through him. Not much — just a thread — but he felt it.

"Really," he murmured. "What happened?"

"Lariat wouldn't say exactly," said Jules. "But she won't do business with Practical Elegance anymore, so that's the end of them. And Ella Coach is suspended from Coterie. Lavaliere has no more competition."

Serge swallowed a hard knot in his throat. Ella needed him. He had to get to her. It didn't matter how pathetic he felt.

"But that's nothing. Here's the *real* news." Jules turned away from her view of the city and leaned back against the curving glass. "Lariat wants our help this weekend to prepare her estate for a party. A little private meal for the Charmings, followed by a larger celebration."

"That's the big news?" he asked, frowning. "A party?"

"Not just any party." She smiled at Serge and arched an eyebrow. "A betrothal."

"Betrothal!" The word slipped from him before he could control it, but Jules missed his horror.

"I know!" she said, looking ecstatic. "We've done it again — another Charming queen, courtesy of our little shoe. I don't think the prince knows yet, but it doesn't matter. Clement has him well in hand. It's going to happen."

"But they're so young."

"When has that ever mattered in cases like this? The two greatest families in Blue joining hands. It's been a long time coming." She picked up a crystal-handled mirror and ruffled her spiky hair, fashionably disheveling it. She glanced at him. "You're sweating," she said. "What's wrong?"

Serge felt his clammy brow. "I rushed here."

"Good," said Jules. "You don't have a moment to spare. This betrothal party has to be stunning — even better than Clement and Maud's." She shoved Lariat's list of demands at him and collapsed into her chair. "I've got the *worst* headache," she said. "But consult with me on anything you need, babe. You know I'll be right here."

Serge left the penthouse at a trudge, reading over the list. What Lariat wanted would require the efforts of every single fairy at the Slipper. By the time he reached the lobby, he grew dizzy; he had to brace himself on a chair. He felt a hand at his elbow supporting him, and he glanced left, almost expecting to see Jasper. It was Thimble. Her dark blue eyes were serious. "You need help, Serge," she said quietly.

He didn't protest. He let her put him into a chair near Lebrine, who stretched out a tentacle to squeeze his shoulders. He didn't even flinch as salt water destroyed his leather coat.

"Cup of tea?" said Thimble, perching on the low table before him.

Serge shook his head. "I'm . . . going to visit Jasper," he said. He had to tell him what he'd learned about Ella — he owed him that.

"He's not home," said Thimble. "But I can get him and bring him here."

"No." He didn't want Jasper to come back to this place. "I'll meet him . . . where I left him. Tell him that."

He left the Slipper and made his way to the dark, moonlit beach where he'd last seen Jasper. He stumbled down toward the water, dropped down onto the hard sand, and waited.

When Jasper joined him, he alighted several feet away and looked out at the ocean. "You're a wreck," he said.

"Yes."

Jasper was silent for a moment. "There's something you want to tell me," he said. "Something you want me to do. What is it?"

"Ella's in trouble. Lariat Jacquard is trying to run the Coaches out of town. She had Ella suspended from school, to separate her from Dash."

"But she can't!"

"She did," said Serge. "And it gets worse. The Slipper is arranging a royal betrothal party for Dash and Lavaliere. They'll be engaged this weekend."

"*No!*" Jasper was six feet in the air. "We have to stop it."

"How?"

"I don't know — but we'll start by visiting Ella. Come on."

"You'll have to take care of her alone now, Jasper."

"What? Why?"

"I can't fly anymore," said Serge, "and I've lost my magic. You were right. I should have walked away from the Slipper, but I didn't, and now I think my dust is gone for good. It's too late."

The next thing Serge felt were strong hands under his arms, hauling him to his feet.

"Well, *now* you're just being maudlin," said Jasper, gripping him around the waist. "Hold on tight."

He unfurled his great Crimson wings and lifted off, pulling Serge into the sky with him.

Ella

SHE was dressed in black knit from her neck to her feet, and Clover stuffed her hair into a fashionably floppy gray hat that fell low over her eyes. They took her downtown in the carriage, all the way to the lower arts district on the southeastern fringe of Quintessential's respectable side.

"The rest of the band lives on Sharp Street," Clover told her. "The apartment's over the top of a room we use for rehearsals. We'll keep everyone busy upstairs, and you can have privacy."

"I'll watch the window," said Linden. "If anyone's coming, I'll send down sparks, and you can hide." He frowned at her. "Why the look?"

Ella shrugged. "I don't know," she said. "Just — why are you bothering, I guess?"

"You did us a favor with the royal ball," said Linden. "We owe you."

"We also like you," said Clover. "And we remember how it was when Pa died."

"So we get why you're a mess," Linden added, wiping his spectacles on his one sleeve. He replaced them on his nose and peered at Ella. "If you ever want to talk to us, you can."

Ella nodded, touched — and a bit ashamed. Their own dad was dead ten years, and she'd barely ever given that a thought. Maybe she owed them too.

They reached the Current's rental house. It wasn't an attractive building, even in the darkness, and neither were the structures around it. People spilled from the tavern on the corner, rowdy with laughter. No one from C-Prep would be caught dead here.

"Come on," said Linden. "We'll sneak you in."

Clover checked first to be sure that no one was in the downstairs room, and then the two of them smuggled Ella to the door and hustled her through it into quiet darkness. Linden lit two candles, and Clover pulled the hat off Ella's head and ruffled her curls back into shape. Ella looked around. It was too dim to see much, but there wasn't much to see: instruments leaning against the walls, a few small tables, and several chairs scattered about. Otherwise it was bare.

"We'll give you as long as we can," said Clover, taking a candle with her to the stairs. Linden followed. They let themselves in through the upstairs door and left Ella alone to wait. She carried her candle to the window, opened the curtain a finger's width, and watched the dark street.

A carriage rattled over the cobblestones and stopped before the door. A tall figure descended; she couldn't see his whole face because of his hat, but his profile was impossible to mistake. He limped to the door — he was hurt. Ella set the candle on a table and ran to meet him before he could knock. She pushed the door open, grabbed his sleeve, drew him inside, and shut the door as quickly as she could.

"What's wrong?" she demanded. "Why are you limping?"

He took off his hat and glanced around the dim room. Even by the light of one candle, his beauty made Ella catch her breath.

"Where are we?"

"My stepsiblings' place," she managed. "They rehearse here with their band."

"Do they know? About us?"

Us. "Yeah, but I promise it's all right."

He gazed at her a moment. "I can't do this," he muttered, and Ella's heart gave a fearful slam, but he put up his hands at once and shook his head. "I mean," he said, "I have to tell you something." He wrung his hat in his hands. "But it's treason."

"Then don't," said Ella reflexively. "Everyone already thinks —"

He shut his mouth and put his hat on the table. His eyes were tired. Defeated. Like her mum's had been at the end of every long week when her spirits were ground down to nothing. He must be so lonely, she realized. Shut up in that palace with his mum gone away, and he couldn't tell anyone anything or it would all end up in the *Criers*.

Yet here he was.

"Go ahead," she said quietly, deciding. "Tell me whatever you want."

"It's the Jacquards," said Dash, grimacing as he said the name. "I can't stand Lavaliere. But if I won't court her —" He drew a deep breath. "Lady Jacquard will eliminate my father from the Essential Assembly."

For a moment, Ella could only stare at him, unable to grasp what he was telling her. It was too huge. "But . . . how?"

"Through a vote. She wants the kingdom."

"Would the Assembly really let her have it?"

Dash nodded.

"Then *why?*"

He looked at her in puzzlement. "Why what?"

"If she has that much power already, why doesn't she leave you alone? Why does she care if Lavaliere has the crown?"

"It's the ultimate accessory." Dash made a guttural noise. "That's all I am to them. To most people," he added bitterly. "A fancy hat."

"Not to me."

Dash's eyes softened. "I know," he said. "You're like my mother. No, not —" He tensed again. "Not like my *mother* — I mean — where you're from. And where she's from. And how you both —" He came to a full stop. He wouldn't look at her now. "I used to be good. At talking. Like this. I'm sorry —"

"Don't be," she whispered.

He caught her hands and tugged her close. Closer even than when they'd danced. He was so tall that she only came up to his chin; his neck smelled of sweat and new-cut wood, and she could feel the frantic beating of his heart. This was happening. Real. She hoped she didn't mess it up somehow — he had experience with this kind of thing, but she had none.

"Ella," he said softly.

She tilted up her face. "Yeah?" she managed.

His mouth grazed hers, and the low noise that escaped him made her break out in gooseflesh all over. She pushed her chin closer for more. Threw her arms around his neck. His lips parted and she was gone.

Dash

HE couldn't remember where to put his hands. He grabbed her shoulders and then her elbows — he tried to touch her hair, but his ring caught in it, and when he pulled away he yanked one of her curls so hard she gasped and broke from him.

"Sorry," he rasped, cringing. He was destroying this. Really botching it. Telling her she was like his mother — and now he'd forgotten how to kiss.

Ella untangled her hair from his ring with one deft movement, and then she took his face in her hands, mumbled his name, and kissed him so completely that he forgot everything else too.

Serge

JASPER flew them both to Cardinal Park East, staying high above the lantern-lit streets since they could not be invisible. As they approached Ella's house, they saw a pack of royal guards mounting their horses just outside the garden gate. The guards rode swiftly south along the park as Jasper landed on the roof of number 76. He and Serge peered over the side of the building. Ella's father and stepmother were leaving the house in a great hurry, both looking terrified; they ran for the carriage that awaited them at the bottom of the stairs.

"Sharp Street," Serge heard Lady Gourd-Coach say frantically. "It's an emergency — drive as fast as you can." Ella's parents closed themselves in their carriage, and the driver took off.

"The king's guards," said Jasper. "Do you think they're after Ella —" He gasped and stopped.

Serge put a hand to his heart, and so did Jasper, looking startled.

"What was that?" Jasper whispered.

Serge wasn't sure. Ella wasn't calling; he didn't hear her in his head. He only felt a strange, warm pang within his chest — a swirl of emotions that he felt certain were hers, intense and tender together. No sense of fear or panic accompanied the sensation. Wherever she was — Sharp Street, he supposed — she did not realize she was in danger.

"We have to get to her before those guards," he said. "Let's go."

THEY sat on the floor against a wall in the empty rehearsal space. A candle guttered atop a table on the far side of the room. Ella's boots were slung across his legs; his head lay on her shoulder, and she moved her fingertips over his scalp, drawing patterns and making him shiver.

"And then?" she said, prodding him along in the story he'd been telling her. "When you reached the tower?"

"I spoke to the girl first," he said. "Rapunzel."

"Was her hair really a hundred feet long?"

"It was. I even cut a lock of it."

"Why?"

Dash sighed. "Because the curse made me," he said.

Ella was quiet a moment. "What was it really like?" she asked, and when he didn't answer right away, she spoke again. "If I shouldn't ask—"

"No. I want to tell you." Many scribes had asked him to divulge his feelings about the curse, but he couldn't bear to share the intimate details with the world. Ella was different. "It spoke for me," he said. "It said things I'd never thought of."

"Couldn't you ever speak for yourself?"

"Sometimes," said Dash. "Like with my mother. Other times . . ." He took Ella's hand and played with her fingers while he spoke. "The first time it happened, I was eleven," he said. "We were at the horse races with the Shantungs. I was talking with Chemise. And then suddenly I wasn't talking anymore. I mean — I was. My voice was still going. But it wasn't *my* voice. Not my words. It was like there was this — this hand inside my head. Moving my mouth. I started saying things to her — things that were so embarrassing, I couldn't —" Just the memory of it made Dash hot with shame.

"I tried to stop," he said. "So many times, I tried to fight. But I lost. I always lost."

Ella sat back. "That's sick," she whispered. "I'm glad that witch is dead. How did you ever stand it?"

"I couldn't. That's why I went to the Redlands to find the witch. I was desperate — and I got it into my head that maybe the Charming Curse could help me for once. Maybe, if I was so good at charming everyone, then I could charm Envearia into setting me free. But then I met her." His stomach turned at the memory of her predatory eyes, her malicious laughter. "I was stupid to try."

"You were brave."

"I didn't feel brave when she turned me to stone."

"What *did* it feel like?"

"Like filling up with sand," said Dash, shuddering at the memory. "Warm, heavy sand. I have nightmares, sometimes, where it's pouring into me and I can't move."

Ella put her arms around him.

"I don't remember anything after that. A month later, I woke up, because the witch was dead — Rapunzel killed her, my mother said. I sent Rapunzel an invitation to the palace so I could thank her. She never came, though." He tugged at one of Ella's bootlaces. "The *Criers* would pay you a fortune for that information," he said. "They're dying to hear about the curse and the witch."

"I wouldn't tell them."

"I know." Dash leaned against her. "What about you?"

"What about me?"

"What's one of your stories?"

"I don't have stories." Ella shifted. "Not like yours."

"Your father is an inventor — that has to be interesting. I use some of his products myself."

"Seriously?"

"The waterproof trousers are good for sailing. I've had the same pair of Cinder Stoppers on my riding boots for over a year, and they haven't worn down at all. Your father is talented."

"Yeah." Ella didn't look happy about it. "He is. He's always caught up in his next idea. He sketches, and he experiments. Even when he's home, he's working." She leaned her cheek against him. "He's never been around all that much, is the thing," she said. "He used to be a traveling inventor, peddling all over Blue, and even in Yellow and Orange sometimes — but he couldn't get anyone's attention. Then my mum died, and your mum wore the Cinder Stoppers, and the *Criers* made lots of noise, and everybody wanted to buy his stuff suddenly. That's when Sharlyn showed up, saying she had the right connections to turn my dad's good luck into a lasting business." Ella sighed. "And then he married her."

"You don't like her?"

She gave half a shrug. "I embarrass her. She thinks I act coarse on purpose, to aggravate the world."

"Don't you?"

The words were out. He felt Ella stiffen. "I mean," he fumbled. "She—"

"You meant it. Don't try to coat it."

He went quiet.

"Maybe I do," she said after a long moment had passed. "Maybe sometimes I act rougher than I really am — but I didn't start that way. When we first moved here, Dad made me go to C-Prep because Sharlyn said I had to. My first week up there, I was just being me. I wasn't wearing fishing boots to irritate anyone. I just didn't have anything else."

"But you had money."

"I didn't know what to do with it." Ella squirmed a little. "The things people said — not *to* me, you know. But about me. Just loud enough. And the way they looked at me. Like I was so low I ought to be dead."

Dash could well imagine it.

"At the ball, Dimity called me a dog." Ella looked away from him. "Garb said my mother was too. That's what set me off."

If Garb or Dimity had been in the room, he would have flattened them.

"That's who Sharlyn wants me to *socialize* with," Ella went on. "Why should I play along? I've got nothing to say to quints who look down on the people who serve them, like they have a right to judge when they don't have any skills themselves except for sitting around looking pretty —"

Dash flinched, and Ella stopped short.

"I didn't mean you," she said.

"Didn't you just describe me?"

"I only meant —"

"Don't coat it," said Dash, using Ella's words. "It's true. I wouldn't know the first thing about making a living. The day we made that list in class, and I saw how skilled you are . . ." He groped for the right words. "It was embarrassing," he said. "Jousting and sailing? That's what I'm good for? I'm no better than Garb Garter."

"You're *nothing* like him," Ella said vehemently. "You're not cruel. You don't mock people."

"My mother wouldn't stand for that kind of behavior," said Dash. "She never laughed about people behind their backs. She's the only reason I'm not insufferable."

Ella was quiet a moment. "You miss her, hey?" she asked.

Dash nodded. "I wish I could make sure she's all right," he said. "But if I write, my father will know where she is. I don't even know when she plans to come back — or if she will."

Ella squeezed his hand. "She'll be back. She said so."

Dash stared at her. "When did she say that?"

"In the carriage. She told me that running away wouldn't work forever, and that I'd have to come back — and so would she." Ella studied his face. "Do you want her to come back?"

"I don't know. She might be better off away."

"Because of your dad and . . ." Ella bit her lip. "Sorry."

"You can ask."

"Is it true, then? Did he and Nexus Maven . . . you know . . ."

"They had an affair."

She made a noise of contempt. "Dads are so useless sometimes," she muttered. "Not — not that I'm saying His Majesty is useless — I only meant that both our dads —"

"It's fine." Dash tucked his arm around her. "He is useless." He'd never spoken so honestly to anyone but his mother. He kissed Ella's forehead and she sighed, very quietly.

"What are we going to do?" she said.

He shook his head. Not this conversation — not yet. It had been the best night Dash had ever known. He could not accept that it must have an end. He wouldn't go home or back to school. He'd just live here, in this musty room, with Ella.

"I like you." Ella's voice was faint. "So much. I just want to know you better all the time."

"Then meet me again."

"But . . . someone will catch us. Your guards, or —"

"You don't want to?"

"I don't want Lady Jacquard to get the country."

"She won't. I won't let her." He faced Ella, and the trust in her expression made his chest tighten. She believed in him. She was counting on him. For a moment, his voice would not come. "I'm going to do things better than my father," he finally said. "Things that should have been done a long time ago. I'll fight them — the Guild and the Jacquards. I will. I promise."

"I know." Ella cupped his face in her hands and kissed him. Dash's stomach swooped. He caught her by the arms to steady himself and kissed her back.

Serge

JASPER pulled Serge with him over the glittering, lantern-lit streets of Quintessential. "Southeast," Serge directed him. "Cut straight across Harbor Street — there, I see them!"

The guards were directly below them, riding hard. They'd reach their destination in a quarter of an hour. Maybe less.

"Can't you go any faster?" Serge demanded.

"I think the words you're looking for are *thank you,*" Jasper retorted, but he sped up, cutting south toward the arts district. "Where now?" he shouted over the noise of wind in their ears.

"Further south — past Snapping Square."

Jasper had them there in minutes, and he dove lower so that Serge could see the street names. They found Sharp Street where it crossed East Taping Road. They were possibly five minutes ahead of the guards — possibly less.

"Where is she?" Jasper cried, careening over rooftops with dizzying speed.

"Land!" said Serge. "I can't concentrate."

Jasper alighted on a sooty rooftop and released Serge from his grip. Serge clasped both hands to his chest. When Ella called him by name, he was drawn toward her by the magic string that connected her heart to his, pulling him to the place where she was. But she wasn't calling now. All he felt was a faint throb of residual emotion, and he wasn't sure how to follow it. Perhaps if he weren't so weak . . .

"Trust yourself," said Jasper.

"I can't —"

"Don't waste time with that. Give me a direction."

"*You* do it," said Serge in frustration. "She's your goddaughter too — you sense her."

Jasper shook his head. "Whatever we felt earlier is gone," he said. "It only lasted a second for me. It's Blue magic — it works better for you — you *have* to find her."

Serge shut his eyes and strained, desperate for any hint. From below, he heard the raucous laughter of tavern goers. He also heard the sound of a fiddle and somebody singing. The music was coming from directly underfoot.

Ella's stepsiblings. Their band. And Ella too — she was right below him. He could feel it now, the quiet tug at his heart pulling him not east or west but *down*. Relief flooded him.

"We're there," gasped Serge. "You brought us right to her." Without thinking about it, he lifted off with his own wings. He didn't have time to be surprised. He leapt from the building and fluttered to the street below.

Ella

SHE held Dash tight. They couldn't stay forever, but the idea of parting made her stomach hurt. It might be days before they found a way to meet again. Weeks, even. She buried her face in his chest.

"How long can we stay?" she said. "When do we have to go?"

"Not yet." His voice was muffled in her hair. "A little longer."

The front door slammed open, and they flung themselves in either direction as two dark silhouettes flew into the room.

Flew.

"Ella." She recognized Serge's voice. "Is that you? Is the prince with you?"

"Yes," she managed, her heart pounding. "Why are you here? How did you find us?"

"Who are they?" Dash demanded.

"My fairy godfathers."

"Your — but you never —"

"No time," said Serge, crouching in front of them. "Your father's guards will be here any moment," he said to Dash. "We have to get you out. Jasper will take you to the rooftop, and I'll take Ella with me —" He stopped short, and then she heard it too: the sound of horses swiftly approaching on the cobblestones outside. Jasper barred the door.

Dash struggled to get to his feet. "My ankle," he groaned, and Ella scrambled to help him.

At the top of the steps where Clover and Linden had disappeared earlier, the door banged open. Fiery sparks shot down the stairs.

"They're here," breathed Ella. "That's Linden's signal. Serge, please — make us invisible."

Serge stared at his hands. Even by candlelight, Ella could see him sweating.

"Yes you can," said Jasper, though no one had spoken.

Hoofbeats clattered to a stop outside the door. There were jangling thuds as men dismounted and boots struck ground. Serge clenched his fists and made a noise as if he was trying to lift something that was much too heavy for him.

"Open up, by order of His Majesty the King!"

The guards began to strike at the door.

Serge

Ella's fear was palpable. She needed him. The prince needed him too. The bangs at the door were heavy and insistent — any moment, the king's guards would be through. "I'm so sorry," he gasped. "Forgive me."

Jasper laid a hand on his arm. "You are her godfather," he said quietly.

Serge cringed, despairing. He knew what he was supposed to be. But how could he summon what was no longer there?

"And I can tell you absolutely," said Jasper, "that you are *not* out of magic."

Serge blinked at him. "That's impossible, you can't know —"

"But I do." Jasper leaned close and whispered to him. "I feel it as clearly as any emotion. Your magic is there, right where it's always been — use it."

Serge clenched his fingers tight. He shut his eyes. He felt the tingle of something deep in his gut. Something bright and old and familiar. In a moment, he felt the tingle in his palms too.

Jasper was right. He could do this. He was not dry — he still had power.

The wooden door cracked down the middle.

"Now," gasped Jasper, squeezing Serge's arm tight.

Serge opened his hands. He flung dust into the air, and it settled on all four of them as the king's guards kicked the door in. They stomped into the barely furnished room, swinging lanterns ahead of them and staring around, but they could see neither the two humans nor the two fairies who huddled against the wall.

"Stairs," said the front guard, and he climbed them. He slammed his fist hard against the upstairs door as the other guards followed behind.

The door opened and Ella's stepsister, Clover, stood in it, looking as though she wanted to appear annoyed. Serge could see, however, that she was afraid. The guards could likely see it too.

"Hand over the prince," said the front guard.

"I haven't got him, sir," said Clover.

"Where's Elegant Coach?" barked the guard. "According to her stepmother, she should be at this address." He held up a note. "Where's Clover Sourwood-Gourd?"

"That's me, sir."

"So you wrote this letter. Where's your stepsister?"

Serge felt Ella's terror. Felt her hand grasping for him, closing first on the edge of his wing and then on his sleeve. Dust seeped from his palms in reply.

"I think she went out for a walk," said Clover.

The guard shoved his way past her into the apartment.

Serge grabbed Ella's searching fingers. He snapped his own, and they were upstairs in a badly furnished but rather artistic-looking apartment full of tarnished candelabras and humans in their twenties. By the looks of it, they had recently been eating; now all of them stood rigidly around the dinner table. Serge steered Ella invisibly among them as the guards filled up the place.

"Tell us where she is," said the guard with the deep voice, kicking over a chair as though he'd find Dash under it. "We know the prince is with her."

Serge pushed Ella into a tiny privy chamber at the back of the apartment. When they were inside it, he made her visible once more.

"Get out there," he whispered. "Now!" He gave her a push.

Ella stumbled from the privy chamber into the sitting room. Clover and Linden jumped at the sight of her, while the rest of their band just stared.

"Uh . . . hey," she said.

Serge watched from the privy, still invisible, holding his breath. The front guard approached Ella, his bushy eyebrows furrowed.

"Thought you were out for a walk," he said.

"No," said Ella. "Just in the privy."

The Current glanced at one another as the guard peered over

her head into the darkness at the back of the apartment. "Where's the prince?" he demanded. "Is he back there too?" He pushed past her.

Before the guard could reach the privy, Serge snapped his fingers and vanished.

Dash

An invisible hand grabbed his and pulled him out into the street, and then he was flying five — ten — twenty feet above the ground, dangling by his wrist from the grip of a fairy he couldn't see. But he had glimpsed him in the room below, and his eyes and wings had glowed terrifyingly crimson. Afraid to fight lest he be dropped, Dash let the Crimson fairy deposit him on the roof of the building without a struggle, though he groaned when his weight came down on his ankle once more.

"Jasper, where are you?" It was the same voice that had spoken to Ella downstairs, close by, though he couldn't see anyone.

"Right here," said Jasper, who still had Dash by the wrist. "With the prince."

"Your Royal Highness." Dash heard footsteps crunch closer. "My name is Serge. I'm the fairy who found you in the Redwoods after Envearia turned you to stone, and I was there in the palace when you woke. Do you remember me?"

He did now. "Yes."

"Good. I'm one of Ella's godfathers. Jasper is the other. We're going to take you home."

"You can't leave Ella."

"She's downstairs with the band. It's in everyone's best interest that she bear out her siblings' story that she's been here all night — and that she has no idea where you are."

Dash's wrist was released. He heard more footsteps, followed by Jasper's whisper from several feet away: "The Coaches are here."

Dash limped to the edge of the rooftop and looked down. There were Ella's father and stepmother, bolting from their carriage and into the room where he and Ella had just been. From the open apartment window below, Dash could hear Ella's voice, then Spaulder's.

"I don't know where he is."

"Don't lie. We've been watching you, Miss Coach. We know what you're about."

"She *is* here!" came a woman's voice, rich and full of indignation. Ella's stepmother. "Exactly as my daughter's note said she would be. Ella, these men think you're with His Royal Highness — but I don't see him."

"Right," said Ella. "'Cause he's not here."

"Then that's all there is to it," said Lady Gourd-Coach. "Gentlemen, are you satisfied?"

"We'll need a thorough search," came Spaulder's voice. "His Majesty's orders. You two, comb the back garden. Bevor, let's check the roof."

"Lady Gourd-Coach can handle it now," Serge whispered, pulling Dash away from the roof's edge. "Jasper will carry you. Let's go."

Serge

WITH the prince's direction, they came to the top of the tower nearest his rooms. Jasper passed Dash's hand into Serge's, and Serge snapped his fingers, bringing the prince into the palace, right to the center of his firelit bedchamber. He made the boy visible with a flick of his dusty fingertips, and Dash looked down and patted his torso, clearly glad to see it there again. He sank down on his bed, wincing, and bent over to prod at his ankle.

The prince's valet entered the room, gasped, and pelted away in the other direction. In minutes, King Clement strode through the door. He grabbed Dash by the collar and wrested him to his feet, making him shout in pain as his weight came down on his injured ankle.

Serge retreated to the window, still invisible.

"I *know* where you were," the king shouted, shaking his son with every word. "I don't care that no proof has been found of it. If you so much as glance at the Coach witch again, you'll be in contempt of your king — not your father — your *king*. I'll throw you in prison — no, I'll throw *her* in prison. And I'll make sure she suffers."

He flung the boy away from him; Dash stumbled back and fell onto the bed once more.

"If Lariat finds out that you went missing tonight — and she might, given how many places my men had to search and how many people know you were out playing around — we're *finished*. Not that you have any idea what that means! I was a fool to think you understood the stakes." The king paced about the room. "You've never had the pressure of managing that wretched Assembly — you've never known responsibility. By the time I was your age, my parents were dead and I was on the throne. If I had my fun, I deserved it — I *earned* it. I was a man, in charge of a country. What are you? A boy obsessed with a dingy little wharf rat!"

"Call her one more name . . ." said Prince Dash quietly.

"And what? You'll strike me?" The king advanced on him. "Since you can't be trusted to manage yourself, it's time to make things official. You and Lavaliere will be betrothed."

The prince jerked. His face turned white. "What?"

"You'll be promised to her," said his father. "The scribes will be made aware, and the business will be known across Tyme."

"I —" Dash shook his head. "I won't propose."

"You won't have to. I've already made arrangements with Lariat."

The prince pushed himself to his feet, wincing. "Father," he pleaded. "Don't."

"You made your choice," said the king. "Now pay the price."

"Please."

"Your time with the Coach girl is finished," said the king. "Done. Until after the wedding, at least — once things are settled, pursue whomever you like."

Prince Dash's face went from white to red. "You think I'd ever be like you?"

"You already are. Look at you, with Lavaliere on one arm and a peasant on the other —"

Dash lurched toward him. The two of them stood nearly nose to nose.

"There's no way out, son," said Clement. "Resign yourself."

"There's a way out." Dash's fists were clenched. "I could tell you where my mother is. Then you'd call off this betrothal — wouldn't you?"

The king's expression sagged. For a moment, the room was so utterly silent that Serge froze, afraid to so much as flick his invisible wings.

"Yes," Clement said faintly.

"You would." His son eyed him. "Even if Lariat calls the vote against you?"

"Just tell me. Please."

"No." The prince smiled. "I won't give up my mother and the monarchy just so you can have what you want. One day, I'm going to be the king this country needs, unlike you —"

Clement struck him across the face, and Dash staggered back, holding his cheek. The king strode out of the chamber and slammed the door behind him.

Dash sank onto his bed. He put his face in his hands.

"Your Highness," Serge ventured. Dash gasped and looked up. Serge made himself visible, and the prince's eyes lighted on him.

"You — you heard all that?" he said. "You were here?"

"I was here."

"So you can just," said Dash, licking his lips, "come into the palace? Invisible?"

"We're not in the business of assassinating monarchs," said Serge. "You needn't fear."

Dash peered at him. "You're Ella's godfather. You were my mother's too."

"Yes."

"Then help me — please help me. Get me out of this."

The boy's handsome face was so full of desperate hope that it gave Serge pain to answer him. "There's little I can do," he said. "The arrangements have been made. Lady Jacquard's party this weekend is a betrothal dinner for you and Lavaliere."

The prince gave a hoarse, unhappy laugh. "I'll be married in two weeks, won't I?"

"No. Not for a long while, I imagine."

"Then you don't know Lady Jacquard," the prince replied. "Or my father." He gave Serge a pleading look. "There's really nothing you can do? No magic that can —"

"Change Lady Jacquard's mind?"

Dash nodded.

"Even if I could use such magic, I wouldn't," said Serge. "Your choices are before you, dreadful as they are. You must do what you believe is right."

He heard his own words as he said them, and he knew they were not only for the prince.

Dash stared down at the floor in defeat. "I didn't even get to say good-bye to her," he mumbled. "Will you tell her — tell Ella —" He halted. A blush came to his cheeks.

"Write to her," said Serge gently. "I promise not to read it."

"You'd deliver a letter for me?" Dash asked, looking up at him.

"I only wish I could do more," said Serge, and he waited by the window while the prince took up his pen.

Ella

WHEN the guards finished ransacking the apartment on Sharp Street, they finally had to admit that His Royal Highness was not present. They slammed their way out, leaving disarray behind. Clover and Linden coolly answered all their mother's questions, sticking close to the truth and never hesitating, and eventually Sharlyn gave up and told Ella to get in the carriage.

"Those guards really expected to find the prince with you," said Ella's dad as the horses drew them toward Cardinal Park. "They said the two of you have a habit of sneaking around together, and they've found you all alone in classrooms, hiding from the others. They even said you were alone in a garden at the royal ball. What's happening, Ell?"

She was silent.

"From now on," said her dad, "when you're up at school, you'll have to avoid him."

"Earnest, really, this is the prince. She can't just drop him —"

"I'm suspended from school," said Ella dully. At least the trouble she was about to get into would stop them from talking about Dash.

"Suspended!" cried Sharlyn. "What happened?"

"Nothing. Lavaliere lied and said I attacked her during sports."

"What did you do?"

"Nothing," said Ella again. "But I'm kicked out for a month."

"A *month?* Oh no they don't. We are not paying that kind of tuition so that they can deprive you of an education. No matter what you did —"

"Which was *nothing.* Dad, you believe me, hey?"

Her dad glanced at her and pushed back his dark curls. "You've been so secretive lately."

"*I've* been secretive? Who knocked down our cott?"

"Stop it," said Sharlyn. She sat with her hands clasped in her lap, one thumb meditatively stroking the other. "You're lying," she said.

"I never *touched* Lavaliere Jacquard —"

"I believe you on that," said Sharlyn. "But you're lying. So were Clover and Linden. The situation is simply too extreme. The Jacquards abandoning Practical Elegance — royal guards showing up at our home — and a suspension too? Where there's smoke, there's fire."

Ella did not reply.

"Ella." Sharlyn's voice was almost gentle. "You're in deep water now. If you have a relationship with the prince, then you're in a very serious, very political situation, and you'll need help to navigate it. You have to tell the truth."

For the rest of the ride home, Sharlyn pressed her, but Ella didn't speak a word. An hour later, she was in bed and had already put out her lamp when she heard the fairies' chime. She sat up and lit the wick again, and Serge and Jasper appeared in her room, looking tired and grieved. Jasper perched on her bed and took her hand.

Serge knelt at her bedside. Ella heard his words as though they were coming to her from a great distance. Betrothal. Lavaliere. He handed her a letter Dash had written. She held it tight, pressing the wax seal with her thumb.

Betrothed.

"But he can't be," she heard herself murmur.

Jasper's face was a mess, his tears becoming minuscule frogs that leapt from his face only to vanish in bursts of smoke. "Oh, Ella," he choked.

"This is intolerable," said Serge angrily. He got to his feet. "That boy has potential, but he's being traded off like a gambling chip —"

Ella put a hand to her stomach, feeling suddenly like she might retch. The thought of Dash trapped with Lavaliere, unhappy and alone, cut straight through her numbness. She had to watch him live that life, and that was bad enough. But he had to do it.

"It will change him," said Serge, shoving back his disheveled hair. "He'll be forced into a role, and he'll play it, and eventually he won't have to play anymore. He'll *be* it."

"Serge." Jasper gave him a hard look, and Serge paced furiously away to the window.

"Don't open the curtain." Ella got to her feet. "Guards are watching the house. We saw them when we drove up."

Serge pivoted, his little wings sticking tautly out from his back like two slivers of ice-blue glass.

"We so much want to help," said Jasper. "What can we do?"

"Help Dash," Ella said at once. "He'll be so unhappy if he has to marry her — can't you — can't you somehow —"

Serge looked sick. He shook his head.

Ella looked down at Dash's letter. "Then I'd like to read this in private," she said.

Jasper nodded, sniffling. "Of course."

"We'll see you very soon," said Serge gently, and with a faint *snap!* the fairies were gone.

She opened the seal.

Ella ~

It's true what Serge told you. I'm betrothed. I could get out of it, but it would mean giving up the country. We both know that can't happen.

I want, as you said, to know you better all the time. There's nothing I want more. But I can't see you again, no matter what I want. I would try, but my father made it clear that if I'm caught, he will take it out on you. He mentioned prison, and I'm sure he means it. I won't put you in that kind of danger.

Since this must be the end for us, I want you to know what you've meant to me. You have changed me, Ella Coach. You have altered the way I see my position, my country. Our country. The person I was a few weeks ago did not deserve to call you a friend; today, I hope that I do. Just as I hope that, when I am king, my actions will make you proud.

I will miss you. I will never forget you. Farewell.

Dash

She sank down on the bed and read it again, and then once more, until she felt convinced that it was true. He was getting married. They could never see each other. It was over.

But one day he would be king. A good and benevolent king. And according to him, she'd had a hand in that.

Ella scrubbed the tears from her eyes. She kissed the letter and put it away in her desk, then sat down and took up her pen. Dash was brave enough, and strong enough, to do what he was doing. She would be strong enough to finish their project on her own. She'd see it through — and she'd get her dad and Sharlyn to listen. Just because she wasn't royal didn't mean she couldn't act: Practical Elegance employed hundreds of people, and she was in a position to better their lives.

She reached into her schoolbag, pulled out the speech that she and Dash had drafted, and began to make revisions.

Serge

HE brought them to the park across the street. They materialized, invisible, not three feet away from a royal guard. Silently, keeping hold of Jasper's arm, Serge fluttered deeper into the trees until the guard was far behind them, and when they came to the fairywood at the center of Cardinal Park, he plunged into it.

Immediately, the world around them changed. It was no longer night. The park vanished, replaced by a misty whiteness full of slender, silvery trees. Here he made himself and Jasper visible.

"You'll have to help Ella without me," he said. "Just for a few days."

"How can I? There are guards watching her window."

"I'll make you invisible, and you can stay that way until I come back again."

"Back from where?"

"The Slipper."

"But," said Jasper uncertainly, "I thought . . ."

"I have unfinished business," said Serge. "The betrothal party."

Jasper stared. "You're not seriously going to help with that."

Serge shut his fingers over his palms, which oozed, quickly and thickly, with the dust that had just hours ago been impossible for him. He flexed his wings, which were no longer heavy or sore. He knew the right course — it stretched before him, clear and simple. He would go to the Jacquard Estate, and he would do what he should have done months ago. Years ago.

"When I'm through at the Jacquards', I'll be done with the Slipper — and I'll be in trouble," he said. "Big trouble. I'll come and find you, but then we'll have to hide. Tell me now if you don't want to be involved."

"Then you're really quitting?"

"Yes."

"Are you prepared?" said Jasper anxiously. "Because it's going to get ugly. I never told you how my grandmother reacted when I left her. She tracked me everywhere I went, and she sent waves of enemies to try to recapture me —"

"Are you trying to talk me out of this?"

"No!"

"Good," said Serge, feeling more confident every moment. It had been ages since he'd felt this certain. "The next time I see you, I'll be . . . well." He wasn't sure *what* he would be. He had never envisioned his future without the Slipper in it. "Perhaps we'll do that thing you mentioned when we were down in Eel Grass," he mused. "Go from cottage to cottage, helping those in need."

"That would be lovely," said Jasper, who still appeared distressed. "Be careful."

"I'll see you in a few days. Watch over Ella." Serge paused. "Was it true what you said on Sharp Street?" he asked. "Could you really feel that I still had magic?"

"No," Jasper admitted. "I just knew that you needed to hear it."

Serge nodded. He made Jasper invisible and left the fairywood.

At dawn on the day of the betrothal, an army of Blue fairies arrived at the Jacquard Estate. By midafternoon, it was a world of beauty only magic could make real, its balconies bedecked in twinkling fairy lights, its windows spilling over with waterfalls of ripened flowers in every shade of blue, its grounds aglow with thousands of tiny lanterns that hung in midair.

Serge dismissed the Slipper staff and went up to Lavaliere's chamber. He found Lariat sitting with her daughter on a chaise as they reviewed the guest list together.

"Fortunately," Lariat was saying, "the Shantungs have declined."

"Why did you even send them an invitation?"

"Because it would have looked spiteful not to — it doesn't matter. Cameo Shantung has finally realized that her place in society isn't at its height." Lariat shot Serge a white smile. "Everything is perfect," she said. "Beyond lovely. I don't know what I'd do without you."

Serge permitted himself a little smile. "What's happening with Cameo?" he asked, curious.

"You didn't see this morning's *Crier?*"

She handed him a copy and tapped a fingernail against the headline: *SHANTUNGS TO VACATE ANCESTRAL ESTATE.*

"Cameo Shantung and Maud Poplin, both out of my sight in the same month," Lariat said with a sigh. She pushed back her sharp, dark fringe. "Finally, luck is with me. Of course it wasn't *all* luck." She returned to sit beside her daughter. "*You* remember, Serge."

"I'm sure I do. What are you thinking of?"

"Ten years ago or so, Cameo wanted to start using gnomish devices to unroll the silk cocoons," said Lariat. "I went to the gnomes myself to get the same deal, but they're such a strange lot. They said they'd made their arrangements with Shantung, and they didn't want to trade with anybody else." She snorted. "Not very business minded of them, but you know how unreasonable magical creatures can be. Not *you,* of course."

Serge frowned. "That deal with the gnomes never went through," he said. "Did it?"

"Oh no. I made sure that the Assembly outlawed that little bit of horror. Those devices might have doubled Shantung's business — can you imagine? Disastrous." Lariat laid a jeweled hand upon her daughter's shoulder. "Every careful move has been worth it," she said. "Finally, we'll have a Jacquard queen, and the Gourd-Coaches will be out of this city in a matter of weeks. You've won." She leaned in to kiss Lavaliere's cheek, but her lips did not touch the girl. "Be good tonight," she said softly. "Get his promise. No mistakes."

Lavaliere nodded.

Lariat went for the door. Serge spoke, because he had promised himself he would speak. He would try first. One last time.

"Your daughter's condition is worse, Lady Jacquard," he said.

Lariat stopped moving. Her fingers curled like claws.

"Much worse," Serge pressed. "I know you don't want to hear it, but it's the truth. Lavaliere needs real treatment soon, or her infection could be fatal."

Lariat glanced back over her shoulder with eyes as cold as stone. "I told you I didn't want to hear this again," she said. "Did I not communicate clearly?"

"You did."

"Then spare me your opinion. Do your *job*."

"Yes, ma'am," said Serge quietly. "I will."

She left the chamber. Twill took out the pain cream and glove, but Serge motioned her away. "Leave us a while," he said. "I want to speak with Lavaliere in private."

"I know what you'll say," said Lavaliere when the door fell shut. "But I don't care. You heard my mother. Do your job."

"My job is to help you."

"Then take the illusion off, make the pain go away, and let me get betrothed."

"Lavaliere."

"Shut *up*," she said, and she got to her feet, but she swayed and fell back down again. She shut her eyes and slumped back — for a moment, she fell unconscious. Serge flew to her at once and grabbed her shoulders.

Her eyes fluttered open. They were bleary. "What happened?" she murmured.

"You fainted." He felt her throat. "Your heart is racing. Are you dizzy?"

She shook her head very slowly, as though to move it caused her great distress.

"Just do my face," she whispered.

"You need a Hipocrath."

Lavaliere winced, and her head fell against Serge's shoulder. "As soon as I'm married."

"The wedding won't happen for years!"

"Mother says it will be soon," she said. "I'm so close."

"You need help now. Tonight. Don't you want to live?"

"I want . . . to be betrothed."

"Your mother wants that, not you."

"I *do* want it." Lavaliere sat up suddenly. Her voice was rough, unlike herself. "I want the crown. *She* couldn't get it — she missed. I won't miss."

"Do you really hate your mother that much?"

Lavaliere looked at him with eyes that did not belong to a young girl.

"Then don't die for her," said Serge. "Listen to me. You don't have to go to Port Urbane. I can find somewhere in Lilac. Somewhere secret and private. There are so many lakes up there — so many little islands — you could be completely hidden. Let me take you."

"What, now?"

"Yes."

"But what would you tell my mother?"

"Nothing."

"You'd kidnap me?" Lavaliere whispered. Her eyes were bright. Full of fear — and hope.

"I'll spread a rumor that you're deathly ill and had to be taken away for special treatment by the Exalted Council," said Serge. "It's practically the truth. Once the rumor is out there, your mother will have to play along or risk exposure. You'll be able to take off the illusion and recover. When you reappear in Quintessential in a few years, you can tell all your friends how you barely escaped death. They'll hang on every word."

Lavaliere's head tilted slightly. She was listening. "What about Dash?"

"You don't even like him."

She played with the tie of her Prism silk dressing gown. "And my mother?" she said.

"There will be nothing she can do. She won't disinherit you, if that's what you're worried about — you're her only child."

Lavaliere laughed under her breath.

"Even if she does," said Serge. "You'll be far from her. You'll be alive, you'll be strong, you'll get to make all your own choices, and I *won't* turn my back on you. I'll help you all the way to the end, I swear on my wings I will. Please, Lavaliere." He took her hand in his. "I'm your fairy godfather. *This* is my job. Let me rescue you."

For one beautiful second, she seemed a breath away from saying yes. She opened her mouth and leaned toward him.

And then she shrank, and her eyes clouded as though she'd seen some future before her that she could not bear. "Stop talking to me!" She pushed Serge away from her with both hands. "Don't you ever dare speak like this again, do you understand? Fix my face — and do it *now*, or I'll tell my mother everything you said!"

He had done everything in his power. Offered her everything he possibly could.

"It was your choice," he said. "Remember that."

Lavaliere turned up her face and shut her eyes, and Serge tore the illusion from her.

Her face was as horrific as he feared. The sores covered her mouth now. And her eyelids. She was so disfigured that no one would ever recognize her.

"Get Twill back here," Lavaliere commanded, but Serge did not go to the bell.

Instead, he took her hand and kissed the back of it.

"Good-bye, Lavaliere," he said.

Her eyes snapped open. "What?"

"I won't come back," Serge said gently. "I can't hurt you any longer."

"But you *can't* go!"

Serge went to the balcony. He heard Lavaliere's footsteps chasing him across the carpet — heard her gag as she caught sight of herself in one of the many mirrors around the room.

"Wait," she moaned. "At least cover me back up first —"

"If I do that, you won't be able to numb the pain. I won't trap you in that agony."

He leapt up onto the wide, white balcony railing. Below him, fairy lanterns illuminated the lawns, awaiting Prince Charming and his proposal.

"My mother will ruin you," cried Lavaliere. "She'll destroy you in this city — in every city!"

He knew it. Just as he knew that Lariat would find someone else to cast the illusion. His departure wouldn't end this abuse. One or two of the other fairies at the Slipper could step in for him and cover Lavaliere's face, but none of them knew her looks like Serge did, and none of them were as talented as he. The differences would show. There would be rumors.

"Don't leave me," Lavaliere shouted as Serge flew from the balcony, out toward the sea. "Mother! *Mother!*"

He flew to the Slipper. When he arrived, he went to the penthouse and withdrew from his pocket the letter he had already prepared. He knew that Jasper would tell him that this part was unnecessary and that he should simply turn his back. But he was a professional.

"Serge," Jules said when he entered. She laid down her *Crier*. "I thought you'd be with Lariat. How's the estate? Ready for royalty?"

"Breathtaking," said Serge. He took his pocket watch out and laid it on her desk, along with his bluebell chime and his letter. He drew breath, and for one second — just one — he nearly reconsidered. The Slipper was so beautiful at sunset. In a moment, all he had worked for would be lost to him.

He thought of Lavaliere's face, and he shuddered.

"I resign," he said.

Jules's eyebrows flew up. She laughed her husky laugh. "Oh dear," she said. "Rough day with the human elite? Sit down and tell me. I'm sure we can fix it."

"I don't think so."

"Babe." She smiled at him. "We've been together a long time. More than half your life."

"Two-thirds of it."

"See? I *know* you. You love this Slipper. You'd never abandon it."

"I cleared out my office."

"Relax. I'll call Thimble. She'll get you a nice glass of gold tea."

"I filed my severance papers with Lebrine."

Jules's eyes narrowed. "She didn't say anything to me."

"I just handed them to her," said Serge. "No one knew this was coming. Don't take it out on anyone but me."

"Take it out?" Jules laughed again, but this time the sound was cautious. "What kind of monster am I all of a sudden? You want to quit? Quit. It's a free shoe."

"Thank you." Serge went to the door.

"Serge. Get back here. We obviously need to talk."

"I'll talk, but only for a moment," he said. "I have an ultimatum, and you're not going to agree to it. When you don't, I'm going to leave."

Jules came out from behind her glass desk and stalked toward him, her eyes glittering.

"An *ultimatum*?" she said. "What in Geguul is wrong with you?"

"Lariat Jacquard is killing her daughter," said Serge. "I won't be her accomplice any longer."

"You want me to assign someone else to that job?" said Jules angrily. "You're putting me in an impossible position, and you know it. Lariat will put up a fight —"

"I'm not asking you to put someone else on the job," said Serge, and Jules's wings relaxed. "I'm asking you to cut ties with the Jacquards. Completely. It's Lariat or me."

Jules's mouth dropped open. "What did Lariat say to you?" she demanded. "What do you think you know?"

"I know that I was almost lost," said Serge. "But I don't blame you for that. Much as you contributed, it was entirely my own fault. I should have resisted."

"Serge. Listen to me."

On Jules's desk, Serge's pocket watch had grown so hot that it was smoking.

"That'll be the Jacquards," he said, pointing over her shoulder.

Jules ran to her desk, teetering on her heels as she went. She snapped up the watch and clicked it open. "What did you *do*," she breathed, turning on him.

"My job."

"If you jeopardized this betrothal, I'll ruin you," Jules hissed. "I'll crush you. Your reputation in this town will be destroyed — and not just in this town. All over Tyme."

"So I've been told."

"Get back there *now*."

"Good-bye, Jules. Don't waste your time threatening me; there's nothing you can say, and I imagine the Charmings are already on their way to the party."

Jules was at her desk, ringing her chime, shouting for Thimble, and trying to read the pocket watch all at the same time. Serge pressed the button for the Slingshot, and the door slid open.

"Best wishes to you in making wishes come true," he said.

He stepped into the Slingshot, and the door slid shut.

Ella

At number 76, the week passed in relative quiet. Clover and Linden traveled out of Quintessential with the band to play at parties in other towns. Sharlyn visited Coterie Preparatory School to protest Ella's punishment, but Madam Wellington would not budge. Not only did Ella have to serve out her full suspension; at the end of it, she would be subjected to a disciplinary hearing, with the Jacquards and several other donors present.

"She thinks she can expel you," said Sharlyn when she relayed the information to Ella. Her eyes were flint. "But I'll be prepared. That woman doesn't know who she's dealing with."

Ella had a feeling she didn't mean Madam Wellington.

She spent her nights knitting, attacking one project after another. She started a floor-length rope vest for Clover, because it was similar to something she'd heard her stepsister admire once. She finished a tunic for Linden, and into its one sleeve she knitted a long, skinny pocket where he could stow away his drumsticks. She even started a skirt for Chemise Shantung, whose family was apparently leaving Quintessential. The one decent girl her age she'd met in this city, and now she'd be gone.

She visited Chemise that weekend, with her own knitting in hand as well as extra needles and wool. A maid brought her into the parlor, where Chemise sat in a wheelchair, her feet wrapped in thick bandages and propped up before her. In her lap was a skein of lavender wool. In her hands, crochet hooks. She looked up at Ella and smiled. "I'm so glad you came," she said. "How have you been?"

"How have *you* been?" Ella replied. "You remembered how to crochet?"

"I needed a project." Chemise glanced at her feet. "So I asked my mother to remind me how it's done."

Ella sat beside her. "Your mum crochets?"

"Mother can do all sorts of things. She can even spin silk."

"Really!"

"So can my sister," said Chemise proudly. "I'm expected to learn too. Shantung has a history of artisanship, you know. It's important to understand the things you sell . . ." She faltered. "Not that we're selling much anymore," she said. "It's so strange. I can't believe we're truly leaving Quintessential after seven centuries."

"Then there's no chance of saving the company?"

"Shantung isn't closing completely. We're keeping one workshop to take care of the few clients we still have." She looked warmly at Ella. "Like Practical Elegance," she said. "Your family's contract with us makes a great difference."

"I'm glad," said Ella, and she honestly was. "I brought wool to show you how to knit," she said, holding up her offering. "But you look busy enough."

"If you know how to spin silk, I'd like to start learning that," said Chemise, laying aside her crocheting.

"I didn't bring my drop spindles, or I'd teach you."

"We have those," said Chemise. "I'll call for them. And some tea." She rang the silver bell that sat beside her on the table.

✦ ✦ ✦

At home that afternoon, Ella rehearsed her business proposal with Jasper, who had come to sit with her every afternoon, invisible. Serge wasn't with him, and he didn't explain why.

"Thanks for drawing these," she said, looking at the design sketches Jasper had made for her. He had been with her for a few hours already — longer than usual. Ella knew why. She was trying very hard not to think about it. "You make my ideas look so much better."

"Your ideas," said Jasper, "are *sensational*. I've never liked big knits, but when I see how *you* interpret them? I'm converted."

"They'll know I didn't make these," said Ella, holding one of his illustrations up to the lamplight. It sparkled. The colors were so vivid they didn't seem real.

"Tell them it was Dash."

Ella flinched.

"I'm sorry."

She attempted a casual shrug. "I have to get past it, hey?" she said. "No choice, is there."

Her room was quiet. She could just see the depression in the cushion of her desk chair, telling her that Jasper was sitting there.

"Tonight," came Jasper's voice, very softly. "In an hour. That's when —"

She shook her head. She put the sketches with the rest of her proposal in a sleek leather portfolio that Jasper had given her for the presentation.

"I think you're ready," said Jasper. "Let's see what you're going to wear."

Dash

IN the carriage on the way to the Jacquard Estate, King Clement was quiet. Dash looked out the window at the sea. His injured ankle was propped on the cushion across from him. He wasn't supposed to put his full weight on it until tomorrow; he had a crutch for tonight. It would spare him having to dance with Lavaliere, at least.

That he had to marry her was still unreal to him.

His father opened a flat black case that he held in his lap, revealing an array of lustrous jewels. "When you ask her," he said, "present her with these. They're tradition. I couldn't find the ring — your mother must have taken it with her."

"I have it," said Dash. "I won't give it to Lavaliere."

"It passes from queen to queen."

"No."

King Clement shut the case. "You know that I don't want this for you."

"Then marry Lariat."

"Is that what you want? Queen Lariat?"

Dash did not want it. Lavaliere was the better choice. It was an awful future to look forward to, but it was not as bleak as living under Lariat's direct rule.

The Jacquard mansion shone in the falling darkness. Two footmen opened the carriage doors, and the prince and king descended together, Dash with his crutch, limping. Scribes crushed in around the royal guards, shouting questions. On the steps, King Clement turned and raised a hand, and the scribes gazed up at him, ears pricked, pens poised.

"Stay near for an announcement," said the king. "This is a special night."

The doors of the mansion opened. Framed within were Lariat and Lavaliere, pictures of beauty and splendor — in dress, at least. Lariat's smile was unmistakably pinched, and Lavaliere looked strange, Dash thought. She was the wrong color.

"Tans must be back in fashion," muttered his father. "I'm not sure it suits her."

It wasn't just the tanned skin. Something was out of place. Her nose. Her mouth?

They reached the top of the steps.

"Your Majesty," said Lariat. "Your Royal Highness — poor thing, what's happened to your ankle? Let us get you to a comfortable chair."

"I suppose you won't be able to dance," said Lavaliere, and as her lips moved, Dash saw that even her teeth were strange. Unnaturally white.

"No."

"What a pity," she said. "But we'll be able to watch everyone else enjoy themselves."

For the rest of our lives, Dash thought, and he limped his way inside.

Serge

JASPER'S door flew open at his knock. Both of them were invisible, so Serge could not see Jasper's expression, but he could see that his Academy boarding room was bare.

"I already moved out. I'm ready to hide." Jasper's hand found his arm. "Are you all right? What happened at the Jacquards'? At the Slipper?"

"Not here," Serge said.

They flew to the harbor. In the darkness between the barnacled legs of one of the shipping piers, Serge made them visible, and by the time he had finished telling Jasper everything that had happened at the Jacquard Estate and in Jules's penthouse office, Jasper's wings glowed so fiercely that Serge cautioned him to dim it down a touch.

"But I'm so proud of you," Jasper whispered. "And so happy for you."

Serge's wings warmed and gave a gratified flutter.

"I have a hiding spot for us," said Jasper. "Let's go —"

"Wait." said Serge. "Help me. What Lariat said about the gnomish devices — there's something wrong with her story."

"You think she lied?"

"No, I think she was too truthful. She said she went to the gnomes and asked them to make her the same deal they'd made with Cameo. They refused. A month or two later, the Assembly passed a law blocking all gnomish machines from being used by the Garment Guild."

"So Lariat sabotaged Shantung."

"The point is, how did she *know* to sabotage her? How did she know to visit the gnomes? Lariat shouldn't have had that information. That deal was secret. I only knew about it because I was Challis Shantung's godfather. I worked in the Shantung mansion. I reported every Shantung secret straight to the Slipper."

Jasper gaped. "Why?"

"Because I'm thorough!" cried Serge. "I've always been meticulous in my reports. Anything I learned on any client visit was filed with Lebrine."

"So Jules knew about Cameo's plan."

"Yes."

"And you think she told Lariat."

"I think it's far bigger than that. Tonight, before I left Jules, she asked me what I think I know. And the more I dwell on that, the more I — hold on." Serge flicked his fingers and created two long scrolls in midair, from memory. The first list, he titled *Members of the House of Mortals*. The other, *Glass Slipper Clients, Past 20 Years*.

They matched. In all but a few names, the lists matched.

"We've been spies," Serge whispered. "Collecting government secrets for Lariat Jacquard. We've been in every Assembly household, reporting things back to Jules. That's how Lariat knows exactly when and how to ruin her competitors —"

"It's how she controls the votes in the Assembly," said Jasper, taking hold of the lists, which glowed sharply silver in the darkness. "It's why she can overthrow the king."

"*I* did this," said Serge in disbelief. "When I think of the secrets I've recorded — the things she knows —" He pressed both hands to his stomach, sickened. "Everyone in the House of Mortals has something to hide, and Lariat knows every whisper. Anyone who goes against her risks public humiliation and financial destruction."

Jasper ran a fingernail along the list of Assembly names. "This is simply diabolical," he said. "Worthy of my grandmother."

"I thought Jules got greedy for the attention after she made Maud queen — I thought that was why the List was full of nobles. I never realized there was more to it. But of course — of *course* — it all started after Clement married Maud," Serge said. "Lariat has been plotting to undo him ever since."

"We have to expose this." Jasper handed back the lists. "We'll go straight to the Assembly members. Tell them they've been used."

"They're all at that betrothal party."

"Cameo Shantung isn't."

"You're right." Serge rolled up the lists. "Let's go."

They flew to the Shantung Estate. The great house was dim within, and mostly empty. Packed crates filled the parlor. The only furniture not draped with a sheet was a tall glass display case, holding the exquisite glass slippers that Serge had made for Challis ten years ago. Florals had been in fashion then: blues, purples, and greens married vividly in blooming iris flowers of glass. The small glass dots that Jules had insisted on affixing to the slim heels were their only imperfection.

The butler brought Serge and Jasper deeper into the house to a small office where Lady Cameo Shantung waited, standing amid her shrouded furniture. She could have been her daughters' older sister, with her heart-shaped face and smooth black hair. Only her exhausted eyes gave her age away.

"Serge." She nodded to Jasper. She did not look pleased.

"I apologize," said Serge. He closed the door behind them. "We wouldn't trouble you so late at night if it weren't serious."

Cameo's face grew fearful. "Challis?"

"No, not your daughters. I'm sure they're both well."

"Chemise isn't," said Cameo sharply. "Her feet haven't healed, and no Hipocrath can tell us why. Whatever magic was in that Ubiquitous acorn may have damaged her permanently."

"I'm sorry," said Serge. "So very sorry."

"You're the first to say so," said Cameo. "Not one of the rest of them has been here since the ball. Not *one* — except for Ella Coach, who has known Chemise barely half a year but has more compassion than the people who have known her all her life. Lariat Jacquard sent us an invitation to come and dance at her home tonight, however." Cameo's nostrils flared. "How generous."

"It's Lariat Jacquard I'm here about."

"Skies, isn't she done with me yet? I'm barely in business, I'm leaving the city, my daughter can't walk — what does she want? My face?" She laughed. "She's been jealous of my face since we were ten years old."

"Please, Lady Shantung. Listen."

Cameo sat erect on a sheet-covered chair. Quickly, in simple terms that embellished nothing, Serge explained the situation.

Cameo's face barely moved. "Why tell me this now?" she asked.

"Because it's not only your house that Blue fairies have served in. It's an extraordinary breach of confidentiality for me to show you this list of our clients, but since this information has already been compromised . . ."

Cameo took Serge's lists and compared them. Within a minute, she looked up.

"So this is how she does it," she whispered. "I always wondered. People despise her, yet they do whatever she says — I knew it must be blackmail, but this . . ." She paused and looked from him to Jasper. "Why did you participate in this?" she asked. "Why would you do it?"

"I had no idea that this was happening until tonight," Serge said. "You have no reason to trust me, but it's the truth."

Cameo pursed her lips. Momentarily, she shook her head.

"It can't be right."

"What?"

"You couldn't have known about the other deals Lariat blocked. The gnomish devices were only the beginning. I contacted the Prism Keepers Association of Lilac to explore my options there, but Lariat shut that avenue down as well, long after you finished your year with Challis."

"Are you sure?"

"Positive. There were other deals, but there was no other fairy in the house after you. She must have gotten the information another way."

Jasper spoke. "She could have left magic in the house," he said. "Something Serge placed here without knowing it?"

Serge's blood slowed. He *had* placed something in the house.

"The glass slippers," he whispered.

Jasper and Cameo both drew breath.

"All our past clients have a pair in their homes, and you're not the only one who displays them in a common area." Serge shook his head. How could he have missed it? How could he have been so fooled? "Jules always puts a finishing touch on them — a glass dot. She calls it her signature, but it could be listening magic. Do you ever conduct business in your parlor?"

Lady Shantung flushed suddenly. "The private things she must have heard," she muttered. "The completely private — that's an abuse of magic power." She glanced at the closed door. "And she's already heard this conversation," she murmured. "She knows that we know."

"I seriously doubt it," said Serge. "Jules is not the fairy she used to be, and those shoes are at the other end of the house."

"Lady Shantung," said Jasper, crouching beside her, "are you aware that Lariat Jacquard has enough votes in the House of Mortals to push King Clement out of the Assembly if she wants to?"

"What can I do about it?" Cameo demanded. "The Assembly barely listens to me anymore — and now I know why."

"Take the lists, Lady Shantung," said Jasper. "Spread this news to everyone you can. You know better than anyone which Assembly members might be swayed away from Lariat's side, and she'll never suspect a strike from you. She doesn't think you'll fight her."

Cameo Shantung raised her chin. "Doesn't she?"

"You've packed up your estate," said Jasper. "She thinks you're beaten."

"Actually, in her words," said Serge, "she thinks you've finally realized that your place in society isn't at its height."

Pride blazed in Cameo's face, and she put out her hand. "Give me those lists."

Ella

IT was Sharlyn, still in her dressing gown, who brought the morning *Crier* to Ella's door. Ella could see the enormous headline from where she lay.

BETROTHED! PRINCE CHARMING TO WED LAVALIERE JACQUARD.

Sharlyn sat on the edge of the bed. "You knew this was coming?"

Ella rolled toward the wall to hide the wetness in her eyes.

"I don't know how close the two of you were," said Sharlyn. "Or how serious it was between you —"

Ella pulled a pillow over her face. Sharlyn waited through Ella's shuddering and spoke again only when she was still.

"I'm not here to intrude on your feelings," she said. "I know there's nothing I can say." She reached out a hand as if she might brush back Ella's hair, but she stopped and retracted it. "I doubt I can help, but I have to ask. Is there anything I can do?"

Ella pushed herself up to sit against the headboard, and she wiped her sticky, tearstained cheeks. "Actually, yeah," she said. "I wanted to ask you something. Remember how I told you I wanted to show you a business proposal for Practical Elegance? It's done."

Sharlyn glanced curiously toward Ella's desk, where the proposal lay. "Is that it?" she asked. "Would you like me to read it?"

"No, I want to present it to you and my dad."

"So you'd like a meeting with us?"

"Yeah," said Ella. "I would. As soon as you're both free."

"Your father's rearranging the displays over in the shop today," said Sharlyn. "But tomorrow we're both available. If you feel up to it by then, why don't you meet us at one o'clock, down in the office?"

"Yeah, grat —" Ella stopped. She would do this right. "Yes, thank you," she said, more carefully. "I'm up to it. I look forward to our meeting."

SERGE

JASPER led him to a neighborhood near the wharf, in a part of Quintessential that Serge had not seen for many years. They landed on the roof of a crumbling old government structure, long abandoned, with a disused bell tower erupting from its leaking stone buildings.

"Fly?" said Jasper. He pointed to the top of the tower. "Or walk?"

"Walk," said Serge, whose smaller wings were already fatigued, and he followed Jasper up the dilapidated spiral stair. "What is this place?" he asked.

"It's Gossamer's," said Jasper. "And the others'."

"Others?"

"You had your secret clients and your meetings with Jules," said Jasper. "I had projects of my own."

They reached the top of the steps. He knocked once, then twice, then thrice on a wooden door, and the edges of the door glowed with golden light. It opened, and they flew into the bell tower.

Serge looked around in awe. Gossamer's place was in the most unfashionable area she could possibly have chosen — which was very like her — but inside the bell tower, she'd created a world of beauty. The tower looked like the fairy glade where Blue fairies hatched and returned to fade. The same soft hanging moss, full of shimmering lights; the same warm, enveloping blue mist. The only things missing were the big speckled eggs.

Gossamer greeted them, dry-eyed for once.

"You're certain about him?" she asked Jasper, eyeing Serge with distrust.

"*Beyond* certain," said Jasper. "He quit the Slipper *spectacularly*. Wait till he tells you."

Gossamer did not appear convinced.

"Gossamer, forgive me," said Serge. "I sided with Jules, and she made a fool of me — of all of us. The Slipper is more poisonous than any of us knew."

This was too intriguing to be denied, and so Gossamer drew them further into the mist-shrouded bell tower, toward a meeting space arranged with cushions and pillows. On these, to Serge's surprise, sat a dozen or so godparents and employees of the Glass Slipper — including Thimble, who beckoned for Serge to sit with her. He alighted on the empty cushion at her side.

"We were just discussing the future of godparenting," said Gossamer, settling on a pillow beside Carvel and Georgette, both of whom gave Serge sheepish looks. "You have news for us?"

Everyone looked at him, suspicious and expectant.

"You think you've been working for Jules," Serge said, "but for years now, all of us have really been working for Lariat Jacquard." They were quiet, but their faces filled with horror as he explained what he had discovered, and how.

"Skies," said Gossamer. "Humans will never trust us after this."

"They'll be angry," Serge agreed. "By now, Lady Shantung will have spoken with a few of the families. Eventually, the news will leak. Humans can't keep secrets."

"Apparently, neither can fairies," said Thimble angrily. "Why, oh, why didn't I quit twenty years ago? How many times have I wanted to do it — how many times have I asked myself, 'Thimble, what are you doing here?' "

The whole group chimed in at once with their agreement.

"Every fairy still with the Slipper has to be warned," said Serge. "Lebrine too. We have to tell them all the truth about what's been happening — they need to know they're being used."

"But they'll be furious," said Thimble. "They'll all want to leave the Slipper at once. Where will they all go? What will happen to the godchildren?"

"The fairies will come here," said Gossamer. "And we will start again, without Jules. As for the godchildren, it's high time we moved on to help those who actually deserve us."

"Wouldn't that be nice," sighed Carvel.

"It's what we all came to the Slipper to do," said Georgette. "There's no reason why we shouldn't do it."

"But what will Jules *do* if she's left with no one?" Thimble cried. "She'll come after us all, and she'll — she'll —" She stopped. "There's nothing she can do. Is there?" She looked at Carvel, who shook his head.

"I'll head to the shoe and get the word out," he said, getting to his feet. "Jules still thinks I work for her. This is as good a way as any to quit."

"I'll go too," said Thimble, but her little blue hands were shaking. "I guess this means we're really finished," she said. "After this, we won't be able to go back. Oh, why do I feel so dreadful about it? I *want* to quit — what's wrong with me?"

Jasper flew to her side and put his arm around her. "You've been there a long time," he said. "You used to do good things there. Of course you feel torn."

Thimble nodded gratefully and went with Carvel out of the tower.

"You're like no Crimson fairy I've ever encountered," said Gossamer, watching Jasper. "And I mean that as a compliment."

"It definitely is one," said Jasper.

"What should we do now?" asked Georgette. "What's our next step?"

Serge glanced around the room. "Our next step is to find bigger headquarters," he said. "There are about to be quite a few more of us."

Ella

THE following afternoon at one o'clock precisely, she went downstairs and found her dad and Sharlyn working in their office. Her dad was drawing something — plans for an invention of some kind. Sharlyn was bent over a list of figures.

Ella cleared her throat. "Is this still a good time?" she asked as they turned to the door.

"Ell," said her dad, glancing over her business clothes. "You're looking slick, hey?"

Sharlyn sat back in her leather chair and removed her pince-nez. "Earnest, she made an appointment. She's here to present her proposal."

"The school project?" Her dad's brow creased. "The one you did with the prince?"

"It's not a school project," Ella replied. "It's a real plan for restructuring our workshop and wage practices while keeping Practical Elegance profitable."

"Very serious stuff," her dad joked. "You're starting to sound like Sharlyn here."

"Come in, Ella," said Sharlyn. "We're listening."

Ella looked down at her portfolio. It was sweaty — she hadn't realized how hard she was gripping it. She inhaled a shaky breath and exhaled a stronger one, then did it one more time. She touched her necklace charm for luck.

She started her speech.

"Practical Elegance is a family employer," she said. "Two-thirds of our employees are the sole financial support for their families. The welfare of hundreds of children in and around Quintessential, Coldwater, Stodgeside, and Eel Grass depends on wages earned in Practical Elegance workshops. As parents, both of you are well aware of the weight of that responsibility."

She spoke slowly at first, afraid she would forget the words — and then, as she gained confidence, she found herself speaking freely, sure of what she believed, even if she couldn't quite remember how to say it.

"We've already untied ourselves from Jacquard," she said when she got that far. "Maybe it wasn't our intention, but we did it, and we're better for it. Now we need to take our commitment to family welfare even further. Garter is disgraceful in their treatment of laborers. They employ eight-year-olds, and they work them for ten-hour shifts. At Batik, the youngest workers are nine, and just last year, half a dozen of those children lost one or both of their eyes to backsplash accidents at the dye vats. Afterward, they were put out on the streets, blind."

Her dad's face betrayed discomfort. Sharlyn's was impassive.

"Practical Elegance has contracts with both Garter and Batik," Ella went on. "Which is the equivalent of supporting their cruelty, which I know none of us wants to do. The good news is that we don't have to. The alternatives might not be perfect — but take Loden Woolery, for instance. Like Practical Elegance, their youngest employees are fourteen, and like Shantung, they offer at least a minimum of help to their people who are sick. Still, nobody does as much as they should. Practical Elegance will be the first. We can set the standard. We can demonstrate to the Garment Guild how skilled laborers ought to be valued. We can make our workshops safer than any others, and we can offer better benefits than any other company." She straightened her shoulders and braced herself. "As long as we change our ideas about what it means to make a profit," she said. "We'll have to take less as a family."

Sharlyn's neutral expression flickered.

"We'll also have to raise prices in our shops," said Ella. "But people *can* pay. We just have to educate our customers so that they know they're buying from the best business on the Avenue. Take a look at this sample budget, and you'll see what I'm suggesting."

Sharlyn put on her pince-nez, and she and Ella's dad studied every one of Dash's carefully written columns of sums.

"This is incredibly informative," said Sharlyn. "I didn't know half of these numbers. Where did you get these financial details about our suppliers and competitors?"

"Prince Dash looked in the Garment Guild records."

Ella's dad let out a low whistle. "It's good to have friends."

"Exactly." Sharlyn turned another page. "Still . . . these changes are extreme."

"That's why we made a timeline," said Ella. "Turn the page and see. It can all be done in a year. First, we stop the Garter contract —"

"Garter stays," said Sharlyn. "Shantung already adds a major expense. Switching to Loden is impossible."

Ella bit down on a retort. She had promised Jasper that she wouldn't get angry and throw away all her hard work. They wouldn't listen to her if she went on the offensive now. "Not if we live more modestly," she said, forcing her voice to stay even.

Sharlyn removed her pince-nez once more. "I understand," she said. "You feel it's unjust that your friends in Eel Grass don't have your money and advantages. I think it's admirable that you're so aware of your good fortune. But it's not wrong, or unethical, for you to enjoy that fortune. Practical Elegance has succeeded on your father's genius and my business understanding — and that's fair. That's called reaping what you sow. We *should* benefit from our efforts."

"But we don't need a house this big," said Ella. "We don't need two carriages, or to live on the park, or have servants either."

"The servants might feel differently about losing their jobs," said Sharlyn.

"Fair enough," said Ella, rattled. She hadn't thought about that part, and she didn't have a ready response. "But your offices don't have to be over the shop on the Avenue, do they? What if you moved them to Ragg Row instead?"

Sharlyn did not look eager to agree.

"I don't see how it'll work, Ell," said her dad, who was still frowning at a list of replacement supplies. "Some of my inventions depend on materials from the vendors you want to cut — and they're big sellers, those products. I'm proud of you, though, for putting all this together. Bet you get a top score, once you get back up to that school of yours, hey?"

He was still thinking of this as a school project — he wasn't listening.

"I have new design suggestions," Ella said, opening her folder. "They'd replace those products, and they're based on things you already want to make. If you'd just look —"

"You've given us plenty to discuss for now," said Sharlyn. "Save the design ideas for our next meeting. When you're calmer."

"I'm calm!" she said, louder than she meant to. "And I'm not even halfway through!"

"Don't shout at your stepmother."

But it was all falling apart. "If you'd just move the office to Ragg Row —"

"I won't move the business to an area of the city where clients don't feel safe."

"If it's not safe, then how can you ask people to work there? They get there in the dark of morning, they leave in the gloom of night —"

"You've done very well, Ella," said Sharlyn, in a tone that suggested there would be no further discussion. "Now, control yourself. Don't let anger ruin your hard work."

It was too late for that. Ella slammed her folder shut. "I don't get you," she said. "Yesterday morning you acted like you cared. I actually thought you might take me seriously."

"You make that very difficult," said Sharlyn. "Not only because of your temper, but because you won't allow me to know you."

"I went shopping with you the other night, didn't I? I'm dressed up the way you like, I'm making friends with Chemise —"

"Everything I know about you is just a guess. It's a hard position to be in as your guardian. It makes it difficult to stand up for you to people like Madam Wellington. It also makes it difficult to trust you."

"Oh, so if you trust me, you'll be able to hear what I'm saying?" Ella retorted.

"Let's try it and see."

"What do you want to know?"

"Why you're so angry with me, for a start," said Sharlyn. "You bristle at everything I do or say. It can't just be because I married your father. I don't expect you to feel comfortable with my presence and your mother's absence, but you've known me for a year and a half, and you still —"

"My *mum*," said Ella, "is why I'm angry. I can't believe you don't *get* that."

"She had a hard life," said Sharlyn. "And a harder death. But you can't blame me for what happened to her —"

"Maybe not you," said Ella recklessly. She pointed to her dad. "*Him* I can."

Her father stared at her. "You blame me," he murmured, "for Ellie?"

"Where *were* you, Dad?" Ella turned on him and searched his face. "When she was working like that, when she was dying — where were you?"

"Trying to make a living, for both of you —"

"No, stop *saying* that. You were away, following your dreams and doing your inventions, and *I* was at home trying to make a living for both of us. *I* did what needed to be done, not you."

She had never intended to tell him this. Her mum had made her promise not to. But maybe it was time to break that promise.

Her dad glanced uneasily at Sharlyn. "I don't know what she means," he said. "Truly."

"Perhaps she'll tell us," said Sharlyn. "Ella?"

"Mum made me swear I wouldn't," said Ella, keeping her eyes fixed on her dad. "She thought it'd hurt you if you knew. But if you knew, you'd know me better. You both would. And maybe you'd understand."

Her dad looked terrified. Ella set aside her folder. She pulled up a chair to sit facing him.

"If this is about Ellie," he said, "working in that shop . . . Ell, I know they hit her. I know things about that place I wish I didn't know. You don't have to tell me again."

"It's not about Mum," said Ella. "I told you. It's about me."

She tried to figure out where to begin.

"When I was little," she finally said, "I used to go with Mum to work." Her voice sounded strange to her. She had never expected to tell this story. "She started at Jacquard when I was just three," she said. "I didn't understand that if I messed up the silk, I'd get us both in trouble, so Mum had to distract me. She gave me Prism cocoons to unroll, to keep me from pushing my fingers into her spinning and ruining it."

The office was so quiet that the clock in the parlor could be heard ticking, even though the door was shut.

"There were other kids in the same room," Ella went on, "but they were tied to their chairs, and they were paid to work. I got to sit with Mum on her mat, because she told the manager that she'd pay for anything I ruined. But she couldn't actually pay, so she kept giving me cocoons to keep me busy."

She took a deep breath and watched her father's face. "You were gone peddling," she said. "When your inventions didn't sell, Mum had to find a way to pay the bills. And I was unrolling silk anyway. So finally she gave in, and I started working full-time, like the other kids. I was four."

Ella's father's face slackened.

"I was good at it," said Ella. "Really nimble and fast. I could get the whole cocoon unrolled in one long strand. I'd go to work with Mum at six in the morning, and we'd stay until eight at night. Sometimes ten if we needed to catch up on expenses. I got blisters and they'd pop, and if I got blood on the silk, I'd get beaten. Finally, I built up calluses." She held out her still-rough fingertips to show him. "When I was five, they moved unrolling up to a different floor of the shop, and I couldn't sit with Mum anymore. They tied me up like the other kids, and they hit me just as hard. For a couple of years it was like that."

Her father looked like he might be sick.

"When I was seven," Ella said, "I started at the village school, and then I could only work half days. Then, when I was eleven, it all stopped. Mum wouldn't let me come to the workshop anymore. She said I had to study and get a scholarship to the University of Orange, so I could get out of Eel Grass. But a couple years later, she got sick."

She paused to gain control of her voice.

"I tried to quit school and go to the Jacquard shop in her place so she could rest and get better. But she was so stubborn, and she felt so guilty that I'd ever worked in that shop in the first place. The sicker she got, the more she wouldn't let me help —"

This time, a longer pause was necessary.

"Ellie never told me," her dad whispered. "How could she never tell me? I thought it was just her, making ends meet. I would have stayed in Eel Grass and worked at the docks."

"Mum was afraid of that. She said you were worth the sacrifice, and someday people would see how great your ideas were. She was right, hey?"

Her dad covered his face with his hands. "If *she* wanted to sacrifice — but to do it to *you* —"

"Dad." Ella knelt before him. "You can't change how it was. You can't change Mum's decisions. What you *can* change is Practical

Elegance. This is what I'm telling you. This is why, to me, this is no school project. When you choose Garter, you're saving money on wool by putting their people through the same degrading things Mum and I went through — and you can't do that. If that kind of life wasn't good enough for us, then it's not good enough for anybody. No one deserves it. We can't support it."

Her father's back heaved.

For a long time, there was stillness in the office.

"I have an idea." The interruption came from Sharlyn. Ella turned to find her stepmother looking at her with uncharacteristic softness. "I want you to come and inspect our workshop," she said.

Ella's heart leapt. "You do?"

"You have experience," said Sharlyn. "I personally believe that our shops are run well, but you'll know better than I."

Ella stood. "Can I go through every room? Can I interview employees? Can we make changes right away?"

"Yes, yes — and yes. Within reason."

"What's reason?"

"I honestly don't know," said Sharlyn. "We'll have to discuss things as you discover them. But I will seriously consider every suggestion you make."

"But if people are sick," Ella pressed, "we'll help them."

"Yes," said her dad swiftly. His voice was rough. "Yes, we will."

Sharlyn slipped quietly out of the office.

"I'm sorry," her dad whispered once they were alone. "I'm sorry I wasn't there. I'm sorry I didn't know. I'm sorry I haven't listened —"

"Dad, stop," she said, though it was everything she'd wanted to hear from him. "We'll make things better now, hey?"

He shook his head. "I'll never forgive myself."

He began to cry.

Ella took his hands, and something in her chest — something that was hard and hot, old and angry — loosened, like the opening of a fist. It wasn't gone, and perhaps it never would be, but it no longer gripped her by the heart. Her dad had been wrong. Her mum had been wrong too. They both of them had done what they believed was best. She could hold the past against her dad forever, or she could forgive him. Forgive them both. Move ahead.

"Mum was wrong not to tell you," she said quietly. "I'm glad I did."

Dash

THE betrothal party had been a waking nightmare. Dash felt as though he had not really lived it; he had merely observed the events. Lavaliere had pretended happiness — or perhaps she'd been genuinely emotional; he'd seen her eyes fill with tears at one point when they were sitting together and watching the others dance. Lady Jacquard had fawned so triumphantly over him that his dignity had barely survived it.

He had not been forced to propose; his father had made the arrangements for him, just as he'd threatened. That was one mercy, at least. The other was that no one really expected him to show great affection for Lavaliere. Quintessential understood that the match was political; he had been able to get away with simply holding her hand. Even Lavaliere herself expected no more.

The next evening found him cooped up in his chamber, trying to figure out a way to get a letter to his mother, when a folded note slowly floated down in front of his face and landed squarely before him. He jumped up from his desk, whirled, and reached into the empty space around him, but there was nothing except a fluttering of the curtain near his window. Whoever had been there a moment ago — and Dash thought he knew who it was — was gone now. With shaking fingers, he picked up the note, which was addressed to him in messy handwriting that made his heart beat twice in one go. He fumbled to get it open.

Dash,

I know this is a risk I shouldn't take, and I won't do it again. But just this once, I had to tell you.

I shared our business proposal with my dad and stepmum, and they listened. It took some doing, but they listened. They're not going to fix everything all at once, but they're going to let me inspect the workshop here in Quintessential and help them see what's wrong. Real changes will happen, and I'll make sure they happen right away. It's such a good start. It will change people's lives. I can't wait to begin.

Thank you so much for everything. For hearing me. You've changed me too, you know. I was so angry, and I felt so lost here. Now I understand what I have, and I know what I need to do. I don't want to run from this city anymore, because my work is here. Just like yours. Even if we can't be together, we can still work toward the same things. In that way, at least, we can always be near each other.

Your loyal friend always,

Ella

He ran a fingertip over her name. Had he really helped her? Given her something? He was glad if he had. She had given him so much.

And she was really doing it. Inspecting workshops, making people listen. Changing lives. She was doing more without a crown than he had ever tried to do with one.

He tucked the letter under his waistcoat, close to his heart, and he went to his father's office, determined.

"I want to participate in the Assembly," he said before his father had even looked up from his desk. King Clement raised his head.

"Concentrate on the wedding," he replied. "You have enough to do."

"You're the one who wants me married," said Dash. "You plan the wedding. I want to do something useful. I'm attending the next session with you. There are things I want to discuss with the House of Mortals."

His father smiled faintly. "You want to bring up your labor questions."

Dash lifted his chin. "What if I do?"

"You'll have a riot on your hands," said his father. "The issue is volatile, and you have no experience with politics. I can't let you have the floor."

"Maybe not right away," said Dash. "But eventually, I *will* have the floor."

"When I die and you take the throne, you mean."

"I'm coming with you, Father. I'm not going through with this wedding if I can't have something out of it."

"It's a little late for demands, son. You're already betrothed." The king considered him. "Still, it's true, you ought to see how it's all managed. When you finish your studies at Coterie, you can begin attending sessions with me."

"I'm not going back to Coterie," said Dash. "I want tutors here at home. And I'm not waiting. I want to see how things work *now* —"

"All right, all right," said his father, waving him off. "Tutors, Assembly sessions. Make of your youth an endless parade of isolation and aggravation, if that's what you wish — just go and be angry and passionate somewhere else, would you? I'm busy."

Dash left him, satisfied.

Her dad and Sharlyn kept their word. A few days after their meeting, Ella rode with them to Practical Elegance on the Avenue. Her dad showed her every new product in the store and told her which ones she could expect to see in progress at the Ragg Row workshop. Reversible coats with detachable sleeves, adjustable boots that went from thigh to ankle height, scarves that doubled as hunting nets — even a bright yellow children's jumpsuit that had been treated with a secret compound sourced from the mines of Crimson, to make it glow.

"So parents can find their children more easily in crowds," said her dad proudly. "Part of our new line of gear for the All-Tyme Championships this summer."

Ella fingered the paper tag that was pinned to the little suit. Seven hundred nauts. And they'd have to raise it to nine hundred, according to her business proposal. For a moment, looking down at the price, Ella doubted that her plan would ever work.

But the quints around here could pay anything.

Ella gazed around the shop at the words that were painted above the various sections. *The Authentic Equestrian. The Authentic Sailor. The Authentic Mountaineer.*

"What's all that about?" she asked Sharlyn. "The authentic stuff?"

"It's important to give customers something more than a product," said Sharlyn, obviously pleased to be asked the question. "When they shop at Practical Elegance, they're not just buying quality goods. They're buying an identity."

"An identity?"

"Wearing our clothes, they can imagine themselves as true athletes — true survivalists. If we can give them that feeling, then we'll have customers for life."

Ella looked down at the paper tag. "So . . . what if we shifted our identity a little bit?"

"In what way?"

"What if we tried making people feel like they're not just athletes and survivalists — they're also good?"

"Good at what?"

"No, *you* know," said Ella. "Kind. Virtuous. That sort of good. What if we could make them feel like every time they spend money with us, they're saving people's lives?"

Sharlyn looked curious. "Go on."

"We're using Shantung now," said Ella as the idea began to flesh itself out in her head. "It's costing us more, so we want customers to pay more for it, right?"

"Yes . . ."

"So we could sew a tag or sear a stamp onto all of our products that include Shantung silk. A symbol that shows that *this* silk is made by fair labor, so it's special. Then everyone would be able to see, when the customers are wearing it, that they're the sort of people who really care about the poor. Basically, we give them bragging rights. Let them show off how generous they are."

"Interesting." Sharlyn tilted her head. "That's very, very interesting."

Upstairs in the privy, Ella changed her clothes and let her hair down. When she emerged, Sharlyn looked with surprise at her faded old traveling outfit.

"You changed," she said, failing to keep the disapproval out of her voice.

"It's to wear in the garment district. I'll catch a public carriage from here — there's one in twenty minutes. How'll I get into the workshop? The manager won't recognize me. Can you write me a letter?"

"We'll visit the workshop together."

Ella rejected this. "If I show up in a plush carriage with you, nobody in that workshop will talk to me. I mean, they'll *talk* to me, but only 'cause they're scared. They'll think I'm just a quint." She paused. "I mean, I'll be intimidating. I need to look like I belong."

"You may have a point," said Sharlyn. "But you can't go to Ragg Row alone. Quintessential is not Fulcrum. You'll be targeted and robbed."

Ella held up rough fingertips to silence her. "I memorized the carriage route last night. I know what I'm doing."

When Sharlyn would not give in, Ella appealed to her dad and he backed her. But Sharlyn looked unsettled as she wrote Ella a letter of admittance to the workshop.

"Be careful," she insisted. "I don't care how experienced you are — you go straight there, you come straight back. I want you here again by noon."

"It's nearly an hour's ride," said Ella. "I'll need time for the inspection, and to interview the employees, and to ride back. I'll be here by the time you close at six."

Reluctantly, Sharlyn agreed. Ella was off.

Dash

THAT morning, Lavaliere stayed behind from school, and he took her to Farthingale's to let her choose her wedding jewels. Scribes followed their carriage like a pack of starved hounds, but Dash's new bodyguards kept them well back. The one benefit of this despicable betrothal was that the king's guards no longer followed him, and Dash was allowed to choose his own protectors. He selected the guards who had cared for his mother, and chose Tanner as his footman.

In the carriage, Lavaliere leaned back against the cushion beside him, eyes closed. She still looked wrong to him, Dash thought. He couldn't understand how a person's face could be so different, out of nowhere.

He sat up at the sensation of the carriage coming to a halt. Tanner opened the door; the guards blockaded a path into Farthingale's. The scribes shouted from beyond them.

"When is the wedding, Your Highness?"

"Will you be married at sea, like King Phillip? End the curse the way it began?"

Tanner went before them to open the door into Farthingale's, and the guards shut the scribes out to wait on the Avenue. Lavaliere reviewed the offered jewels listlessly. Every few moments, she winced and pressed her fingertips to her temples.

"Are you ill, my lady?" asked the clerk who attended her. "May I get you anything?"

"No," she said with a glance at Dash. "It's only the scribes. I suppose I'll have to get used to their shouting." She turned her attention to a sapphire cluster.

A small girl who was in Farthingale's with her mother approached the royal couple with a flower. She curtsied prettily and offered the flower to Lavaliere. "I want to be a princess just like you," she said.

Lavaliere took the flower and kissed the child's head, and the little girl grew rosy and ran back across the shop to her mother. The lady bowed her head to Dash, and he felt sick. This was just the start of it. Little girls all over Blue, rich and poor alike, would want to be Lavaliere. They'd admire her. Love her. Copy her.

Ella came into his head with sudden force. *They copy you, you mean.*

She was right. They would copy Lavaliere not because she was a Jacquard, but because she was his betrothed. He was giving her the stage. He could choose what kind of role she would play.

He could choose his own role too, he realized slowly. He could lead the scribes in any direction. He didn't have to be just Dash the Betrothed while he waited for his father to give him a chance in the Assembly — he could do more. He could start the fight now. Just as Ella was doing.

He leaned against one of the jewelry counters, watching Lavaliere and thinking.

Once she selected her jewels, they returned to the carriage, scribes shouting at them all the way. Lavaliere waved, giving them a glimpse of a lavish ring that she had chosen, and then she held out her hand for assistance at the carriage door. She leaned heavily on Tanner while Dash studied the scene before him.

Lavaliere and her jewels did not matter. But there were things that did. People didn't hear about those things because the scribes paid no attention to them.

But they would. If he led them to things that mattered, then they would attend.

He beckoned for Tanner as an idea began to take shape.

Ella

Ella disembarked from the carriage and looked quickly around to get her bearings. This part of the city reminded her of Fulcrum; all dingy gray buildings with few windows, like prisons. The people going into them wore patched clothing and tired expressions; their postures suggested they had long since given up dreaming about another life.

The Practical Elegance workshop on Ragg Row was not far from the riverfront. Ella made her way down the docks and past the cargo boats, where laborers unloaded great boxes of raw wool and live

Prism-silk pupas that still had to be boiled. Ella cut up Knot Street and across Cobbler's Alley, toward her destination.

When she reached Ragg Row, her heart began to pound. She walked along the squalid street, packed from end to end with workshops, each one butting up on the next, four and six stories high. She saw Shantung Silkworks, smaller than some of the others but with more windows, and then Garter Woolmakers, vast and soot-blackened, eating up almost the rest of the block.

There, across from Garter, was the smallest building on the street, with the newest bricks. *PRACTICAL ELEGANCE* read the sign above the narrow front door, and Ella hurried toward it, digging into her bag for her letter from Sharlyn.

Dash

THE carriage left the Avenue but did not go west to the Jacquard Estate. Instead, it went east toward Arras Wood and the Thread River.

"Why are we going this way?" asked Lavaliere, frowning as they came to the northeastern edge of the wealthy neighborhoods of Quintessential.

"It's a surprise," Dash said.

They rode through the wood and over a bridge, passing the old bulwarks that had been built around western Quintessential during the time of the Pink wars. Beyond these military walls, the city landscape changed dramatically. Stainless, impressive grandeur gave way to seedy hovels. Moth-eaten rags were tacked over the windows like curtains; the windows themselves were just empty holes in the walls. The carriage traveled up onto the rutted embankment, and the wheels struck hard against every bump in the earth, rattling them.

Lavaliere sat flat against her seat, wearing an expression of terror.

"Where are you *taking* me?" she demanded.

"Just wait," said Dash, but he too was repulsed. He had never traveled to this side of the river except on journeys out of the city, and then the curtains of the carriage had almost always been pulled to spare him the view. The gutters flowed with filth, and the people who walked along them looked sinister to him. They bowed as the carriage passed them, but in spite of their show of deference, Dash feared them and the desperation with which they eyed the silver wheel spokes and the jeweled carriage door. His reaction embarrassed him — was he really afraid of his impoverished subjects? He imagined what Ella would think of him if she knew.

"I want to turn around," said Lavaliere.

"Why?" said Dash. "What's wrong?"

"Look outside," said Lavaliere. "*That's* what's wrong."

"This is for the wedding," said Dash.

At the mention of their union, Lavaliere calmed somewhat. She pulled the carriage curtains closed with two sharp jerks. "Tell me when we get there," she said, and she leaned back again with her eyes closed, wincing.

Ella

THE door of the Practical Elegance workshop stood open. A thin, gray-haired woman in a long apron guarded it, holding a charcoal stick in one hand and a ragged scroll in the other.

"Name?" said the woman without looking up. "You're late."

"Ella Coach," said Ella. "Earnest Coach's daughter."

The woman looked up, eyes sharp and fearful. "My lady," she said uncertainly.

"It's just Ella." She handed over Sharlyn's letter. "No one's in trouble, I promise — I just want to look around."

"I swear we follow every rule, my lady."

"Really, it's all right," said Ella warmly. "I'm not inspecting the people. I'm looking at the shop itself. I want to make improvements to it."

"Improvements?"

"The kind that might help people, I hope," said Ella. "It's for a school project," she added, to make herself sound less threatening.

The woman relaxed an inch and slid her charcoal stick into the pocket of her apron. She handed back the letter. "I'm Amice, my lady," she said. "I'll show you around the workrooms."

They visited a small room on the ground floor first, where laborers were busy at cobbling benches. It was nothing like Jacquard had been — the products Practical Elegance made were intricate and technical; they required a variety of materials and many kinds of skill. The tools and workstations were unfamiliar to her. Ella went into the room and smiled at the workers who glanced up. A few smiled back. She did not, after all, look particularly out of place, and they had no idea who she was.

She followed Amice between two rows of benches down to the far end of the room, counting the windows as she went. The space was small but not stuffy; it would be worse in summer, of course, but a breeze moved freely through the room, making it more comfortable than she remembered Jacquard being.

The stools the workers sat on, however, were wobbly and appeared uncomfortable. That could be remedied. She took out her papers and made a note, aware that heads turned surreptitiously toward her as she did so.

"Is that glove protecting your hand properly?" she asked a woman in the corner. "Do you need a new one?"

"Can't afford a new one," said the woman.

"Then you were asked to buy your own work gloves?"

The woman shrugged. "No one asked," she said, "but no one gave me any either."

Ella noted this too. "Tell me a little about the tools you're using," she said to one of the young men who was bent over a boot, struggling with an implement that looked a bit dull to Ella's eye. "Are they sharp enough? Strong enough?"

The young man looked suspiciously at her. "I'm doing the best I can," he said.

"I know." Ella pointed to the tool in his hand. "What's this? And does it work as well as you want it to?" The young man hesitated, then briefly named the things on his table and admitted that there were better tools available.

On her way back through the room, Ella moved slowly, studying each employee and trying to determine their ages. There were men and women both, cutting and hammering, most of them of an age to be at work. But there were a few, Ella thought, who were too young to be spending their days inside, making boots.

"How old are the youngest workers?" she asked Amice as they left the room.

"Fourteen, my lady."

That was a lie, Ella decided. The youngest was eleven, tops. His parents probably had no choice but to send him. Perhaps someone at home was sick, and the family needed extra money to pay for treatment. Or maybe the boy was orphaned. But child welfare was a larger issue, and one that Ella alone couldn't solve. It was a problem for the Assembly. The king. It was something that Dash would confront someday, she hoped. Some changes would have to be slow.

Ella inspected the rooms on the second floor, and the third. The top floor was a sewing room and held the largest number of workers. They were bent over long tables, some stitching together yellow fabric pieces that gave off a faint glow, others hard at work tatting the scarves that doubled as nets. The dye from the yellow fabric had a strong, unpleasant smell, and Ella's eyes smarted. She made a note of it.

A wet cough from the far corner of the room sent a chill up her spine. Ella hurried to the far corner, where the cough had come from. The sick woman was easy to find; she had her fist pressed to her mouth, and her face was as red as her hair from holding in the spasm. When Ella reached her, the woman could no longer hide it; she turned her head to the wall and coughed until blood spattered on the bricks.

Ella crouched behind the woman, who was panting, and she laid a hand on her shoulder.

"What's your name?"

"P-Pelerine."

"You shouldn't be working, Pelerine," said Ella very quietly. "You have to rest, or the roop won't get any better."

Pelerine gave her a wild look. "It's just a cold," she whispered, rubbing a handkerchief over the pink spittle on her lips. "Anyway, who are you?"

"Someone who knows what I'm talking about, hey?" said Ella. "You have children."

"Yeah."

"How many?"

"Three."

"That's three children who can't do without you," Ella said.

"They can't do without food either," said Pelerine bitterly, fishing a Ubiquitous acorn out of her apron pocket. She cracked it hard against the worktable in front of her, and it transformed into a lozenge. For a brief second, the lozenge sparked, and Ella reared back — the whole table was covered in thread that could easily catch fire — but Pelerine smothered the spark with her palm. She stuck the lozenge in her mouth and rubbed her burned hand on her apron.

"Makes my throat feel better," she mumbled. "I'll be fine now."

But she wouldn't. Ubiquitous lozenges only quieted the roop. They didn't cure it.

"Come with me," said Ella. "Bring your things. You're not in trouble, I just want a word."

She took Pelerine down to the tiny closet of a room that served as Amice's office. She confessed she was Earnest Coach's child, and she told Pelerine her history. The young woman stared at her in amazement.

"You really worked for Jacquard?" Pelerine asked when Ella was finished. "I've never been to the shop in Fulcrum, but the one here is a nightmare, hey? Twisted place. I worked there two years, then got lucky and got this job — it's leagues better here, I can tell you. Nicer place, better pay, shorter hours — everyone would rather be here."

Ella was unfathomably glad to hear it.

"How many people here have roop?"

Pelerine twisted her dirty handkerchief in her lap. "They'd hate me if I told you."

"How many?" said Ella. "Please. I won't let anyone starve, I *won't*. No one should die like this." She took out her purse and fished out the healthy stack of nauts that she had brought with her in case of finding sickness. She pressed the money into Pelerine's hand. "Here's my proof," she said. "I'll take care of you, all right? You go back to your cott and recover, and your job will wait for you. On my honor, it will. Tell me where you live, and I'll visit every week and be sure your children have what they need."

Pelerine stared down at the money.

Then, suddenly, she bent her head and wept.

"You're — like a fairy godmother," she choked. "Like a dream."

"I'm not," Ella whispered. "I should have come here months ago to see what I could do."

Pelerine didn't seem to love her less for this. She reached out and clutched Ella's hand. When she had recovered herself, she told Ella everything she knew about the people in the workshop who were sick and suffering. Ella took careful notes. This she would not discuss or negotiate. This would change tonight.

She sent Pelerine home. There was more to do here — she would come back tomorrow — but for now, she had enough to get started. Once out on the narrow street, she picked her way carefully over the broken cobblestones and down along Ragg Row to the next intersection. She was about to head for the wharf when she heard a man's rough, leering voice call to her from across the way.

"Didn't they want you at Practical Elegance, bobbin?"

Ella glanced up. A short man with bruise-colored bags under his eyes stood leaning against the corner of a building that consumed the whole next block.

The short man beckoned to her. "Looking for a job, hey, lovely?" he asked, baring his yellow teeth in a smile. "There's always room for talent at Jacquard."

Ella's stomach turned over. She looked up at the building across the road. Its walls were old and crumbling, and thick with grime, and it had almost no windows. From the outside, it was worse than the shop in Fulcrum, like a great stone tomb. She wondered just how bad it was within.

Some force within her compelled her to cross the road. She had to see it. See if it was really as bad as she remembered — or worse. She'd never have another chance to get inside this place.

"Yeah," she heard herself say, "I need a job."

"Name's Neats," said the man, thumping his chest. "You?"

"Kit," she said.

"Walk with me, Kit. Let's see if you're fit to be employed."

She followed him into the Jacquard workshop.

THE carriage stopped, and for the first time, he thought of turning back. He could imagine what lay outside, but he did not really know. It scared him.

He was sure it would scare Lavaliere. He was counting on her reaction.

"Are we there?" Lavaliere opened her eyes. "Finally."

Tanner opened the door, and Dash stepped out onto the dim, narrow street over which the Jacquard workshop loomed, a massive block of rotting, ominous stone. For a moment, he couldn't focus on anything but the assault on his senses — the sound of something dripping, the moisture in the fetid air, a pair of churls chewing some dead, rotten animal near the doorstep.

"What is that *smell?*" said Lavaliere from within the carriage.

Dash reached in for her hand, and Lavaliere stepped onto the street. Above the black door directly in front of them, the word *Jacquard* was painted in small red letters on the grimy wall.

"Surprise," he said.

"What is this?" Lavaliere stared at her surname. "Where are we?" She gazed without understanding at the enormous building before them. Around her, the scribes were equally confused.

"Is this where your mother is hiding, Your Highness?" ventured one of them.

"No, mule, it's the Jacquard workshop," scoffed a plump scribe. "Haven't you ever been in this district?"

Dash was surprised that any of them had.

Lavaliere's mouth, meanwhile, had opened in dismay. "You brought me to Ragg *Row?*" She looked terrified. Revolted. The scribes watched her every movement.

"This is our future," Dash said. "We should see it together." He glanced at the scribes. "I'd like a few of you to follow us inside." The scribes came back to life, shouting to be chosen.

"I'm telling my mother," Lavaliere said.

"Yes," said Dash. "Please tell her I'm interested in her life's work." It wasn't really a lie. He had no trouble saying it. He even managed a smile.

Lavaliere threw his hand away from her. Red-faced, she climbed back into the carriage and slammed its ornate door on him. This the scribes noted with glee, and Dash scanned the group of them to select his ambassador to the *Criers*. His eyes settled on the plump scribe who knew what a workshop was. She was busy looking up and down the street and taking notes on their surroundings rather than paying attention to Lavaliere's tantrum.

"What's your name?" he asked, nodding to her.

"Nettie Belting, Your Royal Highness," she said, stepping forward.

"You wrote the Coach story. The good one."

"Thank you, sir," said Nettie, looking flattered. At the mention of the Coach name, a few of the other scribes cocked their heads and did a bit of scribbling.

"What else have you written?" asked Dash. "Anything I'd know?"

"The Rapunzel story, sir. I interviewed her at the Fortress of Bole a few months back."

He remembered that one. On the whole, it had been a decent interview. Mostly substantial. Just a bit of gossip for dressing.

"Nettie," he said, "follow me." He beckoned to a few other scribes as well, and they hurried to attend him. Sure of his purpose, Dash marched up to Lariat Jacquard's workshop, with scribes right behind him.

NEATS beckoned Ella into a tiny, low-ceilinged entrance hall and locked the door behind them. He ducked into an open room with an oil lamp burning on the desk; the smell of its smoke did nothing to disguise the sour stink of sweat and mold that filled the air. He came out again with a ring of clinking keys and a shabby, poufy cap. "Put this on," he said, tossing it at her. "Keeps your hair from getting mixed up with the silk. We don't want polluted goods."

Ella loathed the thought of wearing it: Long ago, she'd gotten lice from one of these caps, and she'd spent nights in front of the fire, her mum picking through her curls strand by strand for every louse and nit. She'd always brought her own cap after that. Having little choice now, however, she donned the one Neats offered and tucked all her hair in. Her scalp crawled.

Neats walked her to the dark, narrow stairwell.

"What're your skills?" he demanded.

"Unrolling silk and spinning it."

"Your fingers are too big for unrolling."

"I have lots of practice."

"Good. One of our girls stopped showing for work. I need a replacement."

Ella hoped the girl wasn't dead.

"Let's go." Neats jerked his chin at the stairs. "Fifth floor. Haven't got all day."

Ella put her foot on the first wooden stair, which was water-stained and in danger of caving in. At the landing of each flight of rickety steps, they passed doors that were bolted and padlocked shut from the outside. Neats checked each lock, jingling his keys.

On the uppermost floor, he unbolted the door. The air that exhaled from the room was putrid with sickness. Ella looked in. It was a long, rectangular slab of a room with a few narrow windows so dirty that no sunlight broke through. Half of the chamber was packed close with people of all ages, kneeling on threadbare mats and spinning at their wheels, many of them smothering coughs as they worked.

The other half was full of children.

They sat beneath the windows at long, low tables heaped with boiled cocoons. None of them dared look at Ella, not even the little ones, who were tied tight to their chairs with short lengths of splintering rope.

Neats steered her to the end of the children's tables. She was the oldest among them by at least five years. Ella sat, trying not to disrupt the work of the girl on her left and the boy on her right. A dull knocking could be heard from the stairwell.

"Better see who's here," said Neats. He picked up a cocoon, dropped it on the table in front of Ella, and slapped her on the shoulder. "Now get to work." He left the room, shutting the door behind him. Ella heard the bolt on the outer door scrape as Neats locked them back in.

She looked down the table at the children in her row. The little ones seemed so uncomfortable, their bellies pressing the ropes, their skinny faces sweating in the shadowy light, their fingertips raw.

"Neats'll hit you if you don't start," whispered the boy next to her.

Ella looked around. "There's no floor manager up here?" she asked.

"Hasn't been one for months," the boy said. "But don't think about slacking. Neats is quick, and he'll be back."

Ella's fingers moved automatically, finding the end of the pulsing thread and prying it free, then ever so carefully guiding the tip of her finger along the fragile line of it, pulling it with one hand while her opposite fingers unrolled the cocoon.

A little girl at the next table began to cough. Her bony shoulder blades made dents in her loose brown smock. Ella crushed the half-unrolled cocoon in her fingers.

Why had she come here? What good could she do here? She had no authority to change Jacquard Silks, she couldn't make them stop this — she couldn't even admit she was here, or she'd be arrested for trespassing. Even if she could rally the workers and march them all out of here, what would be the real result? Homelessness and starvation?

The girl coughed again, smothering the wet noise in her arms. Down at the farthest end of the children's table, another child joined in the coughing fit, her stomach straining against the rope that held her in place as she seized. They were trapped. Just like she'd been.

And she could not rescue them.

Dash

It took several minutes for someone to open the front door of the Jacquard workshop. When he saw Dash's royal coat, the troop of scribes, and the uniformed guards, his eyes popped and he bowed low.

"Your Royal Highness," he croaked.

"Are you the manager?"

"I am, sir, I am — name's Neats, foreman here at Jacquard. How may I serve you, sir?"

"I want a tour of the premises. To better understand the business of my future wife."

"Yes, sir, of course." Still maintaining his uncomfortable bow, the man shuffled to the side to let Dash enter the building.

The place was narrow, dark, and damp, and smelled worse than the street outside. Mice skittered down the corridor ahead, but Dash made himself proceed in spite of his disgust. Nettie followed close behind his guards with the other scribes behind her, and Neats shuffled at their heels. One of the scribes peeled off from the group and left the workshop, holding his nose.

"Quite a few stages of silk production are handled here, sir, quite a few," said Neats, sidling in front of the guards to unlock a door. "In this room, you'll see our weavers at the looms, sir."

Neats pulled the door open. The long, narrow room that Dash peered into was dim and musty, filled end to end with looms. People hunched uncomfortably on low stools, leaning very close to their work to have a hope of seeing it.

"This isn't where the story's at," he heard one scribe whisper to another. "Who cares about dirty workshops? I'd rather see if I can get a word from Miss Jacquard." The other scribe nodded agreement, and the two of them backed out of the room.

Dash pointed to the windows, so blackened that they blocked daylight. "They're filthy."

"I'll have them cleaned, sir," said Neats at once. "Tomorrow."

Dash didn't see why they ought to wait. Neats had a dirty rag tucked into the back of his belt; Dash snatched it from him and went to the windows himself. He climbed onto a chair and drew the rag down a stripe of the first window. It barely made a difference. He spat on the rag and tried again, applying more pressure as he swiped at the dirt, and he was pleased to see a streak of bright glass appear as a result of his effort. He spat again and wiped another clean streak, and another. As he did, the sun broke through. The people at the looms looked up to see what had caused the rise in light. Their eyes fell on Dash and his guards.

The people's hands stopped moving on their looms. They stood, some of them with great difficulty, bracing their backs with their hands. They bowed to him.

Nettie scribbled furiously, sweating to catch every detail. Dash's voice failed him completely as he gazed down upon his subjects. What could he say to these people whom the Charmings had so long neglected? Nothing. Even the Charming Curse would not have known how to talk its way out of this. Only action mattered.

From his perch upon the chair, he spied another locked door at the far end of the room.

"What's that?" he asked, pointing.

"Another room, sir. For the boiling vats." Neats went and unbolted the far-end door.

Dash stepped down from the chair and followed. "Why do you lock your workers in?"

"It prevents theft, sir," said Neats. "Silk's precious, you understand. Some of it's Prism — plush as jewels. I also check their bags when they go. Employer's orders."

"Couldn't you hire more supervisors instead?"

Neats's eyes shifted away, and his already ruddy face turned blotchy. "True, sir, true," he muttered. He shoved open the door that separated the rooms, and now Dash knew why the air in the place was so moist; steam billowed from the open chamber, oppressive and hot almost to scalding. The workers here were mostly eclipsed by the fog, but Dash could see their chapped skin, red brows, clouded eyes. They dumped baskets of wriggling cocoons into the boiling water, and the water splashed back, burning them. They merely flinched and kept stirring.

Dash approached a boy who might have been nine at best.

"How old are you?" he asked, and when the boy saw his crest, he bowed low.

"Your Royal Highness," said the boy. "I'm —" He glanced up and saw Neats. "I'm fourteen," he finally said, trying to make himself look taller.

Dash did not contradict him. "Your name?"

"Singer, sir. Singer Mantle."

"My middle name is Mantle."

"I know, sir," said Singer.

"You go to school?"

"No, sir. My brother Raglan teaches me," said Singer. "He works upstairs, but sometimes at night, when he's not too tired, he reads to me."

"What does your brother do?"

"Spins, sir."

Dash pulled a twenty-naut piece out of his pocket and gave it to Singer, who was dazzled. "Take the day off," said Dash, and when Singer looked fearfully at Neats, Dash placed a hand on his small shoulder. "Your job is safe," he said. "I know your name. Go."

Singer bolted from the unlocked room.

"How many employees do you have here?" Dash asked as he strode out of the boiling room and back toward the entry corridor. The weavers watched from under hooded eyes as he passed.

"Close to six hundred, sir."

"How many under fourteen?"

"Oh, sir, I don't know exactly, sir —"

They left the looms, and Neats locked the door behind them. His hand shook; his keys jangled. Dash knew that the man was deciding whether to tell the truth.

Nettie's pen moved fast, giving him more courage.

"Don't lie," said Dash in the silence. "I'll go in every room. I'll see them for myself."

"Two — ah — two hundred," said Neats. "Roughly two hundred."

"How young is the youngest?"

Neats swallowed. "I can't say for certain."

"Where are they?"

"They're on the top floor, sir — doing simple stuff, I promise you. Once the cocoons are boiled, the little ones unroll them —"

"With their little fingers." Dash turned to Nettie, who was now the only scribe left with him. He didn't know when the others had gone, and he didn't care. If they couldn't see that this was a story, then they wouldn't know how to write about it anyway. "I'd like to see them, Nettie. Wouldn't you?" He strode to the stairs and climbed to the fifth floor, the stairs creaking beneath his weight as he went.

Ella

SHE took another cocoon from the table; this one she unrolled smoothly and put aside the fiber when it was done. Her fingers, now older and less practiced, were slow. Her fingertips tingled by the fourth strand, and she knew that if she pressed on, her old calluses would throb. She pulled a fifth cocoon from the pile, then turned her head at the sound of the lock and bolt being moved on the other side of the chamber door.

"You'll see them here, sir," came Neats's voice. But it was now a servile whine.

Prince Dash of the Blue Kingdom stepped into the doorway, glittering in the gloom. He all but filled the narrow frame, and he was too tall for the door; he had to duck to enter, with guards behind him, as well as a scribe. All of them turned toward the children, their faces grim.

He had come. He'd told her he would try. But he had really done it — he was here, he was *seeing* this. Relief flooded her so intensely that she almost lost her head and called out to him, but she caught herself just in time. If he saw her and spoke to her, if he made them notice her, then Lariat Jacquard would know she had been here and she'd take it out on Practical Elegance. Sharlyn was going to kill her, kill her, *kill her*. . . .

On the other side of the room, people stumbled from their spinning mats to their feet and bowed to their prince. Ella prodded the children on either side of her. "The prince," she whispered. They gasped and sprang from their chairs to bow, all except the littlest ones, who were held in place with rope. Ella stood and ducked her face, now grateful for the cap that covered her hair. She clasped her hands in front of her to stop their trembling.

Dash's heavy footfalls approached the children's tables, and Ella curtsied very low to hide behind the boy beside her. A short silence, and then — "I'm not sure this work is simple," he said in a voice more commanding than Ella could remember hearing it. "Here, Nettie. Try it."

Ella looked up from under her lashes and saw Dash toss a Prism cocoon to the scribe who was with him. Both of them attempted to unroll the silk, both without success. Dash fumbled with the fiber, his fingers too large and inexperienced to manage it. He pocketed his ruined cocoon, knelt beside the smallest girl, and tugged on the rope that bound her. "Does this hurt?" he asked.

The girl flicked her eyes to Neats. She shook her head.

Dash untied it anyway and threw the length of rope at Neats, who barely caught it.

"I want the children's names," said Dash, and Nettie obeyed at once, moving slowly along the tables as she collected personal information. Ella tensed when she drew near.

"Name?" Nettie asked her.

"Kit." She stared at the floor.

"Surname?"

"Don't know. Orphaned."

Nettie leaned closer. "There's plenty you could tell me, isn't there?" she whispered. "Meet me at the Hook and Eye when your shift is over? I won't put your name in the *Criers*."

Ella nodded to get rid of her, and Nettie moved on.

"Untie the rest," Dash said to Neats. "Now."

"If you please, sir, I'll be fired if I do, sir. My employer —"

"I'll speak with Lady Jacquard," said Dash furiously. "Tonight." He strode farther into the room, coming closer to Ella until he was level with her. She ducked her face completely, breathing hard.

"Open this," said Dash, nudging a locked door with his booted foot. Ella hadn't noticed this door at all, and she was surprised to see, when Neats got it open, that inside it was another workroom just as long and dull as the one she was in, full of more spinners on mats. She heard the crack of a Ubiquitous acorn as someone within took a lozenge. She expected Dash to enter and continue his inspection.

But he didn't. And when he suddenly turned back, she wasn't expecting it.

He caught her eyes and drew a sharp breath. She bowed her head, making the slightest *No* motion with her hand. He came closer anyway. She saw the toes of his boots in front of her.

"Why — are you here?" His voice was hoarse. "You're older than these children."

"Kit's new, sir," said Neats. "Just started today."

"I see," Dash said. Ella wondered what he thought she was doing. She'd probably never be able to tell him. From the adjoining workroom came the sound of another acorn cracking, as Neats shut the door between the rooms and locked it once more.

A moment later the prince was gone, with his followers behind him, and the door to the stairway was bolted shut again as well. When he left, no one sat. They looked at one another in wonder.

Then they began to murmur. For the first time since arriving, Ella felt something in the air that was not hopelessness or decay.

"What was that about?" asked an older girl who had a spinning mat across from the children's tables. She jerked her tanned chin at Ella, smiling. "He's lovely, hey?" she whispered. "Just like in the *Criers*. And he paid you attention, lucky."

Ella was hardly fit for speech. She drew a deep breath to control herself, but the stale air did nothing to help her. It smelled of sweat and spit and smoke.

Smoke.

Ella was not the only one who smelled it; several people in the room put their noses suddenly into the air like dogs.

Then the first scream came from behind the locked door.

Dash

THEY were on the fourth-floor landing. Neats was looking for the right key. Dash stood staring at the hinges of the door, his heart galloping. He had never expected to see Ella there. He had to invent an excuse to go back.

Then screams filled the stairwell. They were sudden and many; he started violently and looked above him, where the terror was coming from, and then the desperate thuds began. People were beating on the door of the locked workroom. Crying out for help.

"Fire," said one of his guards. "I smell it."

Dash ran up the shaking steps two at a time toward the door behind which Ella was trapped. He grabbed the padlock that held the bolt in place and turned to demand the keys from Neats.

Neats was gone. Only the guards were behind him — and Nettie, who looked frightened to death.

The screams in the locked room redoubled suddenly, now full of pain as well as fear. Frantic, Dash smashed the bottom of his boot against the padlock.

MOST of the workers ran for the door to the stairs. They crushed against it, banging and screaming, smothering one another. Only a few went to the door of the adjoining workroom and tried to smash the lock to let out those who were on the other side.

They had no heavy tools. Ella tried the lock with her fists and her feet, but she didn't have the strength to break metal. A man pushed her out of the way, a thick wooden pipe ripped from a spinning wheel in his hand. He smashed it frenziedly against the padlock, and others joined him, tearing pieces from their own wheels and beating on the lock until it began to give.

When it fell, the man lifted the bolt; the door slammed open and he was flattened by a stampede of terrified spinners from the other room. They stepped on one another, leaving bodies beneath their feet as they surged to the far door. Ella leapt onto the nearest table to avoid being caught in the undertow, and over the tops of their heads, beyond the door, she saw the fire.

It had consumed most of the wooden floor in the next room, cracked and devoured the spinning wheels, ignited the piles of silk upon the mats. People were crowded at the windows, trapped by the flames.

People on fire.

Jumping to the street.

Ella got her wits back. She ran atop the tables, kicking baskets of cocoons out of the way, until she came to the chairs at the end, where the smallest children were wriggling, crying, trying to untie their ropes. She dropped beside the first one, fumbling, clumsy — she couldn't do it fast enough — they would all die like this —

She grabbed her necklace. The call burst from her in a scream.

Serge

SERGE, SERGE, SERGE!

He gasped, shot through with cold terror, and leapt to his feet in Gossamer's bell tower, where some fifty fairies had gathered to discuss the Lariat Jacquard situation.

"Ella," he and Jasper said together.

"Everyone, come!" ordered Jasper, hurtling to the window.

Serge soared from the bell tower, following the pull of Ella's fear upon his heart. She was near. He only hoped she was near enough. He veered steeply downward toward the rooftops of the workshops below. The other fairies followed at once, and they sped, all of them, over the top of Knot Street and across Cobbler's Alley to Ragg Row, where Serge dove lower still, and turned.

They saw the fire from the end of the street.

"GO!" cried Serge, and the fairies rushed in as though they were themselves on fire.

Ella

FLAMES leapt in the adjoining doorway now. Tongues of it lashed into the workroom, reaching for the spinning mats. Smoke rolled in, acrid and black, and coughing fits joined the cacophony of screams. Scores of people pushed against the locked door to the stairwell, clawing and crying, while Ella's fingers moved, slick with sweat, on the knots that bound the children in their chairs. She could not fail. No shaking, no mistakes. Every knot she had ever untied had been for this. All around her, the freed children begged her for help; they needed comfort; someone had to tell them what to do next, but the only thing to do was run, and the door would not give.

Dash

HE smashed his boot against the lock again, cursing. Among the chorus of screams on the other side of the door, children were crying, their terrified keening unbearable to him.

"Stand back," said one of his guards, sword out. Dash stepped aside, and she bashed the lock twice with the hilt. It gave. The door slammed open, and a sea of screaming laborers crashed through it — the guard was buried underfoot on the stairs and Dash was shoved to the railing, Nettie beside him. It creaked against his waist, threatening to break and send him plummeting into the stairwell.

He struggled to get his left hand to the door. His fingers found the wooden bolt, which he seized in a grip like stone. The stairway filled rapidly, everyone pushing downward, everyone pounding together on the stairs. Wooden steps cracked and fell through; ankles were trapped by broken boards. Dash heard the railing split behind him — felt Nettie fall back. Before she could fall to her death, he grabbed her forearm in his right hand.

With a groaning heave like a ship at sea, the stairs collapsed.

Ella

THUNDER cracked that was not thunder; from the stairs came fresh screams. Ella's head snapped toward the door just in time to see people falling through the open entryway into the empty stairwell where stairs no longer stood.

No stairs. No *stairs.*

Only jumping from the windows was left.

Panic finally gripped her. She tugged in vain on the knot that trapped the very last child, blinded by the sweat that filled her eyes.

"Jasper Jasper Jasper," she sobbed. "Serge Serge Serge —"

Smoke darkened the room, even as the fire in the doorway flamed brighter, catching the first row of spinning mats in her room.

Serge

BLACK smoke billowed from the rooftop of the Jacquard building. Some mortals lay crumpled on the street like laundry; the few who had survived were moaning, broken. Two girls stepped together onto the sill of a fifth-floor window. They looked down in terror at the street — then, licked by flame, they screamed and leapt.

Serge shot toward one falling body, Gossamer toward the other — they caught the girls but had not enough wing strength to do anything but break the fall. Both fairies spiraled toward the street, barely holding on to those they hoped to save. The girls toppled from their arms and onto the cobblestones, screaming in terror — but alive.

Dash

HE dangled in the empty stairwell, gripping the bolt of the door with his left hand. His arms burned as though his muscles were tearing apart. Nettie had him by the right wrist, dangling lower than he. Her fingers were sliding. She wept. He tried to lift his arm with Nettie on it, but she was too heavy. His shoulder popped out of its socket at the strain, and he shouted.

Nettie cried out as one of her hands slid from his wrist, her nails tearing at him as she lost her grip. She screamed and dug into his wrist with her other fingers, catching hold again, but barely. And soon it would not matter. His left arm was trembling. Out of his control. His hand began to slip from the wooden bolt.

SERGE

MORE jumpers plummeted; more fairies went to them. Serge flew to the top-floor windows, blew them open with an outward thrust of his palms, and burst into the room. Smoke hung like a haze; he ducked low to get under it. In half of the room, flames leapt high. Spinning wheels cracked. Silk hissed.

"SERGE!"

Ella. She was crouched in the corner with a group of children who could not run away. In the open doorway near her, where there should have been a stairwell, there remained only a few broken boards, leading nowhere.

A hand gripped the bolt of the open door, but the fingers were sliding. In seconds, whoever was dangling there would fall.

Serge hurtled toward Ella, Jasper toward the slipping hand.

ELLA

SERGE'S face was the most beautiful sight of her life. Beside him, a fairy with dark blue skin held out her hand to the children.

"Hold on to me," she cried, and several grubby hands flailed to get into hers. She gripped the ones she could and snapped the fingers of her other hand. She and the children vanished.

Serge reached out his hand, and Ella pushed more children toward it. "Grab on to him!" she shouted. "Fast, fast —"

Three little hands touched Serge's, and he was gone.

THE fingers that caught his wrist were white and slim, but inhumanly strong. Jasper — the same fairy who had carried him to the rooftop on Sharp Street. Jasper seized hold of Nettie with his other hand, and he beat his great crimson wings, rising high enough to bring both Dash and Nettie parallel with the workroom door. Smoke came through it, burning Dash's eyes and throat, but Jasper swung him by his arm straight into the workroom.

He dropped to the floor. His shoulder exploded with anguish as the heels of his hands struck the boards. Orange light flickered, making hazy shadows everywhere; he squinted to see a cluster of children pressing toward the only window that had not been consumed by fire. Their small hands were grabbed by blue ones filled with sparkling dust. Fairy fingers snapped. Children disappeared. One of the fairies grabbed Nettie's arm, and she too vanished.

Jasper flew past Dash toward a girl in a cap who held a limp child in her arms. He pinned the limp child under one arm, used the other to grab a boy around the waist, and soared out the window as the older girl turned back to grab the last few hands that reached for her.

Ella.

"DASH!" she cried, and then she choked, coughing, and pointed beyond him toward the flaming mats. Dash looked behind him and saw an unconscious child buried under fallen chairs and nearly obscured by smoke. The boy appeared peacefully asleep, insensible of the piles of silk that burned ever closer around him.

Light flared suddenly, making the room a sun, and Dash looked up at the source. Above him, the wooden frame that supported the rooftop was aflame. A beam cracked from its place and fell. Children screamed. Dash rolled hard toward the unconscious boy, pain ripping through his shoulder as the burning beam crashed to the floor alongside him.

Ella

SHE pushed the last two children toward the wall to avoid being smashed by the beam, but she could not spare them pain — the fire was too close now. Visible waves of heat undulated in the air. The little ones screamed, and so did Ella — her eyes burned and blurred —

And then blue wings appeared. Blue hands were upon them. The children were gone. Ella pressed herself to the wall in terror as the flames from the fallen beam roared up and trapped her. Just feet away on the other side of the beam knelt Dash, dragging the unconscious boy out from under a pile of chairs. Using one arm, he pulled the boy's body close to him. Chunks of rooftop fell into the room, igniting the few mats that hadn't already burned. Dash curled himself over the boy as embers rained down on his head, and he moaned. Ella could not get to him, she could only get to the window, and she climbed onto the sill. It was burning now, the sill itself was burning — the bottom of her skirt was burning. She looked down at the street, and it did not look so far away, and the air outside was cold. The fire singed her legs. She leapt from the window of the Jacquard workshop.

Jasper caught her.

The last thing she saw as he bore her away from the blaze was the blur of Serge's wings as he hurtled past them toward Dash, dodging falling flames.

Serge

HE didn't dodge them fast enough.

When his left wing caught fire, he felt it in every part of himself, and he screamed, contorting as he reached out for the kneeling prince and the boy he was clutching.

The roof crumbled and caved in. Flaming beams tumbled toward the prince. Through blinding pain, Serge seized him by the sleeve and snapped his fingers.

The last three living creatures on the fifth floor of the Jacquard workshop vanished in a cloud of blue dust.

Ella

HER heart beat like a wheel in a rutted road, jarring her body with every uneven strike. Jasper set her on the cobblestones and extinguished what remained of the fire on her skirt, and then he soared once more into the burning building.

Above the narrow street, smoke had turned the sky black. Ashes fell like snow upon Ragg Row, where all was chaos. Bodies lying still. Bodies twitching. Bodies alive but burned beyond endurance. Children sobbing in the gutter across the road. Fire bells ringing and sailors from the wharf running, bearing buckets of river water, staring up at the blaze they could not reach.

"Raglan," screamed a boy. He knelt by a charred body that lay splayed upon the stones. "Raglan, get up . . ."

Ella hobbled to the boy and stooped behind him.

"It's dangerous," she choked, her voice dry and burned. "We have to get out from under the windows. Come with me."

"Raglan — Raglan —"

The boy buried his face in the dead man's chest and would not be moved.

Serge

He brought the prince and the child to the street and collapsed on the cobblestones.

"Your wing," cried Gossamer, flinging fairy dust at it. The flames sizzled and died, and Serge moaned. "Try to flutter," she said grimly.

"It feels — dead —"

"If you feel it, it's not dead."

Serge fluttered and roared at the pain of it.

"There are hundreds still trapped," she said. "The fire's still burning. Stay right where you are and help put out the blaze while we keep up the rescues." She raced back into the building.

Serge closed his fists to replenish his dust, and he summoned a wave of water. He sent it tumbling toward the flames.

Dash

A sailor took the unconscious boy from under Dash's arm and splashed water on his face. Dash looked wildly around him for the faces he knew. His guards. Nettie. Ella.

Clutching his dislocated shoulder, he searched the frantic street, calling their names, becoming more desperate as no answer came. At last he tripped over Ella, who knelt at his feet with her arms around a boy he recognized. Singer.

Ella looked up at Dash, her eyes bleary with exhaustion. "He won't leave without his brother," she said.

Dash knelt to pick up Raglan, but his shoulder flared with pain so acute that he shouted and grabbed it with his other hand. "It's out of joint," he managed. "I can't."

A sailor in the street dropped down at once beside him. "Your Royal Highness," he said. "Could I help?" Dash nodded, expecting the man to pick up the body. Instead, the sailor took Dash's upper arm in his weather-beaten hands. "I can put this back in," he said, "but it'll hurt. Bad. With your permission, sir?"

"Do it," said Dash, and he clenched his jaw and threw back his head, hissing as the sailor thrust his shoulder back into its socket with one agonizing shove. The haze of pain dimmed.

"Thank you," he said to the sailor. "What's your name?"

"Marl, sir."

"Marl — would you carry him?"

Marl picked up Raglan, and Ella helped Singer to his feet. As they limped away together, out of range of the fire, scribes moved in around the group of them, clustering close.

"Are you in pain, Your Highness?"

"What did you see inside?"

"GET BACK!" Dash roared, advancing on them with aggression he had felt for years and never used. The scribes scattered, yelping. "Look around you!" he shouted. "Help these people!"

The scribes stumbled away.

Ella

IF the fairies hadn't come, it would have been much worse. That was the only comfort she could give herself. Thanks to the fairies, in half an hour, every living worker had been evacuated from the Jacquard workshop. In an hour, the fire was out. It had destroyed the entire fifth floor and a section of the fourth. Families came running to find their own people. Wail after wail of grief pierced the air. Bodies were lined up like lumber along the street.

Soon more fairies arrived — many dozens of fairies — who took up the work of recovering bodies and assisting lost children and the wounded. Ella helped them however she could, and so did Nettie, who asked the victims gentle questions as she brought them water and bandages.

Dash remained across the road on a doorstep, holding Singer in his lap. Singer was motionless, his face buried against Dash's injured shoulder, and though Dash looked pained, he kept hold of the boy and did not move.

Ella found Jasper in the crowd and brought him to Singer's side.

"Hi, Singer," said Jasper, crouching down. "Ella told me about you. I'm going to take good care of you and get you something to eat."

He led the boy away.

"You're burned," Ella said. Dash's bare head was livid with a handful of small, bright red scorches. "I'll get ointment —"

"I'll be taken care of," he said flatly. "Don't waste the supplies."

Ella dropped down upon the step beside him. Together, they stared at the destruction before them. The dead had to be carried away. The orphaned had to be provided for. Workshop repairs would take months, and some who had lived through the fire would starve in a few weeks when they could find no other work.

"You were heroic," she said. "Saving that boy upstairs. He was awake when his mum came looking for him — I hope you got to meet her. She wanted to thank you."

Dash covered his face and began to cry.

Dash

ALL those people dead. His guards too. Dead. That was his fault — he'd killed them, bringing them here. Lariat Jacquard had killed them. He wept, and Ella hugged him close. Being near her again was such comfort — even here, in all of this. He put his arms around her and hid his face against her neck.

"It was terrible," he managed, his teeth chattering though he was not cold. He couldn't control it. "Even before the fire started. So much worse than I pictured."

"Yeah," she whispered. "But now you know. Now you *really* know."

He nodded and held her tighter.

When she suddenly pulled away, he looked up, confused, and was shocked by the sight of the king's carriage. It stopped before them in the street, and Dash was caught wet-faced and unprepared as his father descended.

King Clement strode to the doorstep and crouched before Dash, his face ashen. "You're alive," he said. He seemed not even to notice Ella. "The guards rode back to raise the alarm — they said you were in the fire."

"I was," said Dash, startled by this show of fatherly concern.

"What in Tyme's name were you doing there?"

"Yes, Your Highness," came a voice that chilled Dash's blood. "What *were* you doing there?"

Ella

LARIAT Jacquard's snarl took her so by surprise that she gasped. Lavaliere stood at her mother's side, her face bizarrely altered, staring at the wall above Ella's head. Tears had dried in tracks down her cheeks.

"Who destroyed my workshop?" Lariat's voice snapped like a whip. She turned her vicious eyes on Ella, just as men in guards' uniforms approached — but they weren't royal. They must have been Lady Jacquard's own security, and they hauled a struggling Neats between them.

"Your Majesty," said one of the guards briskly, bowing. "Your

Highness." He shoved Neats forward toward Lady Jacquard. "We found him hiding on a cargo boat at the wharf, my lady. Hoping to escape, no doubt."

"My lady," Neats whined. "I *told* them not to crack those acorns in the workrooms — I confiscated every single one I saw, and I sent the sick ones home when I heard them coughing. I swear on the Shattering, I did everything you asked me."

Lady Jacquard's eyes held their target. "*You,*" she said to Ella. "What was your role in this?"

Ella's chest constricted.

"That's only Kit, ma'am," sniveled Neats. "Just started working for you today."

"*This* girl got a job in my workshop today?"

"Yes, ma'am. I put her upstairs just an hour before the fire started."

"Where upstairs?"

"On the fifth floor, ma'am."

Lady Jacquard's face lit with triumph. Ella felt the noose slip around her neck.

"No." Dash leapt to his feet. "You *can't*."

"An *unbelievable* coincidence," Lariat Jacquard said, feasting on Ella with her awful eyes. She turned to King Clement. "This is Ella Coach. The girl who attacked Lavaliere at Coterie. I want her arrested for sabotage. And murder."

The king motioned for his guards.

"Get back." Dash pulled Ella to her feet beside him and put his arm tight around her. "Don't touch her."

His father waved his guards forward. Spaulder reached for Ella's arms, but Dash stepped between them.

"I'll fight you," he said recklessly. "I swear."

A few of King Clement's guards forcibly restrained him. The others tied Ella's hands and marched her away, while behind them,

Dash thrashed and swore and shouted for the fairies. Ella heard him calling Jasper's name, and Serge's.

"How dare you?" cried a familiar female voice.

Sharlyn stepped in front of Ella, stopping the guards' march. Ella sagged with relief.

"Where are you taking my stepdaughter?" Sharlyn demanded, her voice hard. "And why? There are laws, aren't there? Who ordered this arrest?"

"His Majesty the King," barked Spaulder. "Stand back."

Sharlyn took Ella by the shoulders. "Say nothing," she said. "Not one word. *Not one.* Do you understand me?"

Serge was with them in a flash, grimacing in pain. Half of one of his wings was charred coal black and ragged around the edges; ashes molted from it when it moved. "Ella," he panted. "It will be all right. I'll do everything in my power. I'll speak to your stepmother — we'll organize your defense. There are witnesses who know you didn't start it —"

"Clear the way!" The guards wrested Ella out of Sharlyn's grip and marched her onward.

They reached the barred door of a military detention carriage, where the guard on her left stopped short with a soft cry of surprise. "Look," he said. "Is that really . . ."

Spaulder turned back, and his heavy chin dropped.

"Skies," he said, his voice almost reverent. "It is. It's Queen Maud."

Dash

His heart leapt. His mother was here.

She wore the same servant's uniform that she had departed in, but at her arrival, the chaos of Ragg Row fell still. She ran from her carriage to her son and took his face in her hands, while the world around them watched her, riveted.

"Let him go," she said.

The guards obeyed her, and Dash stumbled free of their grip.

His mother searched his face with eyes that were swollen from crying, and then she gathered him to her and rocked him. He slumped. From the safety of her arms, he saw his father's awe-struck face.

"Maud," said the king in wonderment. "You read my letter?"

She let go of Dash and turned on her husband. "Don't think for one second that I traveled here because of it," she said. "I came because I saw, in the *Criers*, that without my knowledge or consent, my only child, who is not of age, is *betrothed*." She looked at Lady Jacquard as if she were a roach she had found on her pillow. "I arrived at the palace to be told that his life was in danger. Now I find guards assaulting him in the street when someone should be tending to him? Look at him, Clement. He's burned. Explain yourself."

The street was silent. The only thing moving was Nettie's pen.

"Take your daughter home, Lady Jacquard," said Queen Maud when the king said nothing. "I will take my son." She turned her back on Lariat. Dash had never loved his mother so much.

"Your Majesties," came a desperate voice from beside them. It was a thin man in fine clothes that sat awkwardly on him. Dash recognized the man — he'd met him at the ball.

"This is Ella's father," he told his mother. "Father arrested her, but she's innocent. He has to let her go."

Ella's father looked at him with grateful surprise and a measure of alarm.

His mother looked at him with curiosity. "Ella who?"

ELLA

THE guards loaded her into a detention carriage that smelled of vinegar, and they untied her hands before slamming the barred door shut and locking it. The wheels began to turn. They were really taking her to prison.

Dash broke from his parents and bolted toward her. "Stop!" he cried, but the carriage did not stop. He leapt onto the back lip of the carriage, which was barely wide enough for the toes of his shoes to find a perch. He grabbed hold of the bars — then groaned and let go with one hand. "There'll be a hearing," he panted through the window. "I can't make him listen — I'll come to see you —"

She grabbed his hand. The carriage thumped down hard into a ditch in the street. Dash lost his grip and stumbled back onto the cobblestones, and the carriage turned a corner, cutting him off from her view.

Ella sank to the floor and curled up on her side, too frightened and exhausted to pretend more strength than she had. She shut her eyes. The moment she did, harrowing images jumped into her mind, and she cringed against the horrors she could not unsee. Her eyes opened again, staring through the bars of her small jail, as the carriage rattled toward the prison that awaited her beneath the halls of the Essential Assembly.

SERGE

DUSK fell, and still they had not carried every body from the stairwell.

One hundred and seventy-one. That was the death toll. Some had burned, others had suffocated in the smoke. Several had been trampled underfoot. Many had jumped to their deaths. The rest had died in the collapse of the stairs.

Serge had never done work so terrible as moving the bodies. He had been too young to fight against the Pink Empire, but this, he felt certain, was as grisly a scene as any from the war. As he worked, he grew accustomed to the pain that shot through him every time he moved his wing. It was small penance.

He looked down at the body of the girl he had just carried from the stairwell. She was Ella's age, and he recognized her face. She had been one of Lavaliere's personal maids, but she must have lost her position and ended here. If only he had been paying attention, he could have helped her. Saved her.

"Meet me in my carriage," said a cold voice behind him. "Now. I'm owed an explanation."

Serge laid the dead young woman in the street, beside the others. He straightened her apron and brushed back her hair.

"I'm busy," he said.

Lariat Jacquard gave a laugh that would have frightened him a week ago. "How long have you been undermining me?" she asked very quietly. "How long have you been serving Ella Coach?"

So she had seen them together. She'd seen him fly to Ella's side. She wanted dirt on Ella now. He didn't have to be Jasper to know that.

He went back into the workshop without giving Lariat any answer. When she left, he did not know.

Several minutes later, Jasper joined him on the street. "She's going to hurt you," he said.

"Who, Lariat?" Serge shook his head. "She'll certainly try, but she hardly matters now."

Jasper pursed his lips. "I'm going to take a short trip," he said after a moment. "I'll be back in time for Ella's hearing."

"Why? Where are you —"

"Just trust me?"

Serge nodded, and Jasper lifted off. The dark sky absorbed him.

DASH

THE fire at Jacquard was news before the *Town Criers* even reported it. It spread rapidly outside of Quintessential and traveled up and down the coast of the Blue Kingdom, then beyond its borders.

Dash would answer no one's questions but his mother's. To her, in private, he opened up his heart. He told her of Ella and the ball, of their school project, of their feelings for each other. He told her of the terrible betrothal, and the workshop, and the fire.

His mother listened well into the evening, attentive to every word. When he was finished, she took up the sapphire ring that Ella had returned, and she gazed at it.

"How funny that it should be the same girl," she murmured. "And that her godfather should be Serge." She looked up at Dash. "You've known her a very short time, Dash, and the accusations against her are serious. Don't involve yourself unless —"

"She's innocent," he said. "And I —" He looked away from his mother's watchful face. "I need to visit the prison. If you ask Father to let me, he will."

"I'll speak with him."

But even when Queen Maud requested it, King Clement refused to allow Dash access to Ella. Furious, Dash shut himself up in his room.

He was surprised in the middle of the night by Serge, who entered his chamber invisible in search of certain evidence. Dash was still in possession of most of the Garment Guild records, and the fairy rifled through the crates until he found whatever it was that he needed. He also promised that, when Ella's trial came, he would be there to interfere if it was necessary.

The day after the fire, Nettie Belting's story broke. *Criers* boxes across Tyme were filled and refilled as everyone in every nation devoured the story behind the whispered rumor.

JACQUARD IN CINDERS
PRINCE CHARMING AND 600 LABORERS TRAPPED IN DEADLY BLAZE;
BLUE FAIRIES RACE TO THE RESCUE

It was a story both substantial and scandalous. Little children trapped in a burning building, the horror of death and destruction, heroic fairies, Prince Dash courageous, corruption at Jacquard, the arrest of Ella Coach, and the return of Queen Maud.

Dash read it, and his eyes jumped all over the page, afraid of what lies they might find. But along with the sensational details, Nettie had delivered all the depth he could have hoped. The conditions of the workshop were described — its locked doors and diseased quarters, its bound children and rotting stairs. No one who read the story could miss the truth: Lariat Jacquard was a monster, and nearly two hundred corpses lay at her feet.

The House of Mortals called swiftly for a hearing to determine Ella's role in the fire. Within a week, the hearing was organized. The day it began, thousands of laborers from all over the kingdom converged upon the government; they surrounded the walls, cursing and weeping, waving flags that read *FREE ELLA COACH*. The army forced them back to let the royal carriage through, and as it rolled along between their ragged bodies, the people chanted Dash's name. Not his father's.

His mother pressed his hand.

The Assembly Hall where the king presided was a great, round chamber with a vaulted ceiling made of pale blue glass that was cut like an enormous jewel. Tiers of box seats, silk-curtained and velvet-lined, ringed the curving walls: one seat for each member of the Assembly. At the top sat the House of Magic — fairies, Hipocraths, and a few Kisscrafters of unusually significant power. Immediately beneath them sat the most influential members of the House of Mortals: the Garters and Gussets, the Batiks and the Panniers, the Trusses and the Farthingales. Beneath these seats, in descending rings of boxes of decreasing size, were those whose wealth did not reach quite so far. In the center of the bottom rung sat Lady Shantung. Only the gallery benches were below her.

Across from this theatre of power, raised up separately on an astonishingly high blue marble dais, three grand seats glimmered beneath a mist of magic light. On the left sat Exalted Nexus Maven, First Chair of the House of Magic. On the right sat Lariat Jacquard, First Chair of the House of Mortals. In the center shone the royal throne, ornate with jewels and silver, with a back that stretched up as high as three tall men. At the sides of this ostentatious display, two smaller thrones awaited the prince and queen.

Dash took his place on the right, between his father and Lady Jacquard. His mother stood on the left, between her husband and Nexus Maven. The Exalted Nexus inclined her head to Queen Maud, but the queen neither looked at the woman nor returned her gesture.

King Clement sat. So did the rest of the Assembly. The hall fell silent, but from outside, the ceaseless chanting of the labor class was clearly audible. Already, the Relay had begun to record the session: He sat in a trance at his table upon a small platform near the Nexus's side of the dais, his Exalted amulet resting upon his doublet, his hand moving faster than humanly possible across sheets of special parchment as he communicated every detail of the hearing back to the Exalted Council.

"Bring in the accused," bellowed King Clement.

From between the low gallery boxes across from the dais, the doors of the prison cellar opened. Dash's heart lurched. Half a dozen unnecessary soldiers bullied Ella to the center of the floor, where two unadorned chairs waited, facing the dais. Dash was startled by the sight of her in prison clothes and chains, looking as much like a criminal as Lariat Jacquard could have wanted.

Ella glanced back over her shoulder and up into the lofty gallery. She recoiled from the hundreds of hard faces that stared down at her. When she turned again, her eyes found Dash, and he thought he saw, just for a second, how frightened she was — and then the guards shoved her into her seat and bound her to it, as if she were any threat. Her stepmother, Lady Gourd-Coach, stepped forward from the gallery and took the seat beside Ella. Behind her, Ella's father sat in the front row, visibly sweating. His stepchildren flanked him, grim-faced.

King Clement opened a small, gilt-edged scroll and raised his voice above the sounds of the furious city outside. "In the case of the Jacquard fire, Elegant Herringbone Coach is charged with trespassing, sabotage, and the murder of one hundred and seventy-one citizens of the Blue Kingdom. If guilty, she will be sentenced to life imprisonment. Elegant Herringbone Coach, how do you answer the charges laid against you?"

Ella's eyes glittered as if they still reflected fire.

"Not guilty, Your Majesty," she said in a soft, subdued voice that was unlike anything Dash had ever heard from her. Even her southern accent had all but vanished.

"She lies," said Lady Jacquard, settling back in her chair. "Bring in Rolo Neats."

SHE sat bound to the chair as Neats was marched into the chamber. She tried not to feel the hundreds of eyes that glared down on her, or the ropes that cut into her arms, or the sweat that rolled down her neck. From outside, she heard the sound of Dash's name being called by the people. She heard her own name too among the cries. No matter what lies Lady Jacquard told, the people of Blue knew the truth.

But they couldn't keep her out of prison.

Sharlyn had been permitted to visit the prison as her advocate — just once, and very briefly. Before their time together expired, she made Ella swear to be composed. She was not to speak unless she was questioned, and then she was to speak properly, with not one breath of insolence.

The guards released Neats's arms and stepped back, leaving him so close to Ella's chair that she could smell the filth of him.

"Mr. Neats, you oversee my Quintessential workshop."

"S'right, ma'am." He bowed low to Lady Jacquard. "Going on eight years now."

"During that time, has there been a single death there?"

"Not one," said Neats. "You take good care of your people. No one could be more grieved by the deaths of those laborers than you."

Lady Jacquard touched her heart. "Thank you," she said, and Ella had to fight to hide the outrage she felt. "Please tell the Assembly what happened on the day of the fire."

"This girl said she needed a job," said Neats. "Said she had experience unrolling cocoons, so I put her on the fifth floor. Then the fire started."

"How soon after she reached the fifth floor did the fire begin there?"

"Within an hour, my lady."

"And you had no idea that this girl was Ella Coach?"

"She lied, ma'am. Said her name was Kit."

Lady Jacquard raised her eyes to the Assembly. "It cannot be coincidence," she said. "Ella Coach gives a false name, sneaks into my workshop, and in less than an hour a fire breaks out right beside her? Ella Coach set that fire. She despises me, as she despises us all. At the royal ball, she called us murderers. White-hearted witches. And why?" She lanced Ella with her eyes. "Because I gave her mother twelve years' employment. A heinous crime indeed."

Ella clamped her teeth together hard and thought of Sharlyn's warnings. *She will bait you. Expect it. If you rise to it, she wins.*

"She trespassed on my property," Lariat went on, passing pale fingers through her sharp fringe and smoothing it aside again. "She lied to gain access to a workshop where she knew that she would never be allowed if she gave her real name. Once inside, she set fire to it, purely to punish me. The lives of nearly two hundred people were nothing to her." She turned to the king. "Sir, I am ready to call my next witness."

"Very well," said King Clement. "Lady Gourd-Coach, have you any response before we proceed?"

"I have, Your Majesty. Thank you."

How Sharlyn could sound so calm, so nearly cheerful, Ella did not know. Her stepmother hefted a dense pile of parchment from the sleek bag she kept beside her, then stood and stepped forward. "Lady Jacquard, you claim that if Ella had given her real name, she could not have gained access to your workshop, yes?"

Lariat barely inclined her head.

Sharlyn arranged her pince-nez and consulted her stack of parchment. "But she *did* give her real name when she worked as your employee," she said. "Here are the labor records filed in the year 1083. E. H. Coach, Fulcrum. She was eleven."

The Assembly murmured, and Ella's breath quickened. She hadn't known Sharlyn was going to tell them this. She permitted herself a brief look at Dash, who was staring at her.

"Here is the file from 1082," Sharlyn went on. "When Ella was ten. In fact, Garment Guild records show that you employed Ella Coach regularly starting in the year 1076. When she was four."

Dash's face slackened.

"You're confused," said Lady Jacquard. "That's her mother's name listed in the files."

"Her mother never took the Coach name. Here it is: E. Herringbone, listed separately, also at the Fulcrum location."

"And how do we know these records are legitimate?" Lady Jacquard demanded.

A flush rose in Dash's cheeks, and Ella knew at once how Sharlyn had gotten the labor files. He glanced up to his left, and she followed his gaze to the top of the chamber, even above the House of Magic's high seats. There, perched in a ring around the cut-glass ceiling, were a host of Blue fairies, including one with a plume of white-blond hair that waved perfectly over one eye and a wing with its top charred black.

Beneath her collar, against her skin, the charm on her necklace grew warm.

"I assure you, these are official records." Sharlyn handed the files to a page, who ran them up the steps to the royal seat for the king to review. King Clement flicked through the evidence, then turned furious eyes upon his son.

"For seven years," said Sharlyn, her voice as even as a blade, cutting through the noise in the chamber, "Ella Coach unrolled cocoons in a Jacquard workshop. She spent much of her childhood bound to her chair by people such as Rolo Neats, just as she sits bound before you now."

The noise in the Assembly Hall redoubled. Snatches of conversation could be heard, some sympathetic, others unpleasant.

Disbelieving. Amused. In the highest mortal tier of the chamber, someone laughed.

"Thank you for further proving my point, Lady Gourd-Coach," said Lady Jacquard. She wasn't as good as Sharlyn at hiding her real feelings; her smile was too sharp to be genuine. "It is now clear that Ella Coach's grudge against me is far longer and more personal than I previously knew. The fire was her vengeance."

"Rolo Neats," said Sharlyn. "How did the fire begin?"

"I was on the stairs," he said. "And I heard —"

"Did the fire start on the stairs?"

"Well, no —"

"So you don't know how it began."

"I heard screams," he insisted. "From the fifth floor, where Ella Coach —"

"You saw nothing," said Sharlyn. "Correct?"

The man looked nervously up at Lariat. "She's in Jacquard one hour, and a fire starts," he said. "S'proof enough, isn't it? What are the odds?"

"They are twelve thousand to one," said Sharlyn. "Ella Coach has spent nearly twelve thousand hours of her life in a Jacquard workshop. That is twelve thousand opportunities to set fires — and yet, somehow, no fires were ever set. Still, you would swear that she set *this* fire, although you did not see it and although she was locked in the same room with it, unable to escape, on the fifth floor of the building?"

"I'm just telling you what I know!"

"Where did you go when the fire broke out, Mr. Neats?"

"I ran from it like anyone would."

"His Royal Highness did not run."

The Assembly Hall went quiet. Neats's chin trembled. Dash gazed straight ahead, face flushed. On the other side of the king,

Queen Maud stared at Rolo Neats as though she would have preferred him dead.

"Did you unlock any doors before you ran?" Sharlyn demanded.

"There wasn't time."

"And yet there *was* time for His Royal Highness to return to the fifth floor without you, risking his life to free those who were trapped there, although he had no key. Because when you ran, you took your keys and left your prince behind. Didn't you?"

The queen made a low noise of fury. Neats looked to be on the verge of blubbering.

"Why *were* those doors locked, Mr. Neats?"

"To prevent theft!"

"Are there no floor managers to oversee that?"

Neats glanced at Lariat in terror. "There have been, in the past. But they've gone off and left me on my own, see, and I've had to make do by myself."

"For how long?"

"Going on a year," whispered Neats.

"A year?" Lariat Jacquard leaned forward. She looked genuinely surprised. "Neats, it is your duty to hire a full staff. You have been given adequate funds with which to do so."

Neats squirmed, still blinking back tears. "I tried," he whined.

"I would venture a guess," said Sharlyn to Lariat, "that rather than hiring an appropriate number of supervisors, your Mr. Neats has been pocketing two or three salaries in addition to his own, and locking the doors to make sure he wouldn't get into trouble for it."

Sharlyn turned her back on the royal dais to address the full Assembly.

"Look at him," she said. "Here is Lady Jacquard's great witness to Ella Coach's guilt. A man who did not see the fire start. A cheat who embezzled from his employer. A beast, who, to save his own skin, left Prince Dash to act as foreman and unlock those rooms. Rolo Neats abandoned six hundred people in a burning building, and near two hundred of them died the most gruesome deaths that I have ever seen."

"And *that*," said Lariat Jacquard, looking relieved, "is entirely on his head. I had no idea that he was locking those doors!"

"If you did not know for a year that your foreman was placing your employees in danger, then that is very much on *your* head, Lady Jacquard," said Sharlyn. "You own Jacquard Silks, and you hired Mr. Neats. Your neglect made his abuses possible."

Lady Jacquard's expression was smooth as wax, except for her eyes. They gleamed with hate.

"I am ready for the next witness." Sharlyn took her seat beside Ella and removed her pince-nez. Her hands were steady, her face implacable, and if Ella had not been bound to the chair, she would have flung herself at her stepmother and hugged her tight.

Serge

EVERY Blue fairy who had witnessed the Jacquard fire had been summoned to the hearing by the House of Mortals. They perched at the height of the chamber, looking down on the proceedings in silence. Serge watched as Lavaliere was brought forward as the next witness.

"Where's Jasper?" whispered Carvel, beside him. "I thought you said he'd be back."

Serge could only shake his head. It had been a week, and Jasper had not returned from wherever he was.

"Where's Jules?" whispered Thimble on his other side. "She's never missed anything this sensational. Do you think she's afraid to show her face?"

Serge thought exactly that.

"She attacked me in the changing room at school," Lavaliere was saying now, in a voice that trembled for effect.

"Show the Assembly the injury that Ella Coach inflicted," said Lariat.

Lavaliere held out her forearm and pushed up her silk sleeve. Four long, red scabs glared from her skin. The Assembly gasped, and she swayed on her feet. A guard caught her elbow.

"My poor darling," said Lariat. "Please tell the Assembly what happened next."

"She pushed me down and I went unconscious," said Lavaliere, leaning against the guard for support. "I've always been afraid of her, but . . ." She paused.

"Yes?" her mother prodded.

"I tried to be kind. Because . . . Ella is so new here. Now I wish I'd spoken sooner. If only I . . . If only I had shared my fears . . ." Her eyes closed. "All those people might still be alive," she managed, and then her voice broke, and she began to weep.

"Ella Coach uses violence and intimidation to achieve her goals," said Lady Jacquard, gesturing toward her daughter. "She targeted Lavaliere, who was alone and vulnerable. She attacked the laborers in my workshop, who were unaware of a trespasser in their midst. She is a bully who takes advantage of those who are weaker and cannot defend themselves."

Serge's lungs constricted suddenly with fury that did not belong to him. It was Ella's emotion: She was close to bursting with anger. In reply, his heart grew warm within his chest. It filled him with a bittersweet gladness he could hardly contain.

I'm here with you, he thought. *Be calm. Take one deep breath, and then another.*

He saw her shoulders relax. Saw her fists uncurl. He only wished he could as easily soothe Prince Dash, whose face was mottled with all the fury that Ella could not betray.

"Lady Gourd-Coach," said the king. "Have you any reply?"

"Indeed, Your Majesty. Thank you." Sharlyn rose, and the Assembly leaned forward in their boxes — hoping, Serge was sure, for another sensational interrogation.

"Miss Jacquard," said Sharlyn. "Who witnessed the scene between you and Ella Coach?"

"Dimity Gusset found me bleeding on the floor."

"But who witnessed the attack itself?"

"Ella caught me alone," said Lavaliere. "She didn't want witnesses."

"I ask you again: Who witnessed the scene between you and Ella Coach?"

Lavaliere glowered at her. "No one," she murmured, holding out her arm again for a moment before it fell limply to her side. "The proof is here."

"That only proves you were scratched," said Sharlyn. "Not who scratched you. Why, it could have been anyone. You could have done it yourself."

"Ridiculous," Lavaliere mumbled. "Why would I hurt myself?"

"You seem unwell, Miss Jacquard," said Sharlyn. "Even faint. Are you in pain?"

Serge saw Lariat's expression freeze. Saw her hands clutch at the arms of her chair. "Those questions do not pertain to this hearing," she said. "Your Majesty?"

"Lady Gourd-Coach, have you further relevant questions?" asked the king.

"No, thank you, Your Majesty."

Sharlyn took her seat as a guard supported Lavaliere to the top of the dais and helped her to sit beside her mother. Her head lolled to one side and rested against Lariat's shoulder. "There, there," Lariat murmured. "Sit up, darling."

Lavaliere dragged herself into an upright position and leaned back.

"With his Majesty the King's permission," said Lady Jacquard, "I would call him for questioning."

DASH

A shocked murmur raced through the Assembly, and Dash whipped his head toward his father, but the king looked unsurprised. Apparently, he'd known this was coming. He rose from his seat, golden in his official uniform, the crown shining upon his blond head.

"You have my permission, Lady Jacquard," he replied.

The lady stood and curtsied. Dash sat between them, rigid.

"Is it true, sir," said Lady Jacquard, "that you have questioned Ella Coach's loyalty to the Blue Kingdom?"

"Yes," said King Clement.

The wind went out of Dash as surely as if his father had struck him. Was this what he would do to save the crown? It was one thing to arrange a bad marriage, but to convict an innocent person of a crime she hadn't committed — it was going too far. The throne wasn't worth saving if it had to be saved like this.

"And is it true," said Lady Jacquard, "that you asked His Royal Highness Prince Dash to keep an eye on Ella Coach's activities at school, in order to discern whether she might be, in fact, a threat to the nation?"

"Yes."

"And what did you discover?"

King Clement cleared his throat. He opened his mouth.

Dash spoke forcefully, the only word that came to him.

"No." He was on his feet. "*No*," he said again, louder.

"I have no choice," his father whispered, barely moving his lips, as every person in the House of Mortals leaned toward the royal seat, trying to hear him. "The kingdom will be hers if—"

"It's already hers," Dash retorted, his voice rising with every word. "You do everything she says. Just put the crown on her head and call it finished."

There were gasps. Shouts of muffled laughter.

King Clement blanched. "Be *silent*," he commanded. "Or be carried from this chamber."

Dash glanced at Ella, resumed his seat, and did not move.

"What did you discover, sir," Lady Jacquard continued, "about Ella Coach's loyalties?"

"Clement," Dash's mother said softly.

The king looked from Lariat's face to Queen Maud's. The queen held his gaze for a long, silent moment.

"Your Majesty?" prompted Lady Jacquard.

King Clement's eyes stayed fixed on his wife. "I have determined," he said, "not to divulge any information that I may — or may not — have learned about Miss Coach."

Lariat's mouth opened.

"It is not in the best interests of the country's security," King Clement continued, "to discuss such matters in an open hearing."

"But your knowledge of Miss Coach's activities may have a significant bearing upon the outcome of this hearing," said Lariat angrily. "Do you intend to let a murderer walk free?"

"I will answer no further questions on this subject," said the king, and he sat down.

Queen Maud looked at Lariat and smiled.

"Your Majesty," said Sharlyn, rising. "If you won't testify, will you allow your son to do so? He is an eyewitness to the fire, and the only person in this room who saw Ella Coach before, during, and after the blaze. It seems only just that he should speak."

King Clement's handsome face shifted; malice lit his eyes. Ella saw in a moment what a terror it would be to have him for a father. "You dare suggest that I am unjust?" he said, his voice rough. "No member of my family may be summoned to speak in any hearing without my consent, and I do not give it. That is all the explanation you require."

"However," said Sharlyn, hefting a wide, leather-bound volume from her bag, "there is a loophole." She opened the large book, and Ella squinted to see the gold-lettered title.

His Majesty's Government

Charter of Assembly Regulations

"Here," said Sharlyn, balancing the charter with one hand and raising her pince-nez with the other. "Statute thirty-eight. 'In any trial wherein the defendant faces capital punishment or life imprisonment, a member of the House of Mortals may call for a vote to demand the testimony of a royal family member, if such testimony is believed to be necessary.'"

"But you are not a member of this Assembly, Lady Gourd-Coach," said the king. "You are not even a sworn subject of the Blue Kingdom. You are a citizen of Yellow Country whose tie to this nation is only by marriage, and the sole reason you may stand here as Ella Coach's advocate is that you are her guardian." His eyes swept Sharlyn from her hair to her feet. "Your own monarchy having been twice conquered and ultimately abolished," Clement continued, "you are unschooled in the traditions of royalty. Be seated. I have indulged you long enough."

Ella watched Sharlyn's face, expecting to see embarrassment or anger there. Her stepmother gave King Clement the slightest smile, and bowed her head. "As you wish, Your Majesty," she said, her tone perfectly even, and she took her seat without betraying a flicker of the fury Ella knew she had to feel. *That* was self-control — and because of it, Sharlyn came off looking as though she knew more about royal manners than the king himself.

Ella sat up straighter in her chair. She would stay calm. She would show herself the equal of any of these people. She caught Sharlyn's eye and nodded, just barely. Her stepmother's eyes glinted.

Lariat Jacquard rose, stiff-backed, from her grand chair.

"Whether or not our king and prince testify," she said, "I have proof enough to teach you that Ella Coach *is* disloyal to the Blue Kingdom. Her treason goes much deeper than any of you comprehend. I will show you exactly how Ella Coach intended to escape the fire she set, and just how serious a threat she and her conspirator are to the welfare of our kingdom."

Conspirator. Ella glanced at Sharlyn. What could that mean?

Lady Jacquard gestured to the grand doors on the right of the hall, which opened to reveal a short blue woman in a glittering blue dress.

"I call the Blue fairy Bejeweled, Director of the Glass Slipper."

SERGE

HIS heart stumbled at the sight of her. Gossamer flitted to his side at once. "What is this?" she asked. "What have they planned?"

Serge had no idea. Whatever was coming, it was not good.

Jules fluttered to the dais steps and stood before King Clement and his First Chairs, wings shining, hair coiffed, heels high. "How can I help you?" she said, and her husky voice filled the Assembly chamber.

"Bejeweled," said Lariat. "You employ a fairy called Serge."

Gossamer gripped his fingers.

"Until recently I did," said Jules. "He resigned the day before the fire."

"How interesting. And why did he resign?"

"At first, I wasn't certain," said Jules. "He had served the Glass Slipper for eighty years, twenty of them as Executive Godfather. I was very surprised by his sudden withdrawal."

"But you let him go?"

"It was his choice." Jules shrugged. "Sometimes, a fairy simply has to fly."

The Assembly liked this. They chuckled affably at her joke.

"Did you know at that time that Serge had affiliated himself with Ella Coach?"

"No."

Assembly members stuck their heads out of their boxes and looked up to catch a glimpse of Serge. He did not so much as flex his wings; he would not let them see his alarm. Ella's panic swelled alongside his own, but he could not comfort her now. He had to keep himself in check.

"What did you know about Serge's association with Miss Coach?" asked Lariat.

"Only that I forbade it," said Jules. "His apprentice wanted to work with her, but her name wasn't officially on the List."

"Tell me about his apprentice."

"Jasper is a Crimson fairy and the grandson of the fairy queen Opal of Cliffhang."

A murmur of alarm made its way through the Assembly, and now those who were looking at Serge narrowed their eyes, suspicious.

"You allow *Crimson* fairies among your ranks at the Slipper?"

"There's never been one before," said Jules. "But he seemed genuinely promising."

"And on the day of the fire," said Lariat, "Serge's bond with Miss Coach became clear?"

"I wasn't there," said Jules. "But the Blue fairies who spoke to Nettie Belting all said that Serge and Jasper both received Ella's call."

"And that means that Serge and Jasper were both her godfathers?"

"Yes."

"Did Ella Coach know that it was possible for her to set a deadly fire in a locked room and yet escape from it?"

"Oh, absolutely," said Jules, waving a blue hand. "Nothing to it, with fairies on your side."

"But why would Serge take her side?" said Lariat. "Why would a Blue fairy align himself with a traitor to his nation?"

"Because he's a traitor himself," said Jules. "Bring in the glass slippers."

Dash

He had no idea what was happening. How had a trial about a fire suddenly become about a fairy? And why were there dozens of guards now filing in rows across the chamber floor, each of them bearing a small pillow topped with a pair of glass slippers? The members of the Assembly came to the railings of their boxes to look down and see every detail. For the first time all day, Lady Gourd-Coach looked bewildered.

"I now call upon the fairies of the Glass Slipper," said Lady Jacquard, and her voice rang out in the chamber, victorious. "All except Serge. The rest of you have been summoned for one purpose, and that is to identify, among these many slippers, the ones that you created for your own godchildren. Stand beside those slippers now."

For a moment, no fairy moved. They all looked at one another and then at Serge.

"Come," said Nexus Maven, rising to her feet. "Do your duty."

The fairies descended from the ceiling like falling leaves, radiant in the blue light that filtered through the cut-glass ceiling. They fluttered over the sparkling shoes that rested on the tasseled pillows, frowning and hunting. One fairy landed beside a pillow. Another did the same. In a minute, they had each found at least one pair that they had created, and they looked up at Lady Jacquard, all of them obviously uncertain.

"What is the purpose of this?" said a dark blue fairy.

"Gossamer," said Bejeweled. "Did you make those slippers?"

"Of course I did," said the dark blue fairy. "You know I did."

"No, no, babe. Did *you* make those slippers?"

Gossamer frowned. She plucked the slipper from the pillow, inspected it, and nodded. "These were for Oxford Truss two years ago. What are you getting at?"

"Is that what the slippers looked like when you finished with them?" Bejeweled demanded.

"Not quite," said Gossamer. "They were changed slightly."

"Who changed them?"

Gossamer glanced up at the only Blue fairy who remained perched above the House of Magic. "Serge did," she said.

"What did he change about them?"

"The heels," said Gossamer. "He disagreed with their height, so he fixed it."

"How?"

"With magic," said Gossamer, snorting. "What else?"

"Carvel," said Bejeweled. "Did you make those slippers for Tiffany Farthingale?"

"Mostly," he replied, looking quite nervous.

"But what happened?"

"Serge changed the toes. He thought mine were out of date."

Bejeweled asked another fairy, and then another, and they all answered in much the same way. The fairies grew agitated and the Assembly grew restless — except for Cameo Shantung. Her dark eyes were alert, following Bejeweled's every movement.

"These," said Bejeweled, plucking an amber pair of shoes from a small pillow, "are the glass slippers that Serge made for his own client, Loom Batik. Here are the ones he made for Chelsea Brogue." She went on down the line, naming dozens of Serge's godchildren, every one of them the son or daughter of a member of the House of Mortals.

"If the House of Mortals would indulge me a moment?" said Bejeweled, lifting a sparkling pink slipper into the air. "Raise your hands if Serge has ever been inside your home."

Half the hands in the Assembly Hall went up.

"Thank you, Bejeweled," said Lady Jacquard. "Fairies of the Glass Slipper, we are grateful for your assistance. Serge excepted, you are dismissed from this hearing."

"Dismissed?" said Gossamer indignantly.

"Dismissed," said Nexus Maven. Ribbons of light moved around her hands, humming. Threatening. "The fairies of the House of Magic will escort you from the chamber if necessary."

The Blue fairies of the Glass Slipper looked deeply offended, but they filed out through the grand doors. Dash watched them go, wondering if all of them had really left. They were magic, after all. They could make themselves invisible. He remembered his father saying something once about wishing he could put iron bars on the Assembly Hall windows, but the House of Magic wouldn't hear of it, since their magic would be hampered too.

The guards closed the doors behind the fairies of the Glass Slipper. Now the only fairies left in the chamber were Serge and those few who were members of the House of Magic — including Bejeweled.

"Every pair of glass slippers is finished by the same hand," said Lady Jacquard. "Serge's. He has been in many of your homes, and his slippers have been in the bedrooms and parlors of every family in the House of Mortals. He has had unparalleled access to your private lives."

The Assembly looked nervous now. They glanced around at one another.

"Bejeweled," said Lariat, "what did you learn about these slippers after Serge resigned?"

Bejeweled sighed gustily, and her gaudy gown glittered. "It's just too awful," she said. "I can't even bear to *say*."

But she looked, Dash thought, as though she were enjoying herself a little too much for that to be true. And when she glanced up at Serge, she couldn't keep a wicked smile from her face.

"You might as well come on down, babe," she said. "Your game is over."

Serge

He did not move from his perch. He could barely hear Jules over the sound of his own heart beating. He knew what she was about to say; he knew, and he didn't know how to stop her. It didn't really matter if she ruined his life. They could bring him up on charges, but he was a fairy. He could fly from here and live out his life in peace somewhere that wasn't Quintessential.

But Ella . . .

"Serge infused every pair of these slippers with illegal magic," said Jules. "Listening magic. He has spied on every member of this Assembly."

The Assembly boiled quickly to a froth. There were shouts. Threats. Serge's wings were numb; he couldn't even feel the burned one aching.

Jules and Lariat had beaten him to it.

He didn't know how they'd discovered that he knew about the little glass dots. Perhaps Jules had overheard him telling Cameo through Challis's slippers. Perhaps Cameo had trusted the wrong person, and that person had run to Lariat. It didn't matter. He was neatly framed.

"And so you see? Ella Coach had an accomplice," said Lariat. "A traitor with wings who could bear her safely away from danger. A traitor who passed our national secrets to his so-called apprentice, who is a Crimson fairy and the heir to Queen Opal of Cliffhang. Serge and Ella Coach have been working together to destroy this kingdom — and that includes setting the fire in my workshop. Thank you, Bejeweled. Your testimony has been invaluable."

Serge's velvet jacket felt small and tight. How would they recover from this? How could he save Ella now?

Where was Jasper?

Ella

THEY were going to lose. They couldn't, but they were. She didn't believe for a second that Serge had done anything wrong — Lady Jacquard was only making things up about him.

But the Assembly was angry. Hungry for blood.

"Have you any response, Lady Gourd-Coach?" said King Clement.

Sharlyn rose slowly. "Bejeweled," she said in a voice that, for once, was not quite calm — Ella caught the edge of fear in it, and it terrified her. "When Serge flew to the Jacquard workshop to rescue Ella

Coach, he brought with him more than fifty fairies. What did they do when they reached the blaze?"

"Plenty," said Bejeweled with a *pff* of disinterest. "Saved the children, put out the fire. Made themselves look like heroes."

"You don't think that saving children and putting out fires is heroic?"

"I think," said Bejeweled, putting a hand on her glittering hip, "that it's awfully convenient that fifty Blue fairies were waiting just a few blocks away from the fire when it happened."

Sharlyn was silent. Ella could almost hear her thinking. "Can you prove," said her stepmother after a moment, "that there *is* illegal magic in the slippers?"

Ella sat up slightly. It was a good question.

"You'd have to be a Blue fairy to hear anything through the shoes," said Bejeweled. "But let's have a test." She beckoned to the House of Magic. "A little help?" she said, and she handed off a slipper to the first Blue fairy who volunteered. She gave the other slipper in the pair to Sharlyn, and the fairy volunteer left the chamber. Sharlyn whispered something into the shoe.

"May your branches bear fruit," said the fairy when he returned. "Is that what you said?"

Sharlyn nodded, and Lariat Jacquard sat taller. Beside her, Lavaliere was dozing with her eyes shut and her mouth open. Ella looked away, disgusted by her indifference.

"How do we know it's Serge's magic in these slippers?" Sharlyn demanded suddenly. "How do we know it isn't someone else's?"

That was a good question too.

Bejeweled only snorted. "You mortals think we can do just *anything*. It's sweet."

"What do you mean?"

"It's impossible to tell whose magic is whose," said Bejeweled, ruffling up her spikes of hair with a swipe of her blue hand. "Sure, you get a few fairies and Exalted who can sense the difference between fairy magic and witch magic, and so forth. But narrowing a particular bit of magic down to the individual maker? Almost nobody can do that. Serge has tampered with every pair of shoes that's come out of the Slipper for years — and all his friends admitted it." She glanced up at the king. "Am I done here?" she said. "I feel done here."

And then the whole Assembly gasped with one voice as Lavaliere Jacquard toppled out of her chair and down the dais steps, limp as rags.

Serge

He soared down to Lavaliere, knelt on the steps, and felt for her pulse. Her heartbeat was sluggish. Fading.

"Don't *touch her.*"

He ignored Lariat — it was cruel to expose Lavaliere before all of the nobility, and he knew it, but the girl was near death. If the illusion remained, then no one could help her. He stripped the magic from Lavaliere's face and cried out at the sight of the bloody, welted mess she had become. Her features were dissolving.

"I need a Hipocrath!" Serge shouted. "Quickly!"

Serge could hear people gag, smell the sourness of sickness rise as nobles retched into their silk curtains and velvet chairs. The Blue fairies of the House of Magic bore Physic Nostrum down from his box and deposited him at Lavaliere's side. The small Hipocrath crouched and held his blue palms over her. "Geguul," he murmured. "What is this sickness? Cankermoth — but the toxin here is deeper . . ."

"Cankermoth," Serge confirmed. "Since the bite, two years ago, Lavaliere has been wearing an illusion I made for her, at Bejeweled's orders. But beneath the mask, her condition has deteriorated. It causes her pain beyond endurance, but though I have appealed to her mother to permit Lavaliere to get treatment, she has repeatedly refused."

"It is in her brain and heart," said Physic Nostrum. "She may be lost." He raised his thin voice. "I need everyone with me who has any healing power. Now."

The Blue fairies of the House of Magic bore more Hipocraths down from their boxes, along with Kisscrafters who had the healing touch. The fairies lifted Lavaliere in their arms.

"Help her," Serge said. "Save her."

The throng of fairies and healers tore from the chamber.

Those who were left turned their eyes on Lariat Jacquard.

Dash

LARIAT'S face was ghastly. Greenish gray.

Lavaliere's countenance had looked like pulp. Wet, bursting flesh. Ella looked at him, her eyes shocked and questioning, but he shook his head. He had never guessed what Lavaliere was hiding.

"He attacked my child!" said Lariat suddenly. She pointed down at Serge, who still stood on the dais steps, staring at the door through which Lavaliere had vanished. "He burned her with fairy magic! You all saw him do it, do not let him confuse you — remember what he *is*. A traitor, a menace. He inflicted those welts in order to blame me for them —"

"It was a cankermoth infection," said Lady Shantung clearly from her box. "Physic Nostrum confirmed it."

"Your Majesty," cried Lariat. "Nexus Maven! How can you let this happen?"

"How can you remain here," said Dash's mother quietly, startling him, "when you have just been told that your daughter is near death?"

The Assembly fell silent.

"Maud," said the king, pleading. "Leave it."

"No. I ask her this question as one mother to another. How can she sit in that chair while her child bleeds?"

"I stay in this chair," said Lariat, "because unlike some people, I understand that my duty to my country is greater than my duty to my*self*. I serve this House and this kingdom. *I* do not abandon *my* position. *I* do not run from what pains me. I stay and search for truth."

"This hearing serves your interests," said Queen Maud, "not the kingdom's. If what you want is truth, then here it is: Your daughter suffers from a village pestilence, and you would rather see her dead than admit it."

"Maud."

"Clement." Dash's mother removed her crown and smoothed a hand over her coronet of yellow curls. "I should not have abandoned my position as I did — Lariat has a point there. So let me be official now: I resign my post." She set the crown on her throne and looked at Lady Jacquard. "There is what you covet," she said. "Take it."

"Maud —"

She ignored the king. "I will go to your child," she said to Lady Jacquard, who sat unmoving. "I will comfort her while she is healed — or while she dies. She needs a mother. Any mother. But a good one would be best, so keep your seat."

Dash's mother left the dais. His father tried to catch her hand, but she avoided his grasp and swept from the chamber without a look back.

THE Assembly did not know what to do with itself. The king deflated in his massive throne. Lady Jacquard's expression was empty. Jules made her way to the doors.

"Your Majesty," said Sharlyn gravely. "Serge must be permitted to speak."

Jules glanced back.

"Serge committed treason," said Lady Jacquard flatly. "He has no right to testify."

Before Sharlyn could fight this pronouncement, the grand doors opened and the chamberlain of the Assembly entered with two guards behind her. Serge's wings throbbed with joy — and tensed with fear. The guards had Jasper between them, but a black silk band was tied around his eyes.

"Your Majesty," said the chamberlain. "This Crimson fairy says that his name is Jasper and he is Ella Coach's other godfather. Do you require his testimony?"

Jasper's masked face turned directly toward Serge as though he were a beacon of light. He gave him a little smile.

"Absolutely not," said Jules.

"No," said Lariat at almost the same moment. "We will not hear him. He is a spy who wishes only to delay the vote on Ella's guilt, I am sure."

Out of the corner of his eye, Serge saw something strange: a streak of shimmering crimson. He glanced down to find that it was coming from his sleeve. Swirling cursive glowed deep in the velvet, a luminous red embellishment.

I brought you a surprise witness. This faded, and another line of cursive appeared as the guards wheeled Jasper around. *I had a little feeling it might be necessary. Statute 144.*

Relief and terror flooded Serge together. It was the perfect solution. It was also a dreadful risk.

Miss me?

"Yes," Serge murmured, and Jasper's little smile became a beam as the guards towed him from the chamber.

Serge shut his fists, summoned his dust, and visualized the message he would send to Lady Gourd-Coach.

Ella

"THE moment of decision has arrived." Lady Jacquard's face was smooth again, and some of the color had returned to it. "All in favor of ending this hearing —"

"Stop," said Sharlyn. "Wait." She stared down at a bit of parchment in her hands that had not been there a moment ago. It appeared to be written in silvery script, and it changed the expression on Sharlyn's face from one of grave concern to one of energy. Determination. She looked like herself again. "I would call another witness," she said in a tone so confident that Ella's courage was halfway revived.

"Only if this Assembly permits it," said Lady Jacquard, and she shot a warning look out at the Assembly boxes. "All in favor —"

"But Your Majesty," said Sharlyn, opening the Charter of Assembly Regulations. "It is the law. According to statute one hundred forty-four, if there arises a question of magic that cannot be settled by the House of Magic, then any being with the power to settle the question *must* be permitted to give testimony." Sharlyn clapped the book shut. "Lady Jacquard wants the Assembly to assume, without proof, that Ella Coach has been working alongside a traitorous fairy," she said. "But the question of *whose* listening magic is in those glass slippers still remains."

"Bejeweled says that the question cannot be answered," said King Clement.

"But I say it can," said Sharlyn. She drew a deep breath. "I call Queen Opal of Cliffhang."

SERGE

A little girl — or what looked very much like one — came into the chamber, led by two guards who were unable to mask their fear. Jasper's grandmother was even paler than he, with giant white wings that swirled and marbled behind her like living opals. Her hair fell in long, iridescent white sheets on either side of the mask that obscured her eyes, and her exquisite black gown trailed behind her small frame, making her look like she was playing dress-up in her mother's mourning clothes. Her crown was high and sharp, its peaks set with rubies as crimson as blood. As she walked, she gasped intermittently — little laughs or little sobs, Serge could not be sure which.

So this was what Jasper had left behind. The very sight of her made Serge shudder.

"No." Lariat Jacquard sat back against her chair as though she would have liked to vanish through it. "Your Majesty, do not allow it."

"The charter," said the king. His voice was dry.

"A monarch of the Crimson Realm has no right to decide matters of the Blue Kingdom —"

Queen Opal released a torrent of shrieking laughter that broke from her red lips in a spray of crimson light arcing toward the dais like fire from a dragon's mouth. Dash and Ella cried out, and they weren't the only ones.

The fiery light vanished. Queen Opal's hands flew to her mouth.

"I promised to be good," she said from behind her fingers. Her sweet, girlish little voice turned Serge's wings cold. "If I'm naughty, I can't have what I want, and I *want* it. . . ."

Clement stared down at Opal, arrested. Serge wondered, with some dread, what exactly it was that Opal wanted.

Dash

DASH could not tear his eyes from the Crimson fairy. She had transfixed the entire chamber — nobles and magic beings alike sat motionless in horror.

Lady Gourd-Coach spoke. "Your Majesty," she said to Opal. Her voice was impressively neutral. "Welcome, and thank you for bestowing your gift upon this hearing. I understand that you, alone among all magic beings in Tyme, are proven to have the ability to tell whose magic is whose. Is this true?"

Opal smiled, showing child-size teeth that shimmered like tiny opals in her mouth. "Ask the Nexus." She turned her masked face toward Nexus Maven. "*She* knows . . ."

Maven stood, her hands now surrounded by nimbuses of bright, changing light. "Queen Opal has the power you describe," she said. "She also has the power to hypnotize every mortal in the room. If she is to remain here, she must be properly restrained."

The Nexus lifted the side of her hand with a sharp movement, and a whip of light shot from it, humming. It traveled like lightning toward Queen Opal, who gave a short, soft laugh. At this sound, the ribbon of light changed direction, returned to its maker, and lashed the Nexus to her throne.

"Seducer of kings and Exalted," said Opal, wagging a finger at Maven. She passed her tongue over her small teeth. "Trader of secrets. But you will never take Keene's place on the Council, no. . . . Your power is too small."

Nexus Maven's dark face showed no blush, but she turned away as far as she could. No one moved except the Relay, whose hand never stopped racing over his pages, recording every breath.

Opal laughed breathlessly and turned her blindfolded face directly toward Dash. "Fascinating," she whispered, taking a step toward him. The hairs on Dash's arms stood up. He flattened himself against the back of his chair, expecting someone to step between himself and Opal, to protect him. But no guard moved, nor did any member of the House of Magic, and the Nexus stayed bound in her seat. No one would intervene.

"Prince of Blue. Jasper told me about you." Opal advanced another step toward him. "You went to the workshops," she said. "A pretty, pampered palace child, but you seek wretchedness. Ugliness. Why?"

Dash could not quite catch his breath. Was he supposed to answer her?

"His Royal Highness is not testifying in this trial," said Lariat Jacquard, her voice barely audible.

Queen Opal fixed Lariat with a sightless stare. "I'll get to *you*," she hissed. She returned her attention to Dash. "Answer," she said. "Why did you go to the ugly places?"

"To —" He glanced at his father to see if he would stop him, but the king said nothing. Dash realized he was free to speak. "To understand."

"Understand?" Opal bared her teeth. "Tell more."

"To see what it was like," he said. "To see the workers there."

"To gain what?" said Opal. "Did you want to see how low the low people are, so that you could feel highest of all?" She giggled. "The low people are very low, aren't they?"

"No, I went because —" Dash licked his lips and glanced up. The whole Assembly was looking at him. There was still fear in their faces, but their eyes were curious too. They wanted his answer. Here was his chance to say what he wanted to say before the Assembly without his father or Lady Jacquard's interference. Nobody would tell Queen Opal of Cliffhang that she could not question him. "I learned that the people in the workshops were badly treated," he said. "I decided to help them if I could."

Opal tilted her head. "Did you find what you sought?" she asked. "In the ugly places?"

"I found locked doors," Dash replied. "Rotting stairways. Children tied to chairs. Sick people cracking Ubiquitous acorns to hide the roop, so that they could continue to earn a wage and support their families." He looked up at the Assembly and cleared his throat. "I *saw* Ella Coach on the fifth floor, before the fire," he said clearly. "But she was in the east room. The fire started in the west room, when a Ubiquitous acorn sparked — every surviving eyewitness who spoke to Nettie Belting agrees on that. Ella Coach couldn't have gone into the west room. The door between those chambers was locked."

"Ella Coach, Ella Coach," said Opal, swaying back and forth as though to some music that only she could hear. "Always Ella Coach. But *you* are betrothed to the Jacquard girl." She smiled widely, and her opal teeth glimmered. "Still a Charming," she said. "Courting all the girls you can, curse or no curse . . ."

"I am not betrothed," said Dash clearly.

The Assembly gasped.

"Because your bride-to-be is full of cankermoth poison?" said Opal with a strange, delighted sob. "You would dispose of her?"

"That betrothal was never real."

"Dash," his father said weakly. "Stop . . ."

"No." Dash addressed the Assembly and not Opal. "Lady

Jacquard demanded the betrothal," he said. "I had to agree to marry Lavaliere or forfeit the crown."

"Lies," said Lariat quietly. "Slanderous lies."

"She thinks she can turn you all to her side," said Dash. "She thinks she can make you vote with her to annul the monarchy. And maybe she can. Maybe now that I'm telling the truth in front of all of you, she'll do it. Maybe she has you all by your throats, like she had me."

"She does," gasped Opal, whose smile was ghoulishly wide. "She does, she *does*. . . ."

Dash watched their faces. The highest families, far above him, were hardest to read, and he knew they would also be hardest to win. The Garters and their like would never turn on Lariat. But there were plenty of other faces that registered uneasy understanding. The Trapuntos and the Whipcords. The Kalamkaris and Quebrachos. The Gomesis, the Bixis, the Cloques.

"I went along with her because I was afraid," he said. He passed his handkerchief over the top of his damp head again. "But I'm done. I was a puppet for the Charming Curse. For *years* I said whatever it wanted — did whatever it wanted. It was magic that I could not fight."

They were silent. Listening hard. Queen Opal too.

"But I can fight this," he said. "And I won't be a puppet again for anything." Dash looked at his father. "Not even a throne," he said, and he sat down. He was finished.

Serge

SERGE watched the prince's eyes roam jerkily around the room. The boy's hands shook; his face was blotchy with effort; his whole shorn head gleamed with sweat, and he downed a draught of water like he'd just run ten leagues before pressing the silver goblet to his forehead.

Ella's eyes never left him. She very nearly radiated light.

"Your Majesty." Sharlyn addressed Opal once more. "If you have no further questions for the prince, may I ask you to examine the glass slippers? Can you tell us whose magic is in them, and what it does?"

Serge held his breath, and Queen Opal held out her hands. "Give, give," she begged. "Let me feel. . . ." Sharlyn put a red glass boot into her grasping fingers. "Mmm." Opal caressed it. "Pride. Precision. Him." She pointed to Serge. "This is his work."

"Is it listening magic?"

"No, it's pretty, *pretty* magic. . . ." And then Queen Opal found the back of the heel, and her fingertips passed over the little glass dot. "*Here*," she hissed. "Dirty magic. Tucked into this little . . ." She felt it with her fingers. "Blob," she said, grimacing.

"All the slippers have those dots on them," said Sharlyn, picking up a silver sandal woven from thin strips of glass. She traded it to Opal for the red boot. "Try this one."

Opal's girlish fingers found the dot again with ease. "Same," she said. "Pretty magic in the shoe, dirty magic in the blob. Ugly magic. Listening magic."

Opal pivoted suddenly and pointed an unwavering finger at Jules.

"Her magic," she said. "She is the spy."

Jules laughed shortly. "Nice try," she said. "But you're lying. Your grandson Jasper obviously told you what to say."

Queen Opal hissed. Red snakes slithered from her lips and vanished in bursts of red smoke. "I, lie to you?" Her girlish voice was breathless. "To gain what?"

"No idea," said Jules. "But you can't prove you're telling the truth, can you?"

Queen Opal's little masked face swiveled toward Lariat. "You *pay* Bejeweled to place the dirty dots on all the slippers," she said, and Lariat could not quite control her jerk. She turned her sightless face to the Assembly. "That is how the Jacquard mortal sees into your secrets," she said, and giggled. "That is how she knows when to twist the little knife. So you *have* to give her your loyalty. Your votes." She giggled again. "Your pride."

"It's a lie," snarled Jules.

"They know it i-sn't," sang Opal. "They know it's tru-ue. . . . *Long* have some of them wondered how the Lady knew their secrets, and *oh*, how they wanted it to stop, stop, stop. . . ."

Members of the Assembly glanced furtively at one another, then began to talk low among themselves. Opal had convinced them — or many of them, at least. Serge could see it in their eyes when they looked down at Lariat and Jules. They were livid.

Jules's wings fluttered. She lifted off from the ground and made for a window, but a group of Blue fairies materialized in midair. Gossamer. Carvel. Thimble. They blocked her exit, and Gossamer flung a healthy cloud of fairy dust into her face. When the smoke cleared, Jules was gagged. The fairies dragged her down to the floor and held her while she struggled, and one corner of Serge's mouth lifted in an irresistible smile. The situation was quite serious, of course. His own mentor was a traitor to the crown. The Glass Slipper was ruined. It would be a long time before Blue fairies earned back the public trust.

But Jules was finished. He only wished Jasper could see it.

"All done," said Queen Opal. "Where is my Jasper? He promised, he promised, and I was very good. . . ." She stumbled toward the chamber doors.

Jules desperately flung out both her hands. Her palms were patchy with a paltry layer of wet, clumped fairy dust. A faint blue shimmer erupted from them and chased after Opal. Serge squinted, trying to make out what the shimmer was supposed to be. It was small and disjointed and vaguely dragon-shaped.

Queen Opal stopped dead, and her crimson mouth curved downward in disgust. Just before Jules's blue shimmer touched her back, Opal closed her great white wings, pinning the shimmer between them. She threw back her head and laughed, then opened her wings again, releasing a great Crimson dragon, three times her own size. The Assembly screamed with one voice.

"Fly," cried Opal, and her creation shot straight at Jules. It barreled toward her head, its crimson maw wide. Jules scrambled backward, wide-eyed, unable to scream through her gag — and then she fainted in Gossamer's arms.

The crimson dragon vanished. With a shriek of laughter, Opal flew from the Assembly Hall.

Ella

THE moment Queen Opal was out of the room, everyone in it came to furious life. The magic that had lashed Nexus Maven to her throne faded, and she fled the chamber without a word. Sharlyn sat beside Ella, gripping her shoulder. Assembly members clamored for Lady Jacquard's explanation.

"Nothing has been proved," she said, and the Assembly quieted somewhat to listen. "That creature was brought here purely to confuse you all — and you are letting her."

In her box, Lady Cameo Shantung rose. "On the contrary, much has been proved," she said. "Lariat Jacquard — not Serge — has been spying on all of us, with the help of the Blue fairy Jules. Ella Coach's guilt, on the other hand, cannot be proved by anyone. I call for a vote to determine Ella Coach's fate. House of Mortals, light your lamps if you are with me."

Assembly members reached for the orbs of golden fairy light ensconced on the railings of their boxes. One by one, as members of the House of Mortals touched them, these lamps changed from gold to blue.

Ella's mouth dried up as she counted ten blue lights, then twenty. Nobles looked around to see who else was voting, and hesitant hands became decisive. Now there were thirty, forty, fifty . . . She couldn't look directly behind her to see the others, but she thought there were enough for a majority.

They were going to vote.

King Clement unrolled his gilt scroll. "Elegant Herringbone Coach is accused of trespassing, sabotage, and murder," he read out.

Ella's head emptied. Sharlyn clutched one of her hands, and Serge alighted beside her and clutched the other one. She gripped their hands with all her strength.

"Those among you who believe her guilty," said the king, "light your lamps."

Ella craned to look behind her, but she couldn't see well enough to determine anything. She heard Serge and Sharlyn both counting under their breaths, and then Sharlyn gave a shout of triumph.

"Then I declare," said King Clement, without enthusiasm, "that Ella Coach is hereby found, by the House of Mortals, to be innocent of the charges laid against her."

Ella heard her dad's strangled cry. The noise of many voices swelled in the chamber, and she barely had time to understand the verdict before she was crushed between her dad and Sharlyn.

"Ell," sobbed her dad, kissing her cheek. "It's all right, it's all right —" He untied the knots that bound her to the chair. The moment she was free, Ella leapt to her feet and flung herself at her stepmum, who held her tight and rocked her. Clover reached over the top of her mother to ruffle Ella's hair, and Linden clapped her shoulder.

"Ella."

At the sound of Dash's voice, she pulled free of them all and turned to him. He was still flushed and slick with sweat. "I'm glad —" he said, and stopped. His voice was hard to hear under the din that filled the chamber. "I'm relieved," he said, louder. He stopped again. "You're free," he said hoarsely.

"You too."

Dash grinned, practically blinding her. She reached for his hands. He took one of hers in both of his and turned it over, palm up. To Ella's great surprise, he lifted her upturned hand, bowed his head over it, and kissed her callused fingertips with reverent gentleness.

Tears pricked her eyes at the gesture.

"When you're recovered from all this," Dash said, keeping her hand clasped in his, "I hope we can — that is, I hope you still want to —"

"I do," said Ella, so eagerly that she felt herself blush, but she couldn't help it. It was all she could do to keep from flinging herself at him.

"Soon, then," said Dash, who was red-faced himself. "As soon as I can, once things are —" He stopped and glanced toward the dais where King Clement and Lady Jacquard still sat.

"Yes," Ella agreed, squeezing his fingers. "Soon."

Dash kissed her hand again, bowed to her family, and gave her one last devastating smile before retreating.

Serge

IN spite of his aching wing, he soared into the waiting area outside the Assembly chamber, wanting to find Jasper. Jasper had to see the outcome; he deserved to be part of it — if he hadn't convinced his grandmother to come all the way from Crimson to testify, things might very well have gone a different way.

But Jasper was nowhere to be found.

"I move to call another vote," said Cameo Shantung from within the hall. "To determine whether Lariat Jacquard is fit to continue as the First Chair of the House of Mortals. All in favor?"

Serge fluttered to the other end of the antechamber and opened one of the doors, but Jasper was not in the entry hall either. It was dim and quiet.

"Lady Lariat Jacquard and the Blue fairy, Bejeweled, have criminally trespassed on our privacy," called Cameo's clear voice. "We will draw up formal charges at a later date. Light your lamps if you agree to the removal of Lariat Jacquard from her post, effective immediately."

Serge went to one of the stained-glass windows and peered out into the Assembly gardens. Beyond them, commoners were still chanting at the gates, but there was no Jasper — or Opal either.

A moment later, Lariat Jacquard exited the Assembly chamber, flanked by two royal guards. She passed Serge without looking at him. The guards locked the doors behind her.

Serge turned to fly back into the Assembly chamber but stopped when a gleam of crimson light caught his eye. He looked down and saw a word glittering faintly — almost imperceptibly — deep in the velvet of his sleeve.

Good-bye.

Six Months Later

DASH

THE Poplin School for Children was a marvel of magical architecture. Its buildings of stone, glass, and wood were plain and simple but possessed a curious beauty; they seemed to spring from the landscape around them — tall grasses, wide beaches, high dunes. With the help of the Blue fairies, they had been erected in just four months. The school graced the shore just north of Salting, half an hour's ride from the Corkscrew.

Today marked the Poplin School's official opening, but the orphans of the Jacquard fire had lived there for weeks already. Despite their grief, they were still children; dozens of them shouted and laughed at the windows of the boys' dormitory, flinging fairy dust into the courtyard garden below. The glittering dust settled in branches and upon leaves and petals, filling the trees and flowers with tiny fairy lights. The sun was setting now. Soon the garden would look spectacular.

And most of Quintessential would be in it.

"Is this right, sir?" asked Singer, tugging at his doublet to make it straight.

"Perfect." Dash crouched. "Ready for your speech?"

Singer shrugged, his face pensive. "'Fraid I'll cry."

"Want me to stand with you?"

The boy nodded gratefully.

Dash left the dormitory and made his way to a driftwood bridge. It arched over a saltwater pond and ended at the headmistress's cottage, where he knocked.

His mother threw open the door. "Oh, good," she said, shutting the door behind him. "You need to get dressed." Dash followed her as she wound her way carefully through more than a dozen children to get to the back of the cottage. She sidestepped two boys playing jacks in the hall and went into the room where Dash slept now when he visited.

"There," she said, pointing to a set of new clothing that was laid out on his bed. "Serge stopped by with some royal regalia that he thinks is more your style. I rather like it." She paused before leaving to reach up and smooth his hair, which he hadn't shaved off since the fire. Most of it had grown back in, but it was patchy in a few places where the burns on his scalp had gone deep.

His mother stepped out, and Dash dressed slowly. It was harder work without a valet. When he was done, he turned to the mirror, and his heart gave an uncomfortable thud. Dressed in a golden doublet and royal-blue sash, and with waves of hair upon his forehead, he looked just like the portrait of Great-Great-Great-Great-Great-Grandfather Phillip.

His mother knocked and entered, now gowned and jeweled, with his crown in her hand. She stopped cold when she saw him. "You look so grown," she managed. "So much like —"

She didn't say his father, but he knew.

"He's not coming," said Dash. "Right?"

"No, he stayed in Quintessential. He's giving me space, just as I asked him to," said his mother, smiling a bit sadly. "He thinks if he does what I want, I might go back to him."

After Lady Jacquard was ousted, Dash had expected the Assembly to give his father the same treatment. But having turned their backs on Lariat Jacquard, the nobles of Quintessential were in no hurry to reform anything else. King Clement remained in the seat of power, whether he deserved it or not. Dash was grateful that he himself could still hold the royal seat one day. He'd have his chance to preside. To guide change. Lady Cameo Shantung now sat in the First Chair of the House of Mortals. The Assembly had elected her by a huge majority.

"Corsages are a country custom," said his mother, bringing his attention to a little circlet of flowers that sat on his pillow. "When you see Ella, put it on her wrist. Here, practice on me."

His mother extended her arm, and Dash did practice, though suddenly his hands were prone to trembling. For him and Ella, this night was not only a charity event. It was their first official public appearance as a couple, and the scribes would be on top of them.

"You'll be fine," said his mother as his hand slipped and he crushed one of the little flowers into pulp. "Everyone's behind you."

"Are they?"

"They love your honesty. They want you to do well."

Dash toyed with the circle of flowers. "Will the House of Mortals ever accept her?"

"Not all of them," said his mother. "But they didn't condemn her."

"Some of them tried." He would never forget which ones.

"Don't be vengeful, Dash. It doesn't suit you."

"But will they ever stop — *baiting* her?"

His mother was quiet a moment. "She's easy to bait," she said. "I say that with respect. I like her very much."

He knew it. His mother's approval of Ella was so complete that it made him nervous.

"Certain people will always want to see if they can pick a fight with her, and there's little she won't fight for. It makes her vulnerable." He nodded. "But you're only thinking of your own circle, Dash, and while they're powerful, they're a very small group. Think of the larger kingdom. Your subjects adore her — she's princess in their hearts already."

That made him nervous too.

"Poor Lavaliere," said his mother with a sigh as she arranged his hair and settled his crown. "I went to visit again. It's certain now that she won't recover her vision."

Dash felt almost no pity. Lavaliere had done her best to put Ella in prison for life. "She did it to herself," he said.

"But she's so young." His mother's eyes were wet. "She had no guidance. It tears me apart to think of her mother, living free in Lilac after what she did to that child."

Lariat Jacquard had fled to her family's winter chateau, where she was enjoying every luxury she was used to. She'd been barred from the House of Mortals, her Guild license had been revoked, the Assembly had repossessed Jacquard Silks, and Lariat had been made to pay reparations against the fire — but she walked free. It infuriated Dash. He tried to tell himself that, for Lariat Jacquard, being exiled from high society in Quintessential was the worst possible punishment, but he couldn't be contented. When he was king, murderers like her would rot in prison.

"But then, perhaps she isn't free. Perhaps the Lilac fairies will take notice of her. One never knows with them." His mother smoothed his sash against his shoulder. "I'm going to check on Tallith and the buffet," she said, repinning the Charming crest to the sash so that everything hung straight. "People will arrive at any moment. Where is Ella?"

"We're — meeting." He looked down at the little circlet of flowers in his hands.

"Well, don't be too long *meeting*," teased his mother. "Remember to show up for the party."

Ella

SHE watched from a window of the upper floor of the girls' dormitory as the first few Quintessentialites stepped into the courtyard. They looked suspiciously around as though they could not believe in the beauty of the place. On the stage at the side of the courtyard, beneath blue blossoms that hung from the outstretched branches of an Amitelle, the Current began to play.

Kit nudged her. "You're not nervous about a bunch of quints, are you, Ell?"

But she was. It was one thing to make a business proposal to her dad and Sharlyn — it was entirely another to share her ideas with these people.

"When are you going to get dressed?" said Kit.

"When are you?" Ella retorted.

"This is it." Kit wore the Shattering Day dress she'd had since she was ten. It was tight across the bodice, the waist sat at her rib cage, and the skirt hung barely longer than her knees. Her skinny legs were lost in a pair of old boots. "I've got these, though," she said, and withdrew two Ubiquitous acorns. "Bought them with my wages — one's a gown and the other one's shoes —"

"No!" Ella snatched both acorns from her. "You'll get burned to a crisp."

"Maybe these ones won't crash."

"That's what my friend Chemise thought, and now she can't walk."

"Fine, then." Kit looked down at her old dress. "This is it."

Ella carefully deposited the Ubiquitous acorns in the trash bin without cracking them. Then she opened the trunk she'd brought from Quintessential and lifted out a garment she'd knitted for Kit. The silk yarn she'd chosen from Shantung was extremely thin and delicate; the resulting fabric was light as cobwebs, and Ella congratulated herself that it was really beautiful. It ought to have been. It had taken her the better part of a month and left her hands good and sore.

"Wear this if you like it," she said.

Kit's eyes shone as she took the gown by its straps and held it up before her. "You made this?" she said softly. "For me to keep? Really?"

"'Course it's to keep."

"But it must've taken ages — I can't, it's too much —"

"Please," Ella urged, and she all but shoved the gown over her friend's head. It cascaded just to the floor, iron gray, accented with slender, pale brown braids of silk that made up the thin straps and crossed over the bodice. The armholes turned out to be a little too big, but Ella pinched some of the fabric together at the back of Kit's shoulders, and then it was perfect.

"I can pin them tighter," said Ella. "Don't worry, it'll be fine."

Kit swayed back and forth to watch the skirt swish. "You're brilliant, you know that?" she said, touching one of the silken straps. "What did you make for yourself?"

"Well — nothing. I designed something, though, and commissioned it."

"Oooh, listen to you, all plush."

"I know." Ella fidgeted. "But knits are coming into fashion, and my dad's doing a new collection for Practical Elegance. He hired some really quality knitters to make up the samples, including this. . . ."

Ella heard Serge's chime. Quickly, before he arrived, she changed into her dress. It was light, bright blue, with material as thin and fine as Kit's, and the skirt was full, hanging in a hundred soft pleats to the floor. It pooled just a little around her feet and trailed behind her in a train. Slim white cables framed the bodice, then blossomed into an intricate, structured pattern that decorated part of her collarbone and arced over one shoulder, like jewelry made of silk. She clasped the woven belt around her waist, and the knit hugged her curves just so.

A faint cloud of blue dust popped suddenly into existence between them, and Serge materialized, looking impeccable — and deeply admiring. "That gown is a dream," he said. "I couldn't have imagined anything more beautiful myself."

Ella rolled her eyes. "Yeah, you could have."

Serge smiled. "Fair enough." He turned his attention to Kit. He fitted the straps of her gown and replaced her boots with slippers for dancing. Gray pearls appeared at her ears and throat, and Kit touched them with reverent fingers as he dressed her locks in a complicated braid that fell over one shoulder. "There we are," he said. "Happy?"

Kit stared at herself in the mirror. "You're so kind," she whispered. "I can't believe you're real. Both of you. I have to show Mum —*thank* you —" She bolted from the room.

Serge shook his head. "Rapunzel's coming," he said, brightening. "I got a letter back from the Green Commonwealth just yesterday. She'll be here tonight with a friend."

"Oh, good!" Ella said. "Dash has been wanting to thank her in person. What's she like?"

"Refreshing," said Serge. "Nothing like the Coterie girls." He surveyed Ella's gown. "I just have one little idea. Do you mind?"

Ella did not. A cloud of fairy dust burst around her, and she looked down to find that Serge had filled the soft folds of her skirt with tiny lights that moved and glowed within the thin blue silk, like she'd netted a thousand silver fireflies. Lights glittered from the white cables on her bodice and shoulder too.

Serge arranged her curls into a soft, high twist. "Jasper told me exactly how he wanted it," he murmured. "He was extremely specific — two pages of instructions. You'd think I hadn't been dressing hair for eighty years. . . ."

"How is he?" Ella demanded. "When are you going to see him?"

Serge's face clouded, and his singed wing flicked in agitation as it always did now whenever Jasper came up. "I've told you," he said. "When your year with me is finished, I'll go."

"And I told *you* —"

"Hush." He settled the last curl and turned Ella toward the mirror. "There."

She tensed at the sight of her reflection. The way her hair twined around her head, twinkling with lights, it looked like a jeweled crown.

"Exquisite," said Serge quietly. "Every inch a princess."

Ella tried to swallow her terror. She couldn't do this. She couldn't stand next to Dash in this gown, with this hair, and pretend to be this person when everyone knew she wasn't. When she knew she wasn't.

"There will be people down there tonight who want to make you feel as small as they are," said Serge. "Don't let them. Smile at their barbs. It's the worst thing you can do to them."

Nausea slithered in her guts. But she drew a deep breath and let it out again.

"Great White skies," came a reverent voice from the door, and Ella turned her head to see Sharlyn gazing at her, one hand at her throat. "We have to make that gown part of the collection. People are going to want to buy it tomorrow."

"It isn't practical."

"But it could be," said Sharlyn, approaching. "Your father might even be able to illuminate the skirt himself."

"Or make it removable," said Ella. "It could double as a sleeping sack or something, if it was waterproof."

Serge left them alone together, and Sharlyn offered Ella a small box, white and ribboned. "Don't open it yet," she said. "Wait for your father. Earnest?" she called toward the door. "She's all ready. You can come in."

Ella's dad came through the door and stopped, looking dazed. "Ell," he managed. "You're a princess."

That word again. Desperate for a distraction, she opened the box in her hands. Within lay a pair of earrings different from any jewelry she had encountered. They were clusters of some organic material — seeds, perhaps — russet and lacquered to shining.

"I don't know if you're familiar with the custom of planting trees for the dead," said Sharlyn. "In Yellow Country, when a loved one dies, we bury them with seeds. Fruiting trees grow from their graves."

Ella nodded, twisting one of the earrings around in her fingertips and watching the seeds pick up the light.

"My first husband is buried near my old home with the rest of my family," said Sharlyn. "In the ancestral orchard. It was hard to leave those trees, but for your father, I could let go."

Ella glanced up, listening.

"What I didn't know then," Sharlyn went on, "was that Earnest had taken a liking to our tradition. He planted pomegranate seeds at the head of your mother's grave in Eel Grass, almost two years ago."

"I know," said Ella, surprised now. She looked at her dad. "I thought Sharlyn wanted you to put that tree there."

Her dad shook his head. "My idea," he said. "And it's unusually early, but your mum's tree has already fruited. Those earrings are made of the seeds that came from that first fruit."

Ella couldn't see the seeds now. Water filled her eyes and blurred them. She gripped the earring. "These . . . are from Mum?" she mumbled.

"In Yellow, we believe that the dead only bear early fruit if they're completely at peace in the Beyond," Sharlyn said. "So wear her seeds. And know that she's happy."

It was her dad who stepped forward to gather her in his arms, but Ella drew Sharlyn in as well, and for a little while, none of them could do anything but hold each other. Eventually, her dad drew back and helped her put the earrings on, his fingers shaking. He gave her a handkerchief, and she tried to fix her face as voices and music rose upon the evening breeze. A glance down into the courtyard showed that the garden was growing full.

Ella kissed her dad and stepmum, and she hurried down the back stairs of the girls' dormitory. She sidled around the headmistress's cottage and out behind the primary school until she was just beyond the Poplin grounds, on the quiet dunes beside the sea.

He was already waiting there, shining in the twilight, so splendid that she faltered when she saw him. His crown glinted on his golden head in the last rays of the setting sun, and it took her a moment to convince herself that he was still just Dash — that the rest was only costume.

When she reached him, he grabbed her hand ungracefully and shoved a corsage onto her wrist, mauling a good number of petals to death as he did so. "You," he said. "Look —" His eyes lingered on her hair, her eyes, her gown. "Ella," he rasped.

She relaxed. That was more like it.

"Then it's all right?" she asked, stepping back and twirling. "Good enough for the quints?"

He pulled her to him and gave her his wordless reply.

Dash

THEY were in definite danger of forgetting the party. Ella laughed breathlessly and pulled away from him. "We'll be late," she protested. "And I can't afford to mess up." She suddenly looked anxious, and he offered his hand. She took it. Hers was clammy.

"It will be all right," he said.

"Will it?"

Dash shrugged. "Well," he said. "It will be over, at least. Eventually."

Ella laughed. "You're a real comfort," she said, nudging him.

As they walked back toward the courtyard, the noise level swelled and the music grew louder. Ella pushed a bit closer to him as if he could shield her.

"How long before I get used to this?" she asked under her breath.

He shook his head. He didn't know. This had always been his life.

Together, they walked under the flowering archway and entered the courtyard. The Current played a fanfare. Golden sparks shot into the air. Everyone turned to look at them as the scribes began to call out.

"Dash! Ella! When will the two of you be married?"

"Does your father know where Nexus Maven is hiding?"

"Have you read Nexus Keene's official report on the Jacquard fire?"

Dash looked toward this sensible question and found Nettie Belting on the other end of it. He smiled. "Nettie," he said. "Congratulations on your award. Did you really meet with Exalted Nexus Keene?"

Nettie grinned. "I did," she said. "He gave me a private audience and a commendation for investigative excellence. Couldn't believe it. Thrill of my life."

"Well done," said Dash. "And well deserved."

Nettie beamed. Dash led Ella away from the entrance and into the crowd of Assembly and Guild families, some of whom approached them warmly. Others opened up their circles as Dash and Ella passed, soliciting their attention. But several of the upper-tier families stood back at the edges of the courtyard, and Ella heard malicious laughter from more than one clustered group. She tried to stay focused on the Trapuntos, who were very kind and who had a great interest in labor reform.

As they left the Trapuntos behind, Dash cleared his throat and motioned with his head toward the buffet tables.

"I'm going to say hello to my aunt."

"And I'm going to check on the worktables," said Ella. "Meet you in a bit?"

THEY parted ways, and Ella headed toward the back of the fairy-lit garden, where a great tent had been erected. Inside it, Mrs. Wincey and Chemise were organizing the charity work, helping other guests with sewing and knitting projects for the children of the school. Before Ella reached the tent, someone spoke from the throng of glittering Coterie students to her right.

"If it isn't Cinderella, all scrubbed up." This was followed by a laugh. "Bet it took a lot of soap."

Garb Garter. She kept walking.

"Which is it this time, *hey*?" Garb continued, his voice needling at her back. "Did you buy that gown, or did you *labor* over it?"

"She didn't buy it," came a bored-sounding reply. Loom Batik. "I looked everywhere for knits that are actually fresh, but I barely found anything. She must have made it herself."

Now Ella did stop, just outside the tent's opening. She turned to Garb and Loom and the cluster of students who stood with them. All of them waited, looking half excited, half afraid. They expected her to shout. To curse.

"That's so kind," she said, smiling with all the warmth she could muster, just as Sharlyn would have done. "I designed my gown, but it was actually made at Practical Elegance — all except the fairy lights, of course. If you're interested in something *fresh*," she said, looking at Loom, "I can show you how to knit. Then you could make exactly what you want."

Loom looked halfway intrigued by this notion.

"You want us to follow you into that tent," said Garb, "and knit?"

"Only if you want to," said Ella, whose smile was starting to hurt her face. "Enjoy the dancing if you'd rather. And thank you all so much for being here tonight — it means a great deal to the children."

Giving her best imitation of Queen Maud, she swept away into the tent.

Dash

Aunt Tallith hugged him, ruffled his hair into a mess, and put him right to work filling up the drinks that needed replenishing. He enjoyed the looks of shock and befuddlement that met him as he handed people their cups.

"Oh — sir!" said Tanner, wincing when he realized who was serving him. "Let me take over for you, please —"

"No." Dash pushed the cup into his hand. He'd asked Tanner to attend him on this trip to the Poplin School only to surprise him and set him free in Salting for the night, with an invitation to enjoy the party. Now he held out a cup to a girl with a pustule-marked face, whose arm was laced through Tanner's.

"Grats, sir," she said shyly.

"This is Kit Wincey, sir," said Tanner. "Ella's friend. She works for your aunt at the Corkscrew — we met when I came down here on your orders."

Dash bowed. "A pleasure to make your acquaintance," he said, and Kit's face turned so red that he thought she might burst. Tanner pulled her away, and within a few minutes they'd abandoned their drinks and were dancing together. They swayed to the music in the village style: her arms about his neck, his about her waist.

It looked fun. Simple. Dash searched the crowd for Ella. He caught sight of her across the courtyard and raised a hand to catch her attention, but she was speaking with Lord Quebracho. She touched her belt and gestured with her hands as though she were braiding something. Looking impressed, Quebracho offered her his arm; a moment later, they were standing before Dash on the other side of the buffet.

"Your Highness," said Lord Quebracho. "Your companion has a sharp mind for business." He patted Ella's hand. "And an eye for style. No wonder she has risen so far above her unfortunate birth."

Ella's face fell. Dash didn't trust himself to say anything.

"I'm pleased to make a donation to the children this evening," said Quebracho, insensible of his insult. "From what Miss Coach tells me, your plan for Garment Guild reform is a strong one." He looked at her. "I hope you will contact me when you assemble a board of directors."

"I'm honored you'd consider it," Ella replied.

The moment Quebracho bowed and left them, Dash put a protective arm around her.

"He meant it as a compliment," she said. "I can't let it bother me."

"There's nothing wrong with your birth."

"And he's one of the nice ones." She glanced around the party. "Imagine what the others are saying." She snorted. "Never mind. I've heard it all — and it doesn't matter. Our plan *is* a strong one, and once it catches on, they won't be able to ignore it. Not even the Garters." She took his hand and pulled him closer to the music. "Dance with me?" she said, and when Dash took her by the waist, she looked up in surprise. "What, village style?" she teased, putting her arms about his neck. "Honoring your southern roots? Your mum must be so proud."

He leaned close to her. "Just showing the quints how it's done, hey?" he said, and Ella burst out laughing.

Serge

SERGE watched from the sidelines as Ella twined her arms about Dash's neck. Dash whispered something that made her shout with laughter. He grinned in reply and twirled her under his arm.

How he wished Jasper could see them.

"*Here* he is! Serge!"

He turned to find a bedraggled pair of partygoers standing behind him, wearing festive, fancy clothes that were half shredded, as if they'd been through a battle.

"Rapunzel!" said Serge, torn between delight and concern. "What happened? Are you hurt?"

"My *feet* are." Rapunzel lifted one off the ground and flexed it, and Serge saw that her shoes were caked in mud and her stockings were torn. Her hair hung past her belt, tangled and damp. "I didn't think it would take so long to get here, but we got lost, and I really should have worn the boots you gave me and not these pointy things. I don't understand how these are supposed to be dancing slippers. They're barely walking slippers — I have to sit down." She looked around for a chair, and when she didn't immediately see one, she flopped down to sit in the dirt, while lavishly arranged people all around her stared in horror. "That's better," she sighed blissfully, and she wiggled her feet out of her shoes.

"Sorry we're late," said her friend Jack, picking a small pinecone out of his hair and flicking it to the ground. "We meant to be here yesterday, but we had to keep changing directions."

"You walked here?" said Serge, blinking at them. "All the way from Maple Valley?"

"No, we used my ring," said Rapunzel, holding up a hand to show him. "The Woodmother gave it to me. I can use all the fairywoods."

Serge's eyebrows shot up. He'd never heard of any mortal being given such a thing.

"But fairywoods are confusing," said Jack. "We've followed that ring to a bunch of places we never meant to go. We found the mines of Crimson —"

"There were auggers! They had axes," Rapunzel added.

"So we ran back into the woods and wound up in the coldest place I've ever been, so I'm going to guess it was New Pink."

"It was beautiful," said Rapunzel reverently. "Those huge white mountains — and all the frozen waterfalls."

"And then we found a misty lake, and I think we heard a mimic crying —"

"And then we saw a unicorn!"

"And finally," said Jack, looking down at his clothes, "we got stuck in some kind of briar labyrinth that — this is going to sound crazy — but I'm pretty sure it tried to eat us. I don't know where that was."

Serge gaped. "That," he said, "is on the Isle of Bad Endings. You went there? And returned alive?"

Jack's face sagged, but Rapunzel only looked curious. "What's the Isle of Bad Endings?" she said. "I've never heard of it. Jack, you never told me."

"I can't believe I didn't think of that," whispered Jack, looking gray. "All right," he said, crouching down beside Rapunzel. "You have to let me help you with that ring."

"I'm getting better at it, aren't I?" said Rapunzel, crossing her arms so that Jack could not touch her ringed finger. "I can do things by myself."

"Fine!"

"Good! Then I want to travel back to Maple Valley alone and see if I can get there."

"You can't wander all over Tyme alone — you could get hurt, or killed —"

"You know who you sound like, don't you?" said Rapunzel, and Jack shot to his feet and turned away from her, wounded and furious.

Serge couldn't follow the particulars of this conversation, but he understood its tone. "You're both exhausted," he said, inserting himself gently between them. "And hungry, I imagine. Can I get you something to eat?"

Neither of them spoke.

"At least let me introduce you to Prince Dash, Rapunzel. He's very much wanted —"

"Did you say Rapunzel?"

Dash stood nearby with Ella, and when he saw Rapunzel sitting on the ground at Serge's feet, he bowed low. She stayed where she was, with her face turned away. Serge thought he heard her sniffle.

"Ella Coach," said Dash, straightening up again. "Meet Rapunzel, who killed the witch and set me free."

"Hi," said Ella, studying Rapunzel with a slight frown. "Nice to meet you. Everyone's glad you could come. . . . Are you all right?"

"I'm fine," said Rapunzel distantly.

"Then would you like to dance?" asked Dash, and he offered his hand.

Rapunzel finally looked up at his face. When she saw him, she turned pink.

"Did you really come to my tower?" she asked him.

Dash nodded.

"And you cut my hair?"

Now it was the prince who blushed. "Yes," he muttered. "Sorry."

"Never mind. I don't care." Rapunzel wiped her nose on her sleeve and gave him her hand, and he pulled her to her bare feet and escorted her to the dance floor, leaving her mud-caked pointy slippers behind.

Jack watched her go, his expression tight. "She's right," he said eventually. "She should do what she wants." He pivoted away from the dance floor. "Thanks for the invitation, Serge — I think I'll grab some food after all." He made his way to the refreshments.

Ella watched Rapunzel with Dash for a moment. "Well, *she's* not what I pictured." She shook her head and tucked her arm through Serge's. "Go to Crimson," she said.

This caught Serge so by surprise that he had to blink rapidly to keep his emotions organized. "In six months or so," he said. "I promised you a year. How many times —"

"Look, I'm not trying to be rude, hey?" she said. "But I don't want you to stay any longer. Not for me."

"Your mother wanted you to have my support."

"What more do I need?" She nudged him. "Anyway, we're not contractual, remember? We're official, you and me. And Jasper too. That won't change just because you're both in Crimson."

Serge was quiet, wrestling with himself.

"He's lonely," said Ella. "His letters are awful."

"I know," Serge murmured. "He's so cheerful it's depressing."

"Please go to Cliffhang and make sure he's all right," said Ella. She clutched his arm suddenly. "But stay for my speech first?" she whispered. "Don't leave until I'm done."

"I wouldn't miss it," Serge replied hoarsely. "And if you ever need me —"

"I'll call. I promise." Ella touched the *E* at her throat, and Serge felt in his wings a throb of emotion that was both hers and his.

"It's time," he said, pointing to the stage, where the Current had just stopped playing. The musicians cleared away as Maud Poplin climbed the steps to address the assembled party.

"Here it comes," Ella whispered. "Wish me luck."

"You don't need it," Serge replied. "But good luck, Ella. And thank you."

"For what?"

He kissed her cheek. "Go on," he said, and he gave her a gentle push toward the stage.

SHE barely heard Queen Maud's introduction. She saw Singer climb to the stage and was dimly surprised to see Dash go with him. He stood at the boy's shoulder, and Singer pulled a slip of paper from his pocket and read his speech to the silent, expectant crowd.

"Tonight's party is many things," he said. "Most important, it's the official opening of the Poplin School for Children, which is a really special place. It's where all of us who — lost people in the Jacquard fire —" He stopped. His chin hardened and trembled.

Dash put a hand on his shoulder.

"Where all of us who lost people in the Jacquard fire," Singer continued in a whisper, "have found a home and an education. The garden we're in tonight is dedicated to my brother, Raglan Mantle, who thought education was important. The Raglan Mantle Memorial Garden is a place where we can come to remember the people who loved us, and who died working for us. We're so grateful for your donations to our school, and for everything you've done to support our futures. Thank you."

Healthy applause met this speech, and Ella saw that more than one pair of eyes was wet.

Some faces, though, wore smirks — the Garters' among them. They, and a few other old families, stood at the back of the crowd with arms crossed and noses high. As Ella climbed to the stage and Singer left it, their disdainful amusement was palpable. She felt like she was swimming through it.

"Ladies and gentlemen," she said when she reached center stage, "thank you for coming here tonight." She would be steady. Calm. She had been in front of these people before, with more to fear than ridicule. She'd made it through the trial, and she'd make it through this. "I realize that this was a long way to travel," she said. "I won't take too much time away from the pleasantries — and I hope you feel, as you look around you, that your donations are going to an excellent cause."

"Miss Coach!"

Ella looked into the crowd and saw, at the back, that a skinny scribe was waving to her. He was standing with Garb Garter. "Yes?" she said, because she had little choice.

"I hear you designed that gown you're wearing," said the scribe. "That right?"

Ella nodded, wary.

"And you're an experienced knitter, wouldn't you say? You can spin too, can't you?"

She nodded again. "I'd be glad to answer any technical questions a bit later," she began, but the scribe was talking again.

"It's just that you seem to be skilled at weaving together all sorts of things," he said. "Silk thread, pretty gowns, social ladders that let you climb as high as the palace . . ."

There were big laughs from the outer edges of the garden. Shocked ones from the middle. Ella was rigid. She sought an answer, but nothing came to her. Nothing she could say out loud. For a long, deadly moment, she was dumb, and the laughter in the crowd turned to murmurs. Entertained. Pitying.

At the back of the crowd, she saw Serge's wings flicker. At the front, Sharlyn and her dad were watching her with tense, anxious faces.

"I appreciate the thought," she replied, keeping her voice nice and even. Almost cheerful. "But it's not quite accurate, hey? I wish I could say I'd climbed here myself. Maybe then I'd feel like I deserve all this. But no — I was lifted here. Queen Maud wore my father's Cinder Stoppers, and Lady Sharlyn Gourd took interest in his genius, and my world changed. It was nothing but luck, really. I could just as easily have spent my life locked in one of those Jacquard rooms. That was my childhood, and I was inches from it being my whole future.

I'll never forget that." She paused. "And what maybe you can't understand is that I'd never want to."

She could hear the crickets singing on the dunes beyond the school, but in spite of the utter silence, she knew her answer had been a good one. At the back of the crowd, Nettie Belting scribbled furiously beside the skinny scribe who'd stuck his foot in it. He wasn't leering now.

"Nettie Belting has called me a hero," said Ella, slipping straight back into her prepared speech. "But while you won't find me contradicting anything else she's written, I have to correct her on that. I'm a survivor, not a hero. Heroism doesn't just happen all at once in an emergency — it's a series of daily actions. It's in the decisions we make that affect other people, and it's within all our grasps.

"The Garment Guild," she said, "first made this country great." She looked around at all of them. "The symbol of the Blue Kingdom is the spindle, because we rely upon it for the wealth and security of our nation. Your contributions to Blue, and your ancestors' contributions before you, are immeasurable. Your families expanded this kingdom along the Tranquil Sea. You funded the military that kept us safe during the Pink wars. And today, you provide the largest and steadiest source of employment in the Blue Kingdom. Perhaps you feel that no more can be asked of you."

They waited, hanging on her words now.

"But I'm asking anyway," said Ella. "Because a tragedy like the fire at Jacquard can never happen in this country again. It sullied our name. The Blue Kingdom has a new reputation across Tyme — and it's not the one we want. It's not the kind this country has ever stood for. You're the ones with the power to overcome it — you and your customers.

"With that, I'd like to introduce to you a new label, for textiles and garments, that I've developed in partnership with your future monarch, His Royal Highness Prince Dash."

Ella held up a paper tag, and the people in the courtyard narrowed their eyes trying to see it.

"This tag," she said, "says 'Fairest of the Fair.' It's a new way of communicating to your customers that *you* are heroic — that you care about your employees and you treat them with respect. This tag proves that you value your employees' skills enough to pay them real wages. You give them leave when they're ill, or when their children are. You don't lock doors on them, or let the stairs rot out under them.

"Our charter will be written by a board of business directors, as well as a new council of workers, who will be present to advise the board about the needs and concerns of laborers. Any Garment Guild business that can prove it meets Fairest of the Fair's standards will be granted a special license to attach these tags to their products, as well the right to use a special symbol that can be stamped or sewn onto the goods themselves. This way, people will know when they spend their money that they're supporting real heroes who believe in the dignity of labor. Better yet, they'll get to wear the Fairest of the Fair symbol right on their clothes, and show off the fact that they're heroes too." Ella smiled a little. "So everybody benefits, hey? Because if you can make people feel heroic, then you'll have customers for life."

Many people in the courtyard looked intrigued. Gratified. Ella waited for the whispers and murmurs to die down. "Thank you."

The crowd in the courtyard burst into applause. Not everyone joined in it — but most did. Far more of them than she would have expected.

"Ladies and gentlemen!" Clover's voice rang out from behind her, across the glittering courtyard. "This next song is dedicated to our little stepsister here. I've been threatening to write one about her for months — now seems like the right time to make good." The audience laughed indulgently, and Ella froze. "You've all heard of the

Cinder Stoppers," Clover said, lifting her fiddle to her chin. "We call this one 'Cinderella.' "

Linden's drumsticks came crashing down in a blaze of bright white sparks as the Current struck up a song — a triumphant, feverish tune that matched the excitement in the air. Their singer belted out the lyrics.

I'm not here to please you, but I know how to save you
And when I'm dead, you'll come to plant the seeds upon
my grave,
And you'll say
Cinderella — royal blue
Cinderella — let me follow you

A wonderful, awful flush of heat consumed her. She left the stage and hurried to Dash's side, where she tried to hide herself behind his height.

"They listened," he said quietly, beaming down at her. "You did it."

"*We* did it. We started, anyway — there's so much more to do —"

"And we're going to do it." Dash glanced toward the crowd, where scribes were fighting their way toward them. "Here they come. Are you ready?"

Ella had no sooner braced herself than the scribes began to pelt them with questions — even a few *real* questions.

"Who will be on the board of Fairest of the Fair?" one of them cried.

"Has anyone already been licensed?" shouted another. "Who's making the decisions?"

"Your Highness! We saw you with Rapunzel on the dance floor! New romance brewing?"

"Miss Coach! Will you reform Practical Elegance too? Or will you give your dad special preference?"

Ella and Dash glanced at each other. They clasped each other's hands. And then they turned toward the scribes and started talking.

Jasper

HE'D been fighting the brackling since midafternoon, and now the sky was red behind the high and peaked black rooftops that circled the crumbling courtyard.

There was something in the wind these days that Jasper did not like. Something heavy and unquiet. It had troubled him since he'd returned to Cliffhang to fetch his grandmother. At first he'd thought he was imagining it — that it was just Cliffhang being horrible as usual — but then he'd returned to Quintessential for the hearing, and he'd felt it there too. An ugliness, faint but certain. It dragged at the edges of his wings. He could not determine what it was, or where it came from.

So he focused on rooting out bracklings.

The foul, well-dwelling beast that squatted before him was utterly revolting: a purple, tonguelike creature, densely wrinkled and pocked with flaring suckers that spat long, barbed tentacles at him every time he tried to advance. Jasper soared to the right to avoid another lashing and flung a handful of salt at the monster. The brackling scuttled behind the well, using its tentacles like spider's legs. It clambered quickly up to the rim again and tumbled down toward the dark water.

"Oh no you *don't* —"

Jasper lunged for the well, grabbed the flask from his belt, and poured lemon juice into the water below. The fresh draught of citrus repelled the beast; it screamed and leapt into the courtyard once more. Jasper poured his remaining lemon juice around the rim of the well so that the brackling had no way back in. The beast screeched in fury. "This is it," Jasper said. "You're going to *shrivel.* I've killed twelve just like you this month, do you hear me? This well is not yours! It belongs to these people!"

The brackling skittered across broken cobblestones, through the glaring beams of the red sunset. Jasper soared after it and hurled salt down upon it. This time, he hit the creature dead on. Salt sank into its furrowed purple flesh with a burning *hiss*; fetid steam billowed from its suckers as it stiffened. As it died, it shot two tentacles up into the air toward Jasper, who dodged and missed one of them. The other sliced his face. He howled in pain and stood there, stung and panting.

Another well clean. Another neighborhood provided for. There was certainly plenty of work to do in his grandmother's miserable duchy. No end of vile creatures to weed from their shadowy corners, no end of mortals to rescue from peril.

From atop one steeply tilting building that was missing its upper floors, a woman peeked over a ridge of cracked stone, watching him. For just a second, Jasper met her eyes and felt the frantic patter of her emotions.

Don't hurt me. Don't hurt me. Please leave me alone.

She ducked out of view, and misery cut him to his heart. The mortals of Cliffhang would never turn to him for help. No matter what he did to prove he loved them, he would always be a Crimson fairy, and they would always, always be afraid.

"Miss me?"

Jasper gasped. Whirled.

Serge stood in the dark, decaying courtyard. Against the gloomy silhouettes of the broken buildings, he was sharp and bright as the moon.

"You're here," Jasper breathed.

"Are you honestly surprised?"

"I . . . *am*."

"I thought you'd sense me from leagues away."

"I *should* have." Jasper absently rubbed his wounded cheek and winced. He'd forgotten the salt and lemon on his hands. "I was busy."

"I can see that." Serge flung fairy dust at him, and in a moment he was dry, dressed, and neatly bandaged.

Then Jasper glanced around and gasped. Serge must have been overflowing with fairy dust, as Jasper's appearance wasn't the only thing that his Blue fairy magic had set to rights. The cobblestones around his feet were smooth and bright. The well was mended — its rope and bucket were restored — the water that shone in the bucket was clean and pure.

Tears sprang into Jasper's eyes.

"Here." In his still-sparkling fingertips, Serge held out an unusual flower — crimson and black, with blue petals blooming at its heart. Jasper took it, realized it was knitted from silk, and clutched it to his breast.

"Ella made this?" he whispered. "For me?"

"And this one for me," said Serge, tapping the knitted blossom in his buttonhole. It was pale blue, but the petals were edged in charcoal that exactly matched his burnt wing, and there was what appeared to be a crimson stain on one side of the bloom.

"How is she? How was her speech?"

"I recorded it for you with an Ora sponge. I thought you'd like to hear her for yourself."

"Oh —" Jasper threw himself at Serge and hugged him tight. "I'm so glad you're here," he whispered. And then he felt, without meaning to feel it, exactly why Serge had come to Cliffhang. He pulled away, dismayed. "But you *can't* stay," he cried before Serge could say anything. "It's a dreadful enough place to visit — I won't let you *live* here."

Serge's wings flickered. The one with the charred edge gave an extra beat. "You promised Opal you'd come home if she testified at the hearing," he said. "You told her you'd stay in her realm until she fades. Didn't you."

Jasper said nothing. He hadn't wanted to answer that question, no matter how many times Serge had put it to him in letters. Answering meant admitting that he was back in Cliffhang for good.

"I know you did," said Serge. "So. If you're allowed to give up your dream to save Ella and me, then surely I'm allowed to keep you company in return."

"It isn't right. It isn't fair."

Serge raised a pale eyebrow. "Why not? We can do our work here, can't we? Start our own service like we talked about? From what I understand, Cliffhang is a nightmare for mortals. We'll be busy for years and years."

"You don't understand." Jasper lifted off and flew to the peaked and sooty roof of one of the buildings. Serge followed him. "*Look* at this place."

At the western horizon, the great shadow of his grandmother's castle loomed over the duchy from its perch upon a deadly cliff. Countless towers protruded like fangs into the crimson sky. Between them and the castle, the black city sprawled, dank and listing, half of it propped up at dangerous angles by whatever magic anyone bothered to spare, the other half falling to pieces. As Jasper gazed out at it, he felt again the whisper of something wrong in the air. Something unnatural.

"There are no systems here," he said. "No Assembly, no Guild, no House of Mortals. Quintessential is a haven of benevolence and mercy by comparison."

Serge surveyed Cliffhang, his expression grave.

"I'd never want to be the reason you were miserable," Jasper said. "Don't stay unless you think you can be happy here."

Serge stared out at the derelict city, silent, but so full of emotion beneath the surface that Jasper could read him as easily as ever. The patter of Serge's heart swept through him. Tense. Afraid.

"We'll never save them all," Serge murmured. "It will be thankless. Heartbreaking."

"I know." Jasper bit back a sigh. "So —"

"So I'm where I ought to be."

Jasper looked up at him, startled, and Serge smiled just a touch.

"Right where I'm most needed," he said. "Shall we begin?"

Acknowledgments

Thanks to the following people for their contributions and kindness:

Ruth Virkus for challenging the clichés;

Cheryl Klein for combing out the snarls;

Kristin Brown for spinning and knitting instruction, and for cartography extraordinaire;

Colin Flanigan for firefighting consultation;

Heather Mbaye for sewing expertise;

Sally Virkus for knowing that durability is the most important thing in life and sewing;

Judy Brough and the gang for loving my children and making it possible for me to parent, teach, and write;

Melissa Anelli, Maureen Berberian, Lisa Campos, David Carpman, Ben Layne, Jennie Levine-Knies, Kathy MacMillan, Geraldine Morrison, and Devin Smither, for providing critical feedback;

My teaching colleagues, especially Christy Bowman-White and Claire Waistell, for unstinting enthusiasm and support;

My students, past and present, for your energy and inspiration. You are lovable, you are capable, and you have the power to do great things.

About the Author

Megan Morrison is a middle-school drama and language arts teacher as well as a writer. She cofounded the Harry Potter fan fiction site the Sugar Quill, and has been developing the world of Tyme since 2003. She lives near Seattle, Washington, with her family. Please visit her website at meganmorrison.net and follow her on Twitter at @megtyme.

Catch a sneak peek at the third adventure in the world of Tyme, in

TYME #3

TRANSFORMED

The Perils of the Frog Prince

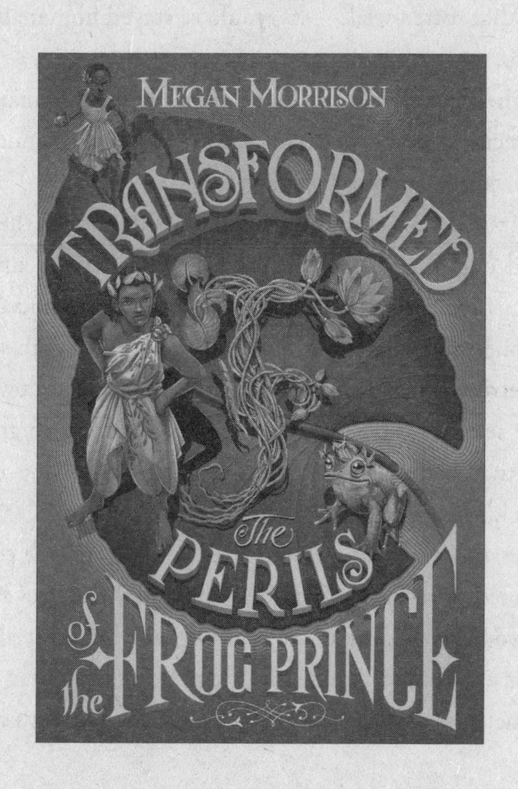

FIFTEEN months.

Fifteen months, one week, three days, and about two hours. Syrah had felt every minute. Every minute that he hadn't spent hibernating, anyway.

He sat on a large, wet leaf, staring up at the rain and regretting, as he often did, the night that had brought him to this pass. It was Deli's fault, he thought bitterly for the hundred thousandth time. If Deli hadn't been such a witch, then he never would have ended up like this. He would never have been thrown out by his family or tricked by that rotten well — he would've stayed human, like he was supposed to.

He sighed, just barely, as he thought of being human. He had never appreciated how wonderful it was. He'd had hands. A voice. He'd worn clothes and eaten cooked food.

Out of the corner of his bulging eye, Syrah noticed the scuttle of a shiny red bug. Instinctively, he turned his head and unrolled his tongue. It still surprised him how efficient this method of hunting was. The bug was in his mouth in an instant, and Syrah swallowed. His eyes retreated into his skull and pressed the food down into his throat. He settled his belly and the undersides of his thighs into the rainwater that had collected in the leaf he was sitting in, and he absorbed a long cool drink through his skin.

It was strange, what a person could get used to. He could never have imagined drinking through his skin, and the idea of swallowing live bugs would have once made him gag, but he did it all the time now, and it wasn't anything, really. He preferred catching those tiny fish he sometimes managed to grub in a stream, but bugs were easier to find, definitely more appetizing than snails — and one did what one had to do to survive.

Fifteen months as a frog had taught Syrah plenty.

"Come here, Prince Frog."

Syrah hopped in a circle and looked up at the blond teenager who had been his protector for the past eight months.

"Ribbit," he said fondly, and Rapunzel smiled down at him.

She was a good kid. Not perfect — she'd nearly let him freeze to death, once — but she cared about him, and in her possession, Syrah felt safe. Much safer than he'd been without her — and much safer too, now that he was normal-sized. During his first few months as a frog, he had remained as tiny as the wishing well had made him, so miniscule that even minnows could have eaten him. Certainly enough of them had tried. Fish, birds, kittens — these were now the creatures of his nightmares. During the first months of his ordeal, mouths had lunged for him, claws had swiped at him, beaks had swooped to pierce him — and worst of all, enormous spiders had pursued him, their crazed, clustered eyes shining, their pincers raised like monstrous daggers. Syrah had never been afraid of spiders, but being the size of a thumbnail had altered his perspective. When he was human again, he would crush every spider he encountered. He would be the mad spider crusher of Tyme, exacting his revenge on every eight-legged creature. His sister Bianca would give him one of her speeches about how all creatures exist in balance. He would eat a bowl of live spiders in front of her face to shut her up.

Several strokes of good fortune had finally landed him in Rapunzel's pocket — though they hadn't felt like good fortune at the time. He hadn't felt lucky at all when a brook had washed him into a line of irrigation, which had carried him to a river, where he'd nearly been dinner for the fish. He hadn't felt lucky when he'd finally washed up on shore and overheard a pair of hunters discussing the best game in the Redlands, which meant that he was a terrible distance now from Cornucopia.

On the other hand, it *had* seemed like luck when he had accidentally found his way into the glade of the Red fairies. Surely, he'd thought, they would notice him. They would recognize that he was human, and they would help him. But the Red fairies had been consumed in their war against the witch Envearia. They had been haggard with fear, their magic had been weak, and they had paid no mind to the spellbound frog in their midst.

And then Rapunzel had come to the fairy glade — and so had Jack, who noticed Syrah, and scooped him off the ground, and gave him to Rapunzel as a birthday present. The best moment of his frog life so far had come when the Red fairies restored Rapunzel to her human size. Inside her pocket, Syrah had grown into a frog the size of a fist, and his relief at the change was still fantastic. He was big. He was visible. He could crush most spiders with a single, vicious hop. Still, even as a normal-sized frog, the world was too treacherous for him to risk traveling alone. He'd been biding his time all these months, and now he was close. *So* close.

Rapunzel crouched before him now and extended her hand. Syrah hopped into it, and when his belly touched her palm, he felt and heard the thoughts inside her mind. *I wish Witch could see me at the* ATC, *I miss her and it hurts, it hurts — Why can't I work this stupid ring? I don't want to miss the tournament.*

This too was something Syrah had gotten used to — or almost.

It was still strange, absorbing people's inner lives just like he absorbed water to drink. He doubted it was something all frogs could do — magic had made him a frog, after all, and so magic had also made him a little bit magical. It was a handy gift. It had allowed him, the first time Rapunzel ever touched him, to discern that he would probably be safe in her care.

Now he stayed near her wrist and carefully avoided touching the fairy ring that flowed around one of her fingers. More than once, he had scraped his belly against the ring by mistake, and it had overwhelmed his mind with visions he could hardly bear. The birth of the Olive Isles as they burst from the sea. The first stars, flung violently into the night sky. And a great blackness — a living, breathing, unknowable blackness, hidden beneath a hill. Tyme's oldest secrets were in that ring, and he wanted no part of them.

"Are you ready to go?" Rapunzel asked.

Syrah replied with his most affirmative croak, and Rapunzel set him on her shoulder, where he settled comfortably and surveyed the world from a proper human height. He was more than ready to go. He could scarcely wait another moment. Rapunzel and Jack were on their way to the All-Tyme Championships in Yellow Country. There, Syrah would finally find people who remembered him as a man. People who would help him.

"You're still using that ring wrong," said Jack. "Let me see it." He shoved his black hair to no avail. It fell down again immediately, shiny and straight, half obscuring his narrow black eyes.

"The Woodmother gave it to me," said Rapunzel, rubbing the ring. "And Glyph said the trees would teach me where to go. If I just keep trying —"

"Come on, you've had a thousand chances," said Jack. "Let me try."

Syrah clung to the last scraps of his patience. He had never been long on patience, but his time with Rapunzel and Jack had forced him to build some.

"Just wait!" Rapunzel cried, flipping her long braid back over her shoulder and nearly smacking Syrah in the face with it. He pressed closer to her neck and avoided the slap. He was attuned, by now, to her hair-throwing fits; he almost never got hit anymore.

"Here's a map," said Jack, shoving a Ubiquitous one into Rapunzel's face. "Here's where we want to go." He thumped the town of Plenty in Yellow Country, on the shore of Lake Tureen. "And here's where we are now," he said, crumpling the map into a useless wad and shaking it at Rapunzel. "We have no idea! The opening ceremonies are going on right now, and the delegates' feast is *tonight*. I told you we should have taken that carriage when we were in Smoketree. At this rate, you'll miss the whole competition." Jack shoved the map into his rucksack.

Rapunzel held up her hand in front of her eyes and turned it back and forth. The ring glinted. "I don't *want* to miss it," she said. "Purl is traveling all that way to see me play jacks."

"And Tess and my mother."

"But I need to figure this out by myself. Without any help. It's important, Jack."

"Why?"

"Because it *is*." She dropped her ringed hand to her side.

Jack sighed. "Let's just walk until we find a town," he said. "Then we'll take a carriage."

"Wait — where's that book you brought?" Rapunzel asked suddenly. She made an impatient gesture with her fingers. "The one you borrowed from your mother."

"Why?" Jack asked, but he was already digging in his rucksack. He found the tattered little book and handed it to Rapunzel. The lettering was so faded that Syrah could barely make out the title. *Edible Plants ~ An Illustrated Guide.*

"This says where different plants grow," Rapunzel said, flipping through it. "We're in the middle of the woods somewhere, so if we can figure out which plants these are, can't we figure out *where* we are?"

Syrah croaked appreciatively and bounced on Rapunzel's shoulder. Yes. A reasonable idea.

Jack looked impressed. "Sounds good," he said.

Rapunzel had already found a useful page. She put her finger on the picture and peered at the nearest patch of flowers. "Does this look right to you, Prince Frog?" she asked.

Jack rolled his eyes, but Syrah croaked his agreement anyway. The flowers in the woods and the flowers in the book were the same. Marigolds.

"And they grow in . . ." Rapunzel squinted at the page. "Well, in summer, they grow all over the place," she said, disappointed. "Orange, the Redlands, the Crimson Realm, Yellow Country, the Blue Kingdom, the Lilac Lakes, Commonwealth Green . . ." She turned the page. "Never mind, this doesn't help."

"Yes it does." Jack had come to stand next to Rapunzel, and he peered at the book alongside her. "Pick another plant — there are tons around here. We'll keep identifying them until we narrow it down to the place where all of them grow. Like that mushroom there. My mother warned us not to eat those."

"Huh," said Rapunzel. "I'm sure I've eaten mushrooms that look just like that."

"You'd be dead," Jack replied. "Those might look like morels, but they're not." He reached over and flipped pages until he reached a page toward the back of the book. It listed several poisonous plants that were easy to confuse with other, edible plants.

"Bluepeace," Rapunzel murmured, dragging a finger down the page. "Hemlock, juggetsbane, moonseed . . ." She pointed to a drawing of a mushroom. "This one? Slumbercap?"

Jack peered at the drawing. "Yep," he said. "See? The inner lining has a silver cast, it says." He plucked one of the mushrooms from the ground and turned it over. Sure enough, its inner folds shone faintly silver.

"Crumble the dried mushroom into hot liquid," Rapunzel read aloud. "Slumbercap will dissolve, emitting a silver curl of steam. Even a small amount of slumbercap may cause extreme difficulty breathing. A few mouthfuls of the poison will result in paralysis of the lungs. Death by suffocation will occur within minutes." She shuddered. "Well that's not very nice."

"None of these are," said Jack, tossing the mushroom away. Syrah watched it fall and made a mental note not to hop on any of those. He didn't want to go absorbing that stuff. "But the point is, these mushrooms grow in Violet, and then down across the central belt of Tyme." He pointed to the book. "The Republic of Brown, Yellow Country, and southeastern Blue."

"Between that and the marigolds, we're either in southeastern Blue or in Yellow Country," said Rapunzel, looking hopeful. "That's closer to Lake Tureen than we thought." She flipped through the book until she came to a drawing of a tree, and she looked up at the ones that shaded them. "These are birch trees, aren't they?"

Syrah hopped. They definitely were.

Rapunzel laid her palm against the peeling white patches of the nearest birch tree trunk. "Birch," she said, consulting her book again briefly. "Now, where do you grow?"

The ring on Rapunzel's finger began to glow.

Syrah's eyes bulged. He hopped repeatedly on Rapunzel's shoulder, but she was too busy reading to pay attention, so he leapt from her shoulder to Jack's. Jack turned his head, caught sight of Rapunzel's ring, and gasped.

"Your ring," Jack said urgently. "Look."

Rapunzel stared at her finger, then lifted her chin and looked up into the slim, leafy branches of the birch they stood beneath. Syrah looked up too in fearful wonder.

"My ring is warm," Rapunzel murmured. "Jack, hold my hand." She leaned toward the tree, keeping her ringed hand pressed to it. "Birch?" she said, almost shyly. "Hello there, Birch."

There was no wind, but the birch leaves rustled musically. The ring glowed brighter.

"We're trying to go to Plenty," said Rapunzel. "Could you show us the way? Please?"

Silvery fog rolled swiftly toward them. It enveloped them, so thick that Syrah could not even see Rapunzel's neck in front of him. The fog coiled into long, thick funnels of silvery whiteness, then burst silently into smoke and dissipated. When the mist cleared, the landscape had changed. They were still beside a cluster of birch trees, but these ones grew along the side of a wide road that descended into a valley. Beautifully tended farms nestled together like a great pastoral quilt on either side of the road, rolling toward a bright blue lake that shimmered in the distance. Syrah began to bounce on Jack's shoulder. He knew this vista. He'd traveled this road. They had reached the ATC. Here, he would find his family. Deli's family. Nexus Burdock. Somebody who knew him.

"These are birches too," said Jack, looking around.

"Is that how it's done?" Rapunzel looked up at the leaves. "I can travel from birches to birches, or maples to maples, or willows to willows?"

"We could make a map," said Jack. "A tree map."

"Yes! And then we really could go everywhere!"

Syrah barely listened. Too ecstatic to stay perched, he bounced into the dry grass and boinged in jubilant circles. His misery was nearly at an end. After fifteen months of grueling patience, somebody was going to make him human again.

Rapunzel touched the nearest tree trunk.

"Thank you, Birch," she said.

The branches overhead gave a satisfied rustle. The ring's glow dimmed.

"We still have to hurry," said Jack. "The invitation says the feast tonight is formal. You need to get changed."

Rapunzel looked down at herself. "I can't wear this?"

"It's an official event. They expect you to get fancy."

"Then you have to get fancy too."

"Fine."

Rapunzel and Jack eyed each other for a brief moment, and then Rapunzel blushed. She pulled her hand from Jack's and strode off down the hill. Syrah bounced frantically after her, croaking as loudly as he could. If she forgot about him now, if she left him behind and some family of weasels popped up and ate him —

"Come on, Prince Frog."

Jack scooped him up, and Syrah's panic ebbed. For a moment, pressed against Jack's palm, he experienced his mind as well. *She's getting better at all this — She didn't need my help at all — She held my hand.*

There was a lot of Rapunzel in Jack's mind lately.

Syrah rode on Jack's shoulder until they reached the bustling streets at the center of Plenty, where he gazed delightedly around, beaming as much as his frog face would let him at the wonderful noise of it all. People eating, kids laughing, babies crying, and the *Town Crier* box pealing over the top of it all.

"Hear ye! Hear ye!"

Jack walked up to the box, put a coin in the slot, and pulled out the tightly scrolled *Crier* that dropped into the undertray.

"Uh oh," he said, frowning as he opened the scroll. "There's some kind of sickness going around the villages east of here. Five people have died of an unknown fever, and there are a dozen others unconscious . . ." He shook his head. "This *Crier* is all bad news. Listen to this: 'Ubiquitous Productions has refused the Exalted Council's request for a meeting, though several recent deaths have been reported . . .'" Jack trailed off, shaking his head. "Crop *rot*. This thing says that some kid fell from a rooftop when her Ubiquitous rope crashed ten hours early. And some other family's house burned down because they got an acorn that sparked — just like the one that started that fire in Quintessential."

Rapunzel looked over his shoulder. "'The Exalted Council's official recommendation is to discontinue use of the acorns until a full investigation can be conducted,'" she read, sounding worried. "But Jack, the only other clothes I have are Ubiquitous ones. What will I wear?"

Jack answered by pointing toward a shop called Practical Elegance. Through its windows, Syrah watched enviously as young people held garments against themselves and looked into mirrors to judge their reflections. He had been like them once.

When they entered the shop, many of the customers turned their heads. Their eyes flickered over Jack's tattered traveling clothes and Syrah on his shoulder, and they raised their eyebrows at Rapunzel's muddy boots and unkempt hair. Some of them whispered to each other, smirking. One girl even pointed at them, then dissolved into a fit of quiet giggles with her friend.

Rapunzel was impervious. "I don't see anything fancy," she announced rather loudly as she glanced around the shop. "Let's go somewhere else."

As if by magic, a saleswoman appeared beside Rapunzel.

"This way, sweets," she said, smiling brightly, and she led Rapunzel through the crowd and toward the back of the shop. Jack went toward a rack of men's tunics, and Syrah looked up at the enormous sign that was pasted on the wall between the tall windows. *FAIREST OF THE FAIR CERTIFIED* it said in fancy letters. *At Practical Elegance, we care for the dignity of our employees. We maintain safe workshop conditions and pay fair wages and benefits.* Beneath this, the royal crest of Blue was seared right into the wall, beside a framed letter signed by Prince Dash Charming, which several customers were reading. A store clerk stood there too, smiling and holding up a small card. "Five percent of all proceeds earned during the ATC will go directly to fund local orphanages," she said. "This charitable outreach is possible in partnership with G. G. Floss of the Copper Door! Make a purchase here, and receive a limited edition luxury truffle! This offer is exclusively available during the All-Tyme Championships."

Jack lifted a paper tag attached to the collar of a tunic. "'Waterproof, wrinkle-free, stain-resistant, travel-friendly, and crafted according to the highest ethical standards — the Practical Elegance guarantee,'" he read. He flipped the tag over and whistled at the outrageously high price. "I could live for a year on that money."

"But they're *so* worth it," said a tall, deeply tanned young man who stood nearby. He had long, dark curls, expertly tousled to look like he'd just emerged from the ocean, and his white tunic was loose and appeared casual, but the details showed that it was extremely well made. The whole picture reminded Syrah powerfully of himself. "They're reversible, and they seriously don't wrinkle."

Jack gave the tanned fellow a dubious glance.

"I wore one practically every day of the ATC last year," said the fellow, "and it's still in good shape this summer, so, you know. Satisfied customer."

Jack turned to him with more interest. "You're an All-Tymer?"

"Cassis Swill. Launchballer for Yellow." Cassis smiled. "You a fan?"

"I'm here with the jacks champion, actually. She's a friend of mine."

Cassis's eyebrows flew up. He lowered his voice and looked both ways. "The witch's kid?" he whispered, leaning slightly toward Jack. "Where is she?"

"Her name is Rapunzel," said Jack, and Syrah heard the edge in his voice.

"Does she still have all the hair?"

Jack's shoulder stiffened under Syrah's belly. "No."

"Too bad," said Cassis, giving Jack a conspiratorial grin. "A hundred feet of hair — something pretty interesting about that, you know?"

"You'd think," said Jack coolly. "Turns out it's just heavy."

Rapunzel burst from the back of the shop like a firework and planted herself in front of Jack. She wore a sapphire gown that made her eyes as blue as an island sky. Syrah couldn't help admiring her.

Neither could Jack. Syrah could feel his pulse racing in his neck. *Go on,* he thought, not for the first time. *Say something. Tell her she's beautiful.*

Jack was silent.

Cassis, on the other hand, spoke. "Looks good," he said, and he took a lazy step toward her. "You're the jacks champion. Rapunzel, right?"

"Yes." Rapunzel jerked her hair away from the saleswoman, who was trying to wind it into an elegant twist. "I like my hair down," she said, and she shook it out. Golden tendrils curled softly to her waist.

"*Nice,*" said Cassis, sweeping his eyes over her. He flipped his hair back from his eyes and jerked his chin toward her in a gesture of approval. Syrah recognized the move. He had used it himself. "So, I'm Cassis. Cassis Swill. You know. Launchball."

"No I don't." Rapunzel turned her back on him without ceremony. "I'm getting this dress," she said to Jack. "It's perfect — look, it comes apart at the waist. The top turns into a satchel if you flip it inside out and button up this end, and the skirt is a waterproof sleeve for a sleeping bag."

"That's pretty handy," Jack admitted. "I should find something like that."

"Right this way." The brightly smiling saleswoman was at Jack's elbow.

Rapunzel took Syrah from Jack and set him on her shoulder. "See if you can get some trousers that turn into a boat," she called as the saleswoman pulled Jack away.